The Happiness of Others

Leon Rooke

The Happiness of Others

The Porcupine's Quill

CANADIAN CATALOGUING IN PUBLICATION DATA

Rooke, Leon.
The happiness of others

ISBN 0-88984-125-X

I. Title.

PS8585.066H36 1991 C813'.54 C91-094750-3
PR9199.3.R58H36 1991

Published by The Porcupine's Quill, Inc., 68 Main Street, Erin, Ontario NOB 1TO with financial assistance from The Canada Council and the Ontario Arts Council.

Distributed by The University of Toronto Press, 5201 Dufferin Street, Downsview, Ontario M3H 5T8.

In the same or different form, these stories were previously published in *The Love Parlour* (Oberon), *The Broad Back of the Angel* (Fiction Collective), and *Cry Evil* (Oberon). 'The Heart Must from Its Breaking' was originally published in *Exile*.

Readied for the press by John Metcalf.
Copyedited by Doris Cowan.

Cover is after a photograph taken by Michael Ondaatje.

Printed and bound by The Porcupine's Quill. The stock is Zephyr laid, and the type, Ehrhardt.

Second Printing.

Contents

Foreword

THIS BOOK draws into one volume some of the stories that appeared in two long out-of-print collections.

The Love Parlour, my first book published in Canada, appeared in 1977 from Oberon Press, in an edition of 500 clothbound and 1,000 paperback copies. *The Love Parlour* contained five stories and a novella, although the novella was not called a novella, and instead was run as three separate stories. In the present volume the novella — rightfully, I think — is called a novella. It has a Mexican setting, has as its title *The Street of Moons*, and takes as its point of departure that particularly American, particularly nasty, sensibility which regards all countries, especially Latin American ones, as adjuncts of their own property, and their citizens as second-class people who ought to be speaking English.

Against a background of pestilence, decay, and death, all of the central protagonists in the story — Madeline, Eleanor, and Señor Gomez — are engaged in the making of certain amendments to their constitutions, certain alterations of vision — changes in the way in which they view themselves and society. I might argue, in fact, that, generally speaking, that is what the whole of this book — and a large chunk of all fiction — is about. The novella's 'For Love of Madeline' section was written in a short burst in late August 1972 in San Miguel de Allende, near the end of a second extended visit to Mexico. 'For Love of Eleanor' was completed later in the year, and 'For Love of Gomez', more complicated in its texture and taxing in its composition, was completed in early 1974, just prior to a third departure to Mexico, this time to Patzcuaro, a lovely town resting beside Lake Patzcuaro in the Michoacán Mountains. The physical lay-out of this town closely resembles the village of El Flores described in the novella, though Patzcuaro has happily been spared the calamities depicted in the fiction. No irony is intended in the 'For Love of' sub-titles announcing each section.

The earliest story reprinted here, 'If You Love Me Meet Me There', was written in Chapel Hill, North Carolina, in 1960, sparked by a next-door neighbour whose house boasted a large Coca-Cola clock above the front door. 'Memoirs of a Cross-Country Man' is a story adapted from a chapter in a novel begun upon my arrival in Victoria in 1969, and not yet finished, nor yet absolutely abandoned. 'Leave Running', perhaps the story here which I might least ardently defend, was written in early 1974, again in Victoria.

Two of the stories contained in the earlier book, 'If Lost Return to the Swiss Arms' and 'Call Me Belladonna', will not be found in the present volume. I think their discarding beneficial to the whole, although for the first-listed of these I retain a certain fondness, since it is one of my earliest stories, written way back in 1958, and was one whose marketing adventures taught the young author a good deal. The story required five years and approximately forty submissions before finding magazine acceptance, then received one of the nation's premier honours through inclusion in the annual O. Henry Prize anthology. Never mind that it was not a notably distinguished story: it was better than the editors rejecting it would have had me believe, and confirmed my already prevailing notion that an editor's rejection (or acceptance) often had little to do with the quality of the considered piece. This lesson provided the stamina, or stubbornness, necessary for the submission of other stories — some included here — a thirtieth or fortieth time.

The second Oberon title this book selects from was published in 1980 under the unfortunate title *Cry Evil* — unfortunate because the contents were not so drab, bleak, or negative as the title suggested. That book, out of print now for more than a decade, offered six longish titles, none called 'Cry Evil' — (there was no 'Love Parlour' in *Love Parlour* either) — and four from that volume are included here: 'The Deacon's Tale', 'The End of the Revolution & Other Stories', 'Biographical Notes', and 'Adolpho's Disappeared and We Haven't a Clue Where To Find Him'. All of these were written in Victoria in the winter of 1979.

Also to be found in this collection are two other stories from a third book never available in this country, *The Broad Back of the Angel.* They are 'Wintering in Victoria', written in 1974, and the title story, done in 1976. Yet another story is included as well, 'The Heart Must From Its Breaking', not published until 1988 (in *Exile* magazine), but written during the same period as the others and placed here for that reason and subtle thematic ones.

My stories began appearing in US magazines in the late fifties and early sixties, at a time when many young writers were insisting that the old short-story imperatives of beginning, middle, and end — as with other rigid conventions — needed revitalization. That the form, generally, without abandoning tradition altogether, required a refurbishing. Eisenhower's conservative hue had largely coloured the social and political life in the US through the fifties, and this same conservative pall was to be seen in many of the literary arts, especially the short story. We were seeking more open forms, fresh angles of approach to material — a new poetics for fiction — while most editors were still expecting the 'well-built', formally repetitious, and realistically endowed works that had prevailed through the thirties and forties.

The one publication that most altered the mode, and which served to groom my generation, was a mass-market paperback called *New World Writing.* Begun in 1952, twice yearly through twenty-two issues it gathered new writing — fiction, poetry, criticism, artwork and memoir — from around the world. Here are some bios from NWW.

> Octavio Paz '... is currently the literary director of an experimental theatre group in Mexico City.'
> Galway Kinnell 'here makes his first appearance as a short story writer ...'
> Anne Sexton 'here makes her first appearance as ...'
> 'The British poet and novelist George Barker's latest work includes *The True Confessions of George Barker* and *Two Plays.*'
> Eugène Ionesco is ...
> Ishikawa Tatsuzo is ...
> Thomas Berger is ...

Samuel Beckett is ...
Saul Bellow is ...
Heinrich Böll is ...
Bertolt Brecht is ...
James Jones '... was recently married and, with his wife, has gone to Europe for two years.'
William Gaddis is ...
Flannery O'Connor is ...
Derek Walcott is ...
Julio Cortázar is ...
Michel Butor is ...
Gabriel García Márquez is ...
'Thomas Pynchon, a 22-year-old New Yorker ... is presently living in Seattle, at work on a novel.'
Camilo José Cela is ...
Joseph Heller's 'Catch-18' is ...
Ana Maria Matute is ...
Malcolm Lowry's *The Forest Path to the Spring* 'here makes its first appearance in print.'
'... Married, with four daughters, Tillie Olson has recently begun to publish her stories.' (In NWW 16, with 'Tell Me A Riddle.')

The writers of the generation beginning and / or emerging during that period, myself among them, were on the prowl for new strategies, new methods of presentation, a fusion of fresh and disparate techniques in the deployment of *story*, stylistic innovation, new skins that one might inhabit, rearrangements in the depiction of place and time and character, a certain discourtesy in the unfolding of plot, displacement of description, new configurations in story structure, a reshaping of beginning, middle and end that more accurately mirrored human thought — were on the prowl, that is to say, for an international insignia, for a revamped, uninhibited muse. 'Models', as the thing these writers were in pursuit of, is too grandiose a word and was, except for Chekhov's stories, an alien, suspect, concept, as they innocently, or deliberately, set out to rejuvenate the form. Raymond Carver, Robert

Coover, Grace Paley, William Gass, Leonard Michaels, Cynthia Ozick, Joy Williams, Joyce Carol Oates, Richard Brautigan, Russell Banks, John Gardner, and Donald Bartheleme are a few on the American side who quickly spring to mind.

By the end of the sixties this healthier attitude towards form had largely won the day. There was a downside, too, of course, as markets for fiction collapsed, but the one had little to do with the other, and 'markets' — nice though they are — were not what had summoned most to the enterprise.

It is not my business, though, to be offering even this scratchy outline of recent literary history, Yankee side. The long and short of this foreword is a simple affirmation of my understanding that a few of the stories in these pages are haunted by the ghosts of authors versed in the traditional way of narrating a tale, or story, or fiction, while others follow a more formally adventurous routing — though not to the extent that I would now — or ever did — think of them as 'experimental'.

Note. When is a story ever truly finished? Each of the works here, in manner large to meagre, has been revised from the original — most often pruned, sometimes added to. Refurbished.

Final note. In 1975-76 I was writer-in-residence at an odd, interesting, bedevilled university in Minnesota. One day in hardest winter a stranger telephoned, and offered his name. He'd read some of my 'stuff', this stranger said, and wondered if I might have a book-length manuscript. If so, he had an arrangement with a certain publisher in Ottawa and thought he might be able to deliver a contract. Was I interested?

'Who?' I said. 'What's that name again?'

'Metcalf', he said. Pause. 'John Metcalf.' Pause. 'Are you there?'

Now here is the same Metcalf, sixteen years later, newly aligned with The Porcupine's Quill and Tim and Elke Inkster, giving resurrection to many of those titles he originally lured out of the darkness. I am pleased *The Happiness of Others* is among them.

Leon Rooke,
8 April 1991, Eden Mills

The Deacon's Tale

HERE'S A STORY.

Although it has been going on for years, the crucial facts are fresh in my mind so I will have no trouble confining myself strictly to what's essential. Nothing made up, have no worry about that. I live in this world too: when my wife, lovely woman, tells me that people are tired of hearing *stories*, they want facts, gossip, trivia, how-to about real life, I'm first to take the hint. So this is plain fact: yesterday my foot was hurting. The pain was unbearable. I was in mortal anguish and convinced I'd been maimed for life.

My wife, naturally enough, was concerned. Now and then she would look in on me: 'How's the foot?' she'd ask. I'd grit my teeth and do what I could to keep from screaming. I hate sympathy, faked or otherwise. Had she come in with a sharp axe to ask whether she could chop it off, I would have felt better. But she was all politeness, you see: 'Is it better? No? Shall I bring you a magazine? Fluff your pillows? Comb your moustache?' Her comments are precious and I want to leave out none of them. According to her, the people in my stories are never polite and nice the way people really are. In my stories it's always hocus-pocus, slam-bang, and someone has a knife at your throat. Turns people off, she claims. I'm influenced too much by TV and radio and by what I read in the papers; in real life people are not nearly so anxious and unhappy as I make out. Put in a little comedy, she says. After all, you live in a pleasant house, you've got liquor in the cabinet, a beautiful wife, and most of our *urgent* bills are paid. Why be morbid? It gives people the wrong impression.

All right, I can see I've already gone astray. All this past history is irrelevant in a story meant to be about my foot. I'm getting too subjective, too interpretive, that's another of my flaws. You sound bitter, she'd say. Just stupidly sarcastic. Never mind that she's scowling in the doorway, grumpy and embittered herself because the bedroom is such a mess. When she's in *her* sick-bed, you understand, she likes everything immaculate: tables dusted, all knick-knacks pointing in the proper direction, flowers smiling from every ledge. Anything less is apt to depress her and I grant you her view is not unreasonable. It just happens that I don't like to be surrounded by that kind of false cheer. If I'm on my death-bed, I want two or three undertakers standing by and if a hearse is out in the garden, so much the better. So:

'Are you in pain?' she asks. 'Do you think you can eat now?'

I groan. I can't help myself. Lovely and generous women like my wife think that all the ills of the world can be cured by a small wedge of cucumber sandwich or a nice salad with a little lemon dripped over the top. My mother is exactly the same and she is still going strong at ninety-five.

'Speak!' she shouts. 'You're the big word-man around here.'

The fact is, although I was starving, I wasn't talking to her just then. We'd had a tiff earlier in the week about my alleged promiscuous behaviour at a party but that's not why I wasn't talking to her. I simply *felt* like keeping my silence. It had nothing to do with my outrage over having been falsely accused. I'm accustomed to that. No, all my compassion, all my sympathy and love and concern, was invested in this wretched foot. I was in agony, I tell you. I was worn out. All night I had been in the grip of a fever — fever and chills — and hadn't slept a wink. None of my medicines helped. Penicillin, codeine, morphine, a bottle of eighty-year-old Scotch — nothing had offered any relief. Meanwhile, she had slept like a princess. Her story would be different, of course. She'd have you think she was up every minute putting hot or cold compresses on my brow. She'd tell you that when she finally did doze off she couldn't get any peace because my hands were all over her. That's not true. It is true that about four in the morning she jumped out of bed shouting. 'Why don't you go and feel *her* up!' — and went running off to another bed. 'What *her*?' I shout. 'That bitch Gladys!' she screams back. Then the door slams and I don't see any more of her until breakfast.

Okay. I see I've fallen into my old trap. My stories don't *move*, she says. That is, they move but they don't go forward. I'm always botching them up with too much extraneous material. *'Who cares?'* she'd say. *'You throw in your mealy-mouthed references to Gladys and expect us to interpret them any way we wish. We're supposed to predict all sorts of dire consequences for these people, for their marriage, because you've invoked some slut's name. Well, it won't wash! Get on with it or shut up.'* That, of course, is what she'd say after first denying that she'd said anything remotely similar to *Why don't you go and feel her up!* I put that part in, she'd claim, only to get the aroma of sex in my story.

'You get into this trouble only because you have nothing to say.'

All right, I've made it clear I had a restless, terrible night. Now she comes in with my lunch on a tray. I'm supposed to comment on how heavenly it looks. She's even brought a little daisy in a vase and has dug out one of the bright yellow napkins she picked up in Mexico. I'm supposed to be touched. She's had to pick this flower from the garden and she's had to wash this napkin by hand and slave over it with a hot iron. I'm not supposed to remember that she's got a trunkful of these faded things or how she came by them. In Mexico, I mean to say, while on a decadent trip with her beloved Arnold, in the days before she met me. I'm supposed to think she's still a lady when in actual fact she's toured three continents with that jerk! Arnold, I should add, is a first-rate story-teller. If you ask her to, she will put one of his platters on the stereo to prove it: 'The Ballad of Johnny Cool,' which hit the Top Forty and became a great movie by the same name. But do me favour and don't take your children to see it.

He's successful, she sometimes tells me, because he knows when to employ dialogue. *'So you've decided to tell us a story about a man with a bum foot. You're smart enough to give him a beautiful, sophisticated and intelligent wife. But right away you impose an impossible burden on yourself. You have him so mad and stupid he can't talk to her. Result, no dialogue. All we get are his lame-brain buckshot musings. It's Dullsville. And I for one couldn't care less about him or his foot. Chop it off indeed. How did he hurt it in the first place? You always deliberately avoid revealing what most people would regard as a most essential part.'*

He got it caught in a crankshaft.

'There you go being cute. You ruin every story you tell with these touches that you think are so cute. Nobody believes for a minute that this character's foot got caught in a crankshaft. Most of us don't even know what a crankshaft is. You will go to any extreme to avoid rooting your story in a basic, common, SHARED *experience.'*

It got caught in an elevator door.

'Not believable.'

A rhino stepped on it?

'Oh yes, any old lie will do. Anyway, by this time it's too late. Who cares? We're not dunces. If I didn't know any better, if I hadn't had to put up with it, I'd never believe your foot hurt at all.'

Forced to, I will tell you what happened to my foot. It was nothing very dramatic. A week ago I was pouring concrete for this absurd gazebo she wanted built on the rocky cliff beside the house. *'Up there, honey,'* she says, *'so we can see for miles!'* Somehow my feet got tangled between bucket, hoe, and wheelbarrow. I lost my balance and fell forty feet on this foot which I'd already sprained when I tried kicking a fire hydrant. Then I had to hobble two miles to the hospital because naturally she had the car, out to one of those treasured lunches with friends whom I never see. After treatment I collared a kind Ladies' Auxiliary person and for ten dollars she agreed to help me get home. I'm in bed, half passed-out, when my wife finally comes in. *'So this is how you build my gazebo!'* she exclaims, and tears out in a huff to see whether I've even started it yet. I can hear her up there stomping about, cursing, kicking rocks down the hill, telling neighbours, *'I knew it! I knew it! He's a lazy sod, he's done nothing and I rue the day I ever met him.'* Meantime, I have revived somewhat and am trying with my bleary sight to find the front door. I'm going out there to strangle her, to push *her* off the cliff. My crutches slip, I topple over, and damned if the same foot isn't banged again. They sweep up my blood and guts and somehow return me to my bed of pain. Naturally she is all remorseful now, and solicitous, and for the next thirty-six hours baby-talk bubbles out of her: 'Does my poor diddums forgive me? Won't my pretty diddums give me his pretty poo-doo smile?' She is so warm and contrite she could cook me in this syrup. Finally, one frostbitten night, I relent and go to put my arms around her in matrimonial harmony: I get her knee in my stomach, a slam of insults, and the next second she's scrambling for another bed. Even if I have chased Gladys, which I deny, it seems to me that our crimes ought to balance out.

Right, so onward, she's now brought the lunch tray in. Ham on rye, a big pickle, a glass of milk, and fresh strawberries under a blanket of homespun cream.

'Eat it,' she says. 'You know what will happen if you lie about drinking whisky all day.'

'What will happen? Let my dark secret out.'

'You'll get blotto.'

'Ho-ho as my Daddy would say. Big deal.'

'Is your foot still throbbing?'

'I don't know. Hit it with a hammer, then I can tell.'

That's enough dialogue for a while. She's got her eyes on my strawberries and has already eaten half the bowl. I'm not supposed to notice that and certainly should not remark on it: she's on a diet. It occurs to me that the reason my foot's in such pain is because the bandage is too tight. No circulation. My foot is puffy and red outside the wrapping, my five toes like shrivelled apple peels. It's one of those surgical bandages, the kind that stretches. I try to reach it, but can't. Every time I move, a thunderbolt rips through my leg and a spike bangs into my skull. My wife takes an interest in my contortions. She's quite bedazzled. Her eyes enlarge. My agony sends the blood rushing to her face. I have her sympathy but I certainly can't expect any help with the bandage from her. She won't touch it. It hasn't been washed in seven days. Nor has my foot. That's just what I don't need: to get trapped in a tub with a hundred-pound foot.

'What can I do?' she asks.

'Nothing,' I say. 'Go away.' Howling pain makes a person rude. I lie still, exhausted; the pain diminishes somewhat. My wife's feelings are hurt, but she insists on feeding me. Each time I turn my head there's another spoonful sliding between my lips. 'Eat,

eat!' she says. 'Your mother tells me she had to feed you this way until you were nineteen years old.' Oh, she knows how to get at a man. She knows how to humiliate him. 'I'm sorry', she next says, 'about last night.' She knows how to make old hatreds live — to make repulsion for one's swollen foot embrace other swollen members too. I must pay for the sins of every man who has ever clawed at her when she wasn't in the mood. 'It's just that I wasn't in the mood.' I raise my head to look at her. What I see are her wet eyes. Luscious, trembling lips. Hair trained by Mister Divine to shroud her face like a tent. *Déjà vu.* I have been here before. And the thought I have now is the same I had then. Better, old sport, that you had married a hag. Staked out the most vile neighbourhood witch and mated with her. One glance at this woman's proud, suffering face and I am hit with instant self-doubt and loathing, I am awash in sentimentality. Old True Love is hooking its claws into me. She's the one who's miserable and misunderstood. *I'm* the brute. We don't need God to remind us of our evil deeds; all we need is another person.

I find myself reviewing this most recent encounter with Gladys. A snaky wink through my bifocals. A tawdry giggle under the tree. And yes, three years ago, a single scuffy kiss in the pantry where a fuse had blown. Crimes microscopic in size but all the same I ask myself: am I not better than this? Would I tarnish reputations, cheapen myself in the eyes of the community, betray this fine woman for the sake of such a pale and fleeting lust as poor Gladys can engender? I tell you the experience gives me pause. I grip the neck of my Scotch bottle tighter and that's a fact.

I got gloomy and distressed. Oh, I plunged into a deep foul mood, no doubt of that. Down there where only mole eyes perceive. Me with stubby legs and no visible neck, chomping on earth worms, aware that my path must take me through solid rock. The same thing happens to her. She sulks, she moans, she sweats: you'd think my flaming foot had been transferred to one of her long limbs. As usual, she combats her depression by lashing out.

'Stop complaining about your foot,' she cries. 'If you mention that goddamned foot to me again I'll scream!'

'But it hurts.'

'Shut up! You didn't appear to have any trouble tracking that bitch Gladys! Or Hilda! What a barge pole *she* was! No, your foot didn't hurt then, you were a four-minute miler so long as you had their buttocks shimmying in front of you!'

Hilda? Hilda *Who? Barge poles!* What on earth can this hysterical woman mean?

'Yes, *you*, you twit! You stump-toed turd!'

Hold on a minute. I can't go on without inserting one tiny aside. My spouse is constantly criticizing me for what she calls my dirty mouth. I can't say a word to friends but that she doesn't first have to chase about the room with her pine-scent spray and cotton for the children's ears. *Reduce the filth*, that's what she's always saying. I get it from bartenders too. *Muzzle it, Deacon, or it's out you go.* I go to a movie, for instance, with naked bodies wallowing all over the screen and language that would drive killer bees to suicide, and if I mutter *Pee on this*, right away I've got six ushers driving me to the door. Fellini can have a hundred bodies copulating in a Roman bath but if I have a couple holding hands in a snowstorm I'm accused of being degenerate. *Yes*, she will say, *but your material has no redeeming quality*. Her friends will nod and grandmothers may come back into the room. So hold on. I'm not to be blamed for *her* filthy mouth. The accusation isn't true in the first place. I learned a long ago to clean up my act. They used to say about my Daddy, that rascal, that he had a mouth like a cat's rear end. You can bet your money I wasn't going to model myself after him.

My wife has no ear for this or any other criticism. Not for nothing has she attended the best schools, known the best people, committed her entire being to this marriage. Her efforts are to be recorded in the Guinness *Book of Records* (under section-heading TOOK MOST CRAP); even now, angels are at work on scrolls to be hung at the Gates of Heaven. I, too, in my dreams, when they are not of dinosaurs and other amiable and extinct creatures, compose encyclopaedic encomiums to this woman:

Mama Fournose — WIFE. *Married to erstwhile stonemason and oral traditionalist known as* Foot. *At great personal sacrifice she fed & preserved this oaf's soul, nurtured his body, saw to it that his house was not overrun with tramps, drunkards, rogues, deadbeats, Hedonists, etc. All this sweet woman wanted out of life was a marriage that would go down in history* (dinner by candlelight each evening of the year — Famous Quote: 'Isn't this romantic!'), *and loyalty. Got neither of above.*

Betroth me, O serpent, to my fate
Let my bones lie still.

A ludicrous sadness overwhelms us both at times. It charges at us with a banshee zeal, routing us from the careful defences we have laid. We pick up the pieces and limp for higher, more neutral ground. Reach for Rule No. 1 of the *Survivor's Guide to Home Warfare*: after any skirmish, win or lose, effect a quick retreat. Tend to your wounds. Keep a fresh whisky close to your left elbow. I must forget what I know of this woman. A college fraternity, in her tender eighteenth year, voted her Most Impressionable Girl; a year later the same group named her Most Desired; competition faltered and within the season a new crown had been bestowed: A Woman Too Good To Be True. What had happened to my beautiful princess to warrant this impossible title? How many dreary days she must have sat, swilling sherry, staring out of windows in makeshift rooms, paced cities like a loaned-out cat, knocked limbs with phantom shapes, yearning every moment for the day when her heart would truly crack and love's childhood dream of her perfect knight could at last draw to its deadly close. *Look, Father, I am a stranger to you now! Look, Mother, at the woman I have become! Oh, lover, I have survived the best and worst you could do to me! Oh, world, send me a man out of your darkness! I have toyed with prince and rabble and am prepared now to wed whatever stranger next steps into my light.*

'This can't go on,' laments my wife.

Most Fashionable now. Her clothes, no less than her black moods, put her at the vanguard of her age. Tomorrow *Chatelaine, Vogue, The Woman's Own Daily* no doubt will call: *We're in a real quandary, honey: this season is it to be mauve or green?*

My rancid foot is killing me.

'Think of something pleasant,' she advises. 'Try remembering your first wife.'

I remember a story that a fellow down at the Motherlode used to tell me. It seems there was this woman down on her luck who one day sat down by a pool thinking she'd throw herself in when this frog suddenly hopped into her lap saying *Kiss me* and she got out her hatchet and chopped off its legs and immediately fried them up on her hibachi and ate them and decided on reflection that she hadn't had such a fine day in years.

All right, forget that story. I can see it's not relevant, what a guy in a beer-hall told ten years ago.

My first wife *was* demented; ever in study of her L. Ron Hubbard; I hardly see how I'm to be blamed for that.

'Or how you wet your bed until you were twenty-one.'

Feeble. Such weak humour will not provoke my ire. Anyway, I have more serious matters to ponder. I've had a suspicion now for several days: my foot is only a symptom of the deeper trouble I'm in. I have some dreaded disease of the blood. That's why my doctor has been so guarded in his report. It's why a simple x-ray was not sufficient. Numerous tests were required: my blood was drained, my urine analysed, my body strapped to numerous unidentifiable machines while four hefty nurses held me down. I am either sick in a most complex way or another patient has been confused with me. I suffer weird discolorations of skin: black here, blue there, a purplish tinge all over. The doctor tells me, *Well. Sir, you drink too much. And you had a wicked fall.* He means to keep the news from me. To let the poor soul have a few happy days.

I'm a normal man, I worry about problems such as this. Yesterday I called a friend of mine, Fromm, a practising psychiatrist. Can you help me, Doc? I asked. Am I in trouble or is this delusion? He refused my case. You're terminated, he said. Deacon, I have bigger fish to fry. *I am at work on a case that could change the entire face of Europe.*

A good man but a dope, what does he know?

My wife is, of course, in on the secret. That explains why twice in the past week she has raised the subject of our financial affairs. *It's absurd, darling, but do you by chance have a secret bank account? I ask because I simply can't figure out where all the money goes.* She wanted me to believe her inquiry could be routinely explained: she had seen a hot item in a dress shop and wanted my enthusiasm before spending what amounted to a small fortune. I might have been deceived. But the next day she brought up the question of wills: *everyone writes a will these days. Don't you think we should?*

It explains too why, on the whole, she's been so nice to me lately.

Nothing she can say, however, will induce me to reveal the presence of my secret account. It's there as a buffer against hard times, and because when my first wife left she cleaned me out. The furniture, my dog, my neckties, my thousand-franc Swiss note, and a Maytag appliance repairman all went away with her. *You deserve it*, she told me. *Say any more and I'll take away that silly toupée you wear.*

Ignore the above. I've read the Book of Job and know when I'm well off.

Her successor is now fluffing my pillows and straightening bed-clothes, polishing the bureau — ploughing like a moose through the trash of seven days. Into her 'White Tornado' housewifery act.

'In case anyone calls,' she says.

Because that is how she is. Although I can go six months in this house without seeing another living soul, and often do, in her mind the front steps are forever packed with visitors queueing to get in. I sink my teeth into my arm, and watch. Women are mad. *All* women are demented. That's what makes them women in the first place. But how else are we to be saved? Who else would go to the trouble?

'Lift your foot,' she instructs. 'You can't rest with the sheets in this untidy state.'

'You expect me to be concerned about sheets when I have only a few hours left to live?'

She laughs. Oh, she has a fine old howl at this. Then she becomes reflective, her cheeks puff, her mouth goes tight, eyebrows leap into her scalp: 'Ah,' she says, 'I've got it. You've been trying to think up a story to tell those deadbeats down at the Motherlode! Haven't you? Is it about your foot? But now you've realized that not even those idiots would be interested in a yarn about a foot, so you've thought to deepen your tale by inserting some nonsense about your approaching death. Or about your first wife running off with your neckties. That's it, isn't it?'

'What is wrong with a story about a foot?'

'The average person cannot relate to it.'

I remind her that everyone has feet. I even laugh because I know the remark is funny. But she does not crack a smile. I can scent the malice of more criticism in the very way she breathes. My wife the acid-thrower.

'Yes, but their feet don't ache. How many of your average listeners have recently been so drunk at ten o'clock in the morning that they've fallen off a cliff? Your stories are merely extended jokes. No meat. No heart. No humour. They are of no consequence.'

I know what she has in mind. She has this theory, for instance, about sex. My stories ought to have more sex. 'But don't make it goofy,' she will say, 'and for God's sake avoid your nasty specifics.

'Or about money. They should be about money. Everyone wants or needs a certain amount of money. You'd have people around you all the time if you ever talked about money. But for God's sake don't make it too intelligent. You always want to appear so smart. It puts people off. You can't stand people knowing you were born a hick and didn't wear shoes until you were twenty years old.'

Well, that's what she says. Actually, I was born in a porter's closet in the Louvre, Paris, France, and didn't go country until I was four, after my parents were killed in a tornado in the Aleutians.

'And don't tell it in that twisty language. Or with that hound-dog face. As for that, you'd be a lot better at it if you stayed sober.'

She pauses there. She doesn't want to go too far, she knows I have feelings. She knows I can be hurt. She sits on the bed now massaging my poor, hot, throbbing foot. Her hands are deliciously cool. Or perhaps it is the other way around. Perhaps her hands are hot and my foot is cold. I can't be sure. That illustrates another of my faults. I have too many *perhapses* and far too many *can't be sures*. 'I like', she has told me a thousand times, 'the simple declarative statement.' Not a busload of adjectives. Although she does not call them adjectives. She calls them 'extra words.' That's understandable, after all I'm the one around here who considers himself the professional. 'I'm the amateur,' she will say. 'Just a darned good Eaton's buyer, just cook, maid and sex object. But that doesn't mean I'm ignorant. If I say your stories stink, they stink.'

She's saying nothing at the moment. In a half-trance she strokes my foot. Her face catches the sunlight and I can't deny she's lovely. She's lovely, she's nice, she's employed. The truth is, my foot may be either hot *or* cold but, more important, the ache is absent. It may be there but I can't feel it. She stares out the window. Placidly strokes my foot. Probably she is thinking about dinner. Or about the new suit she didn't buy after all. I lie there luxuriating, so to speak, in the touch of her hands. They tickle. I like it, I mean to say. Now and then she runs a hand up my leg. Fingers fold lightly over my knee. There is a soft glide along my thigh. Now back to my foot again. Again. Again. Then once more the somnolent climb up my leg. I dare not move. I'd like to, though. I am definitely getting interested. Her hand strokes and my body of its own accord sinks down, trying to urge the hand ever higher. I dare not speak. One wrong word and this moment is lost forever. I'd like to hire a violinist, Isaac Stern perhaps, and give him permanent residence in the attic. For times such as this. I wonder what will happen when she stops looking out the window. What will happen if *she* gets interested? I close my eyes and think: stroke! ... stroke! ... now higher! Higher! *Ahhhhh!* That's the ticket! Nice! Nice...

That's where the sex comes into this story. I thought I'd try it. I wouldn't want it said of me that I'm not open to criticism. My idea, moreover, is that by including it I can kill two birds with one stone. I see it as a nice, positive moment in the lives of these two people. That's another criticism she makes of me. 'You're too negative. People are tired of all the negative crap. Who wants to hear a story about another loser? What's the point?' As proof, she usually drags in that story someone told about two guys buried up to their necks in sand. Or the one I like to tell about four shoe-salesmen who fall into a cave and argue for hours about which of them wears a true size ten. 'Big deal!' she says. Not that I exactly disagree with her on this score. 'People are not a bunch of sows', she will say, 'wanting to wallow or root in another's misery. Or in their own, for that matter. Leave us a little hope, will you? A little dignity!'

She ought to know what she's talking about. She gets out much more than I do, she has her lunches three or four times a week, she's in and out of people's houses and gets to know what they are thinking. When she tells me people want realistic, happy stories, I believe it. I know her remarks are meant to be helpful; I realize some of mine are getting a bit ripe. 'I've heard that,' she will sometimes say. 'You told me that one last week.' And I can imagine her final assessment of this hurt foot piece: *just another sleazy monologue! It's the same old story, sugar, we practically know it by heart.* She will admit too, if pressed, that she didn't appreciate that part about her stroking my leg. It was insulting, it questioned her natural sensuality, and what about her privacy? 'Keep it up, sonnyboy, and roses will grow out of your ears before I stroke you again!'

Don't I honour anything? Is nothing sacred?

That is what she will be saying next. 'But do go on. Don't let me hold up your precious story. Your audience is breathless!' How would you react to such ridicule? Do you think you might momentarily flounder? I'm a professional but that's how it affects me. I get red in the face and can't sit still — the thread is lost, you see. I laugh and try to put a light face on it but everyone can see she's stopped me in my tracks. 'Where was I', I will lamely persist, 'before I was so rudely interrupted?' She will smile knowingly: 'You were talking about how I know more about what people are thinking than you do.'

I plough stubbornly ahead. Sometimes people *will* drop over. They do. They ring up and ask whether they can shoot over —

because they've heard I've been ill or depressed or they haven't seen us lately down at the Motherlode — that sort of thing, all perfectly natural. So we will be sitting down to a drink, eating roasted almonds or cheese or a pizza, say, with these people, and it happens that it is not altogether unheard of for one of them to ask outright for a story. 'Tell us a story,' they will say. 'Let's hear what's been going on with you two.'*Long time no see, Deacon, lay one on me, we're all ears!* That sort of thing. I am, naturally enough, happy to oblige, since I have come to think of myself in those terms. As a storyteller. It's what my mother tells her friends: 'Deacon doesn't do anything, he just tells stories. That's all he does. He could have had a good trade as a stonemason but it seems he's content to let his wife support him.' So I, as I say, am happy to respond to these requests. I get right down to it. *There was once,* I might tell them, *in darkest wintertime, in this most foul time of the year, a man who went about our country with his feet bound in rags, with horrible leaking eyes, and with a great hump on his back in which you would think he carried all the troubles of the world. Now one day, on that very day in which this poor rogue was to breathe his last, on that day a young girl innocent as the dew came dancing along his path.*

As a rule I am interrupted at about this point in the narrative. *She* wants to tell the story. Or *they* do. For her part she doesn't trust me with it. I have, she will claim, already got it wrong. 'You are flogging a dead horse and no one in this company wants to hear it.' What is wrong with it? 'It is pseudo-literary trash,' she informs me. 'A hump, indeed. If we want Dumas we can go to the library. And your young innocent tra-la-la, what garbage!' She will go on to tell me how my plot is to develop: the stupid old bugger bleeding to death in an alley somewhere, our young innocent then walking up and kicking the corpse — because it's symbolic, you see. Both of them rotten and dirty and disagreeable creatures and somehow all of society having to accept the blame. 'Either that', she informs our group, 'or he will have no plot, he will simply have the old fart walking down the street thinking his own vile accusatory thoughts while the girl hovers innocently, symbolically, in the background waiting to be redeemed through true love.

Nothing ever happening, not even any description except the odd streetcorner lamp now and then and maybe dog feces in the gutter. So don't tell it. It won't make any of us feel any better. It won't make anyone want to rejoice that they are alive. So what if people like your ugly hero do exist, you think that's any excuse? What percentage of people in the world do you think your old bastard represents, him with his filthy psychology and his dog crud in the streets? He's probably out hunting Nazis, right? Why don't you tell a story about an average person for a change, one with average wants and needs? I know too that before you're another minute into this oral beauty you'll start trying to make it sound deep, you'll drop vague hints, the situation will get so tangled up and messy we won't know where we are. It's just another of your hateful disgusting creations and we will want to go and take a bath and regret we ever asked you to open your mouth. Gloom, gloom, gloom, that's all you preach.'

The truth is she is better at storymaking than I am. At least if our friends are any judge. They smile and laugh and feed her good lines. In my story, which she appropriates, my sour old man's hump is barely noticeable. She refers to this growth as a *pretty ridge* and speaks of his scarred but ennobled face, his good manners, and benevolent attitude. He meets a nice mature woman at a bus stop who turns out to be the daughter separated from him in a train wreck years before. 'Why, I thought you were dead!' she remarks. Pathos carries the day: for a decade now the daughter has been placing flowers on the grave thought to be her father's. It is this journey, in fact, which has today been interrupted. 'Come home with me,' entreats the girl. 'Mother could not accept your death. All these years she has faithfully waited.' He stops off for a shave; she goes in and buys a new coat she's been eyeing in Eaton's.

I admit her stories make me feel good. I concede that her tales are populated with characters one might willingly invite into one's own home. I am bothered a little by the coincidence of this bus stop meeting, though she waves aside this minor reservation. 'A story has got to be true to life,' she opines. 'Every day I meet someone on the street whom I have not seen in years.' Others agree. They give examples.

'All right,' I argue. 'Even so, you must admit that her version does not sound modern.' This observation is met with instant derision. Hands flap in the air, everyone wants to talk at once. Would I be done, then, with Goethe? Are Sophocles, Dante, Shakespeare to be thrown into the incinerator? A hundred names collide in the air. 'What about Woody Allen? Sam Shepard? Cecil B. De Mille? Would you throw them out because they do not sound modern?'

I try to edge in my one thin line of defence: that I am speaking only of and for the oral traditionalist.

'Spit!' my wife declares. 'You think your kind of oral history is an end in itself; I say look where your lies have got us. Abnormality creates more abnormality. You will have people expecting it of themselves and disappointed when it is not achieved. You will not be content until you have us walking about on all fours. You must encourage us to nobility. You must inspire us. *Inspire* us, you fool!'

I don't know. I can't refute the arguments of these people. I despair. How can I go on in the face of such accusations, such hostility, with a story, for instance, about my miserable foot? Why not give up? Retire into a world of pleasant chat. The only pleasure I have left is to look back with a wet nostalgic eye to the good old days. In the old days I was to be found every night down at the Motherlode. Folks would spin off their stools and clap me on the shoulder, saying, 'Tell us another one, Deacon!' And they'd spin the other way and punch a neighbour, crying,'This guy is great, his stories will put hair on your chest!' So I'd rock on my heels and launch into the first thing that entered my head. It came easy as breathing, I had only to open my mouth and the magic would fly. 'Listen,' I would say, 'have you heard the one about...' and before you'd know it they'd be doubled up, laughing, wheezing, pounding on the floor and falling against walls, or they'd be sobbing, the tears plopping down their cheeks, their poor hearts bursting. 'By God, that was a good one!' they'd say. 'By God, Deacon, that was a pip! What a beaut!'

So I don't know now. The heart has gone out of it. Maybe I need the enthusiasm of those good old days, expectant faces lining the bar, urging me on, quiet as snakes while they waited for what was to happen next and always knowing there'd be a good solid snort of another man's liquor at the end. I don't know. Can't tell. Maybe I have begun to lace my tales with too many non-essentials like that rubbish about Gladys or even that my foot was hurting in the first place. Maybe my whole approach is wrong. I've become fancy, gone twisty in the lingo and the mind. I'll have to think about it. Have to lay off the newspaper and TV for a while. Go easy on the booze. Try to recapture what I had at the start. Go back to scratch. Anyway, that's the advice my wife will give, late at night when I roll hurt and trembling into her arms. 'Stick to a single incident,' she will say. 'Make use of chronological time. Keep it simple. You will get your confidence back in time. I'll help you. If you get into trouble, you know you've always got me here to fix it up.'

Memoirs of a Cross-Country Man

THOUGH THE DAYS ARE HEAVY, the nights they are starry-eyed. The first night at Estalavita Monastery I have terrible dreams which none of whom come true fortunate to say. In the dream I am like the beast being stroked after the long and fearful journey over hills, sweat guzzling off the hide and the hair slicked down, smooth hand on the rump and the sugar cube in the mouth, a cool voice whispering in the deadness of the ear: 'A mangy jackass, him, too bad he have to carry such a heavy load.' The voice in the ear is the talking in my head, the ear opposite asking what was said. And the talk goes on. Each minute of the darkness of the night I wake myself leaping from the bed, crying, *Where am I?* Crying next, *Marguerite, where are you?* Stumbling in the dark to close my arms on air. Falling back inside the rippling dream to say, *Ahh, here she is!* To drift along under the soft waterfall of her touch.

In sleep González is as much awake as he will ever be. And though the days are heavy, the nights they are starry-eyed. I go about Estalavita like a man entombed: working, walking, gnawing on the thumb. As much walking on my head as I am on the feet, half the time not knowing where I am, while the prison of the body and the poison of the well and the sweet harmony of the torpedo acid tubes meet to decide which will make the final claim. Mouth hanging open, the bowels too weak to turn, myself too blind to tell the difference if they do. Our first day at the Pasadoke Hotel Marguerite have said to the fat grinning man behind the desk, 'Where is a good place to get something to eat and drink?' And reach for the comic book to ask again, *Dónda está un lugar bueno para ir a comer y tomar algo* ... and that question now tumble over in my head to make me sick, the thought of drink, of food, the thought of Marguerite. Flushed face and changing smile, oh perfect picture then the happy bride! Now a loss that sickens too. And in the sky a puff of plane exploding the face of my poor mother everywhere.

'Busy yourself,' the good Brother John advise.

I do, I do. I scrub out the pots and pan, plant food in the garden outside the wall, hoe and rake and sweep the trash, scrub down the cell and wash the back of the good Brother John and before the door the apple peel of the bad Brother Sam and look out the way for the lost crazy man who wander in one day looking he say for the search of the holy Grail. Oh, there are all sorts here and I make myself useful to this bunch you bet, never mind the bull, never mind the banging of the head on the stones of the wall, the mutterings of the head in the sleeve, the trampling of the feet on nails ... never mind, I say to myself, for González Manuel he is not so far gone he don't know a good deal when he see.

'Maybe,' I say to Brother John, 'maybe I stay on, turn the spade here, wear me a gown, go barefoot on the soil, grow old and die unbeknown to the loved ones far away who never give a thought to me, I help you all for all my life González is a hard-working mule. González have found his place in the world, never mind this place be a tomb and I blow away to dust if ever I come again to fresh air.'

'You got it bad,' John say, 'but I think you'll live.'

That much they say and more, these crazy men, and even old Brother Sam, sorry as bastard ever was born, always kick you when you scrubbing the wall, punch your nose and starve you naked for the kindest word, even he will have to say in the end *Favour him O Father the poor miserable halfbreed, the poor mangy wop González Manuel, for in my heart I believe he has atoned for his evil and cannot help his stupid ways.*

I look it, that much to be sure, the mangy lowdown wop who steal the hubcaps even while the car is moved, who yank from the mouth the last biscuit of the starving pariah-dog, but who can help what he look who have been through where I have gone? I smack the first bastard say it isn't true and maybe I smack you just because!

In the meantime I work along with the ways of the time at hand. González Manuel he a man of many moods, be something in this world his moods if they last more than the second quick. Even in the dreams sometime I am in trudge with the mushness of the heart, crying up forgiveness for the sorry sonofbitch who poison me at the well, for Marguerite who leave me flat, even for the man in the street I never see ... for all the bastardmen who hit me everywhich time I turn and kick me in the teeth when I am begging please — even him I forgive for a man can afford if he know that somewhere once in the world is a woman like Marguerite who have give her love to him and maybe no doubt would send her best if even she know where to send.

The first day after the sleep I have already become Christian in the concept of the holy brothers of the monastery. A private ceremony with Brother John who baptize me from the heathen way and confess my sins, saying, *Now repeat after me:*

I know Father I have sinned because the heart is a bare and naked bone.

I know Father I am unworthy for my head is like unto a cloud of dust.

Sure, a drunkard he can spit on stone but González Manuel on the safe side will make no fool of God. A man come up slow when he fall where I have been: he come up with a slow look around and a sharp eye to the blind spots everywhere. Smart you bet, never no more the hatrack where the head should be. To the blind spot come the chop that take the head with it to the frying pan. If not the blind side then look out straight ahead. It is the man looking you straight in the eye pretty as you please, saying, *What a nice day, González, howdeedoo, I be glad to help you any way I can, food, drink of water from the well, whatever you could want for I am here to serve* — oh you look out for him, I tell you this, for just when you saying to yourself, *This one good Joe sure as the day I'm born, just the best sonofbitch I ever see* — why just then the bastard will haul out the axe and send your head flying halfway up the mountain top.

It take a time but I have learn: never look a man in the eye. Look at the sky, look at the shoe, stand awhile and shuffle the feet, and when you ready to go, back up and take the long way round. Once you stare the bastard in the eye he good as have you in the cup of the hand.

'I know what you mean,' say Brother John. 'I been that road myself.'

'A man of my nature,' I say to him, 'how he to live his days? Dusting the britches of whoever hand him the broom?'

The brother smile and wave his hand: 'Some men are born', he say, 'to wave the wand, others to record the magic fact, most to slave till the magic comes, to push the dirt and hoard up strength against that time when the dirt pushes them.'

He carve the bread, grinning, easy to see González Manuel is all of him ears. 'You want me to tell you', he say, 'what your life has been, to tell you what death is? God knows, if all the black holes of the earth were placed one inside the other and then you were placed inside the smallest, the blackest of these, then that would be your life up to now. What travels you've had, González, they've all been on the wings of a darkness formed by all the lives you've left behind. Leaving life and entering death in your present state, you'd never know you'd made a turn. The final loneliness distinguishes the living from the dead and I ask you, one poor deluded sinner asking another, where do you think you are now? You're like me, you don't know. Who does? The body does not immediately yield up all its parts, neither expect the spirit to enter into all of hers. Have you entered the room of a dying man? That's what the hush is all about. The crazy doctors can't fix a proper time of death because they can't measure the spirit pull. All those ghostly Helens mucking up the air! González, man is illness personified, how can he know when he will die? Your life has been one long attempt to come to grips with your own passing from this passing world, you've wanted it to be simple as signing your x to the dotted line. Put down the x, you've said, and let the grave be filled. That's why you've invented this stupid story about some bastard at a well trying to poison you!'

Invent! When I am passed out with fever by the well and seventeen days delirious through the screaming sand, falling on my face a thousand times before I face up to falling here? Invent! With the bastard spic buzzards crawling on the head one day and the clothes all gone where the sorry man at the well have stolen even them! Naked through the desert crawling every mile! '*Stupido!*' I say, '*tres stupido!* Maybe you tell me where the invention end?'

John, he carve off the cheese and drink the wine and lean back to study me. 'Oh, nonsense,' he finally say, 'González, I saw you with my own eyes: you crawled into these walls like a man crawling out of a thousand caves. The truth is you like and demand your lowly state, you've got a craving to be the downtrodden man. I submit — goddamn, with all earnestness I do — I submit that the days you lay stinking at the well, the days you crawled sick, hungry and burning across those baking hot miles to this place represented your closest communion with man. If you're honest I believe you'll admit that those experiences were the most satisfying you've ever known, more satisfying by far than this wretched love of Marguerite you talk so much about. Bird brain! You recognized the spirit pull! You hit for that stage of painlessness beyond the pain! While with Marguerite, if my guess is right, you recognized what life could be with all your dark boxes gone, with sunlight on your brow. And being the crazy *hombre* that you are, you recoiled. You couldn't even consummate your wedding vows.'

How he know? The bastard monks they look you in the eye and root the sorry secret out. And now he have that much still he root some more. He stab the knife in the carving board and study my face hard.

'I've been wanting to ask you', he say, 'about all this wop business you talk about. Your blue eyes interest me. For instance I've been wondering, goddamn you, how they got that way. In my experience two figs do not make a peach. But we can go into that another time, I guess: what puzzles me now is why you talk the way you do — that absurd pidgin-English you fill your mouth with. In your sleep — hell, in those crazy dreams of yours! — I've seen you talking straight as I'm talking now. Is it because you see yourself as fool? You refuse to present yourself seriously for fear that seriously you've nothing to present? Is that it?'

What I say? Once in the city by the river when I am with Marguerite she say that very thing to me. You don't fool me, she say, not one little bit. What I *can* say except a man his own lifestyle is all he have. He have more I have *her* with me now. When a man lose the style he go looking for the flair. That gone, then he can go looking for the dotted line, for Mr x to hold his hand. Seven years I been to night school, three years I go to Harvard-Yale, I am in good standing with the American Academy of the Poets and read every word of the encyclopaedia job I sell, not to mention the money I spend to buy the taco stand. The Taco *Ding-Dong* franchise, all of it mine. All the same a man who never know where he get off neither do he know where he get on. At the wedding in the church Marguerite introduce me saying, 'González, you remember Miss Hannah, I'm sure,' and who is it in front of me but a woman I never seen before who smile and say, 'Oh, yes! you're that nice orderly who left Margy the flower in the jar when she was sick!' and to myself I say, 'Me? Where?' Later she take me aside, say, 'Psssst, let's share secrets, let's,' and she say sure she remember me good, good to see me again now, got one good girl I have, be good to Margy, worship her very ground — but listen, she say, never breathe a word to her that I was the one left the flower in the jar, I stole it from that awful grouch Gladys Beer, the lady with the boils, sure you remember her, Jesus what a case!

And then she trip off to leave González tripping on himself, which way knowing where to turn? What hospital? When? I never see you before, Miss Hannah, never see Marguerite as a child sick. One time I work the hospital sure but I am down in the basement blackface shovelling coal to the boiler room, keeping close watch the gauge which the bossman say will blow the whole shebang skyhigh one day. Sure, and never see these people seeing me, leaving flowers in the jar, never setting eyes on Marguerite, you bet, otherwise I marry her long before.

Who is González Manuel is why he talk the way he do but *who is he* is the question yet. God knows a man on the run, a man who leave running every place he go, he not have time to sit back with blowing smoke from the pipe, careful polish of the phrase or spit shine on the shoe! Who you know can speak like the prince when inside he know he is being made the clown?

'You can lead the burro to the water-hole,' I tell that man John, 'but how can he be made to shout *Olé?*'

'If you are a man who has been led there,' he say, 'if you are not stupido as a donkey's rear end, then the *Olé* is every place you look. It's the looking that brings it there. Take my case now: my mother, as sorry a little water-hole as ever you saw — my mother took in strangers for the night. *Way* in, is what I mean. You think that wasn't hard on me? And my Father? My Father killed a man in Richmond, Indiana, another in Bull City, Arkansas, a third in Montreal, Quebec. These are all they traced. Mother spent her best years trying to get me sent to him, saying a boy needed a dad and didn't I need him? I arrived with my bags and a note from her to him in Sacramento, California, on the day he was being gassed! He'd been caught finally but the case was one of mistaken identity. A friend had used his name while successfully murdering three in a family of four. The fourth insisted my father was the man who had sliced the throats of her parents and her brother, aged ten. The same friend who had accomplished this told me so himself, he bought me coffee and pie and admitted he would kill me too if I breathed a word. The surviving girl in the murdered family fell in love with me and I with her, we were to be married but at two o'clock in the morning on the day the wedding was to take place a TWA jetliner crashed into the house of the uncle and aunt with whom she was staying, killing seventy-eight persons on board, not to mention the aunt and uncle and the girl herself. This friend of my father found me in the city of Miami, demanded money from me not because he felt I owed it to him but because he simply was down on his luck and didn't know who next to kill. I pitched him out the window of the ninth floor room of the Sheraton-Plaza hotel but what the police didn't know was that he was dead before he hit the street. True, I swear to God! He'd had a heart attack when he realized through me that death was staring him in the face. A fire in the hotel that night killed another thirty-six and I was a hero, single-handedly saving four people from Idaho trapped in their rooms. A happy story? Listen, my mother shot herself in desperation one evening when one of the strangers wanted to drink rum when all she had was gin. He had dared her to shoot as an example that she cared. I held her head in a towel while he phoned for the ambulance, and fled. That same night in a period of two hours nine women were raped at knife-point within a mile of where we then lived. Upwards of a hundred people witnessed these acts but none stepped forward to halt them and no two witnesses agreed as to what the rapist wore. Need I tell you that man was me? Soon afterward I placed myself as novice here. And my past is saintly compared with the past of most of my brothers here. Now I write psychoanalytic articles for the learned journals and use the small payment to support the works of poverty, celibacy, obedience to our superior grace, and love. Otherwise I pray. I find you refreshing to talk to, González, for you strike me as one vastly unlike myself: you're a victim as I but, unlike myself, it isn't because you've acquired the taint of sin. You can't tell me about your well because I know the goddamn place better than you ever will.'

He stands, taps finger to brow, scrapes crumbs from the jaws: 'A lovely meal. Now come along with me. It's time you met our chief, Father-Padre, who is double father to all the brothers here. Come. Come.'

A man can bleed from the heart, knowing soon it will bleed no more. There come a time when he is willing to kiss the foot of the man who wiped the shoes on the head. If I feel bad then I don't know yet González is a lucky man. The night I make the visit to the Father-Padre is the same night a sane man flees. The Father occupy the cell at the end a narrow hall, dark and cold, up high somewhere in the monastery wall. Up high too a single window which hove in the sun on shiny days, thin beam of light over the bare stone wall, across the bare stone floor, and the very air it is damp, bare and cold. Father-Padre himself resemble no man González Manuel have ever seen, bleak features in the clouded face which afterward I cannot recall to say this is how the Father looked or even this was how he seem. Tall figure in the white robe, bare red toes upon the stone, he does not walk he flows, wisp of dank musty odour moving in the faint darkness of the cell. Down across the brow and winding down past the cheek a wide purple scar looking fat upon the sunken skin, the thinnest man in all the world and tall enough to stoop for doors. Sometime somewhere someone have pull all the nails from the fingers, all the hair from the head and the skin have the colour purple like a man who have come back from the grave and soon to head there again. In his eyes are the calm depths of a man who never dream.

It is cold enough to freeze the nuts between the legs.

You feel unloved, González Manuel? Estalavita loves you. You have been ill-used? We will not ill-use you here. God is nothing, man is less. Are you hungry? In the kitchen there is soup, porridge, bread and cheese. I myself partake only of bread, a raw egg once each day. What we have is yours, what you have is ours. As you have come many have come before. As you leave so will others go. We are one with you, you are one with us.

Father-Padre he does not speak with words, at the end of the cell a writing stand which have a camera set behind. Built into the opposite wall and to the walls of other cells where I work I have found the green face of the television screen which take closed circuit his message every wall. The message unroll on the screen like a man turning the wheel by the hand.

You will have observed I have no crucifix on the wall, no chain around my neck. Who is God if not me — and you? The soul serves, as does the floor for my feet without the need of shoes. Assume I know your thoughts, your trials: each place you have been I have been before. In this cell for seven years I have stood: it is forbidden that I take rest by sitting or lying down. Once each month for one hour I am transported into the courtyard for sun and it has been noticed that where I tread, the grass nevermore will grow. All around us are dying men, the best of these I attempt to summon here as I have summoned you. Call upon me when you wish, make no regard for light or day. If I am here, but gone in a manner you shall understand, do not be afraid. Stay for what length you must, share in what comforts you may find: we are an extension of yourself. In what other way can your happiness exist? We of this order are bound by rule and practice the councils of perfection as best we can. There is no finish, there is no end, and while there is corruption anywhere there can be no perfect human being and for this reason Estalavita has latitudes of grace. Our most exacting rule is our confinement to these walls since in our imperfection we can hurt no one but ourselves. Howevermany light years we remove ourselves from the common laws of mankind these laws remain no less embedded than is mankind itself embedded within the rock and clay and our mixtures within the clouds. I do not mean to be obscure. My whole attention rests not on you or even on the difficulties which brought you here. No person may leave running but something of value is left behind. History is the truth of this and in the running the place we have run to is not better or worse than that place left behind. God is wicked, man is no less. We have passed from darkness into light and into darkness again and with each passing the shadows have not changed. And death makes no room for you. Leave nothing behind when you go. Arriving, nothing will have been there before. You are one with me, I am one with you. Sisters in light are brothers in darkness before. The eye of the storm is brainless, it occupies a centre and is powerful beyond reckoning, it goes where it goes.

The screen is blank now, nothing on it shows. The drum rolls empty inside the screen as the idea flowing outside my head. I am at peace I think but who can call me satisfied? Despite all the good intentions of Father-Padre, González is no nearer to where he was. Face to the spangled boughs of desert scrubs the crooked sky is fading under the cold flush of the rising moon. At this point in the corner the Father stands silent, not one eye move or muscle twitch, he is nothing short of dead. Outside the window a flutter of wings, in the sky a black bird flying for the trees.

And in the corridors of the hall there is the smell of water sweating on the stone, the musky damp of moss around a tomb. I don't know why I think of death but it is what González feel. My own footsteps slide along the wall and come back to me echoes like the walk of someone dead. A man in my state is in no hurry to go fast, no haste to move at all. Black space is at my rear, even blacker is the space before. If I am not dead myself then González have the sense of the dead following slow behind. It remind me of the time I am a child alone in the room, alone in the black house waiting for the mother to come, for the day to come when the ghosts are gone. A man can stop where he is and stare all the way through the black dark to the childhood days to see himself trembling as he tremble then and if he is honest he can admit to himself, González the childhood have followed you each step the way, or even plead inside the heart, Sonofbitch, don't follow me no more.

Housed in the vaults along the corridor walls the dead brothers of the sect. One above the other for all the distance the candle goes. Living with the living is not enough, now I have also I think to live with the dead. And all the time I am wanting to run a long shriek is climbing inside the throat and a busy hand pushing from the rear. For I know something else to come, one more vault to find, my own. *González*, the deathman say — *are you there?* One time maybe I was — but now? In the dark the truth and the lie sleep side by side, face to face: one day when the dark is black enough maybe the lie will turn and run. *González, are you there?* Only Marguerite knows I am. I tell myself now that if she say I have left the flower in the jar and reveal it dry between the pages of the book who then knows better? She or me? Sure the darkness the answer knows but will it tell me?

Oh, the night is busy one I have. Later on the crazy monk who search for the Holy Grail come awake to say, 'Got you now!' The eyelids roll, a second later he is dead. His body it is prepared for the vault within the walls, before the light of morning come it is sealed away behind the stone which read:

All-arm'd I ride, whate'er betide,
until I find the Holy Grail.

If he found it, the brothers say, let it go with him.

'Shit,' Brother John say, 'it takes a crazy man not to know he's had it all the time. The blood of God is never spilled, ours you'll find every day.'

Sure and I come to find the thing in the bed I have been sleeping with is none other than myself. Myself that feels the shape I hold, the shape that will conduct the body over the wall of stones to the level digging earth which say finally HERE HE LIES. The truth is that the trouble with González have finally brought him low. Meanwhile the God who gives life to the biggest fool will say Carry on. When the last trumpet sound still will there be music in the ears ... if not that then a clanging in the head. A natural death, the deathman say, is all the law allows. The dream is in the sleep but what is in the dream? Sometime between the taking of the porridge and the chewing of the bread I find myself, González back at the bridal rooms of the Hotel Pasadoke sending off to the newspaper the classified ATTENTION READERS OF THE NEWS: *When last seen she have blue eyes, about my height, wearing tight-fit English tweed high above the knees. Pantyhose neptune blue, no hat and alligator shoes. Reward offered, write me here, you be glad you did.*

Leave Running

YOU AWAKE, Igor? Igor?

By her side Rose's lover stirred.

Igor the thief, Igor the lover — opened his eyes, saw the sun sliced on the floor.

God, don't you hate venetian blinds?

It wasn't the blinds but the sun that Igor didn't like.

Cigarette, Igor?

Her finger poked his shoulder. Poked again.

Igor?

You know, Rose, said Igor — Rose, you know I never smoke.

No, she said, I didn't know. She poked again but he refused to move. Igor, thief and lover, refusing to turn and look at her.

I've got to go.

He said nothing. She saw him close his eyes, and immediately her own eyes were shut tight.

Flesh is impermanent; let us grieve that it is not forever anchored to these beds. To these afternoons. She lifted a thin arm as if to compel the blinds to close and descend.

I've got to, she said.

Go, he said.

People of Igor's persuasion are trained for this. They come and go, they enter and leave. What they find in between is the only burden they have.

She rested on an elbow — surveyed Igor's room. Drab, sterile, empty — she would find no ghosts here. Her fingers stroked lazily through Igor's hair. All my life people have been leaving me or I have been leaving them. Parents, children, friends. My husband goes to work, my children go to school. Where did I go, Igor, before you came to me?

Igor groaned.

What are you looking at, Igor?

The floor.

She placed an ear against his lips to get these words. Igor the house thief, Igor the break-in man: it was not his habit to speak often or loud. He adjusted his voice only to compensate for whatever noise was occurring within. Within himself, that is, where stealth was the rule. Igor spoke the way he moved: a shadow at the back door. Lift a latch, slither through. Igor the cat burglar is inside your house. Hide your silverware, your TV, put a lock on your bedroom door.

Rose shifted, rolled away from him. His skin was damp, he looked too thin, too dirty. The smell of the thousand closets and basements he had hidden in, passed nights inside, attached itself to him.

One night you awaken, your husband is asleep by your side, you hear a creak in the floor — and there in the dark stands Igor the housebreaker at your husband's dresser, dousing himself with cologne. You watch him in the mirror; minutes go by before you realize he has also been watching you.

I smoke too much. I know I do. Maybe I shouldn't have come.

Maybe, he said.

Across the line of shotgun rooms a gruelling trail of abandoned clothes. The afternoon had a weight Igor couldn't endure. He needed night. Darkness. Then he could slither free.

She fussed, blew smoke across his nose: You're no help at all. In your own way you're just like Talbert. Next time I'll send him. Maybe you'd like that.

Igor lay very still. This woman frightened him. People did who didn't know when or how to shut up.

She had sat up in bed that night she remembered. She had said, Try the *Monsieur de Givenchy*, it's the best in the house.

She stared at his sunken cheeks — Igor, why don't you ever shave? — at his pale flesh, his bones, his thin chest and dirty nails — at the stubble of beard which was blue. Her own cheeks burned.

I get along.

Igor resented this. This woman was silly, it was not her business to instruct him. He could ask questions, too: why have you been following me? What is your purpose with me? But he knew the answers: Rose wanted to be the housebreaker now.

I do okay.

Yes, she said. Her wine-red nails traced along his spine. Yes, I'm sure you do.

He burrowed deeper under the sheet. His rooms held no secrets, contained no evidence; they were furnished as they had come. The rooms, to his mind, were a mark of pride: anyone could live here.

Igor, you don't have to continue in this line. I have money enough for the two of us.

She lifted the sheet off him.

It may be a low-risk profession, she said, but you could still get caught and go to jail.

Igor thought it unlikely. Houses didn't resist; their occupants didn't either. They watched TV, they read, they slept. Wall-to-wall carpets cushioned his steps. He rarely had to search for what he came for. In fact, it seemed to Igor that the houses welcomed him.

That night she had let her husband sleep. Had made no move to reach the bedside phone. Had left her body exposed.

Do you like the *Givenchy*? Talbert's wallet is in his inside breast pocket. Did you find my jewels?

Of course he had fled. And although he had taken a circuitous route in returning here — darting up alleys and across back yards — he had sensed someone in pursuit of him.

After all, Igor, it isn't especially ennobling to be what you are. What did you do with our toaster? Two bucks at a pawn shop?

Igor remained silent and still.

Igor? Igor?

Her voice was a whisper. Igor, listen! Did you hear something just then? Has someone broken in?

The woman was silly; she was playing games. But he turned, looked at her.

Igor? When you go out tonight, I want to go with you.

He shook his head in protest. His fists gripped the sheet.

I'll be careful. I won't even enter the house with you, I'll stay outside and watch, if that will make you comfortable. But I want to see the house you rob. I want to be there when you break in.

She stretched across him, reaching for the ash tray, raking his face with her breasts. He caught a nipple in his mouth, closed his teeth on it. She held her breath, pressed against him.

Harder, Igor. Harder.

Her expression never changed. Finally he let go, licked gently around the wound.

That hurt, Igor. But I have control. I can be quiet. I can walk on cat feet. They will never know I am there. Which house do we hit, Igor? Have you one picked out? Can we do it tonight?

Good second-storey men do not take disciples on. Do not conduct tours for women who have nothing else to do. It takes one man alone to feel out and come to terms with that darkness in which people live.

Take me with you, Igor.

The risks were increasing. Around him, Igor suspected, traps were being laid.

No, Rose. Rose, go home.

AT HOME — at home her husband Talbert was swearing at the piled-up sink, the filthy house — mess of scabby wounds over every minute of this and every other bleeding day. What a goddamn day, where is she? Where? Where are you, Rose? He stormed from kitchen to living-room to bathroom door: stood there pounding on the painted plywood. Nell? Rose-Nell, you in there? I'm coming in! He waited, hearing her scream *don't you dare*; her quick urgency as she flushed the toilet, closed the lid, stood to face him, scowling, near to tears: 'Can't you see it's occupied! Must you always barge right in!' He opened the door to the empty room — to this room empty as every other.

Another indignity spared.

But where are you, Rose?

The floor showed pools of water by the tub, bathing accoutrements overturned. Careless, arrogant Rose had had occasion to wash herself, she could not be bothered to pick up or even to rearrange her debris: oils, milk bath by Xanadu, her Jean Naté lotions, her talcum by Shalimar. Wherever she was she'd be smelling good. Too goddamn good, he thought, cursing her for that part she had left him: tiny dark leg-hairs at the bottom of the tub, his razor on the ledge unclean. He flipped on the tap, washed the Gillette clean. The water pipes clanged, nothing in this house worth a damn.

He followed over the waxed floor a wet trail of feet — entered the bedroom. The closet was open, wire hangers scattered about in a tangle — like live things, he thought, thin idiotic little bastards that had fought among themselves. Clothes had slid free, frothy soft piles of cotton, satin, velvet, acrylic nothings now a rummage load, mummy wrappings above her unmatched shoes. One of the four sliding doors slammed off its rollers: further evidence of flight. And now, here, another pool of water where she had sat at her dressing table preparing her Goddess face.

He sat on her wet, padded stool, studied his own mirrored countenance. In the old days there might have been lipstick messages on the glass: GONE TO SCHOOL, GONE TO STORE (DINNER IN THE FRIDGE). Civilization, he thought, what place have we come to now? With the coming of streets, housing tracts with scrub-yards, the pouring of concrete over every falling mile — with all that, a person could no longer track another human down. All the tracks covered over. They sped from here to there — suburb to city — somewhere in between they disappeared. Carried there — Nell anyway — by salmon instinct, by whatever else was blind in them ... to run against the stream a thousand miles, back to whatever had spawned them, waylaid them, there themselves to spawn, waylay, mingle bodies, mingle ocean oil and Georgia Strait perfumes: plant eggs, rot and die.

Nell?

Rose-Nell?

He sat there, softly speaking her name; he didn't know why.

Stupid, he said. Out of my goddamn head.

On the strewn bed the clothes she'd contemplated and refused. In an age of abundance looking for the one perfect garment for her much-considered flesh.

Zipper me up, Talbert.

Talbert, don't sit there sulking, dopey as a mule.

He lifted organdy frock to hand, buried his face within its folds. Powder, sweat, mould, perfumes: that good closet mulch. Here a stain under the arm, let's throw this one aside. Now another — but no good, observe the broken stitch. Try this one, yard upon yard of see-through Turkish stretch, painted eyes here where breasts would rise. A gift, he remembered, of Christmas last, a small offering intended to ease the strain of times too hard: themselves at each other's throat. Something whimsical and sexy from him to her, notice that hereafter he would try harder to satisfy. With it a card written in Santa's hand: WHEN YOU WEAR THIS HOW CAN I REFUSE? Yet he had, not once but a dozen times. With her clothes off she scared him half to death, another perfect body saying *Satisfy, satisfy!*

He pitched it down. Seventy dollars at Mr Pearl's Main Street store but not good enough for whatever she was doing now. Gone where? *Where are you, Rose?* For a month now he'd come home to find her in blue jeans, ratty knees and drooping seat, ratty bandana holding up her dingy hair — up to her ears in smoke, in a litter of tea cups and her ratty magazines.

Good day? he'd ask.

Up yours Talbert, honey.

What had happened to his perfect bride?

IGOR?

She rolled, stubbing out her cigarette. Hating cigarettes, her menthol mouth. One day I'll put an entire package in my jaws, chew on that: get my fill of the bloody things.

Watch it, he warned — but too late. The tray overturned, scattering ash and stub over Igor and the sheet.

I'm sorry, she said. Clumsy. Maybe I'm nervous. Why don't you wash this filthy sheet.

She fingered ashes and cigarettes into a pile, then placed the ash tray upside-down over the perfect mound.

Now they are safe, she said. And smiled for the very first time that day. Do you enjoy me, Igor?

He shifted, wanting to put space between himself and her. Stroking her buttocks with one light hand while the second stroked to find that shape in the air.

The chemists are wrong. Air is composed of solids — they are invisible but they are there. Ask any break-and-enter man; it is the first lesson learned.

God, she said. Don't you hate these blinds?

He stared gloomily at the floor. Was the sun going down? The window's shadow still angled along the floor, sun slicing through the open blinds. But the blades were less distinct now. Shadows were in retreat. Soon the night would conquer all.

A few theologians are on the right track; soon night will be all there is.

I notice nothing about these rooms, Igor. I couldn't tell anyone what this place looks like, even at the threat of death. The police may wring my neck, they'll get nothing out of me. Do you have any chairs? Rugs? What colour are your walls? I don't know, Igor. I don't know an Igor either. What was that name again?

In Igor's view, she talked too much. She would want to wake her victims: Hello. Igor and I are burglarizing your home.

She might even be violent, for all he knew. Would looting be enough? He could see her shaking her victims awake: Hello. I'm stabbing you now.

Igor, do you know what I'm looking for? In those houses I hope to enter with you?

Igor nodded.

Sure. A marriage better than your own.

AT HOME her husband Talbert sat at her dressing table, balanced on the padded mahogany stool. Another antique, he thought, like myself. He stared at the mirror, said out loud: I see you, Talbert. And leaned close, intending to determine if indeed there was something or someone there:

The person I was, he meant, before I became me.

Good eyes, he said, I see you. I can look into them and believe I exist. But it was because he could remember the good old days

— when he had believed. He settled back, crossed his legs. Fusing within his, her image too.

Where are you, Rose.

A cold dampness on his lower back made him twist about: her abandoned towel, pressed flat now, marring the finish of this ridiculous stool. Inlaid silver no longer gleamed. Four hundred dollars, just six months ago, at the Antique Gallery on Fort Street.

He could place these antiques end to end and they'd reach all the way out of town. But all the way wasn't far enough. What am I doing here? Why do I bother to come home? He didn't know. Time had him floating here. Time would float him on again. Vaguely, he could remember it had been a busy day. His days always were; it is out of jealousy that the night has a thousand eyes. He got up, kicked the stool, balled a fist, stuck it to the mirrored nose: no solace there. He turned and left the room before his anger could mellow into disgust.

The children had come in. In the TV room they didn't look up as he passed — slouching, lingering — by the door. Children, he thought, *my* children! Gloomy lamp-post sons. Do you see me here? Your old Dad? Scratch gravel, Tonto, hi-yo Silver, awayyyyyyyy! What he had only on Saturday afternoons, they now had every day. He resented that, yes, he did. His own childhood had been lived in a wait for Saturday, for the afternoon western, for the evening horror show. Occasionally Frankenstein and the Wolfman still moved behind this glass but the horror had gone out of them and left nothing in its place.

Goddamn TV, he muttered, and kicked the wall. Walked on. You, Talbert, are the monster now.

The metal clamour, metasonic boom, rang in his ears, pursuing him back to the kitchen where he rattled pots and pans, searched for a dish towel that didn't have the stench of decaying food. Liberated womanhood had harnessed him without fanfare to house and stove. Pick up, scrub up, hurry up — dump all your garbage, Talbert, into this pail. Then dump pail over the TV, over the very heads of your rapt-eyed sons. Here's advice, sons: swim into the canned laughter, the metered applause.

Wake up! Wake up!

Goddamn stove. He swiped damp cloth around the metal rings. Around the drunken metal eyes. Slapped it across the enamel top. Stooped — flushing, hurting in his joints — and smeared away at grease, coffee stains, blood — this anonymous scum. Stood and slowly wiped the metal eyes again. Through these eyes one saw into the soul of mankind. These eyes that could work man or woman into an early grave.

Something is wrong with us. It is madness to insist on three meals each day. Or even two. The cattle should eat us.

He turned on the electric eye, watched it go red. What are you doing, Talbert? I am working in a circle. You start here and slowly close it around. At this moment you are about at this point and as you can see, Talbert, things are heating up. We call this, Talbert, the story of your life.

He turned off the element. Watched the eye go cold, and nodded his appreciation: either way it was the story of his life.

Where are you, Rose?

The kids would have to be fed soon. Kids have no dignity, they scream when they are hungry. His had been taught to scream three times a day. He imagined certain conversations he might have had with his own stalwart mother:

What would you like for dinner, son?

A bleeding field of sugar cane. I want to chomp into a bagful of clouds, to chew them and swallow them and float away to be broken up and blown and made to fall again like rain.

You're a shitty little son, his mother said. Why don't you go off somewhere and play with yourself?

A bold, beautiful, prefab woman. She would fold tent and go, flee motherhood better than any other living thing.

His mom: ironing in the raw, pointing her iron at the three weeks of fermenting brew who sat at the kitchen table, elbows at rest among apple peels.

Oh, your mom's a devil, isn't she, son! If God hadn't been tired He'd have worked on her some more.

He? Who is the *He* you're speaking of? Screw, Mama said, your old hook-nosed God! And circled the table, leaving the iron to smoke away the ironing board — leaving all to bend and stick her mouth on his, poke her tongue inside, working to open his fly and place her hand inside.

Dear old mom: she knew how to keep a boy on his toes. Knew how to make those close to her stop and think.

You go on about your business, said mom. Can't you see your father and I have business here? Come on, pa — awake!

Wake up! Wake up!

He applied a last dab of filthy cloth to the laminated counter top: waited a moment, fascinated, as the wet trails dried, leaving nothing there. Except himself and pa and dear old mom. *Where are you, Rose?* He turned, flung the grimy crumb-sodden cloth across the room to the piled-up dishes in the sink.

Wash yourselves.

Then strode back through the dining-room, the living-room, bedroom, sunroom, and hall — making the rounds like a night watchman with a watch on everything but his clock. Wrestled back to the TV and yelled:

You mangy kids! You dope-eyed sons, turn off the set! Off! Get outside! Go on, go! Outside and play! Take your baseball hats, your hockey sticks, your skates, your goddamned —

Aww, Dad, moaned the oldest — we want to see the end of this!

Of what? Do you even know what you're watching?

It's Gilligan's Island, Dad. They've found gold!

Marooned, marooned. Let myself be marooned like that silly twerp, Gilligan: rewound, rerun, to find gold here at five o'clock with these bloody kids. He relented, standing before them with twisting torso, his insides knotting hard — then took a deep breath, kicked air, kicked at Gilligan's imbecilic face — kicked at them. No, no, get outside, I mean it now!

But, Dad.

Don't Dad me and where's your Mom?

The boys raised cherub chins, see-through cherub eyes.

How should we know?

You accuse us falsely, oh the injustice of it, Dad! They eased themselves out of the room, tracking lightly around his fumes. Trekked toward the front door, looking over their shoulders — gave a single anguished cry, and disappeared. Consumed by space — banished — gone into thin air. Silence, a silent flesh-eating house. Blessed lovely silence, blessed, so rare as to make him believe for a moment that he'd never known such silence before. Since before his marriage, before his birth — before ... what? He didn't know. A timekeeper adrift in the universe.

He turned on the TV, sat down himself. Stretched his legs. The image blurred, would that it would ever so remain. Retreated, reappeared. This brainless comedy. Marooned between toothpaste ads, between utter stupidity and total insanity — halfass Gilligan now monkey-struggling through the brush, having lost the pirated hoard once found. Dung, dung, said Talbert.

Oh God, what manure!

Is this why Nell had escaped the house? Why she dunged herself out in fine dress and monkey-perfume? Who could blame? A smart woman, Rose. He kicked at Gilligan, aiming for the crotch — succeeding only in jostling the set. Gold glittered in three tides of Quasar green. He took off his shoe, set foot to rest against Giggigan's — Gooligan's? — Gangugee's? — monkey jaws. Did Gilligan have a wife? A child somewhere?

Do you know where they are?

Canned laughter erupted from the set, swimming up his leg, into his head. A drink, I need a drink, he said. A shot, doctor, of your best canned heat. Fire embalming fluid into my veins.

He remained seated, lacking the wherewithal. Good old-fashioned wherewithal. His eyes ached. His very goddamned eyelids ached.

My very goddamn eyelids, doc.

IGOR?

She thumped her cigarette into the ash tray at the slow rise and fall of his chest.

People are nicer when they're happy. Igor, let me come with you?

She held the hot tip of the cigarette an inch above his skin.

Igor, I'm warning you.

MY VERY GODDAMN EYELIDS, Talbert said. Outside — outside he heard a car breezing past, screech of tires, horn raking the neighbourhood. Goddamn horn, goddamn neighbourhood — what was it this time, who were they looking for? He struggled up, stumbled to the window, peered through. Nell?

It didn't sound like Nell's car but was it Nell?

Rose-Nell, have you come home? Back to people who love you?

But it wasn't Nell. Down the street a boy in a hard hat sitting easy at the wheel of an open yellow Porsche — back from the squint-eyed dead, back from the rotting heart of the city to look up old school chums, to say, Chums, that's how it was. To roll back the sleeve, spit on the needle, say, Shoot it to me, Chums, right here. Talbert flipped the curtain aside, flexed his muscle, stared at his trembling arm.

This one's a downer, doc.

Now I'm a crazy nosy old bat with one shoe off and one shoe on. I'm losing it, doc. Down where the Porsche had drawn up, romped a long-haired smiling girl, arms performing a flute dance to the honking horn — now hitting the street in hiphugger boots, tassel-strung leather coat, a shriek that split his ears. She hurled herself across the car's low-slung hood, the driver slid low, geared, spun tires, shot off with the speed of a killer whale.

Praise Love, young love, thought Talbert — Old Burp Gun, Burp God Love, mother of us all.

Nothing like a hot date with a man who knows his wheels.

He wrenched back to his chair, kicked horizontal bars out of the TV face — sat down. Oh to be down on the street, to be off and away, with such an ornament on my hood. To have this instead, this orbit within the Burp God womb, to feed on pep pills, supermarket fluff and bleach, the usual piss politics. To be ever within arm's reach of war, six million Jews, Fascist pigs as heads of state, snipers in the tower, madmen in the trees, how many crazy C. Mansons Mylaiing how many other poor sonsofbitches in how many other villages all along the trail. All along expressways and byways, from the heart of the city to the heart of the city dump.

Nell, Nell, I need you, Nell!

Dad, Dad, you dirty Dad!

The boys came running in, piling in on him, thumping at ribcage, shoulders, head and shin — tugging, poking hard. Out of joyous rage that they had been deceived, that he had supplanted them at the forbidden set.

Dad, oh, Dad, that's not fair.

Whoa, he said, settle down.

They punched and pulled, yanked at his hair, joined in a death grip on his throat.

Say you're sorry, Dad.

I'm —

What are you saying, Dad?

— sorry, boys.

They climbed up him, snuggled in. Snuggled close. To touch something alive and warm. Do you remember, sons? This is the way a real person feels.

What's your favourite, Dad?

My favourite what?

Your favourite program, Dad. I know what mine is.

Where's your mother, boys?

Oh, Dad, not that again!

Idiots-at-large, idiot image of Rose and him — and we are responsible for what they might become. If I were taken for ransom how much would they give to have me back? Four dollars from their piggy-bank, if it interfered with no plans of theirs. In a reasonable age he would be thrown into chains, be dragged to jail, taken up and hanged. In a reasonable age. They stared a moment at the changing show. Here Comes Lucy was coming on fast — another can of worms.

I'm hungry, when's dinner, Dad?

I don't know.

What're we having, Dad?

Disappearing Mom.

Aw, Dad.

She wasn't coming home. Nell had wised up finally and gone away for good.

She's gone, he told the boys. From here on out we're on our own.

Oh, don't be silly, Dad, don't worry so much.

Do I worry, Rose? Rose, am I worried now? He went to his closet, pulled out his lumberjack coat which smelled of smoke and fish, of grass and wood. Pulled on his box-top game warden's badge. Felt for his wallet, forgetting he had misplaced it somewhere.

Where are you going, Dad?

To find Nell, he said. Maybe she's out there on the road, run down by a yellow Porsche with a girl on the hood. Maybe she's up there in the hills, run down by a rampaging moose. Out there in trouble, just waiting for me to appear. You guys behave, get your dinner, put on your pyjamas, do your homework, go to bed, don't sweat it, I'll be back soon.

Don't worry about us, Dad.

He went outside, stood in the yard. It was dark now, a reversed smog bowl in soft romantic illumination above the city.

Where to begin?

IGOR? Is it safe? They are not asleep.

Igor lifted the latch. Slid through. Here he was in control, no one could instruct him. He was the master of these dwellings. She entered behind him, holding her breath. The house seemed hollow, ghost-occupied. The darkness in which she moved was alive, breathing — welcoming this intrusion.

Where are you, Igor? Igor, shouldn't we wait until they go to bed? I hear children, Igor.

Igor's hand closed over her mouth. You have to rush these houses, he said. You have to show them who is boss. His voice was so quick it snapped: Igor the housebreaker filling the skin of Igor the languid lover.

Igor, whose house is this? Igor, I can't see.

You have to feel it, he said — or go home.

She reached for him but he was gone. She stretched out her arms, felt about, could find nothing. It might have been a cave underground, a black box empty except for her. She moved. Nothing scraped, nothing fell. She moved with purpose now, confident that in this utter blackness nothing would get in her way.

The house even feels familiar. I can do it, Igor. I find I have a talent for this.

Again Igor was beside her, this time a light touch on her arm. His whisper matched her own: Yes, you're doing well. Let's go. Let's see what kind of life we have here.

She clutched at his sleeve: I *know* this house, she whispered. It's amazing, Igor! I was made for this work! I can feel the life of this house pulsing in my blood! What next?

But Igor was no longer there. Gone without a sound, a man who could see — who could read — the dark. Where are you, Igor?

She advanced timidly, quivering with tension, her hands outstretched against the dark. In a hush. But the house seemed to hum, to vibrate, as though welcoming the intrusion. How weird, she thought. How exciting. It is as though every room, each nook and cranny, is in willing partnership with this violation. Who lives here? she wondered. What kinds of lives do they lead? What do they know that I don't know? It was not their possessions, their material goods, that she wanted to carry away with her. But their very *lives* that she would steal from. To borrow what *works*!

Stairs, now. She started up. *Hello!* she whispered. *Yoo-hoo! Are you there?*

It wasn't the entering, she decided, that was hard. It would be the leaving. Why not stay awhile? Hide away in the attic, in closets, under the bed. Get to know these people.

Adolpho's Disappeared and We Haven't a Clue Where to Find Him

WE HAD NOT SEEN ADOLPHO for the whole of one month and were beginning to wonder if evil had not befallen him. It must have been about two weeks ago that Skoals, in response to a casual inquiry, remarked that Adolpho was just the sort of innocent, airy person to whom evil was ever liable to occur — 'the plucky, dim-witted sort', he said, 'who will step into a thug's net with his eyes wide open and not know he's been done wrong by until he wakes up at the bottom of a well.'

Nettles objected to this unkind assessment of our friend's character and wanted to know whether Skoals had any cause for suspecting violence had been done him. 'No more than you,' Skoals told him, laughing in that mirthless way he has. 'No more than any one of us.' There seemed sinister intent in this odd comment and for a moment our group fell silent. Then Nettles could stand it no more and in a loud voice emphasized that, speaking only for himself, *he* knew nothing. 'Our friend has simply dropped off the face of the earth,' he lamented, appealing to me, 'but he's a resourceful fellow, I don't suspect he's come to any harm, do you, Philby?'

I felt unaccountably exhausted and could not bring myself to contribute anything useful to the discussion. That is the way I have been of late: as if an incomprehensible maze has opened in front of me and I have stepped involuntarily into it.

'Oh, I expect the bloke will show up in time,' amended Skoals. 'I mean only to point out that criminal acts against those of our station are becoming more and more prevalent. You will recognize, I might add, that Adolpho's habit of going about with a full purse was quite well known.' I suppose each of us gathered around the Statacona fire at that moment patted his breast pocket, for if Adolpho had the habit so did we.

Our servingman Mole at last arrived with fresh drinks, and Skoals felt obliged to ask him whether he could account for

Adolpho's mysterious disappearance. In a splash of rude monosyllables, that oaf professed to a total ignorance of our affairs.

'Gawd,' said Nettles after the man had gone, 'from the way he acts you'd think he never heard of old Adolpho.' A few more remarks were passed on that sullen, impenetrable creature as we tossed back our brandy. It was a slow night at the club, the place being deserted save for ourselves and a clique of newer members, all rogues, and so vulgar and disreputable that no proper gentleman will have fellowship with them. They had been gathering all evening round the fireplace some thirty feet from us, taking quite the best chairs and generally conducting themselves as if they had a direct line to the Queen's bedside.

Then Gerhardt, whom we knew only in a nodding way, decided to make himself familiar. He padded up and stood the longest time by our table, breathing hard and smoothing down his moustache like a diamond merchant. We were finally moved to inquire what the deuce was the matter with him. 'I have news,' he said gravely. Before we could tell him to peddle it elsewhere he rose on his heels and declared that Adolpho had been abducted. 'Yep,' he said, 'ransom note came this afternoon. Thrown through the wife's window, I hear, tied to a stone.'

Skoals's eyes sought mine but I looked away, feeling a surge of nausea. I scarcely saw Gerhardt. I could hear the lick of flames in the fireplace, the clink of glasses, a murmur of voices, but what I was most aware of was the moose head on the panelled oak wall above us. Old Adolpho had donated it to the club.

'How much?' demanded Skoals. 'What figure have these reptiles asked for?'

Gerhardt shook his head in what we took to be abject misery, leaving us to our anxiety while he meditated on the ceiling. 'Have to dig deep,' he finally grumbled. 'All of us. The culprits want a ridiculous sum. Poor Orpha will never be able to raise it.'

Gufstaffson kicked out his stubby legs, stood and strode to the fire, there throwing himself in a slouch against the stone facing. Skoals was scrutinizing Gerhardt with an expression of dreamy consternation. Like him, I couldn't make head or tail of Gerhardt's story. I felt a deep fatigue at that moment — rancid and bitter vision of all the evil set loose upon the world.

'Yep,' said Gerhardt, 'that's the upshot of it. A dangerous business we have here.'

Eventually I became aware of Nettles's hand resting on my knee. He peered at me over his spectacles, his flesh pale as a skinned rabbit, his eyes actually moist. 'What can we do?' he whispered.

We were all in partial shock. I guess it rang in our ears, the coincidence of having just speculated on the possibility of harm coming to our friend.

Gerhardt lifted his arms in a gesture meant to emphasize his magnificence, his voice now booming: 'I'm good for a thousand! What about you gents? I know your group was as tight as quails nesting. I know you won't let Adolpho down.' He thrust his open palm at me. 'How much can we count on from you, Philby?'

I noticed my shoe-laces were untied and reached down painfully to set the loop in them.

My heart was pounding. I've not been in the best of health lately. These days I take my physician's advice seriously: *You've got many good years ahead of you, Philby, if you'll just learn to relax and enjoy yourself. No necessity for you to lead a dog's life any more.*

'You know we can't do enough for old Adolpho,' I heard Skoals remarking. One of the rotters across the room laughed, but when I looked up they were all hidden behind their papers. Nettles and Gufstaffson were whining that their funds were all tied up, any other time they'd happily add to the war chest. Nettles puffed on his cigar. I wanted to lift a foot and kick him.

'Times are unpredictable,' he muttered. 'Our group is not exactly sitting on the treasury, whatever the rumours.' Gerhardt ignored these declarations, though his scorn was apparent. He was still tumbling his fingers under my nose, entreating a donation. I started to speak but my throat went dry and I shrugged my shoulders helplessly. Skoals jumped back in.

'Like to hear more about this ransom note,' he stated gruffly. 'Don't pay to give in too easily to such ruffians. How do we know they haven't already done in old Adolpho?'

Gerhardt's lips curled away from his teeth, his features became truly malevolent. I realized in that instant that he was something other than the noisy upstart we'd taken him to be. He was treacherous and unpredictable, a man to watch out for. Even as I was formulating these thoughts the transformation was continuing. His frog eyes sluiced shut, his lips compressed, his cheeks ballooned, his face turned cherry red. He went high on his toes, trying to keep whatever it was inside. Then his lips shot open and a monstrous laugh suddenly erupted. '*Haw-haw!*' he cried, spurting saliva ... and '*Haw-haw!*' ... and the laughter kept spewing. Tears streamed down his cheeks, he clutched his sides and bent over wheezing, yet those mad *Haw-haws* continued to rain down on us.

We thought the man had gone stark raving Jupiter.

He took to pointing at us and each time his nasty frog eyes opened anew, his guffaws burst forth in greater volume. *Haw-haw-haw* now and *Haw-haw-haw* and more of it, the contemptible dog. After a time we came to realize that the entire club was laughing with him. They were thumping their knees and collapsing in fits against the walls, a bunch of randy hyenas. 'Can't do enough *haw-haw*,' wheezed Gerhardt, 'for old Adolpho *haw-haw* ... times unpredictable *haw-haw* ... not sitting on the treasury *haw-haw-haw!*' It was an embarrassing few minutes, I don't deny it. Gerhardt finally howled his last and dispatched himself over to where his cronies were collecting. Their laughter gradually subsided, though the atmosphere worsened. The club became a black, reeking miasma; suspicion and hostility seemed to engulf us all. We were aware of the spread of sinister whispers and could hear the isolated, anonymous catcall.

We ignored such boorishness as best we could. We realized that Gerhardt, by this action, had proclaimed himself leader of the opposing Statacona faction, that his was precisely the kind of low-born, debased element against which we would have to contend as long as we persisted in our efforts to uphold and perpetuate the club's time-honoured standards. 'We have given the Statacona our best years,' fumed Skoals, 'and this is how they repay us. It would have been a shambles long ago but for Philby and our crowd.'

Shortly after Gerhardt's exhibition our group dispersed. Gufstaffson provoked a mild astonishment by declaring his intention to go that evening and solidify relations with his often estranged wife. Skoals and I thought it best to withhold comment on this reunion. Nettles was more than a little angry and hurt by the suddenness of this announcement. He fell into a gloom and went off soon afterward.

Left alone, Skoals and I brought our heads together in a brief conference. 'What do you make of it?' he asked.

'Of those two?'

He shook his head irritably. 'No, no,' he whispered, jabbing a finger toward Gerhardt's crowd. 'Adolpho. That gang of cutthroats over there.'

My mind refused to move. For a moment I couldn't think what he was talking about.

'Have we reason to worry?' he asked. *He* was worried, I could see that.

'I don't know,' I managed. 'This is deep water we've got into.'

He nodded, lapsing into momentary silence. I watched Mole clearing cigar stands at a nearby corner. The man's baggy breeches were soiled at the knees, his cuffs damp and rolled, as if he had been out digging in a field. 'I don't see why Gerhardt pulled that trick,' muttered Skoals. 'He hardly knows Adolpho, surely his whereabouts are of no concern to that wretch.'

'He thinks we've done it,' I said, looking squarely at Skoals. 'He thinks we've done old Adolpho in.'

Skoals's face dropped. He looked haggard and appalled, an old, old man. It was a face, I thought, that might have been staring at me from a grave. Then his eyes lit up, he found a bright refuge in wit. 'I didn't,' he murmured. 'Did you?'

My own smile felt pasted on my face. I was too tired for Skoals's lame humour. Nor did I receive his remarks so innocently as perhaps he intended them.

A minute or two later we shook hands and he took off.

I pulled my chair nearer to the fire and put my feet up and contented myself watching the flames. The three neighbouring chairs forming our cove remained vacant, even those members of long-established amity avoiding me, aware no doubt of my disdain for the pious oaths they would feel called upon to utter. I couldn't have tolerated any decrepit wag coming along to tell me that I and my friends had been wronged, that rogues like Gerhardt should have their hands fitted with thumbscrews, that this nasty business would soon blow over. Blast them all, I thought, blast the whole kit and caboodle to hell, I thought, and sought to relax, sliding deep into the cushions, closing my eyes which recently seemed to be running to water more and more. . . . I found myself humming a soft, jagged little tune I hadn't thought of since my childhood. The tune had to do with two young, foolish lovers who become separated while on a long journey. Evil times befall them, the years pass. The heartsick maiden is deceived into marrying a dreaded woodsman, ancient and embittered. Marry him, a witch tells her, and you will be reunited with your lover. It doesn't happen that way and our maiden grows old, weeping. Then one day the woodsman goes hunting and his arrow brings down a deer. The distraught woman sobs at the sight of the animal slung so irreverently over the old man's shoulder. Dress it, he tells her, that we may have food for the winter. Unknown to him, she buries the beast in soft earth. That night her lover comes to her bed, reborn, he tells her, because his love is the warm heart of the deer. They murder the dreaded woodsman and in the morning it is his body which is laid in soft earth. Yet the next night, in the arms of her lover, the woman is ravaged by shame and guilt. She sees herself flying through the sky on a stick. She sees a heartsick maiden weeping by a pool and tells her of a dreaded woodsman living nearby and that if she will but marry this embittered old man she will one day be reunited with her lover.

This ballad tormented me, the words kept tumbling over in my head. However had I come to remember such ridiculous tripe? Its childish melody served as a further insult, mocking me for my vain susceptibility, taunting me for my barren life. The tune was insistent: it bounced merrily through my mind, at the same time hovering outside my skull as if God Himself were its punitive composer. Innocence seemed to have no place in the story, it was not germane to God's little hoax. The maiden, the lover, the woodsman: they were all guilty. Murder is done with the same ease and aplomb as one gathers flowers and the right or wrong of it is not an issue. It was very well, I thought, to have said to Skoals that this was deep water we had got into but, I reasoned, it would get deeper yet. We stood to the side, executed this or that careful motion; in the meanwhile God steered us willy-nilly into His maze of traps. Gerhardt, for instance ... had he actually possessed a motive for his depraved joke, or was he merely giving impromptu expression to the current divisiveness in a club which for a full century had pledged itself to the all for one, one for all concept of charity and brotherhood? Was the rogue in league with the devil, I wondered, or did he know something? The fireplace flames licked gently, shadow-patterns on the lids of my closed eyes, ghost figures dancing without threat. I relaxed under that suffusive warmth, lulled almost into slumber, submitting almost with pleasure to my drowsy contemplation of the nature of evil. It seemed to me that Adolpho's fate was of no consequence, that whatever mercy or violence had come his way evil would continue to stalk us and always with the same abandon and whimsy and steadfast loyalty to absurdity that it had stalked him. Evil wanted only to make us look and feel ludicrous, then it could rest. And we were privileged to have it that way, I reflected. For only in tripe of my song's kind could man be transformed into a beast and back again. We were stuck with the life that had been ordained for us. We perceived our agony and were allowed our brief sojourn, however futile. It was given to us to divine God's scheme and add our laughter to His. This itself was evil, but evil of a sort that alleviated much pain. God no doubt approved of our laughing at Him. It let Him know what *we* knew: that while He amused himself with our lives, and duck-walked us through our maze, other, stronger forces were toying with and ridiculing Him. Stars, rigid after their long waltz, mocked His small power.

I suddenly sensed I wasn't alone. I opened my eyes and found Leland, the club rake, standing in front of my chair, cheerfully smiling, his eyes riveted on me. 'Why the black mood?' he inquired. 'A fellow would think you had lost your best friend.' His polite demeanour, his gay humour, the emptiness with which these remarks were uttered, caused me to sink even more into despondency. I felt my ire unaccountably rising and although I would have liked his company I told him to go away. 'Happy to oblige,' he laughed. 'Mustn't cross swords with our oldest member. When you kick off I'm going to see that we name a footstool after you.' He saluted Adolpho's wall moose, turned his grin on me, then wheeled about and strolled away. I watched his retreating backside, feeling envy for this man who took nothing, not even death, seriously. Adolpho too, it seemed to me, had been like that. Flimsy, arrogant creature floating above life, having his fun with us.

I yearned for the rascal all the same. I drank my brandy down and looked off toward the door, half-expecting to see him there waving his chubby hand in greeting. What I saw was a trio of members in fancy duds whispering importantly and I grasped that they were speaking of Adolpho, of the void his departure left in our ranks. From the hang of their long faces I perceived more: they too were pointing the finger of suspicion . . . *Adolpho is missing, old man. You must tell us where he is!* Evil, I thought, how evil these men are! What prompted them to go about with their scurrilous whispers, their accusations, their foul murmurings behind every chair? They advanced toward me. I closed my eyes, waiting for the hand to descend on my shoulder, for their vile words to fall. Yet no hand touched me and a moment later it seemed to me I had dreamed them there. The logs hissed in the fire, the flames scratched at my lids. I was alone.

It is not in my nature to want to understand what isn't meant to be understood. It was too much idleness doing this to me. It was not having old Adolpho any longer to regale me with his cockamamie fancies, his airy boasts, his buoyant jibes, his concoctions, his endless tales about the enchanted and enchanting Orpha. I missed his capacity for enthusiasm, his facility for finding beauty in the most fetid, puerile pond, pasture or field one ever came across when walking with him.

His moose head held me to my chair. Adolpho, on the occasion of its being hung, had told us how this stuffed head, with its bland and ignorant eyes, had all but brought his house crashing down. Orpha, it seems, had seen such a beast pictured in a book and had mooned over it until Adolpho determined that her happiness was dependent on her acquiring one. He had gone to a far country where the animal roams unfenced, like sad prehistoric cows that are too insipid to fear any person or thing, and he walked directly up to one of these animals, settled to his knees, and shot it in that portion of the chest which rises between its tall front legs. He had the head properly stuffed and mounted and brought it back in a crate to give to his Orpha. She had taken one look at it and fallen into a dead faint. 'Her eyes rolled,' he said, 'her face went white, it was as if she had been made to stand toe to toe with all the wickedness man had ever invented.' For days she was joyless, bereaved. He could see, he said, that Orpha took no pleasure from his gift and eventually concluded that perhaps what the dear woman had wanted was a live beast which could go about unhaltered in the deep woods surrounding their house, and thus provide company when his wife was lonely or made low by her womanly sorrows. So he was presenting the head to the Statacona, he said, making the best of a misguided affair. 'It isn't a moose anyway', he confessed to me somewhat later, after its moose identity had lodged in my mind, 'but a kissing cousin, the North American caribou.' Despite its imbecility, he claimed, the animal had an aristocratic air, dignity of a plodding sort, and would be quite at home in our club chambers.

It is the moose then and remembering Orpha's part in the story that has served to draw me each evening to the same club chair. Under spell of the soothing fire I have only to lift my head and gaze into the gleaming orbs which are the beast's eyes and I am instantly transported, my spirits lift, the thought of evil deeds, the sundry imperfections to which we are heir, all dissolve, practical considerations of everyday life ebb away, and I find myself sharing the innocent, dignified, enchanted world of Orpha and her stolid, benign, antediluvian beast.

As is usual, I ruminated at some length over Adolpho's Orpha, endeavouring to construct in my mind a picture of this elusive, now no doubt besieged and frightened woman. I tried to imagine what she would be doing at this hour: her husband gone the whole of one month and herself abandoned in isolated countryside, probably without so much as a stick of firewood to keep her warm. I resolved soon to go and see her, to let her know that she had a kindred shoulder to lean on. We owed it to Adolpho to do this much for her. I would kindle the fire, sit her down at the warm hearth, pour her the best soporific ... hold the child's hand ... discuss her future in sympathetic, practical terms. Because, despite my fancy which saw Adolpho materializing in the club doorway, my bones knew the man was not going to be returning, that Orpha had seen the last of him.

'*Must go now, old man,*' he used to say.
'*Must go tend my little nightingale!*'

I dozed. I must have, and for some little while, before waking with sticky, wet eyes. A hot sweat lay on my brow. The moose appeared to be holding me in mournful judgement from its place on the wall. The space around me seemed stuffy and sour, the air so tainted with an unknown stench that my first baffled thoughts were of a decapitated, rotting thing that some wretch had placed next to me. Yet I beheld nothing in my vicinity to justify this extravagant sensation. More likely, I reasoned, a rogue of the first order had deposited his rubbers in my fire. Yet when I poked among the ashes I could discern no such pollutant and was in fact much distressed to discover that my fire had gone out. I trembled with cold. The empty brandy snifter had been removed from my hands. My cigar had tumbled from its stand. I found it smouldering on the Persian carpet under my chair. I made an effort to rise. My seat and backside adhered to the leather so that the chair lifted with my person in the second before it clattered down. My head drummed like a racetrack. My timepiece had run down, though I gauged midnight could not be far ahead. The club had emptied, not a solitary member could I see. A sheet of parchment had been left near my chair. Large Gothic script spelled out a single word. ADOLPHO, it said. My initial reaction was one of consternation. I thought: Adolpho has been her, he has left this himself. He has found me asleep and has wanted me to be informed of his safe return....

An immense weariness, wind from a pharaoh's tomb, swept over me; I could not compel myself to think about the matter. A multitude of questions hung like curtains behind which I dared not peer. Why was the Statacona deserted? Had traps been set for me, to spring the moment I stepped beyond the Statacona door? Was Gerhardt lying in wait? Had he conceived stratagems whereby I alone was to be held responsible and punished for the evil that stalks our world?

Even Mole, that cur, was gone.

I could find no one.

This insolvency of character proved a temporary one. I retrieved my hat and stick from the cloakroom, made my way down the corridor and out the door. I set out for a walk in Great Statacona Green, from which our building a century or so earlier had drawn its name. I had need, I reasoned, of a long walk. Far from being too much alone, as had earlier seemed to be the case, I now realized I had of late been too little accustomed to being by myself. My friends had been making too many demands on my time. In recent months, there had always been Nettles and Gufstaffson, Skoals or Adolpho grabbing at my sleeves, waylaying me, inducing me to accompany them on this or that escapade. *A long walk, Philby, a bit of solitude*, I heard myself saying, *and you will be restored to full form. Nothing is so grave as it purports to be. Our fates are not carved in granite after all.*

The night was damp and milky, my feet churned along through cool fog — indeed, it was a fit night for a mariner. Statacona Green, that unkempt lay of land preserved by the Borough Council much in its natural state, stretches from perimeter to centremost point for a distance of close to one city mile. It was to this wilderness heart that I now directed myself. It was here on just such a walk, at just such an hour, in fog bathing us, that Adolpho and I had last been together. Here that he continued his account of Orpha's moose. 'Apparently,' he told me, 'in that country the animal is viewed as legal prey only during certain periods of the calendar. In the space between hunting seasons the animal forgets, his docile, friendly nature emerges anew, and the creature will venture from his home in thick brush and come almost to a solitary farmer's door. You will even see them drawn to outlying city hovels, standing forlorn in this or that open field, lured by the hope of easy food, I should suppose. I saw mine not thirty yards from my hotel. He gave me no difficulty. I had only to load my weapon, advance a few paces, and shoot him.'

I came now to Black Pond in the Green's centre, a pool, it was said, whose depths had never been calculated, and seated myself on the very path of ground where he and I that night had sat. 'Naturally,' he told me, 'for Orpha's benefit I had to embroider the tale. She would have you believe I trekked a thousand miles over snow and mountain trail and that the beast was menacing me.' His voice as he confided this had a melancholy tone quite out of keeping with my knowledge of him.

'How much', I asked him, 'has this expedition set you back?'

'My life,' he groaned. 'My life. My beautiful Orpha remains unhappy, you see.'

The moon that night was as yellow as a round of cheese. It lit up the black water to the extent that I found myself thinking of it as a giant evil eye watching us in cold detachment, although I saw too that this same moon transformed the pool's slime into a pretty field of glass. We sat side by side on the damp, reeking earth there at the water's edge, our images reflected in the glassy surface where our sticks jabbed. It is so dormant, this pond. Ageless. One is tempted into believing there is something almost sacred about a place that can preserve itself unaltered past all the years of one's mortal life.

'She's unhappy, did I say? More to the point, she's in another world. My poor nightingale.' He spoke in a hush, recognizing, I suppose, as much some interior truth about himself as about his lovely Orpha. 'Given all this,' he next asked me, 'in your opinion what should I do? How may I recapture the child's love?'

I had no advice for him.

Once, one cold day when I was a child, my father had brought me to this black water. I dragged a dead limb from the brush — fully forty feet in length it seems to me now — and plunged the long pole in. I pushed it down and down, the pond consumed my stick as if it had been no longer than a witch's broom, and I never touched bottom. It was my moment of truth, a revelation I would carry with me. Horrible, yet fascinating — these depths that are measureless, incalculable. The thrill and the horror I felt at that moment I shall never forget.

It is such a deep pond then. Nor is it a pretty pond. For very good reason casual strollers prefer to avoid the place. Wilderness grows up to Black Pond's shore for three-quarters of its turn, rendering it largely inaccessible. There is that. Moreover, it is a brackish water, half-covered with green slime, and its odour is putrid. Gnats in warm weather hover perpetually over its surface while in the black water itself nothing lives. Now and then a lazy turtle may decide the place is satisfactory. Later you will find his empty casing at anchor under the slime. I often come here. I dislike the place. It offends me enormously. I come here because my father brought me here when I was a child. It was stagnant and repulsive even then.

Adolpho that evening found cause to make one observation about me which I emphatically denied: 'Rot and beauty', he told me, 'in your mind walk hand in hand. The older you get the truer this is for you. Yet you have a romantic disposition, Philby: it gives you pleasure to regard them as a loving pair.' I do deny it. Decay does not interest me. I find no fascination in it. I loathe it, my spirit recoils. I abominate what is happening to my body.

A man should not utter such accusations to one he counts as his friend. I would never have spoken in this fashion to him.

No one has seen the poor devil since.

A FEW DAYS LATER I ran into Nettles on the street. He reported that he'd been in the grip of an unholy influenza and had been keeping indoors. His pallor seemed normal, though I refrained from comment. I cannot say he was as kind to me. He said that I looked distinctly unfit and wondered aloud whether my doctor hadn't diagnosed some new ailment or whether I had been treating myself to a proper night's sleep. Naturally I made light of these remarks.

'Have you any news?' he asked in a low voice, dragging me away from the lamp-post into shadow.

'None,' I said.

'Then all is serene?'

I replied that our affairs had that appearance.

The next day Gufstaffson's houseboy came around with a message informing me that he and his spouse had repaired their nuptial differences and would in the near future be receiving once more. But the letter's contents and his sending of it in the first place I found curiously offensive, and hoped he had spared Nettles this ignominy. Like Nettles, the boy was moved to comment on my visage. Was there anything I required? he asked. Could he run and fetch a doctor to my house?

I sent the imp packing fast.

I took my medicines and nibbled at the light supper my help had left me. I wasn't up to dining at the club.

Skoals, someone told me, was deep into his maps and avoiding everyone.

I had my own affairs to attend to.

The time passed. Finally reassembled, our group exchanged surprised remarks on the oddity of an entire fortnight having elapsed in which not a single member of our circle had visited the club.

Adolpho, it turned out, was still missing.

'Nothing,' said Gufstaffson. 'Not a word. No one has seen or heard from the fellow.'

'Ditto here,' confirmed Nettles. 'It's as if the old boy has dropped off the pier.'

Mole was compelled to come stoke up our fire. He was unwashed, his pig-eyes lit as if by the rigours of an imbecilic brain — an oilish rodent of a man. It was impossible to regard this repulsive specimen without feeling a pang of contempt for the human race.

Nettles dropped his hand on my knee, laughing. 'Calm down,' he said, 'you're in such a state these days.' He yanked his handkerchief from his breast pocket and dabbed it at my wet brow. I kicked at him and the others laughed.

Mole poked clumsily at the fire. He spat at and cursed and jostled the logs, glaring at me when I told him he'd never learn to lay a proper fire. Then Nettles had to chase after the brute to order more drink. The fire was too hot and I had to push back my chair.

I dozed. It was Skoal's voice which awoke me. 'Heaven help me, you're a grim bunch,' he was saying, 'but you'll be more cast down yet when you hear the news I've got.'

Gufstaffson asked what was meant by these words. Had evidence been found as to Adolpho's whereabouts after all?

'Not a bit of it,' Skoals said, dropping into a confidential whisper. 'I've been going through the account book in which Mole records our expenditures. It appears a bolt of pages has been torn from the ledger.' He lowered his voice still further, his expression wary. 'Adolpho's entire account has been removed. We'd be hard put to prove that the man had ever been a member.'

Nettles gave a cry of astonishment. He and Gufstaffson were most keen: what barbarian, they asked, would commit such mischief? What could be the explanation? Skoals motioned their heads near. 'It's my notion,' he declared, 'that Adolpho himself, prior to his disappearance, removed the pages. I suspect the poor devil couldn't pay up!'

They thought this a scandalous suggestion. 'The theory is incompatible with what we know of the man,' offered Gufstaffson. 'Adolpho had his faults, perhaps more than most, but he was hardly the criminal you portray.'

Then one of them was shaking my shoulder. 'Wake up, Philby. Tell us what you think.'

I quietly dropped the news that Adolpho had been into me for a large sum, if this fact was of any significance.

Skoals smacked his hands together, jubilant.

'But Adolpho was well fixed!' cried Gufstaffson. 'He could have bought us all many times over!'

'That's true,' agreed Nettles. 'The rogue spent money like a sultan.'

Skoals murmured something to the effect that a great many rats lived in walls where one could never see them. 'I should remind you', he added, 'of what you must at times yourselves have sensed: that despite his fellowship with us, his way of life — not to mention that of his precious Orpha — remained an enigma.'

They denied this with vigour — as did I, though no one listened — accusing Skoals of singing a different tune now that Adolpho was no longer among us. But on the question of money they were vehement. Only a few months back, they pointed out, Adolpho had been speaking of returning home, of erecting a great mansion for Orpha which would stand for centuries as a monument to her memory. This did not sound to them, they said, like the talk of a man courting ruin.

Skoals scoffed at this, muttering that we had more gold in our teeth than Adolpho could have raised in a year. 'No,' he went on testily, 'our knowledge of Adolpho was confined strictly to what he himself elected to tell us, and I for one took what he said with a grain of salt. The man was a dreamer, a fool, as devious as a one-armed wheelbarrow. I could never make head or tail of his stories. And as for returning home, well, except for Philby who has always claimed this place *is* home, we have spent most of forty years talking of little else.'

Our group went temporarily silent, directing black looks at one another.

Mole tried sneaking by but Nettles threw burning sticks at him until the rodent agreed to bring us another round of drinks before dinner.

Gufstaffson quickly splashed his down and turned surly, feeling that everyone was against him. 'Next thing I know,' he whined to Skoals, 'you'll be saying that I'm a fool and a cad also, or that Nettles is. So what if we do occasionally express the wish that we could go home, or if I for instance wish that my mate for life had been a little more wisely chosen? Just because you and Philby have been bachelors all your lives doesn't excuse you for heaping derision on us and on poor Adolpho just because he was so fortunate in his choice. It seems to me that we ought to be able to expect a bit of loyalty from each other after forty years and that includes loyalty to our missing member. I don't hear Philby saying much about all this. I remember though that he was crying in his cups and running off to see his doctors when Adolpho was talking about pulling up stakes and taking Orpha back to her roots.'

He fell silent but his amazing speech had got Nettles shaking. 'I say amen to all that,' put in Nettles. 'Much has been going on here that I don't understand. There have been nothing but whispers and insults and innuendo since poor Adolpho disappeared.' He paused, a glint came into his eye, and he turned his rudeness on me: 'What happened that night?' he snapped. 'The last we saw of Adolpho the two of you were going for a walk on the Green.'

This brought Skoals angrily to his feet. 'You're whipping a dead horse,' he told this pair. 'Unless you want to straight out accuse old Philby of a dastardly crime I'd suggest you hold your tongues.'

Nettles instantly deflated. He took off his glasses and wiped them, mumbling that he hadn't meant to suggest anything.

'Well, you'd best clam up,' Skoals warned him. 'You know what these Statacona villains would make of talk of that kind.'

Gufstaffson hurried away and returned a moment later with a glass of water which he seemed to think I needed. Skoals patted my arm. 'Ignore the fool's prattle,' he said. 'You know how rabid he can be. Drink it down, old friend, that'll get your juices flowing.'

Nettles offered me his hand but I wouldn't take it.

He and Gufstaffson drifted off to engage in a private conference.

Skoals and I forged the pretence of a smile as a member passed.

'Eavesdropping,' whispered Skoals. 'Reminds me of the war.'

This remark touched me deeply. My eyes flooded. We had been through a lot together, old Skoals and I. He drew closer, our knees all but touching. It struck me that he had aged considerably in the last few days. 'How are you?' he asked. 'Feeling better?'

I nodded. My tongue felt as if it had swollen.

'I've still got that numbness in the limbs,' he confessed. 'My trouble got so bad I had to have a feather mattress made.' His manner was just short of bereavement, as if he feared we both might shove off then and there. 'No need to be touchy about it,' he told me. 'You get to our age you've got to expect a bit of suffering, a few aches and pains.'

I gave an evasive nod, not being really very interested. A curious lethargy had come over me. I had not the strength to lift my hand. Concern for my health from Skoals and these others puzzled me no end. I felt queerly distracted, and I wondered vaguely whether there was not among my acquaintances a conspiracy to undermine my self-confidence.

'Why'd you never marry?' Skoals abruptly asked.

I shook my head dispassionately.

'Ever come close?'

I had no stomach for the topic but hinted at the casual nibble in the past. Skoals accepted this, his own memory nudged. 'Must have been in about my fortieth year', he reflected, 'that I fell in with a near-perfect little woman. Such a delight! Such a pretty laugh, like a string of sleigh bells. Part apparition she seemed.' He laughed. 'I never could believe the little filly was mine if I wanted her.'

I reminded Skoals that I had known him for half a century and asked him why, if this story were true, I had never heard of this grand passion before.

'Afraid you would steal her!' he hooted. 'That's why I never told you. Glad I didn't too, after seeing the way you got steamed up over Adolpho's Orpha!'

I remained silent.

'That's one thing I hated about that fella. The way he had of putting that woman on a pedestal. I got sick of hearing about her, you want to know the truth.' He patted my knee. 'Not you, though. Hung on to his every word. Even crossed my mind you'd gone and lost your heart to the woman.'

I had no interest in Skoals's fishing. My attention was on the moose head. Some peculiarity in the light was causing the entire club-room to be reflected in the beast's smouldering eyes. The heavy curtains, the paintings on the dark walls, the fine leather chairs, the beautiful carpets, the golden span of ceiling — all found distorted replication. Members could be seen slowly moving, small and bent, like black twig-people enacting in silent pantomime a play of sinister description.

Nettles and Gufstaffson soon returned, gesticulating wildly, their rage spilling over. 'The foul dogs!' exploded Gufstaffson. 'The villains!' shouted Nettles. 'There is no end to the deceit in this rathole!' Both were talking at once, a shriek of mad accusations.

'What is it?' demanded Skoals. 'What puts you into this fever?'

Gufstaffson spun on him: 'That vulture Gerhardt!' he roared. 'He's been putting his liquor on our tabs.'

'Not only Gerhardt,' broke in Nettles. 'Others are beginning to do the same!'

'That cur Mole says we shall have to pay, he will give us no satisfaction. I'd like to throttle the swine but there it is in the ledger, page after page: *Two whiskies Gerhardt, charge to Nettles. Four whiskies Gerhardt, charge to Skoals.*'

'Even his dinners!' chimed Nettles. 'We owe a fortune!'

One exclamation fed another until the two were in a proper fit. Their solicitors, they said, would hear of this. They would, for their part, refuse to pay! They would resign from the club, see Gerhardt in chains!

There was no soothing them, our cautious replies only fuelling their rage. They would not listen to us and took themselves off again, intending to round up Gerhardt, to give him a good dressing down.

'Evil,' Skoals muttered when they were gone. 'The man is evil. I fear he will not rest until he has the slime covering us all.'

I lacked the stamina to pursue these issues. I was weary of Gerhardt's skulduggery, I found his very name tiresome. Skoals fell silent, hands folded over his large stomach. I could see he agreed with me. We did not have much longer allotted to us, we asked only to be left alone to enjoy the remainder of our days in peace and quiet. I know that is what I was thinking. All of this business was over nothing: so a man had disappeared, suppose he had been murdered or had done himself in, was that a reason for the ground under us to shake, for our friends to go yelping about like lunatics?

I fell into a sombre, half-mellow mood, remembering my father. An eccentric man, I suppose, though I prefer to think of this as an advantage. In Statacona Green one day he had pointed out to me the tree from which the highwaymen were hanged. The many ropes had stripped the bark and in half a dozen places these ropes had cut deep grooves into a favourite limb. The earth underfoot was trampled firm and the grass refused to grow. My father crouched on his heels, scratching at the earth as he told me this. Flesh rots, he told me. This is what a lad comes to in the end, be he evil or be he good.

I tremble to recall that hour.

When the renegade is cut down, my father told me, the soul comes shrieking from the body and flings itself downhill into Black Pond, because neither God nor the devil will have it. It is the tears of all these doomed souls that had made such a putrid hole of Black Pond.

Horrible! Horrible!

WE SOON WENT in to dinner. I recall a plate of food set in front of me and that I could not eat it. I recall Gerhardt's entry. He was all fine-scented, done up in a velvet suit like a man who gives speeches at a circus. He raised a frequent glass, calling out this or that toast: *To Adolpho!* I'd hear him sing. I recall the laughter that swept the room when he said: 'Old Adolpho is still missing, gentlemen, and we have not a single clue to his whereabouts. Are we soon to see nets dragging our ponds? Shall we unloose our dogs and have them nose the bushes in Great Statacona Green? What fortune awaits the fair and fragile Lady Orpha, woman of mystery?' I recall the fascination with which I studied the faces of my incensed friends: Nettles with his bald head and pink skin, his overlong nose and the wrinkles which made a birdcage of his mouth; Gufstaffson with his eyes like two cave apertures, with his jowls and beard and his great mane of hair hanging about his face like a red lampshade. Obscene! I thought. Have these men been friends of mine? I recall Gerhardt's uplifted glass and his merry voice intoning, *To wickedness, here's to wickedness, my mates!* and it seemed to me my own laughter joined that of others in the room. Skoals gripped my arm and I stared, bemused, at his expression of appalled wonder. Nettles and Gufstaffson were out of their seats, their eyes boring into mine, outraged. I marvelled at this venom, yet could not see how it related to me. Leland entered. He floated by our table, a woman's arm hooked over his. I could hear the rustle of her petticoats and smell her heavy perfume. Her presence struck me as most incredible, for women had never been known to grace our halls. Yet it seemed to me entirely appropriate that Leland had brought her, that she should be here hanging on his arm, her face lit in a smile for everyone. 'What, still no Adolpho?' I heard him call to our table. 'Well, I'll wager he's hanging out down by the public bath, his eyes peeled for a wench! Where else would rakes like us go when we're wanting sport!' He was in his usual high spirits, no one could take offence at Leland. He was our favourite, there was not a man in the Statacona who had not wished to be more like Leland. 'Ta!' now he said to the room, smacking his lips in a kiss. 'Carry on, old beauties! Keep your willy flying!'

The woman laughed; then they were gone.

I could not eat my dinner. It was mutton and had gone cold. I could not imagine how this dish had come to me. I hate mutton. Yet I raised no complaint, I took no offence. I would eat it in good time or I would not eat it and either way it would not signify. I dreamed. Wide awake, staring at my plate, I dreamed. At any rate, I heard Skoals saying I did. I felt a pressure at my elbows and submitted to it. Tables clattered back, people stood. 'Get a physician,' someone cried, 'Philby's finally gone and done it.' My friends were at my side, supporting me, and I let them direct me where they wished. The commotion was considerable and I could not get them to understand that there was no cause for alarm. Everyone seemed in a big rush, flitting this way and that; I could not make them understand that they should remain very still. This seemed essential. I tried to warn them that if they continued in this manner they were inviting danger, their positions were in jeopardy. Their movements and voices I found irritating, distasteful, on the point of being obscene. Faces familiar to me through numerous years I saw suddenly as treacherous, decadent, vile masks designed solely to torment me in this hour.

'He's coming around,' I heard Skoals say, 'move back, give the man air.'

A lap robe fell across my knees.

Figures stood by, murmuring. I stared into my old fire. I detected Leland's woman-friend seated opposite me. She smiled, radiant. Her dress was of scarlet and brighter than the flames.

'This Orpha,' I heard her ask. 'Is she young? Is she beautiful?'

Someone chuckled: 'So old Adolpho would have us believe.'

The Statacona lights did a jig. It seemed to me my feet left the floor.

Members were forming a close circle around the woman's chair, fussing over her. Again I felt an urgency to warn them. I thought it uncanny that they lacked the sense to know that they should remain absolutely still. 'Don't worry about old Philby,' someone said. 'He's a horse, he'll make it.' Another said, 'He's been pushing himself too hard, worried about Adolpho, I would guess.'

That they should speak at all I found to be the height of conceit. Whatever terrible thing was to happen to them they would deserve it. 'Ah, well,' someone said, 'it's been a dog's life and I don't suppose he'll be sad to leave it.'

They went on talking. Above their voices I could hear the woman's waltzing laughter. In a while I could see only patches of her fiery dress.

'Old Adolpho, what a wizard! One never knew when he was telling the truth or when he was making up a tale. To this day I'm not convinced his Orpha exists.'

I felt faint, as if my heart was slowly enlarging.

'It will be different around here', someone remarked, 'without old Philby to cheer us up.'

Everyone laughed.

I could feel my head folding onto my chest and my every limb collapsing.

I PEERED in at Adolpho's black window. It was Adolpho's fault I had not got to know her. He never appeared in public with her, never brought her to any of our functions. 'How unfortunate', I would say to him, 'that Orpha couldn't come. Is her health unstable?'

'Oh, she isn't sickly,' he'd reply. 'Far from it. She's fragile to look at, I grant you, but don't be fooled. Five minutes with her and any man would be eating from her hands. I've seen it happen a thousand times.'

I was quite at sea with talk like that.

THE MOST we would ever see was the pale back of the woman seated beside him as the two retreated in the distance.

'Was that Orpha I glimpsed yesterday?' I'd ask.

'Yes, so sorry you missed her.'

'Thin-skinned as a water reed, gentlemen, a smile to tear out your hearts. Graceful, my word. She could fill your teacup and you would never know she had come near. Oh, I'm happy to tell you about Orpha, I can never sing enough praises to my Orpha! Flesh soft as bird's feathers or bride's bottom, a complexion with a blush to sadden radish or rose, oh she's a marvel, is Orpha ...'

'... About fourteen hands high, eight stone light, a warm breath of a girl! Hair yellow as lemon peel! Wonderful lovely dewdrop eyes that have all the innocence of pearls, oh she's a dream, is Orpha!'

BLACKNESS HUNG like a mirror, extending the black window.

I did not want to pop in unannounced and risk alarming Orpha.

Creatures the size of turkeys flapped like black umbrellas from one nearby tree to another.

The house groaned like a coffin.

Thick, smoking sky widened and darkened.

The door opened.

'Orpha?'

The stench was sudden and overwhelming, an ageless fetid rot spilling out from the unbreathing room. *Horrible, horrible!*

Yet it passed, or was lifted into abrupt inconsequence.

Her small frail hand eased into mine. Her shoulder swayed against me. Musically, her voice rose out of the darkness:

'Is it Skoals?' she whispered, 'or is it Philby?'

'Philby,' I murmured.

'Ah,' she sighed, 'Adolpho told me it would be you.'

Her grasp tightened. I lifted a hand to touch her but where her face should have been I felt nothing.

'He has been waiting,' she said. 'Let us go in now and see him.'

My dream cracked like a window, I cried NO! in horror and sought to pull away but her strength was unyielding, she led me hurriedly along, down and down, through levels stagnant and repellent beyond belief, myself weeping now, sinking with her, shrieking that I was *innocent, innocent!* while all the evil of a thousand days licked at my heels.

If You Love Me Meet Me There

FROM A WINDOW in the room at the front of his house he looks out now across the high-strung weeds to their place. They have come for her. They are taking her away. Finally she is dead.

I had not expected this. I entered this room only because here I have a chair in which I like to sit and my work and my books and these two windows which hold me here.

One window faces the street, the other his driveway and the square pink house where the woman has lived and where at last she is dead.

I have seen only two people although I have been watching for some time. Of course, the others are inside. The Rambler station wagon is parked in the yard. On the street shoulder are two other automobiles I have not seen before. Two men have been standing together near these; now they are moving toward the house. There is a hearse as well — it moves out of the driveway, turns left into the street. It passes my house and is gone.

A moving figure catches his attention — a tall, well-built boy, seventeen years old, dressed now in a white uniform.

Yes, Tom. A bakery worker. He crosses the street, uses my driveway as a shortcut, and takes the path through the field to the house of the dead woman. It is a point of sorrow to me that although the path is directly between my house and that of the dead woman I have never used it. Except for my son, no one in my house ever has. Hello, Tom.

Tom has thrown up a sluggish hand; he has smiled sadly and shrugged his shoulders and moves now slowly along the path to the pink house, his hands deep in his pockets.

I should leave this room. It's terrible my watching this way.

Three times since he has been living here the woman has been taken to the hospital. Each time they have said she would not last the night. Each time she has returned.

Perhaps at any rate she has got what she wanted: to die at home in her own bed. Cancer, I believe that's what I have heard. With her husband she operated a florist shop downtown. I've driven by, seen her there. Arranging flowers, taking orders on the phone. A grey, bony woman with haunted eyes. Christ!

Now the black hearse has returned. It could not have gone far. Perhaps the driver wanted cigarettes. Another car also has appeared. It curves in off the street, passes the Rambler, is halted in the scrubby grass near the front door. The children emerge. The daughter is perhaps eight years old, she holds her older brother by the hand. There is one other child, no more than five, but he does not appear. The curtained windows of the hearse glare in the sun.

What a hot, still day this is. It is sordid of us not to pay our respects. But we hardly know them, that's true. She must have been a fine woman. She and her husband worked hard, they were often together. And the children are well behaved.

The children are skinny and shy. In truth they belong to an earlier time. The house belongs to no time at all. It sits pink in the measureless field which itself extends to a drab stand of stunted pine. Some two or three sheds lean in the back yard. On the outside wall by the front door is a large red Coca-Cola clock, which keeps good time. The husband raises chickens in a small way.

The last time I spoke to him he mentioned two matters: his wife was in the hospital again, was not expected to last the night, and my son's dog had been killing his chickens. I was uncomfortable, could not look at him.

He is aware that the dog has been killing the man's chickens. He has seen a scattering of feathers near the back door stoop and twice has found the dog trotting along with a dead chicken in his jaws.

My wife says to me, 'What does he expect? His chickens are all over the neighbourhood and how can a dog not be a dog?'

It is not the dog that concerns her, nor is it the chickens. She senses in the matter a veiled displeasure with her son and is quick to defend him against these unreasonable claims.

Your dog has been killing my chickens, the man from the pink house says, but it is not the fault of your dog. He's a good dog.

It's a small hound-pup from across the street who starts it all. He gets your dog excited, the two of them begin chasing the chickens. Chickens are fast but they run short of breath. I'll get some birdshot, he says. A shot of that on their rumps and they won't bother the chickens no more.

Come see us, he says — and goes.

—Come see us. Although he and his wife have many times invited us over we've never found the time. She was pleasant, he is too, but somehow their Coca-Cola clock has frightened us off.

He has said to the man on such occasions: Thank you, we would love to come, maybe tomorrow. He has sought to reconcile his personal inadequacy with a desire to be decent, has put on a long face and called: If there is anything we can do, let us know.

The man pauses, answers back: It's all a matter of time, I reckon. Lord knows.

He is resigned to it, you see. He has accepted her death as he has had to bear with the death of his chickens. There is not much he can do.

Well, it's happened now. She's dead. I guess in a way he must feel relieved.

The boy, Tom, is crossing back through the field between the two houses. He throws up a tired hand, mouths a word against the vacant air. Drops his shoulders and slouches on. In her yard at the pink house the young daughter is hugging herself, watching his progress through the tall tufts of grass gone to seed. She spots the flight of two dipping birds and turns in silent study of them. She wears a grey, full-length dress, bunched at the waist, hanging slack on her arms, and someone has put a rose in her dark hair.

She looks old. Anaemic. She looks small for her age but my wife says no, she's about average. My wife agrees she's not right somehow. One night last week I discovered her out front, staring at our house. At these windows here. For a long time she did not move. My wife saw her also, opened the door, inviting her in. She came timidly into the front room, clutching herself.

What is wrong, Teresa? his wife had asked. Can we help?

The girl seemed not to hear. Silent, she stared through the open door at the nursery room, at the cradle in which the baby slept.

She'll fall out, she said at last. The baby will fall out and bang her head.

Oh no, she's safe, his wife said. She's perfectly safe.

The girl's lips trembled, her eyes glanced past theirs.

He says I'll die too, she said. We all do. It's the Will of God.

Then she started backing toward the door.

If we had moved toward her she would have broken into a run. A false word and she might have screamed.

It's dark, his wife had said. Would you like my husband to walk you home?

I love the dark, the girl said. I can go anywhere.

A moment later they had seen her streaking across the field.

Now she stands in watch of that space where birds had been. Her father has come outside to lean against the Rambler station wagon in the yard. He speaks to her and she moves on out of sight beyond the far side of the house. The sun tints his face red; he appears ill at ease in his tight beige suit as he leans in solemn regard of the driver slouched low behind the wheel of the shining hearse. The lawn around him is much eroded, bare red patches of earth interrupting the dusty green. At the rear of the house the girl again appears, dragging by the leg a mangled plastic doll.

Country to the core. Is this what I held against them? A comic pair. He toothless in his overalls, she with her stringy hair and sad skin, and deep woeful eyes.

Come see us, hear!

So like each other, so well-matched that my wife could even seize upon this, use them in her arguments: you'll never change, we're not right for each other, we can never be with each other the way they are over there.

You want a pink house? A Coca-Cola clock by your door?

I want you to love me the way he loves her.

She's dying. Is that the way you want to live?

Looking for a place to rent, they had arrived eventually at this house here. He liked the windows in the room to the front, liked the way one looked out over the street to the grove of trees fanning away there, the way this second one had a view of the wide field leading to the peculiar pink house which was itself backed by trees, and he saw already his desk in here and his books and the heavy leather chair.

We've got to paint it first, my wife said. I want white walls everywhere. Yes, I think it will do.

They were painting in a back room, absorbed in the task, the evening the neighbours called.

'Anybody home?' That's what they said, and came right in, shouting, 'Anybody home?' as they stalked through empty rooms, finally to find us splattered by paint, applying white rollers to the walls.

You'll ruin them good clothes, the woman said.

You've got it looking good and clean, the man said, I'll say that.

They introduced themselves, asked us our names. They stayed a long time, while we stood, my wife and I, the paint dripping down our sleeves.

Well, look at us! exclaimed the woman. Them standing there ever so polite and not telling us to go home so they can get on with their painting.

They kept telling us they knew we would like it here. The neighbourhood was nice and quiet, it was far enough from town to let you hear yourself think.

Winter's hard though, it'll cost you a heap to heat the place. Anyway, that's what the other people said. They painted too before they moved in. Now, come to see us, hear!

We liked them. We gave assurances that once we were settled we'd drop in. For them to do the same any time they wished.

It did not happen that way. Protocol required their visit to be returned and it never was. When the grass got too high his wife worried him until he went out to cut it. The man from the pink house drifted over, spoke of grass and the weather, of his chickens and the floral shop and the changing neighbourhood. At times his wife stood by, smiling and nodding her head — but they found excuses when invited in.

No, supper's about on, but you come see us, hear!

One year now we've been living here. Only lately, from our son, did we learn the woman was ill, that she might die at any time. My wife has many interests. She wanted to plant a flower garden, bought seeds at the store. The man over there saw her clearing a plot, drove to his shop, returned with six potted plants which he presented to her.

The weather turned hot. One burning Saturday she dragged out the hose, watering the plants in the heat of the day. Of course they died. Driving by on the street one day the man noticed this, returned that evening with twelve plants more, which he set out himself.

What are neighbours for? he asked. But next time wait until the cool of the day.

Many days this year the woman has sequestered herself away in the pink house, alone while her husband saw to the shop. Three times this year she has been hospitalized.

I must cook something for them, my wife has said. Perhaps I can offer to look after the kids. But she has stood here at the window with me. We have not had even the courage to express our solicitude. And it's too late now. I can't just walk up to the door and say I'm sorry.

Over at the pink house now three men in dark suits stand by the front door, looking at the clock. Now and then one will dig his heel in the soil, another will stoop, plucking a blade of grass. The man in the hearse has tossed out another cigarette, is sitting up and looking back at the house. The two male children are out back leaning against a chicken coop door. They take drags on cigarette butts picked up from the yard. Spit, and say a word or two, and kick their heels in the dirt. The child, Teresa, has drifted down into the woods.

Thank God, at last!

Outside, his son's dog has moved off his haunches in the shade of the porch and galloped barking to the street. The white Volkswagen floats into sight, his wife's knuckles white on the wheel. It sputters up the driveway, creeping to a stop. The dog's paws scratch at the door on the passenger side. His wife alights, wrestles with her packages, pauses a moment now to study and evaluate the situation next door. The son escapes from the car, gives chase to the yelping dog.

She comes in, a certain poise and talent for these things not yet disguised by her helpless show:

'My God, the stores were like Christmas, I couldn't even go to the toilet without being poked in the ribs.'

'So long as you went,' he says.

She laughs, leaning with her grocery bags as she transfers their weight to the table.

'There are more in the car.'

'I can't go out now,' he says. 'I'll get them later.'

She kicks off her black suede sandals, shakes hair from her face, arches her brows: 'You can't go out now?'

'No. Later, I'll get them later.'

Her mouth struggles with a smile as she reaches under her dress to remove her pants. She steps out of her briefs, flips them onto a counter somewhere, and advances — cooler now, freer — to unpack her goods.

'As you please.'

He goes back to his room, to his windows at the front of the house. His son and the dog are over in the yard at the pink house, in discreet observance of the activity there. A black casket is being removed from the house and the men are having some trouble with it. It leans just a bit; a man has turned his ankle and lost hold.

Stay back, son. Stay out of the way.

The dog sniffs about in the yard, looking from the men to the boy. The dog is no doubt baffled by this interruption in their play. The man in the beige suit trails after the casket, pausing now to ruffle the boy's head. For a moment the boy walks along with him, closely attentive as the men open the gate of the hearse and slide the cruel black box inside. He falls back as the hearse's engine turns, as the dead woman's husband gathers his children, heads them toward the Rambler in the yard. The hearse drags slowly up the street.

'When did she die?'

His wife joins him at the window. She has changed out of her dress, is buttoning up her jeans, has her hair tied babushka-style by a strip of material that also serves as a curtain sash.

'I don't know. Do you think they'll be all right? The man and the children, I mean.'

'If you knew they wouldn't, what would you do?'

She is not interested in any answer he would have to this. She quits the room, is next seen approaching the car.

She's right about me. I can't so much as bring the groceries in. But I had to watch the baby, there's that. I couldn't just wrap the baby up and take her over there.

The hearse moves sombrely by the house. Behind it the Rambler comes, the boy Tom at the wheel. The little girl sits up front and the man and his two sons sit erect in the rear.

There they go.

Fearful of being seen, he steps back from the window, missing the tentative wave of the man inside the car.

In a little while it will be dinner time.

The poor woman, he will say, cancer is such a terrible affair.

She didn't die from cancer, his son will say. Esther had leukaemia, as everyone knows.

20 NOVEMBER: Her windows are always the same. Whether she's out or in I never know. Frustrating, the curtains always drawn. Now and then a pencil of light, no more. I *ought* to know, that's what I mean, just as she ought to know when I'm on the street watching. Her glass is dirty, too. We should clean it some time. Say I am seen walking by and she beckons with a finger — 'I'm so tired, I'm not in the mood, will you help me?' — and I rush up the stairs, we get out the Windex and paper towels and scrub away until the glass screeches in gratitude. That's when I draw the curtains back. Once they are open she'll not notice, they will stay that way. I'll not open them too much, of course — anyone could walk by and look in. They could stand on the barrel in the alley by the grocery and have a pretty straight shot. Probably when at home, on slow evenings, she's often in the nude. Well, not this time of the year, in the summer, I mean. People are less cautious in summer I've noticed, a good warm day they don't want to believe anyone wishes them harm.

I should mail her a postcard: CLEAN YOUR WINDOWS. THEY ARE A DISGRACE. She'd take it as joke, I've seen how she likes to laugh. I like that, it warms me to see her enjoying herself. Surprises me though, somehow I expected her to be more stand-offish, more practical, more mature. Well, at her age. No, she acts like she thinks she's the toast of the town.

Note, wash hair.

Pick up feathers.

21 NOVEMBER: That idea about writing to her appeals to me. I could drop it in her box, walking by, no one would notice. Save the postage, I can't be too careful in that respect. CAME BY AGAIN TODAY, SORRY YOU WERE OUT. Signed, *Anonymous*. No, that might put her on guard. Why invite trouble? Maybe, simply, *A Friend*, that would be better. If she had a phone — she might have

one of course, must look into that — I could ring her up, make a suggestion or two. 'Windows washed, free of charge, our Get Acquainted Special this week.' Probably she'd laugh, tell me I was ridiculous, no one does anything for free. 'I know you only want to get inside. Don't try it, sister, I'm alerted now.' Or she might tell me she doesn't have the time, busy-busy, never a minute to call her own. She might even act nasty, say something rude: 'I can tell *you've* got troubles, but stay away from me, I don't want to get involved.'

Strange, this habit she has of disappearing. Around a corner, *poof!* — and she's gone. It was like that today. Frustrating, what does she do with herself, where does she go? I think I picked up a cold waiting in the alley for her to show up. *Note*, dress more warmly tomorrow.

Shh, *he's* coming.

22 NOVEMBER: The grocer had his eye on me today. What lousy luck that his place is just opposite hers. A nasty sort. Plain to see he means no one any good. I felt guilty — I *feel* guilty — knowing he was giving me those suspicious looks. To deceive him I strolled up the block, then down the other side. A casual walk, smiling, looking at numbers, the sky, anything. 'Me? Oh, I'm only waiting for friends. Supposed to meet them here. This is Richardson Street, isn't it?' I've got hundreds of tricks like that, I know how to avoid trouble. But I'm careful too, I know what it is to talk myself into hot water. The grocer didn't let up, however. Vile man. I couldn't let him get away with it, went inside his shop. Thinking to buy fruit, take the wind out of his sails. Be aggressive, that's one thing I've learned. Don't let them smell fear.

Beautiful pyramids, at least he knows how to stack fruit, his shop is neat. I've seen him when a customer comes along and takes an apple or orange from the wrong place: he fumes. Often he'll rearrange the entire bunch.

'Don't pinch,' he told me. I wasn't sure that's what he said. He's surly, unshaven, vulgar, a big stomach — hardly the sort she would care for. She ought to move, in fact. I could slide a note under her door: GET OUT OF THIS STINKING NEIGHBOURHOOD, IT ISN'T SAFE. I don't feel comfortable around there, I never have, it's much nicer on my side of town. Good clean streets, and although it may only be my imagination, I think people are nicer. She could afford to move, I've seen her spend huge amounts in a single day without blinking. Crazy, you'd think she'd save a little for the future. She doesn't spend it on clothes, unfortunately. Her coat is not nearly as nice as mine. Frequently she's shabby, almost drab. Of course it's the style now, I suppose the other view is that she's right up there with the latest.

'I said don't pinch,' the grocer told me. Rude. I heard him that time, but had the presence of mind to put him in his place.

'Grapes, please. The white.'

He weighed out a pound. 'More? More?' The price, when he told me, was quite a shocker. I went blue in the face. I had to ask him to put some back, which he did. 'More? More?' I showed him all I was willing to pay: one quarter. I thought he was going to spit in my hand. It's disgraceful what food costs now, I don't see how even a small family can manage. Thank my lucky stars *I* never got into that.

Lost *her* again.

The grocer hates me. It didn't matter to him that I bought his wretched fruit.

'I saw you pinching the apples.' *Scum*, that's what he wanted to say, I could see it in his eyes. He was suspicious. *Up to no good, scum like you, wouldn't be surprised if you murdered your mother*, that's what was on his mind. I was afraid he might call the ... police. The *cops*, I almost said. I hate that word, the police should be respected. Anyway, the grocer will remember me now. He might even tell her that I've been loitering around her place. Well, she should be flattered, someone her age.

'You live around here?' he asked me.

'Sure,' I said, 'just around the corner,' although I stuttered, not at my best.

'Fine. But don't pinch. I welcome your business, but don't pinch.'

I promised I wouldn't any more. I hate myself when I allow anyone to ride roughshod over me like that. But why make a scene? Dignity, that's what was required. A dreary man.

All in all, I think I came out on top.

23 NOVEMBER: Forgot to mention this yesterday. When I got home the telephone was ringing. More trouble, I thought, what next? My key wouldn't fit inside the lock, by the time I was inside my caller had hung up. *If* it was my phone. Could have been in the room adjacent to mine. It's true: I *am* always expecting something to happen to me. I'm always expecting someone important will ring me up. Not to *say* anything important, I don't care about that. If they will only say how are you, how was your day, that will be enough.

I put my ear against the wall. If it was the old man's phone he had missed his caller too. That amused me. First that anyone would want to call him, then that when finally it came he had been out. The old fool. One's entire life can turn on a small thing like that — being out when you should be in, being in the right place at the right time. It takes a certain knack. That's what Colonel Dodson is forever telling me. He has, he says, the knack. 'You ought to cultivate it. How do you think I got to be *Colonel* Dodson?' Chest puffed out, one eye drooping like a sleeping dog's. That's Dodson. Yet, it's true, he *is* a colonel, he gets along.

I kept listening for the old man to come in. If he did I'd knock on his door, look him in the eye, say, 'Well, old man, one of us got a call.' Study him. Determine whether he had been expecting to be rung up. I think actually the call must have been mine. He doesn't need a phone; it's been weeks since anyone called him. Maybe. Of course I don't know what happens when I'm out, that's elementary. *To my own certain knowledge, however, his phone has not rung in three weeks.*

Nothing. He was definitely out.

I went to my front window without turning on the lights. I peeked through the curtains. No one there. No one watching my place, that's a relief. Mine are good curtains, I love these curtains, heavy velvet, blue. Lined too. No one passing on the street would ever know what I do in here, they wouldn't know whether I am in or out. But the window was filthy, that surprised me. Not like a window at all, rather like a charcoal sketch of what a window is supposed to be. *Item,* clean your window tomorrow. Get up early, get up by first light, do a good job.

I shouldn't let such grubbiness disturb me. Why get upset about it? I wiped a finger over the glass. Screech! The filth was outside. That made me feel better, not much, but a little.

I had to laugh at myself. I hadn't yet taken off my coat. Three hours home by that time and I was still in my winter gear. I'm usually careful of my appearance, if I say so myself. Clothes reflect the person. You've got to sit up straight, stand up straight, walk with your shoulders back if you want people to think well of you. Throw the world a smart salute. That's what the Colonel would say.

But then he weeps and destroys the whole effect.

I don't know. It comes over me sometimes, settles over me sometimes as unexpectedly and as beautifully as the first snow, as snow on a sunny day — my change. I do change. I feel myself suddenly go beautiful under this heavy coat. I go up another inch on my heels, everyone desires me. They sell my pin-ups at the five and dime. SPECIAL THIS WEEK AT K-MART, FOUR SHOTS FOR $1.

I had to get out of bed to answer the door. I smoothed my hair back, threw open the door, and a man was standing there wearing a white apron, thrusting a box at me.

'He sent this,' the man said. 'Told me you needed it, put dimples in your cheeks. He's across the street, what do I tell him?'

'That's *your* problem,' I said, and slammed the door.

I reacted pretty well, I thought. I certainly handled that problem.

24 NOVEMBER: A lost day.

Got hair done though, looks nice.

25 NOVEMBER: This morning, going out: A bulbous man in his

underwear at a second-storey window holding a doll in his arms. That's what I thought at first, so I went by again. Not a doll, but a small ugly dog dressed in a sort of blue vest. The dog squirmed and barked and the man shrugged at me and had to put it down. 'Haven't seen you in the Scream Room lately,' he shouted. 'You get yourself sorted out?'

People can be so stupid.

She looked especially dingy today. I'm beginning to lose interest in her. That saddens me. Of course she's old. Probably a mistake in the first place.

Today I was extremely bold. I took a table directly beside hers at Ivanhoe's. Big surprise, she usually goes to La Petite Colombe on Broughton Street (well, their stove was out). A man met her there, though it soon became clear that they didn't know each other well. A trial meeting perhaps. They whispered over the table now and then, they had to push the candle aside. Each time he lit her cigarette her smile — wispy, vaguely teasing — went past him and settled more firmly on me. Oh, she knew what she was doing. I gave the smile back, I gave it to her with both barrels. She doesn't frighten me. Nor does the waiter, I have a right to take lunch where I wish. A table to myself if that's what I choose. He was mad, I only had soup, others were waiting to be seated. Their bad luck, that's what I told the waiter. I hate waiters, they're like doctors, they think they can run your life.

I observed the man with her. He seems nice enough. Mildly good-looking. More than enough self-confidence. Not quite tall enough for her. Once he placed a hand on her knee under the table. She let it stay there for five minutes or so, then she crossed her legs and his hand rose calmly back to the table. It was lovely, his motion. Like a butterfly. They were sharing a decanter of white wine. They began enjoying each other. I could see this surprised both of them.

They left together. He walked with her for two blocks, at Fort and Government they stood chatting for several minutes. They shook hands, both laughing. Then he disappeared inside Montreal Trust.

I don't begrudge the expense. I can make it up by leaving off cigarettes for a while.

I took a seat in the rear of the bus, she sat up front in one of those triple seats facing the aisle, those reserved for the elderly or handicapped. That amused me. She had bought a new pair of shoes and occasionally I caught her twisting her ankles about, admiring them. A lovely tan leather, very expensive, but they're too young for her. Hardly her style. Still, she's got nice legs. Legs just don't age so fast, you can't tell a thing by looking at a person's legs.

She looked less tacky, all in all. She had done her hair. She was excited too.

He came by her place at four.

I hate those curtains. I imagine they are like mine, they hide everything, absorb everything, nothing goes beyond them. Even with both of them there anyone would have thought the place vacant.

The grocer, glad to say, was nice to me.

'You again? Be glad when this cold spell breaks. What can I do for you today?'

I think he likes me. I've got to be careful, he might get the wrong idea. He may think I find him interesting. The way he looks at me. I couldn't tell him it was cold, that was why I was hanging around his shop.

'You married?' he asked.

I rolled my eyes and let loose a loud Ha-Ha. It baffled him, he's not overly smart.

'I shouldn't have asked. Person like you would be snapped up quick.' I saw that he wanted to get familiar with me. But he didn't dare, didn't have the courage, he was afraid of what I might do or say, even create a scene perhaps.

'More grapes today? You do like grapes, don't you, that's good, a lot of vitamin C in grapes — though you are too late I'm afraid, that looks like a bad one you have.'

What a fool. They get nervous, they can't help talking a blue streak, they'll pass any stupid remark to make you think they're an average Joe.

My cold *is* worse. My nose is red, it hurts. My head feels like they've been stuffing eggplant inside. I feel awful.

26 NOVEMBER: Stayed in today. No improvement.

Just after two this afternoon someone knocked on my door. Softly, hardly more than brush strokes. I had heard him coming up the stairs but had decided it was the old man next door. I listened for the key in *his* lock. Soft as the sound was, I jumped when it came to my door. I held my breath, the blankets pulled up to my neck. I waited. Finally I heard him going down the stairs again. I peeked through the curtains but he must have kept close to the building when he came out.

I don't know why I say *he*. My first thought was that it was *her*. Creepy, but I do have a cold. I don't want to go through that again.

This morning I noticed a sheet of paper had been slid under the door. I CAME BY, it said, SORRY YOU WERE OUT.

27 NOVEMBER: Surprise, surprise! Actually I was deeply shocked. *He* knocked on my door this afternoon, the old man. Said my coughing was a nightmare to him, he couldn't sleep, he couldn't think. 'Don't you have any medicine? A little cough syrup? You're driving me crazy.' I hadn't even known he was *in*. I thought he had been out of town for the whole weekend. Ridiculous.

Another thing: he isn't old. Not nearly as old as I thought. Forty, forty-five.

'God,' he said, 'you look terrible. I think you've only got an hour to live.'

Up to this moment I had simply stared at him. It seemed to me someone was playing a joke, that the landlady had moved another man into the next room.

'Can't you talk? I know you can cough.'

He was almost yelling at me but he didn't seem angry. Just loud.

'Oh, hell!' he shouted. 'Go back to bed!'

And he pushed me back — he actually put his hands on me and shoved me back — pulled the door shut and went away. Amazing behaviour. It worried me. It crossed my mind that he was a lunatic, that I was in danger. I put a chair against the door. I stood there, ready to scream, staring at the door, certain he meant to come back. He was large, he looked strong, he didn't look to me like the sort who would be able to control himself.

Half an hour later he was back. He stood out in the hall shouting at me: 'I've got medicines! Cough syrup. Juice. Capsules. Tonics. Aspirin. Open the goddamn door!'

I told him to go away.

'You *can* talk,' he said. 'But shut up, you're sick, you're dying. I'm saving your life. Open the door.'

'No!' I said. 'Leave me alone.' He frightened me, he was obviously the violent type.

'Dry up,' he said. That was to himself, I barely heard it although my ear was against the door. I heard him walking away. I breathed freely again.

A minute or two later he strode right inside. He held up a key, kissed it and put it in his pocket. 'Authority,' he said. 'Works wonders. Sit up, you've got a lot of junk to take. Open your mouth.'

He meant it. He had a white sack jammed full of medicines. He even had a tin of Campbell's soup. 'Beef broth,' he said. 'Thin as eel's breath but better than nothing I guess. Don't you have a hot plate?'

28 NOVEMBER: I feel better, thank God. What a bore he's been. He kept my head aching with his shouts. 'What a pigsty! God, open the drapes. Why are there feathers on the floor? Have you been plucking pigeons, eating pigeons? It's against the law, you know. You can't just walk along, bash a pigeon on the head, bring it home and pluck it and eat it. I've wondered about you. You're nuts, is that the case? How old are you? Don't you know better than to live like this?'

Yak-yak, I thought my head would split.

29 NOVEMBER: I'm not going to keep going on this way. He's quite sure he can walk all over me. He dashed in early this morning and moved my bed, with me still in it, over to another wall. I

breathe too deeply, he claims. Everything keeps him awake. Sirens at night, planes overhead, everything. Even the fish in the ocean a mile from here. '*I want silence at night, do you understand?*'

I've asked the landlady to get back her key, I've told her and told her that man is bothering me. She pats my arm. 'Don't worry about it. He's like a moose up there, he throws his weight around. But you're not Cinderella, as I see it this business is between you and him. I learned early in life, don't interfere.'

Impossible woman. Once each month she dresses up, splashes toilet water on her neck, goes in a taxi across town to sit at her husband's grave. No, I don't expect assistance from her.

30 NOVEMBER: Sunshine at last. I know now I can make it on my own, I've proved that much to myself.

I've been lucky, it seems I haven't missed anything. While I've been cooped up over here she's been ill over there. I got that much from the grocer. 'Oh, yes,' he said, 'she's gone through fifty boxes of tissues, hasn't stuck her head out the door in four days, I didn't know you were a friend of hers.'

He was glad to see me, he kissed my cheek and forced a bag of overripe fruit into my hands.

Funny man.

I worry about the Colonel. In a postcard that came yesterday he says he's got his orders, he's shipping out. Big activity in the South Pacific, watch the newspapers for his name. He has a feeling he won't return. Pray for me, he says.

1 JANUARY: I have figured out why I thought he was so old, that idiot next door. He hasn't shaved and his beard must be half an inch long, growing all whirly-whirly and grey on his face. He walks stooped, especially when he's in a hurry, which is the case most of the time. I can't say I respect him but I have got used to the abrupt way he behaves. He thinks he's my daddy, that's a guess. Last night he wanted to know what I do with myself all day. 'First you're here, then *poof!* you're gone, I can't count on you, where do you go all day?'

We were drinking champagne, turning the old year out.

'Got a lover, have you? The old bench-warmer who has finally made it into the game? Cheers, let's meet like this again next year.'

Turning it out, this year that has rolled by day by day and which to me seems fair enough and good enough only when seen that way.

'Ah, you're moping,' he said, 'don't mope!' — and he thumped his chest, saying, 'The only strings we have are those in here.'

Then *he* turned sour, he wanted to know when I was going to pay him back for all the money he's spent on me. 'I'm broke now, lost it all in a Tuesday night poker game. So pay up, you don't get a free ride on my trolley.'

I told him I had no money, he'd have to wait, and he picked up the champagne and went away disgusted with me.

I didn't know what to do with myself, it was too late, too late to go anywhere. I picked up the phone and dialled her but the line was busy, probably she was having a party over there.

Later on he came back. He thinks he's Lord Nelson, he strides right in. I was taking a bath. He sat down on the edge of the tub, sat there with his legs crossed, staring at me. 'I didn't think you washed,' he said. 'That crust looks like it hasn't been disturbed in years. You could sell that mould to a geology lab. Unfold your arms, I want to have a good look at you.'

I let him. It hurt me but I closed my eyes and let him. I don't know what I expected him to do. After a while I opened my eyes and he was gone. The water was cold, I was sneezing again.

It's true about the feathers. If you sit on a bench and the birds strut all around you they ought to expect it. I hate it, that cocky, you-mean-nothing-to-me air that they have, while all the time they are strutting around your feet, pecking up whatever you give them. I despise their throaty sound, that maddening little hop they take when you or another bird does something to vex them, that wooden-legged strut that they have. You're supposed to sit there and grit your teeth and let yourself be humoured by them. I tried to kill one with a rock but they have necks like a rubber hose, they can scoot faster than guinea hens. I stunned one and brought it home folded up inside my coat. It revived and I had to chase it all over my room. It put me in a fury that I couldn't catch it, the chase left me breathless on the floor. I crawled to the door, opened it, but the bird didn't have sense enough to leave. Well, by that time it had squirmed into a corner and lay there on its side kicking out its scaly matchstick legs.

Contemptible creature. It wouldn't have crossed my mind to try to eat it. I'm aware there's nothing to them except gristle and bone. Their bones shred, they're like hat-pins. Anyway I'm nauseous as a rule, there isn't much I can get down.

If the feathers disturb him I hope he knows what he can do, he can get off his high horse and sweep them up in a dustpan, he's God Almighty and can do that and anything else he wants to.

2 JANUARY: God, I've been in a state all day. I must have taken a hundred pills.

I've been staring at this page for two hours.

A dozen times I've gone down to talk to the landlady, I bang on her door and ask her why there's no heat in my room, I'm wearing three sweaters under this coat and still I shiver, my hand is blue on the page.

'Sorry', he says, 'about last night.'

I'm supposed to leap up and throw my arms around him.

'I wish I could get through to you.'

I want my privacy, I want it and expect it and that's all I've ever asked for.

'It's this holiday season,' he says, 'everything is up in the air, people are not themselves, routines are disrupted, you'll be shipshape once everything returns to normal again.

'I know you hear me,' he says, 'your eyes blink when I speak, I know I'm not talking to a dead wall.'

I've been remiss, I haven't thought of her once all day.

I'll survive; I will, that's what I do when nothing else works.

3 JANUARY: People think it's easy. They say, 'Stand on your own two feet, be yourself.' Then they crawl on to say the same to

someone else while the rest of us who can't move remain in our circle screeching at each other.

That's what it was like today.

Yet he's been going out of his way to be nice to me, he promises he won't shout any more. He said that, holding my hand, looking deep into my eyes, and I had to laugh, being incapable of believing he could even *seem* to be so sincere.

'Good. Are we friends once more?'

I remember the first time I learned how easily and innocently one can wound another person, how with the smallest remark one may damage them. I remember my father had only four fingers on his left hand. I remember the winter when I was five years old and how with my play scissors I snipped the extra finger off his left glove and how this wounded him, how my mother took me to a corner and shook me, saying I was a frightful child. How he was the one who felt ashamed.

'I told you once things got back to normal you'd be your old self again.'

He can sit on my tub and look at my breasts, perhaps he can even put his hands on them and he can accept that the scale of this deed is heavy, no apology can erase that, it's a betrayal of vast proportions and this insight is new to him, it's a revelation, he thinks by this recognition he's improving himself, he's on his way to becoming a decent human being, but in fact he's become worse because he will only be looking for his larger meanness now and this will blind him to the fact that it's the legion of trivialities we can't forgive. I don't care if he wants to look at me in the bath, I can even see pleasure in the episode, but I don't want to be studied like a piece of clay unless I have early warning, unless I can believe there's warmth of feeling, coexistence of spirit between the viewer and the viewed.

Dubious developments elsewhere today: I've been invited to join a theatre group, it's official: the Fine Line Players will take the city by storm when they present six weeks from now Odessa del Rey's memory play, *The Suicide Club*.

'No doubt you wonder', the director told us, 'what will happen when you take your problems into the streets. Cheer up, good people, six months from now the house applause will tell you that your harboured secrets hold previous anchor within the breasts of all solid citizens of the town, that's art, friends.'

'Ah Judith, Judith,' *he* tells me, 'put away your scissors, you'll find old Holofernes isn't such a bad guy. Close your eyes, I'll rub your back.'

4 JANUARY: I find it so interesting. The banker had a fight with her today, right outside her front door. She called him dirty names, half a dozen people came outside or stopped in the street to stare, including the grocer whose job, it seemed, was that of timekeeper; each minute or so he'd pull a watch from his apron pocket and whisper to those near him that they had been going at it for eight minutes or nine or ten minutes now.

'Oh, it happens', he said, 'all the time, though usually they keep it indoors.'

The man was meek, he didn't try to defend himself. She saw this as indifference, it was this, I think, that fed her rage. 'An emotional cripple,' she shouted, 'that's what you are!'

I couldn't help laughing, it's a line I have in my play.

She told him she hoped never to see him again, he was lower than low, she ought to have her head examined for putting up with the likes of him. Then she shook her fists overhead and fled inside.

With her gone he tried treating it like a joke. 'Women,' he smiled, 'what else can one expect?' Everyone still scowled at him. No one doubted the fault was his. 'Women,' he muttered, 'there's a difference all right, women are different.' Someone in the crowd hooted, he whirled around on her. 'Don't get me wrong. They are not different from us, just from each other, from themselves. Name me one woman who's the same from one hour to the next?' Women among us began throwing out names: Sonja Henie, Bathsheba, Mary Magdalene, Cassandra, Mamie Eisenhower, the Queen, Lotus Blossom, Little Mary Sunshine, Henny Penny, the names went on.

'That's enough,' he snarled, 'my case is proved!' He strode across the street; at the grocer's door he turned. 'Laugh,' he yelled, 'that proves it too. Name me one man so able to forget himself that he'd cause a disturbance in the street.' Idi Amin, someone shouted. Charles Manson. The Wright Brothers. Jesus, Hitler, the Bee Gees, anyone from Australia, the list went on. 'I can see you're not serious,' he shouted. 'That's another thing, you women don't know how to seriously discuss an issue.' Lizzie Borden, one of the women called. Lucrezia Borgia. Madame Tussaud.

He gave up, sweeping on inside the store. Behind him the grocer paused to consult his watch. 'Fourteen minutes,' he piped, 'a new record for a Friday.' The street crowd cheered; apparently this was old stuff to them. They dispersed. I felt lonely, unsure of where I should go. Finally I went into the grocery.

The man was telling the grocer he wanted a case of sardines.

'Sure,' the grocer replied, 'anything you want, nothing you two do surprises me.'

'I want them delivered to her,' the man said. 'We're having this trouble because of the diet's she's on, she eats like a bird. No protein, how can she expect to enjoy proper mental health? If you have a few frozen steaks throw those in.'

'Anything you say,' the grocer replied.

'Of course I haven't known her very long,' the man continued. 'She's difficult, a difficult case. I drew her a bath this morning, washed her back, even her hair. I was convinced she didn't recognize me. Don't misunderstand me, she has no strings on me, our relationship is innocent, whatever anyone might suppose.'

The grocer took his money, he said he'd deliver the order right away. He winked as he went by me with the goods.

The man decided he'd wait. One of his socks was on inside out, a tie hung from his side-pocket. His eyes were bleary, as if he'd been losing a lot of sleep. 'What do *you* want?' he asked me. 'Who do you think you're staring at?' I drifted back, turning away from him, turning to the bin of grapes. They were beautiful grapes, perfectly formed on their slender stems, their skins so translucent one could see the seeds inside.

A woman came through the door. She strutted to the counter

and from there disdainfully surveyed us, looking from one to the other. 'Well?' she said. 'I'm in a hurry, which of you is running this place? I want eggs and milk and your best roach powder, don't make me wait all day.' The man shrugged, stepping forward. 'Why not?' he said, 'I got my life's start in a store much like this.' He got her milk and eggs but couldn't find the roach powder. 'I see it,' she said, 'down there, lower shelf, the pink box. No, not the big box, the small box, don't you know anything?'

He bagged her groceries; it was then that she announced she wanted to put it all on charge. The man told her he didn't know about credit, she'd have to wait. I thought the woman was going to slap his face. She put the groceries under her arm as if she had already paid for them. The man paced the aisle, he kept running a hand through his hair, now and then pulling out a handkerchief to blow his nose.

The grocer returned. He had brought the sardines back. He put these down and hitched a thumb over his shoulder. 'She wants to see you,' he informed the man. 'She says for you to get over there quick.'

I looked through the store's plate glass. A slither of light showed at her window, I saw her knuckles gripping the drapes, her face staring down on us.

'Is she crying?' the man asked.

'What do I know about crying, no, she's not crying, she was on the phone when I got there. Talking to someone named Judy. You know a Judy?'

The man shook his head, he knew no friend of hers named Judy.

I said I knew Judy but they weren't listening to me. The man didn't appear to be in a hurry to go to her. He smiled stupidly at the woman with the roach powder while the grocer said to her, 'Lady, you want credit, who are you, do I know you, what is it you have in mind putting up for collateral?' He stepped between them, asking the grocer for cigarettes. 'Anything mentholated, brand doesn't matter, whatever's best.' He asked where he might be able to buy flowers, was there a stall nearby? The grocer replied that he didn't know anything about flowers, what was he running, an information bureau? 'You got troubles, take them to the Eric Martin Institute of Psychiatry, that's nearby.'

We all had a big laugh at that.

The man left the grocery, I stepped out behind him. The streak of light disappeared at her window.

'Where are you going?' the man asked, turning on me. 'Are you following me?'

'Of course not,' I said, 'I'm going home, why should I follow you?'

He laughed. 'Excuse me,' he said, 'I'm a bit distracted, I need to be alone and think this difficulty out but can't manage the time just now. Do you mind if I walk along with you? I've got to buy flowers, perhaps a box of candy although flowers would certainly be better, surely there must be a place around here where one can find them.'

'I wouldn't know,' I said. 'I'm a stranger to this neighbourhood.'

'Didn't I meet you last year, Open House at the Institute? You were wearing a red dress.'

'Not me,' I said, 'I look like death in red.'

How peculiar I felt walking with him, nice, I could hear my heels clicking on the sidewalk while his made no sound. The sky had whitened to near chalk and it had turned colder; our breaths formed small bags in front of us and in the time it took to step through one, another was there.

'Are you warm enough?' he asked. 'I like that coat, black suits you. But it looks too thin, you'll catch a cold. You wear a lot of make-up, don't you?'

I wasn't offended, it was clear that he was saying whatever came into his mind while reserving his deeper thoughts for his own problems. I do that sometimes too.

At the first corner I turned; he went on ahead.

'I hope you find them,' I called. 'The flowers.'

'Oh, I'll find them,' he answered. 'I'm not such a kluck as I appear.'

I laughed, I liked him, I hoped his life would be happy.

I felt hungry. For the first time in weeks I had a true appetite,

I was ravenous and walked all the way downtown to a vegetarian restaurant I know about called *Deer Crossing* and there I had split-pea soup in a cup and an open-faced cheese sandwich with bean sprouts sprinkled on it.

I felt listless and sleepy, I couldn't wait to get home.

5 JANUARY: I couldn't write this last night, it was too ludicrous and funny.

When I got back to my place I found a man propped up in my bed.

Someone had left twelve red roses in a vase on my table.

'Who left those?' I asked.

'Be reasonable,' he said, 'I only just got here.'

He was reading my diary.

'You need help,' he said, getting up, 'and you came to the right man.' He thumped the diary. 'What happened to December? Why did you tear out all the pages?'

I didn't rush out screaming. The truth is he looked harmless.

'Who are you?' I asked.

'Sigmund Freud,' he said. 'I've just finished the last page of *Drei Abhandlungen zur Sexualtheorie* and I'm tired, so don't make this any more difficult for me than it has to be.'

'What do you have in mind?' I asked.

He tapped his skull. 'I'm going to cure you.'

'How do you propose to do that?'

'In your case all that's required is an active imagination. Lie down and get busy.'

6 JANUARY: I've moved. I didn't want to but Sigmund said I should.

'New interests, new horizons, *involve* yourself, Judith.'

Here it's nicer, cheaper too, I have the only room on the top floor. From my window I can see anyone coming, or leaving, for a distance of seven miles.

Note, windows wrong size, snip off bottom of drapes.

I've been lucky, right away I've found someone interesting. She's older than me, on the thin side, she's nervous and dresses badly though I don't find her unattractive. I think she's the kind of person one can depend on. I was on the street not two doors down from here, when I heard her telling off a young boy who had bumped into her. An accident, he claimed — 'Lady, I didn't mean to!' — but she wasn't having any of it. 'You don't own the street,' she told him. 'You think you can knock us all down, your kind, and go your merry way, but I won't have it! You're nothing special, it's time you realized that!' She really was in a rage. Although I was on her side I found her behaviour shocking. The boy was helpless, she had him in tears. Finally he broke loose and ran, just a small boy, barely more than five or six.

Well, his mother should keep him home.

She doesn't know what to do with her hair, it's silly the way she wears it, someone ought to tell her. I might slide a note through her mail slot, MAKE AN APPOINTMENT AT HOUSE OF BEAUTY, MR SAXONY IS A WIZARD WITH PEOPLE LIKE US.

We might be good company for each other, I think we could become friends.

Sigmund is staying with me for a few days while looking for work. He says he won't be much trouble and will do his share of the chores. I like him though he's too chummy in my opinion.

That *she* needs my friendship is obvious. She's discontented with herself, she hasn't learned as I have how to cope with life's small realities.

Sigmund says she wants to be useful to society, she wants to be liked and respected.

I say, 'Sigmund, you don't even know her!' and he shrugs, he says, 'I know women.'

She *is* the kind who drifts from mistake to mistake, she *looks* for trouble. For instance, today before her encounter with the boy she was in the dry-cleaning place on the corner arguing with the counterman. 'Your sign says one hour,' she told him, 'one hour Martinizing, it's in all your advertisements, what do you mean I can't have this coat back in one hour?' But all the time I could see the way he was looking at her, he was interested, that much was clear. And *she* was, too, I saw how sweet she got at the end.

Something as a matter of fact may already be going on in that department.

Sigmund says no, he says she's a long way from being ready to make a commitment to anyone.

7 JANUARY: I couldn't leave her like that, I had to go back. The grocer saw her through his window, I must have been pacing back and forth trying to make up my mind. He came outside, he touched my elbow and put a bag of grapes in my hands: 'Take them,' he said, 'don't worry, she'll be happy to see you, I know she will. Take these grapes up to her, she likes grapes, the two of you will get along fine.'

'She's taken down the drapes,' I said.

'Ah well, drapes get dirty, she's having them cleaned, I guess.'

I had in mind a quiet chat. I'd introduce myself and shake her hand, we'd sit down and over tea I'd tell her I knew what she had been going through, that I had been in that boat myself and while I agreed with her that we had to stand up for our rights and be on guard every minute of the day there was no point in going overboard with it, if a man was halfway decent and good to us we should make sacrifices, be forgiving, give them the benefit of the doubt. Yes, she'd say, I see what you mean, I've been thinking along those same lines myself, it's impossible but what else can we do? The discussion would become intense, we'd sit on for hours comparing notes, quite unaware of the passage of time, probably amazed at how much we had in common.

'That's right, go ahead,' the grocer said, 'nothing to be nervous about.'

He was so convincing, I had never imagined he could be such a warm and sympathetic man, he even walked me across the street and opened the door for me. 'Go on,' he said, 'you won't regret it, you'll find you're doing the right thing.'

'Is *he* here?'

'I wouldn't know.'

Climbing the stairs, I had the most extravagant fantasy: her door would open, she would turn with a soft smile, she would hold out her arms. I would glide across the floor and enter her skin. He would embrace *me*!

The door was open.

He was there.

'At last!' he said. 'Where have you been?'

I walked in.

'You look beautiful,' he said, embracing me. 'That Mr Saxony is a genius.'

His hands moved gently over my body. He closed his eyes, moaned and kissed my neck. I closed my eyes too.

'You've done a nice job, arranging those flowers.'

I loved it, I loved what he was doing to me.

'Sure,' he whispered, 'sure you do. You treasure your schizothymia, you rise above the hoi polloi. There is so much *more* to you than there is to other people. But what about me? What about next week or tomorrow or even one hour from now?'

I pressed against him. I thought: *you* say nothing, *she's* the shrewd one, let *her* handle this.

'In the meantime, where does that leave me? What kind of life do I have, what am *I* to do?'

He held me tighter. I could barely breathe, nor could he. He wanted what I wanted: to become one body that contained all bodies, to look out at the world from the settled, comfortable, perfect silence of a single eye, to have no need even to think *satisfied, satisfied, we are all here*!

The Street of Moons

1. *For Love of Madeline*

EARLIER THIS YEAR, in the remote village of El Flores, in the state of Michoacán which is itself remote — in El Flores then, which is one of the many poor villages lying nearby the big lake there (but creeping away from the water's edge in cozy and random turns up the mountain because they have long since learned to distrust the lake during the rainy season — which in El Flores is most of the year) — in El Flores, I say, there appeared one morning, tacked to four trees at the four corners of the Plaza Principal and to the green-crusted statue of Don Vasco around which the crumbling *jardín* is built, these hand-painted signs bearing the signature of the town's most noted citizen, Señor Gómez:

TO THE PUBLIC

EMERGENCY SITUATIONS INVITED

DRAMATIC FORCEFUL PERSONALITY TIRING OF
FAMILIAR BATTEL OF WILS SEEK SUBMISSIVE
ENTROVERTED FAMALE TO SHARE LIFE OF LOVE
WEALTH AND ADVENTURE. APPLY CAFE BODEGA.

The signs were displayed in such a manner that it was possible for one to read them from the outdoor tables of any of the three cafés looking onto the main plaza, and from the fourth side as well. Here stood the simple whitewashed cathedral and its few stalls selling candles and beads and plastic saints which women with covered heads might occasionally buy for twenty centavos.

Madeline, a determined step or two ahead of her companion, Raymond, had read the signs this morning from all four sides, first while circling the plaza in an attempt to delay a decision as to which restaurant they might attend (and thus to delay breakfast which they could not afford or perhaps hoping by such malingering to circumvent the issue altogether), and again when she emerged — to the distress of Raymond, by the way — from the cathedral with a sheet of newsprint over her head. He resented the twenty-centavo expense and insisted, rather querulously, that it was too late for prayer to do them any good. 'Especially', he said, '— especially as we do not believe in God, anyway.'

One might have seen Madeline's thin lips press her teeth, her pale, long arms whip out and wrench the paper into halves. Might have seen her, that is, turn on him in momentary rage, taking quick breaths that stopped short of her lungs and left her skin spotted, her fingers white. (Her tantrums as a child had been intense and regular and, let us say, successful; she was a nervous, opinionated girl, much inclined to quick fits even now.)

'Especially,' said Raymond, who had long since ceased to be frightened of her, '— especially, as you are such a fool that God, if he did exist, would only laugh.'

Madeline, as usual, had not favoured him with a verbal reply. She had hugged her stomach and marched off to the Bodega and sat down.

Now — and for some time now — the two of them had been seated under the portico at the Bodega, Madeline sipping at water she suspected was impure, and Raymond engrossed in the news sheet — rehabilitated with great care — which he could not understand. He looked up, glancing at her, and now looking down at the lake which had risen during the night, volunteered his thoughts in a tired, petulant way: 'I don't see why we have to eat here. I don't see why we couldn't go to the market and get a peso glass of juice or maybe some bananas that would cost practically nothing. I don't know what the hell you think we're going to do about lunch, not to mention dinner. It's times like these — I don't mind saying it — times like this, you gripe my ass.'

Madeline shook her head gently, smiling in a polite way that meant she was either not listening to him or did not care what he did. The smile lingered, if only to annoy him, which fact Raymond realized as he let his gaze pass from lake to cathedral to plaza — as he let himself look anyplace but at her. He knew perfectly well why they were not again at the market-place. Even the sight of it now made her ill. For the past five days she had been suffering a mild *turista* — the pain was not bad but neither would it leave her. Its small inconveniences had first embarrassed her; now the condition made her furious and she would clench her teeth, breathe her short breaths, when asked whether she felt better or worse.

I'll remain calm, the girl was thinking now. I won't let him know how much the very sight of him disgusts and infuriates me. She quietly stretched her hand out on the table beside the silverware which the waiter had brought long before. He had yet to bring the menu which Madeline was anxious for, wanting to see for herself what they could not afford.

As for Raymond, now that he had told her how he felt, he was perfectly content to sit. He believed that if only more people would sit and think and take life easy the world would be a far better place. He was, in fact, capable of believing that if he sat here long enough this morning, thinking and watching and taking life easy, then all their troubles would go away. It was largely this belief — and Madeline's greed — that had reduced them to their present economic status. Between them they had sixteen pesos.

'Where we slept,' said Raymond — but here he paused. A man in a white suit was drifting by, bowing, heavily ringed fingers clutching his lapels. 'Where we slept,' said Raymond, 'it's under water now. But I don't suppose anyone has noticed.'

Madeline did not reply. She was watching two ants on the table. The ants had thus far successfully moved a crust of bread from the centre to the ledge. A third ant had joined them for a while but she did not see it now. One of the two ants was now reconnoitring along the edge, seeking the best route down. Madeline picked up the bread crumb and returned it to the centre. She watched without expression as the two ants immediately began chasing about in broken directions. A fly on her elbow seemed to be watching them. I will not speak to him, the girl thought. I will not talk to him unless it becomes utterly necessary.

A man's shadow fell between their table and the sun.

'Mademoiselle has been to El Flores before?'

The polite, chivalrous voice at an adjacent table made her turn. The fly on her arm lifted away and spun in the sun. The speaker, dressed in his white linen suit, stood tilted off his heels with one arm tucked high behind him. He was very tall for a native of the region — so Mady thought — and she waited to see his eyes which were shielded by a white sombrero.

'Mademoiselle would like perhaps the sights pointed out to her?'

He rocked on his heels and now slung the other arm behind him as well. Madeline could see enough of his face to ascertain the local bones and colouring. The woman to whom he spoke barely lifted her eyes. He might not have been there at all — so her pose maintained — an obstruction between herself and the sun. She was eating a yellow melon and her hand, resting on the Cerveza portion of the Carta Blanca table top, gripped the base of a glass of orange juice as if she thought someone might take it from her.

'I might place me some signs too,' Raymond said. He was staring off across the plaza at nothing in particular. 'Wanted, one good ticket out of here. *Y no vuelta* either.' His eyes swept lazily across the patrons seated at the other open-air cafés, and came to momentary rest on Madeline. She was now looking down Calle de Agua to where a fisherman sat with his feet drawn up under him, mending a butterfly net.

'They don't use those nets for fishing, you know,' Raymond said. 'It's strictly the tourist bit.' He saw Madeline close her eyes, clenching her face tight. He watched to see how long it would be before she breathed. But then he remembered how much this sort of thing bored him and he looked instead at the ants. They had found the bread and now there were five of them. When he observed that Madeline's eyes were open again he reached forward and pressed a finger against the bread, crumbling it into numerous small pieces. He saw Madeline press her hands to her face and he stared a moment, considering whether she would cry.

'The Mesdemoiselles, they are desiring company, yes?'

The man in the white suit was now at another table where two middle-aged ladies sat with their backs to the plaza and the sun. They wore the El Flores rebozos, one orange and the other red, and the El Flores sandals made of white leather stapled crudely to rubber tire soles. Their feet seemed very clean. '*This* Mademoiselle and *this* Mademoiselle, the situation is an emergency, no?'

Neither of the ladies bothered to reply. They were waiting, too. In each of the three cafés around the plaza the *norteamericanos* were awaiting breakfasts, *desayuno*, which might, or might not, arrive.

'Wanted!' said Raymond, smiling and shaking the rigid shoulder of Madeline beside him, '— a one-way ticket the hell out of here!' She shook her shoulder free and adjusted her chair so that she might be just beyond his reach. The movement was not alone enough to satisfy, though she remained in this position briefly. Then she moved her chair again, straightened, and in a series of tight, violent stabs, swept ants and crusts to the floor. Raymond gave light applause.

The sun was suddenly obscured and both looked quickly to the sky — as did most other patrons seated in the cafés around the plaza. The cloud passed. It was too early — even for the rainy season — for rain. Across the way, at La Chica, on grounds leased from the Posado de Don Vasco, a bent woman with a black rebozo wrapped around what was either a dead or a sleeping child, threaded her way slowly through the tables, her palms cupped to receive whatever centavos might be offered. A dark gentleman in rags, holding a tall tin cup such as those milk-peddlers employ, squatted at the entrance way, his feet bound by a clever arrangement of cloth, rope and twigs.

'Maybe we could get our dinero back from them,' Raymond said. 'You think we could?' His voice was soft, as if by such modulation he hoped to serve notice of his restraint. As if he meant to say, 'You can worry but, as for me, I have nothing to worry about.' Or perhaps he spoke softly only because the wind — and the situation — invited softness now.

'Three lousy pesos,' said Madeline. She drank the last of the warm water in her glass to disguise her sneer. To drown the words her mouth yet could feel. She thought: God, I've done it now. Broken my silence, the last weapon I had. And replaced the glass, thinking: What a fool I am to talk to him.

But the man with her did not notice his victory. A young Mexican in a grey, splattered Volkswagen was circling the plaza, the top of his head concealed behind the fringe of a red satin curtain that adorned each window. A plastic Jesus danced from the rearview mirror and a host of other such symbols were attached to a rear window pedestal. The car boasted a Michoacán plate but it was not an El Flores car. He circled the square a second time and pulled up now at the vacant taxi zone beside a sign clearly reading SE PROHIBE ESTACIONAR. He did not get out. A boy on the curb with a sponge and bucket stood regarding him.

'It is his first car today,' Raymond said. 'Ortega is not yet ready to go to work.'

'That is not it at all,' snapped the girl — her chair scraped over the tiled floor and several people, including the man in the white suit, turned to stare at her. 'Ortega knows perfectly well that the man does not want his car washed.'

It was Raymond's turn to sneer. 'Why,' he asked, leaning on an elbow toward the girl, '— why doesn't the man want his car washed?'

'That isn't the question,' said Madeline — her voice snapped right and left and several of the Mexican men seated nearby were nodding their heads. 'The boy isn't going to ask the man if he wants his car washed because the boy knows the Mexican hasn't got a peso between himself and hell.' The men nearby were grinning and nodding though of course they had no idea what she was saying. 'No more,' said the girl, 'than the three lousy pesos you gave those miserable beggars would stand between us and it, between us and anything else you could name.' The men now grinned more widely and passed inaudible comment back and forth between themselves. They did not understand her — *No entiendo? No entiendo? Cómo?* — but before her period of unaccustomed silence they had seen her for many days waving her arms and slicing the air and spitting out a variety of sounds containing the name of her lazy friend, Ramón.

They watched now to see in what manner he would respond — for sometimes he too would wave his arms and screech — but he was instead looking past the Café Alameda to Calle de San Francisco where now they looked too. A delegation of officials from the municipal building had emerged. Three of them wore suits that seemed made of glass, and the fourth, whose clothes did not reflect the sun, was gesturing vehemently.

The man in the white suit, to whom Madeline was giving her attention, was now seated alone at a table away from the sun. He had removed his hat — it rode *vaquero*-style on one narrow, quivering knee — but Madeline could not see his eyes. The jar of Nescafé Instantáneo had been brought him and he was stirring spoonfuls into a large white mug of steaming water.

The waiter passed through the tables and a number of people — *norteamericanos* — shouted for his attention, but he ignored them, again disappearing inside.

'Café negro, café con leche — hell, just coffee,' groaned Raymond, whose own voice had been among those calling for the boy. 'You wouldn't think that's too much to ask.'

'The Mademoiselle would see the sights?' the man in the white suit was saying to no one, '— the Mademoiselle is perhaps only passing through? What does the Mademoiselle desire?'

Other patrons were drifting in and selecting tables or drifting in and standing a while and then drifting out again. Several of those who believed they had been waiting too long at the Bodega were drifting out to go and wait at another café, just as others from the Alameda and La Chica were quitting their tables to come here. The café owners found this practice reasonable: a customer gained for each customer lost. All who truly desired food at this time of day eventually would be served. Moreover, waiters at the Bodega, at La Chica, at the Alameda would not grow restless and haughty and demand more pay, as they had different faces to serve each day. So long as their tips could not be correctly anticipated — so long as the waiters were happy and satisfied — why it might be some time — weeks perhaps — before they terminated their service with, say, the Bodega, for a more promising relationship with the Alameda or La Chica.

The man in the white suit understood all this — he acted like a man who did. Now pouring his hot milk from the ceramic jug, now stirring, now adding spoonfuls of coarse sugar. He was in no hurry. It was easy to see he was satisfied. The sombrero bucked *vaquero*-style on his thin knee, but not because he desired to go anywhere. Madeline, watching him, waited for him to drink, for then he might lift his face — but she was wrong for she saw him now dipping his mouth to meet the rim of the mug, sucking up the liquid between his teeth.

'The café is good, no? *Es bueno? Correcto? Buenas días*, Mademoiselle. The Mademoiselle is in the hot-seat, no?'

Madeline turned. There was no one behind her. The man in the white suit was addressing his remarks directly to her.

'The Mademoiselle has desires? *Sí?* The Mademoiselle is ambitious for the food?' He smacked his hand on the table edge, made a sucking noise with his tongue between his teeth — and immediately the waiter appeared. He lifted his fingers in a casual outward motion and the waiter nodded and hastened off, appearing a moment later with a single menu which he held to his chest until Madeline reached for it.

'Well, grass-uss,' Raymond said, turning to the man in the white suit, 'much-us grass-us, you know.' The man shrugged and turned aside.

Along the cobbled street in front of the Bodega the municipal officials were passing. One or two citizens from Alameda, from La Chica, the owner of the *zapatería*, and the moustached proprietor of the *peluquería*, had joined them. Now they had paused before the Bodega to invite companionship. *Cómo está usted?* The day is promising, no? We have been asking 'Where are the clouds?' It is our intention now to walk to the water and measure its progress during the night. Someone has been saying the lean-to of the Americanos is washing out to sea? Can this be? We ask you! *Mañana*, what height will the water be? It is wise to be cautious, no? And only our duty as good citizens of El Flores. Who will go with us now?

No one from the Bodega joined their group. Its composition was too official for their tastes and, yes, there was another matter. Most

Bodega patrons had been looking across the plaza at the boy with the bucket who had at last approached the man who sat in the car behind the fringed red curtain. They could hear the boy's thin voice and the man's muffled response. The boy was saying he would watch the man's car. For a peso he would see no one stole the hub-caps or the crooked antenna or perhaps even the licence plate. For a peso he would watch it very good. The man was evidently inquiring what need he had of the boy's service when he was himself in the car and perfectly capable of maintaining his own vigilance over the machine. The boy was saying, 'But, ah, you are sleeping much of the time. I could myself steal the hub-caps and the antenna and perhaps the licence plate.'

It seemed — to those watching from the Bodega — that the man in the grey car would have to give Ortega the peso if he wanted to get back to sleep again. Finally the boy got into the car with the man, and the man drove off with him — and none of the people in any of the three cafés understood this at all.

'Was that Ortega who got in the car?' they asked.

'No,' they agreed, 'it was someone else, for why would Ortega get in the car of the man from someplace else? No, it was not Ortega.'

'We agree, yes,' others added, 'but if it was not Ortega who got in the car then where is he now? Where is the bucket and his sponge? No, it must have been Ortega who got in the car for otherwise his sponge and his pail would be near the fountain where they always are.'

'Yes, it was Ortega who got in the car,' they could all agree. After all, he had been seen talking to the man. And, after all, it was true that Ortega could never be counted on. He might very well have got in the car. He would return soon — in an hour or two — before nightfall — and say it was the Saint — El Santo from the cine and the comic book — who was in the car. A few kilometres out of El Flores they had put masks over their faces, and driven thus to other villages around the lake which were not so well prepared for the flood. Whose foolish officials had not had the presence of mind to stir from their chambers and go to measure the level of water. Possibly this very minute Santo and Ortega were pulling goats and cows and children and old men from the swollen lake.

'For that,' they all agreed, 'is the way Ortega passes the day when he isn't charging a peso for the car. And sometimes even then it is El Santo who pushes the sponge.'

Raymond and Madeline had their breakfast by this hour — *bollillos* and *mermelada* — in the sun, to the clatter of dishes and the occasional lifted voice of someone in the street or in the plaza calling to someone in another place. The rolls were stale but they voiced no complaints. For the marmalade was good and more of it than they could eat. Only once did Madeline rush off to the *damas*, but she was soon back, submerging her irritation and the occasional acute pain in a bickerish concern for whether Raymond had eaten more than his share.

A small boy whose patched britches reached his knees loitered by, selling Chiclets which no one bought. A man and a burro saddled with wood came by and stood for perhaps five minutes in the street between cathedral and plaza. When he had accomplished what he set out to do he slapped the flank of the donkey and both moved on a few yards to stand in another place. The cooks left for the market with their baskets and plastic bags, getting ready for the *comida* trade.

The breakfasting people sat on, their ranks thinning somewhat. Some moved to the stone benches on the plaza and some simply went away, while others moved from shade to sun to shade again. The municipal delegation alighted a second time from their red building on the Calle de San Francisco, proceeding with a second measurement of the water's depth, for it seemed no one had recorded the first.

'The situation is perverse,' they said. '*Obstinado*,' the men in glass suits claimed. 'For this, one must — *vigilar de cerca* — keep one's eye peeled!' True, the lake seemed not much higher now. '*Un poco, no más!*' True, the sky did not seem a threat now. But in the meantime — *en el ínterim* — they would keep their eyes peeled, for that was no more than wise. The fourth member continued from time to time to wave his arms excitedly.

The man in the white suit remained aloof from these manifestations of life in El Flores — remained enchanted, or so it appeared, as now and again he might rise and journey about the tables, seeing to this or that Mademoiselle's health, her desires, extending his good hopes, proffering his services. Enchanted, yes, for it gave him not the slightest pause that the women inevitably turned their shoulders to him, shielded their faces, allowed no exchange, uncivil or otherwise, to escape their lips. He sat now with one white boot at rest on the black stand of the shining, brass-edged box of the small shoeshine boy whose own shoes were very dirty. The boy maintained a scowl of deep concentration, his tongue caught between his lips. He had a scab on his ear and infrequently a white hand would shoot up and flick at it as if dislodging flies. The man's sombrero rested low over his eyes; his white coat, meticulously folded, stretched across his lap.

Madeline's companion, Raymond, had left his table — had gone and come and gone again. He was making trips to the bank — the Banco Nacional on the other side of the plaza — and reporting back his progress there. He had been awaiting — they had been awaiting — a cheque for many days now.

'They've got it,' Raymond would say. 'I know they have. My bank tells me they sent it! Of course the Banco Nacional has it. Oh, they're so corrupt, so inefficient! But they've got it, I know they have. I'll have them tear up the place until they find it — where else could it be!'

To these assertions — to his meek eyes which said to her, 'Isn't it true? Don't you find it reasonable, this that I say?' to these Madeline merely returned a gaze of bleak sobriety that lent all the more force to her feelings of indolent outrage. There *was* no cheque. She shifted her chair once more that the sun might not shine directly in her face; she sighed and turned and averted her eyes; she scratched her shoulder and rubbed her lids and wrestled about in the chair until she sat just so ... waiting for him to be gone again ... waiting to see him trot off across the square and circle the statue of Don Vasco and jump the rock wall there where the sign read EXCLUSIVO SITIO NO ESTACIONARSE. Waiting to see him disappear one more time into the apologetic confines of the Banco Nacional. There *was* no cheque. There would *be* no cheque. There had never *been* a cheque. And if the man in the brown suit repeated *Sí, sí mañana, por cierto mañana*, as she had heard him do, then that man was a fool — though perhaps no more than she had been.

She got up now and moved to another table, away from her nest of breadcrumbs and marmalade which had been accumulating flies. She watched the man in the white suit spit on his fingers and relay the spit to his shoes, in apparent dissatisfaction with their glossy shine. The sky struck dark again but the overcast was temporary; the sun was bold behind it and the wind was churning the clouds along at such speed that she could feel the shadows changing on her face. 'Wanted,' she said to herself, 'one good word from the Banco Nacional.'

'Wanted,' she continued under her breath, '— one good wanted, want wanting wanted now.' The speech surprised her: she rarely talked gibberish and never to herself. But there are times, she thought — this might be one of them — when gibberish accomplishes where all else fails. She fixed her shoulder straps and slipped her broad feet into the Cuernavaca sandals and rose from the table. She turned her face a quick moment into the passing edge of sun, blinked, and knotted her fists at her side — and walked over to the table of the man in white who was just then saying to three elderly women waiting for the *cajero* to take their money:

'Mademoiselle can perhaps explain. The Mesdemoiselles would like perhaps the sights to see them now?'

She came to stand between the women and the man. The women were nervous, bleached, new to El Flores. Their money fluttered like lazy hands.

'Señor Goméz?'

The sun, obscured though it might be, was hot on the side of her face and a fly was crawling on her neck — or perhaps it was sweat. She had the taste of marmalade in her mouth. She waited for the man to tilt his sombrero back and raise his head and look at her. The three women drifted away, chatting amiably — laughing now.

'Good morning, yes?' the man inquired of Madeline, in his polite, chivalrous voice, '— you have business, no?' He tilted the sombrero back and elevated his head but Madeline saw that his eyes were closed.

She sat at his table, let her elbows fall, hooking her fingers behind her neck.

'You are fine, yes?' he said. His lips curled into a contemptuous smile. 'It is good to see you again. Have you improved? No more the *turista*, no? Is there yet the difficulty with your friend's money at the bank?' He waved the jewelled fingers across his face and smiled, saying, 'Ah, these banks! They have no humanity, no finer sensibilities, do you think?'

The girl waited for his eyes to open. She thought if ever he would open his eyes and she could see into him — his character, his soul — she could believe she was doing this. She had quite forgotten that such sighting had never served her well. She leaned close now, whispering: 'I've come about the position.' She moistened her lips and spoke again: 'In response to your ad.' She saw his mouth widen — he tilted back his chair and transferred the sombrero to his knee.

'But how unfortunate,' he murmured. 'How do you say it, that the position is filled.'

She watched his closed lids; she could see his eyes quivering and the spread of blue veins in the skin. His cheeks held the faintest touch of red, as though they might have been lightly brushed with rouge. The chair legs came down and she felt his hand fall heavily on her thigh. 'Ah, but the business is concluded, you see. How regrettable! If I had known! For the emergency situation is intolerable, believe me, I am a man who knows. *Lo siento*, Mademoiselle. I am sorry but, as you say it, my hands are tied. You see?'

The girl saw very well. She had been watching him all morning, no one else had talked to him. It was the game he would play. Raymond, too, had his games.

They sat on together. The sun climbed and the Plaza Principal filled and the *comida* crowd began wandering in. The paths of those from the Alameda, from La Chica, from the Bodega, intersected; gossip and news and speculations were exchanged. The lake, it was established now, was very definitely on the rise. Already its rim was touching the first stones of Calle de Agua. The man from the *oficina de telégrafo* was rumoured to have said that three of the more distant villages on the lake were now totally submerged, but this was scoffed at for the man from the *telégrafo* had a weakness for pulque and moreover the service had never been so fast before. Now and then a man would run down and squat on his heels, testing the water's depth — a mimic of the municipal officials — and his friends would laugh and enact similar tests themselves. The odd child stood around its edge tossing rocks or sticks or dung into the cloudy water. Many others were arriving, too, to observe at close hand the lake's rising. The *helados* vendor bypassed those seated in the plaza and pushed his cart down Calle de Agua, while behind him trudged the weathered *chicharones* man, bound in rags, conveying on his head the large basket of fried porkskins and his bottles of chili sauce. The sky darkened and no one appeared to take offence.

Madeline and the man in white had nothing to say about this quickening along their front. At one point she moved out of her lethargy, her despair, long enough to grasp his arm and thereby claim his attention once more. 'But what if it doesn't work out?' she demanded. 'What if you find you can't get along with this person you've taken on?'

The three bells in the three steeples of the church on the plaza toned midday — or some such hour. In El Flores one could never be sure. In another minute — in another five or ten — the more festive bells of San Antonio on the mountainside would reply.

'It might not, you know,' Madeline said. She released his arm and settled back in her chair. 'American girls don't like to take a lot of shit.'

The man grinned. For the first time, Madeline saw into his eyes. 'Ah,' he said, 'but in that event I will have an opening, yes?' He let her go on looking; he let her see what she would see. Then he rose from his table, blinked, gave her a despondent leer — and walked out of the Bodega, bowing wide to the tables, saying, 'Mademoiselle will forgive? The Mesdemoiselles are satisfied?'

She watched him go. She watched him take the steps of the *jardín*, circle the statue of Don Vasco, saunter at leisure down the walkway with its erratic growth of weed and flower — watched him sweep gracefully up the next series of steps and ascend into the winding Calle de la Noche de la mil Lunas. She expected him to turn and wave, to turn and lift his hat, but he did not. He rounded a corner and was gone.

She exhaled, bore down heavily on the arms of her chair. 'He'll take me,' she said aloud. 'He has to, he has no one else.' She continued looking up Calle de la Noche de la mil Lunas. The street emptied into the mountains and there at its top a black cloud had settled. Any minute now the rain would come, perhaps it was already raining up there. Earlier, she had seen Raymond — or believed she had — threading his way carefully up the street of moons with his green backpack filled and their last ten pesos in his pockets. But possibly not. Possibly he was yet in the bank, bluffing the manager with his talk of a cheque that would never come. It was even conceivable — it was not entirely out of the realm of possibility — that any moment now he would come racing across the plaza, waving in his hands more than enough money to take them away from El Flores.

Possible — remotely so — but not likely. In all probability he was up on the mountain now, waving his thumb. Looking out for a man in a grey car. Saying good riddance to all that. Saying to himself, 'What a hassle that Madeline was!'

She prayed for rain. She hoped the rain would thunder down and wash him in a panic off the road.

A few minutes later the rain thundered down. Whipped about by a simultaneous rising of wind, it drove over stones and pelted trees and formed a thick screen over the lake. It drove El Flores — it even drove Madeline, eventually — indoors. Where she remained for perhaps an hour, perhaps more, as the rain did not abate. One might have seen her finally — a lean, white girl, clothes adhering to her frame — streaking across the plaza in the falling rain, bounding up the steps of the cathedral and shaking its dark doors which of course were closed. And then turning, fleeing up the street of moons, slipping on the wet, gushing stones — banging her knees, wiping rain from her face as she ran — but coming at last to the famous tinsel-sheeted door of Señor Goméz. Might have seen her, I say, knocking her frail fists against the door — cursing — though the wind and rain took her cries and the door remained shut. Then to see her sink down onto the stone steps, her body folding, as the rain pelted her and the swollen waters flowed over her feet. For so it was that day, as the first of the hard rains fell, and the lake began its slow encroachment on the town.

2. *For Love of Eleanor*

THEY MET, as was their custom, on the sunny side of the Plaza Principal and crossed in silence over the ruined grounds, passing on their way the attendant *policia* who stood guard over the tiled fountain, for no one was to use it any more. The young policeman murmured the usual greeting of the morning, inclining an emaciated shoulder toward Eleanor, who returned the courtesy with a smile at his vague face and rumpled uniform, while at her side Frank remained absorbed, watchful of where he stepped, for yesterday he had soiled his shoes. It was clear from his expression — clear to Eleanor at any rate, and to the policeman who no doubt shared his view — that he found El Flores now altogether a dreary and disgusting place.

Quite content herself, Eleanor placed her arm lightly on his as they walked together down the high plaza steps toward the Café Bodega, where they came every morning now for the most extended breakfast in all of Mexico.

'Shall we sit outside?' asked Frank, 'or is it too cool for you?' Sometimes it was too cool for her and sometimes it was not, though Frank would have been the first to say that where they sat seemed rarely to be determined by the temperature.

'Oh, outside, of course,' replied Eleanor, 'there is so much to see.' Frank released her arm, groaning inwardly at this display of her good nature — now stepping politely aside to allow her to pass in front of him through the roped entrance to the Bodega. It was a simple hemp rope the Bodega's owner, Señor Gómez, had installed only the previous week, either as a symbolic effort to cordon off his restaurant from the cruel malady attacking the rest of the village or, more likely, as a gesture of discouragement for his many customers who preferred to quit the premises without paying their bills. In any event, Eleanor admired the new rope. It was the same rope that Michoacán peddlers used to secure their goods as they moved from market to market, the same one the local *leñadores* used to bind wood to their donkeys for transport to the houses of the rich *Americanos*. She had seen it restraining the huge alfalfa bundles that the peasants carried on their backs and she had even occasionally seen it holding up a workman's pants. It was very useful rope and it did succeed, to her mind, in giving a certain character to this drab and sexless café.

She took a seat just by the sidewalk and immediately leaned into the leather harness of the chair, closing her eyes to the sun, which for the moment was bright and warm. She pushed the sunglasses up into her hair and drew the fiery red rebozo close around her neck. Frank accepted the chair opposite her, relieved to see her so soon settling down. Perhaps this morning they could have a breakfast without hysterics or posturing or Eleanor's undiminished fascination with death. He was more than a little tired of Eleanor and this morning he felt — not without some pride — a physical depletion as well.

But he was accustomed to speaking to Eleanor with his own wry brand of accumulated humour, and this morning did not know how to begin their conversation any other way. Thus he shifted about uncomfortably in his chair — it was too small for him — glanced about at the deserted tables, and inquired of Eleanor how her breakdown was coming along.

Eleanor sighed.

A cadre of soldiers passed in sloppy, near-silent formation in front of the café and Frank hoped Eleanor wouldn't open her eyes until they were gone. They would be going to the lake, of course, to relieve other soldiers standing guard there, for no one was to use the lake water either. He watched them until they had disappeared, and then he watched the dust settle behind them. He had heard the rumour — though apparently Eleanor had not — that last night the soldiers had been obliged to shoot someone, for naturally the people of El Flores had to have water and not all could be convinced that the lake was now contaminated too.

He saw Eleanor shaking her head, as if to dislodge the stubbornness of some thought or dream. 'My breakdown, Frank,' she said, 'isn't quite what I had hoped for.' She leaned forward, placing her hand on his arm in one of those tender gestures of domesticity which were so familiar to him and of which he so much approved. 'No,' she said smiling, 'I was much happier in my other life, although it was far less interesting. What does one do with a breakdown? Nothing at all — the breakdown, sad to say, is doing it all to me.'

Frank withdrew the cigarette package from his breast pocket and extracted one. He laid the cigarette down on the table top and stared at it dubiously, disheartened by this reminder that he had no more of his usual brand. He had never told her so, but he found Eleanor's breakdown more than a little boring.

'You see,' said Eleanor, 'in my present state I'm not responsible for my actions.' Her voice lifted in laughter and Frank looked calmly about to see if anyone was watching.

The Bodega remained deserted.

A lone soldier walked casually up Calle de Agua and passed across the plaza, but while Eleanor viewed his progress with a slow turn of her head she refrained from speaking either about this soldier or about those others last night who had fired on the man who wanted water.

'Which means, dear Frank,' she said, 'that I am now cured!' Once again she laughed, though quietly this time, rather like a lady, and Frank stared rudely at her exposed teeth, which were perfect.

He offered her a cigarette which she refused, though she picked up the book of matches and lit his.

She deflamed the match by closing her mouth over it.

'I am not amused,' said Frank, in the voice he would have used with his daughter. He jerked the matchbook from her hand and immediately arranged on his face his expression of offended gloom. He vividly recalled that earlier in the year, seated in the lobby of the Posado de Don Vasco across the way, she had lit another match and held it at her white neck until her hair had burst into flames and he had been forced to grab at her and shove her head into his stomach. Only then did he learn she was wearing a wig, for she had slid free of it to stand pointing and giggling at his astonished face as he stood clutching the wig under his smouldering jacket.

'Are you envious, Frank?' she was saying now, '— would you like a breakdown, too?'

He pushed back his chair and stood. 'I can't afford it,' he said — and stalked off to search for Gómez or the waiter.

But Gómez's small, odd office behind the cash register was empty and no one was in the kitchen, although there may have been, for Frank only made a quick search from the door. He had a need — and cause, he reasoned — to preserve his innocence of Mexican kitchens.

He returned to find Eleanor taking the sun, resting her legs on his chair, her head pitched back, and her eyes shut tight. He adjusted the red rebozo judiciously over her shoulders, and applied a fatherly kiss to the top of her head. Then he lifted her legs to the floor, dusted the chair seat, and sat down.

He was content for some time to sit quietly watching her, thinking: *Ah, sweet Eleanor, how odd she is now!* ... quite forgetting that she had been that way from the beginning: sweet and odd and rather fragile and, to him, quite ridiculously impenetrable. Her head swayed from side to side occasionally — beautifully, thought Frank — as if to music — and now and then he allowed a smile as her tongue flicked out and licked over her lips which he had always thought of as too thin but which he saw now were not at all irregular. He found it curious that she no longer used make-up on her face and that the face which he had once believed to be rather course, with its pink powders and mascara and tinted lips, now looked rather lovely with all that removed. It was, however, the fine sweep of her shoulders that he most admired. Eleanor's shoulders — so he once had been informed — belonged in a museum, high on a pedestal with a glass frame and surrounded by a moat of intense flames.

A cool Indian, he thought now — it was a damned shame that she insisted on making life miserable for those who really were quite fond of her and had only her best interests at heart. It really was too bad — so Frank believed — what Eleanor had let happen to herself.

He saw that Eleanor had her eyes open now, and looked where she was looking: toward the carved, high, bolted doors of the Church of Our Lady of the Saints which Eleanor had lately taken to calling the El Flores headstone. The entire plaza had a mood of disenchanted isolation, though the mood was not confined to the plaza alone and indeed included the whole of the village. For one thing, they could see now the quiet preparations of the mourners at the *funeraría* up Calle de la Noche de la mil Lunas — the Street of Moons, as it was called — and the occasional mourner in his sinister black outfit crossing Calle de la San Francisco with flowers to adorn the coffin mounts.

To his surprise Eleanor still did not speak of the death that was all around them. 'Dear, dear Frank,' she was saying now, smiling gaily across at him, 'how is it I have come to know you so well! This morning you have that insufferable gloating air. It amounts to an odour, though I know you bathe. Was it the company you had last night?'

Frank was not annoyed. On the contrary he admitted to some mild pleasure or even pride in these absurd little insights of hers.

'Why, yes,' he told her, 'I did have company last night. An interesting girl, very odd, very sweet. I met her at Maya's opening.'

Eleanor slid lower in her chair and for a moment Frank could hear her breathing — that peculiar way she became sometimes when excited — her mouth open wide, her breath shallow and so tentatively deepening that small white patches surfaced on her skin. 'Oh, yes, Maya,' she said at last. 'That man who paints the dead!' Her voice was light, even somewhat tipsy, and Frank didn't want to talk about Maya or his see-through portraits of the dead.

'It wasn't a bad opening,' he admitted begrudgingly, irritated that Eleanor might think he had attended for anything other than the punch and the people he would see. Over the next several minutes he proceeded to tell her who had been there, what they were wearing, and how they had behaved, about the strong, warm punch and the last-minute difficulties the gallery had experienced with the authorities who had removed all their ice — not caring that Eleanor displayed no interest, ignoring her when she loosened the top buttons of her El Flores blouse and flung the red rebozo aside that her white throat and freckled chest might claim the sun.

Then he told her about the girl.

'But why,' asked Eleanor when he had finished, proving that she had been listening all the while — 'why was she asked to leave?'

'She insulted Maya's wife.'

'I didn't know he was married,' said Eleanor, finding the thought strange. 'What did your girl-friend say to her?'

'She wasn't my girl-friend at that point,' corrected Frank. 'No, she told Maya's wife that the reason Maya didn't paint the living was because she, meaning Maya's wife, was as good as dead herself.'

'That sounds pretty mild.'

'Oh, I don't know. The woman isn't very attractive. She's not very smart either. And she kept Maya away from the punch. In all the time that I was there I never saw a flicker of emotion on her face.'

'She sounds a lot like you,' said Eleanor with a smile. 'But they kicked your girl-friend out for that?'

'No,' explained Frank. 'It was after she insulted Maya. She told him that she didn't like the way he painted the dead.'

'What did Maya say?' asked Eleanor, who was very interested in this.

'Nothing. He doesn't talk much. Not that she gave him much time. She told him what she didn't like about his paintings of the dead is that he faked it up too much. She didn't like his crummy — that was her word — his crummy symbolism, all those hot red roses crushed in the hands, and such. But finally what she found most detestable was that his dead people didn't look dead — that if you opened their eyes and put a fleck of colour in their cheeks they would look pretty much like everyday, normal, living people.'

'I didn't know you liked the outspoken type,' Eleanor said quietly.

'I don't approve of Maya's work,' said Frank. 'I don't see any point in painting the dead.'

'That's too bad,' smiled Eleanor, patting his hand. 'You'd make a very worthy subject.'

Frank turned his blank stare on her and they sat in pensive silence until Eleanor picked the story up again.

'So naturally when she left you left with her because you were one of those without an orchid or a red rose in your hands — no doubt because both your hands were filled with all the tequila cocktails you could carry.'

Frank did not take this comment seriously, though he was amused by the suspicion that Eleanor still expected some kind of physical loyalty from him.

'So that's Nora Meyer Jones,' he concluded. 'A cool Indian, I think you'll agree.'

'Oh, I agree,' replied Eleanor, avoiding his eyes. 'I'm always delighted when you can find someone who will sleep with you.'

For a long spell neither had much more to say. The waiter did not enter, nor did the owner Gómez — nor for that matter did any customer. All this solitude was quite extraordinary and it occurred to Frank to wonder whether others in El Flores knew something that he did not. Across the plaza two sentinels took up positions by the copper-sheeted doors of the Banco Nacional, though why they should want to he could not guess. A child, the boy Ortega who washed the cars of the *turistas* during better times, came to stare gloomily at the policemen holding watch over the fountain at the plaza's centre, but he soon trotted away, and the policeman completed his lazy turn around the fountain, the butt of his weapon dragging heavily at his heels. The street around the plaza was fixed with dry scales of mud, as were the elevated cobbled sidewalks and steps and the lower façades of certain shops. Here and there even now were derelict puddles of water whose scummy surfaces were like strange, flat jewels reflecting back the sun. The trees in the plaza, once so perfectly sculpted and planted in such a manner that they formed a roof over the grounds, were depressingly open and contorted now, ragged and heavy with their coated dust. The stone benches formerly so neatly aligned and securely anchored to the plaza green sat today aslant of their moorings, broken and crumbling; the brilliantly tiled, arched pavilion on which the musicians played for official functions had been entirely washed away. Down Calle de Agua toward the beach the hard mud thickened, its grey surface marred by countless projections that had been abandoned as the lake waters had receded.

Frank, of course, was thinking of Nora Meyer Jones whom he had left asleep on the bed in his apartment. He had become almost totally immune to the ugliness, the grief, the desolation, the sense of inexhaustible doom embracing the whole of the village. Like Eleanor, he retained barely any memory of El Flores as it had been prior to the rain and the lake's inundation — poor and not yet altogether despoiled, timeless and rather lovely — no more than he, or either one of them, could acknowledge anything more than the most illusory of connections with or attachments to their previous life together. Their past lives had simply vanished since their arrival in El Flores, in much the same way that El Flores had itself now been largely obliterated.

Eleanor's thoughts were of the man from Guadalajara who painted the dead. She got up now and went briskly into the Bodega's kitchen where she found a bin of stale *bollillos* that the flies had no interest in. She put three of them on a plate and set about finding where Gómez kept his *mantequilla* or, more likely the *margarina*. She found the butter unwrapped in a dish by the sink with flies swarming over it. The flies were quite listless and many of them she had to wipe aside. She ate the first roll, looking out from the darkness of the kitchen at Frank, who was looking at his nails, and over his shoulder at the young policeman at the plaza's centre, who had now leaned his rifle aside and was seated hunched over on the fountain wall. She had never met Maya but did have an acquaintance with his work. Maya, she felt sure, could find the death in both of them.

A few minutes later she returned to their table, carrying a beer tray that held two cups of instant coffee and a platter piled high with crusty *bollillos*. She had deliberately left the butter behind, out of amusement rather than malice, for she knew that it did not matter to Frank what he had for breakfast so long as someone else placed it before him. He had always taken considerable pleasure in having women deliver food to him.

He immediately halved a roll and bit into it, and turned to Eleanor. 'She's a cool Indian,' he began, 'but it goes without saying that she doesn't have a peso to her name.' Eleanor laughed, as he had known she would. They had enjoyed many of their closest moments together while discussing the various reasons why rich women were never attracted to him.

The sun had passed under and she dropped her sunglasses into Frank's pocket.

The bells in the three steeples at the head of the plaza tolled the tenth hour.

Around the corner from the Banco Nacional a beggar could be seen picking at refuse in the gutter.

They could see, at the *funeraría* on the hill, the health officers dispatched from Morelia in deep argument with the owner-undertaker whose establishment, it was being said, was not burying the dead with sufficient speed nor quite deep enough.

The less guttural bells of San Antonio on the mountainside responded to those in the plaza, and Frank pushed back his sleeve to check the time. 'Only ten minutes late,' he told Eleanor. The procession of mourners — the advancing of the dead, as Eleanor liked to think of it — was further behind than that. For the past several days the march had begun each morning at nine.

The sun came out again and Eleanor reclaimed her glasses, placed them over her nose and leaned back to receive the sun.

'You've changed, Eleanor,' said Frank.

Eleanor replied that, yes, she had.

'I mean your glasses,' he said. 'These are so much more glamorous than those you used to wear.'

'Yes,' said Eleanor, 'I look ten years younger now. How old am I, Frank?'

'Thirty, I believe you said. Twenty-nine? As I recall, the last time we talked about it you weren't sure.'

A boy wearing a dirty *sarape* that dragged at his heels came by and stopped in front of the Bodega to stare at them. He held a black, wet pig in his arms and the pig didn't move and Eleanor was correct in supposing that the pig was dead. She noticed that the policeman was no longer at his station by the plaza fountain and she missed his enfeebled presence there.

'Thirty-one?' suggested Frank. 'You weren't sure.'

He was himself forty-five.

'I'm always sure,' said Eleanor, 'down to the last decimal. The trouble is I never know when to stop counting. What year is this, Frank? Is this the year 1963?' She held her smile for him, wanting to see if he would remember that was the year they had married.

'This is the year 1973,' replied Frank. 'It is the year of hope and innocence and reduced prosperity. It is the year of the Watergate and the year for Nora Meyer Jones and for Frank and perhaps for you, Eleanor. It is also the year death came to El Flores.'

'*El Santo es loco*,' murmured Eleanor, '*El Santo es —*' ... but she couldn't recall the phrase heard so often during these recent days. The Saint is insane, the Saint is evil-intentioned. For in the minds of the citizens of El Flores their patron saint had entered into El Diablo's fearful skin.

The boy with the dead pig finally went on.

'That's what I mean,' continued Eleanor, 'about not knowing when to stop counting. In my dreams the calendar never exactly specifies. But I believe I'm twenty-eight. I feel twenty-eight. Is twenty-eight a good age, Frank?'

'It's a lovely age,' laughed Frank. 'I am myself twenty-eight.'

'At any rate,' said Eleanor, 'it's a nice age for a breakdown.'

With that she turned mopish and secretive and Frank shoved the *bollillos* aside and put on his own dark glasses. Beyond the Plaza Principal up Calle de la Noche de la mil Lunas at the *funeraría* the mourners at last had assembled. They numbered fifty or so at the moment but their ranks would swell as they filed down from the hill. Up there too, if they looked, Frank and Eleanor could see the odd, unattended child at play in piles of rubble. Such piles were numerous: up there and down Calle de San Francisco and Calle de Agua and around the wide street which squared the plaza and in the plaza itself. In the beginning municipal workers had arranged neat mounds of material from street stones uprooted or displaced, but for days the mounds had remained, while the men awaited instructions from the *funcionarios* as to how exactly they should go about repairing the wrecked streets and walks, the eroded walls and various impaired buildings, though at last the rains quit and the lake receded and thus there seemed no need for hurry. The original purpose of the mounds was forgotten; people of the village saw no good reason why they shouldn't empty their ruined possessions and all else they had no use for onto these official mounds. In a period of days all manner of refuse, unaccountable debris aswim in sewerage and stagnating mud, came to form these piles, and over them by the heat of day the insects swarmed and in their hot chambers the maggots bred. So the brackish decaying piles smothered through the week of sun, now sombre landmarks for Eleanor and the painter Maya to enjoy.

Eleanor nodded her head toward the plaza. 'Pancho Villa returns,' she announced.

For Gómez, the man in white, was advancing across the *jardín*. This morning, against the background of ruin and decay, he seemed more outlandishly impeccable than ever, a vision in his bold linen suit and white boots and wide white sombrero. The girl, Madeline, who had been abandoned in El Flores a few weeks before and who now was in his employ, tagged listlessly behind him, her head bowing low either from her humiliation or because it was her present mood. He stopped, waiting for her, and when she was abreast of him he gave her a shove. A few days earlier she would have screamed at him, attacked him with her fists — now she acceded, whimpering, to his demands. It was not known what Gómez did to break haughty American girls; they came to him out of sorrow or need or because they had nowhere else to go and when he had crushed them he would give them a little money and send them on. Now he stood at the fountain, dipping a white handkerchief into the water; he passed the handkerchief to Madeline and pushed back his sombrero and allowed her to pat the wet cloth against his brow. He waved a hand of greeting at Eleanor and Frank seated at his table.

The sound Frank made was almost a snarl, which encouraged Eleanor to reply as she did.

'That man is beautiful. I adore Señor Gómez.'

Frank cursed for the first time that morning. He considered the man unsound and dangerous and certainly evil. It was rumoured that the man made his money from a string of prostitutes in Mexico City and Frank believed it. 'Madeline is a fool,' he said. 'Surely Gómez is not the sole solution to her problem.' He did not bother to inform Eleanor that Madeline had first come to him.

Both turned their attention to the thin American girl wiping the lips of the señor. She had long, straight hair and a strong, squarish chin but everything else about her Gómez had altered. He had taken her out of her homemade frocks, her sandals and Levi's or heavy-hanging gowns, and put her in the clothes he preferred. This morning she wore tight nylon shorts, high blue socks, and a matching blue nylon shirt open to display the Aztec medallion looped around her neck.

She looked, as Frank whispered to Eleanor, like a cross between a Catholic schoolgirl and a New Orleans whore.

But Gómez had not yet succeeded in doing much about her expression. She still her contemptuous scowl and eyes that conveyed her attitude of imprisoned fury.

'You needn't be upset on her behalf,' said Eleanor. 'All her life Madeline has been looking for a way to be deprived.'

Frank said nothing. Women, in his view, were to be ruled — some of them even to be squandered — but only a criminal would want to deprive them of those qualities that were rightly theirs.

'Actually', continued Eleanor, 'they are quite happy together.'

'Oh, I never suggested they didn't understand each other,' replied Frank.

'It's a beautiful relationship,' smiled Eleanor.

'Like yours and mine,' whispered Frank, and this time he was the one to smile.

The señor and Madeline were now approaching, hand in hand. Shadowed momentarily by the sun, his dark body seemed to recede and vanish inside his white clothes.

'What does he do with them', asked Frank, 'when he has no more use for them?'

'Yes,' Eleanor whispered back, 'that would interest you.'

The Mexican entered with a flourish, bowing low to all the vacant tables, spreading his arms, and addressing the empty chairs in his customary way: 'The Mademoiselle would see the sights? The Mademoiselle is perhaps only passing through? At your service, please, what does the lovely Mademoiselle desire?' He careened gracefully through, clicked his heels in recognition of Frank, and bent to kiss the hand Eleanor was already offering him. The señor was always enthusiastic, he examined his women friends with zealous attention to their moods and whims. '*Ola, ola, buenas días*, Mademoiselle, *muy bonita!* — and Death, how is your good friend Death this morning?'

Eleanor giggled, shifting her shoulders free of his warm, scented hands. The girl Madeline swept on inside without a word, securing herself inside Gómez's tiny office with a defiant bang of the door.

'*Ola, señor! Con su permiso?*' He sat down, immediately launching forth to place his hands over Eleanor's knees and wedge his own between them. 'But only one death during the night, Mademoiselle, *uno y no mas*!' He grinned roguishly, though his voice was more urgent than mocking. 'Perhaps our amigo Death is ready to — how do I say it? — *echar pelillos a la mar*! — to bury the hatchet, no!' His hands slid back and forth along Eleanor's thighs. Her eyes gloated, misty from a feeling near to gratitude. She adored Gómez for his sinister vigour, his perverted chivalry. 'Our sainted devil! *Qué mal suerte*! He is tired, no! So many to have died!' He rose, trembling with pleasure, bowing all around. '*Hasta luega, qué se diviertan* — enjoy yourselves!' He spun on his heels and crossed briskly to the office door which they had all heard Madeline bolt from inside. He knocked politely, rattled the knob.

'Go screw yourself,' Madeline replied. Her tone was controlled and remorseless, schooled by years of privileged bitterness.

The Mexican grinned apologetically to Frank and Eleanor, spun a finger at the side of his head, and disappeared into the Bodega kitchen.

'With thousands of superb restaurants in this country,' observed Frank with no more than a trace of irritation, 'and thousands of fine villages, I sometimes wonder how it is I come to be here.'

Eleanor was silent. Whenever Gómez went away something akin to her own hold on sanity went with him.

The procession of mourners was now advancing in slow broken ranks down from the *funeraría* high on the Street of Moons. The white-washed portico under which they sat and which lidded the rows of shops thrusting out to their left and centre seemed to her eyes amazingly clean above the shadowy business fronts and the *jardín* rubble. All the shops were closed, the *zapatería* and the *sombrerería* stall and the *peluquería* where Frank went each week to get his hair looked after. Café La Chica was barred and the Alameda across the way had numerous CERRADO signs attached to its front, as if its owner could not close his restaurant often enough. The *tienda* was closed and the *ropa* where Eleanor had bought her blouse, and *la papeleria* and the tailors' narrow hall.

One of the priest's many assistants had come out and unbolted the doors of the cathedral and another had appeared and bolted it again.

The shining black and windowed coffin mounts that the mourners would be conveying were as yet hidden away. The procession was now perhaps a hundred strong, wrapping forlornly down the thin, winding street, now appearing, now disappearing, while the buildings blended along that height, their walls in the sunlight a single climbing panel of faint pastels. The clay roof seemed joined, a vibrant orange ceiling gently aswim over the town.

Madeline unlatched the office door and glanced around for a sight of Gómez and locked herself again with a brief, violent curse.

The quiet shuffling footbeat of the approaching mourners fell and rose and was obscured again. They would not begin their dirge until they rounded the plaza corner and the cathedral stood in view.

Eleanor, with a slim elegant finger, was spelling out the Carta Blanca beer legend on the table top. 'Yes,' she said, 'and your girl last night, the cool Indian, is she very young?' Her voice was elegiac, remote and wan, although the expression on her face was vacant, simple-minded even, as if her thoughts were of nothing more significant than the flies across the room or a spot of water on the floor.

'Twenty,' Frank said. 'On either side of twenty, I would guess. Attractive, somewhat large — very self-assured. She may be joining us, I hope you don't mind.'

'No, I don't mind,' answered Eleanor.

'But then again,' said Frank, 'she might not.' He grimaced slightly to show Eleanor how matters stood. He was past that age when he could speak with confidence of women's intentions.

'Do you like her?' asked Eleanor.

Frank considered the question carefully. He didn't want to do injustice to either of the women. 'It's a temporary relationship,' he said. 'Nothing will come of it.'

'Why, Frank, how can you say that? How can you be sure! She might prove to be your golden girl, the one you've been waiting for! You might grow to love her, to pine away when she isn't around, the two of you might in fact become inseparable, you might marry and have a host of wonderful children!'

Frank laughed. He leaned back in his chair and laughed, beaming at Eleanor's crude display of mirth. 'I like that, Eleanor,' he said. 'I like that "host of children" business! As if I will ever have another child!' His laughter stopped as suddenly as it had begun, and when he next spoke his voice was gruff, unforgiving in its tone. 'Reminds me of Sarah. How is Sarah, by the way?'

'Our child, Sarah,' said Eleanor, 'is in boarding school.' She was at pains to speak this very clearly. She wanted nothing misunderstood. 'Sarah likes it fine.'

Frank did not say that she ought to. He hoped he didn't need to remind Eleanor what it was costing him.

Eleanor relaxed, reaching over to pat Frank's arm. 'You're a very young man,' she advised him, soothingly. 'You have a lot of time and I see no reason to rush into any permanent arrangement with your young lady friend.' But Frank retained his gloom, thinking it necessary that Eleanor be made to recognize the air of their tainted partnership.

Gómez reappeared. He rattled the doorknob and called to

Madeline and instantly something crashed against the other side of the door. Gómez didn't appear to mind. Again he threaded through the room, remarking to this or that empty chair: 'Mademoiselle would like perhaps the tour? The Mademoiselle is occupied?' He begged a chair's pardon — '*Muy bien — y usted?*' — and sat in one. The simple explanation occurred to Eleanor: it was the tourists and not his own twisted longings that had driven Gómez crazy — the tourists and the *inmigrante norteamericanos* who forced him each day into his cruel white suit.

'The Mesdemoiselles are desiring company, yes? The Mesdemoiselles — how to say it — are lost? *Perdido? Qué pasa*, lovely Mademoiselle?' He went on talking to the empty tables in his usual way. Presently, perhaps, Madeline would come out and sit with him.

Frank was twitching. It seemed unjust, his having to put up with Eleanor's childishness and Gómez as well. Eleanor was batting flies from her face, routinely, as if entranced, and the flies did not appear to object. Frank followed her stare and saw nothing to deserve such scrutiny: a collapsed section of plaza wall and above it the mouth of Calle de la Noche de la mil Lunas. Her look was totally vacant and the enormity contained in such a look never failed to distress him. In this instance, watching her, it seemed to contain by its very absence so much of his life with her, a life that in retrospect seemed hardly to have been his own. He was getting too old for this, had never been comfortable in the presence of a woman he couldn't desire. It amazed him, now that he thought of it, that he could no longer remember what it had been like to sleep with her, quite forgetting that this had been the first memory erased. And Sarah, too. A moment ago he had struggled to recall her name.

Eleanor continued her mindless brushing away of flies. Their own patterns of flight seemed undisturbed. He felt angry with himself — and reasonably so, he decided, for it had been absurd of him to agree to come here and sit with her these mornings to watch this asinine parade of mourners, this senseless passage of the El Flores dead.

He grasped her rebozo and tugged. 'What is it, Eleanor?'

'I was shooing away flies,' she said.

The mouth of the Street of Moons was suddenly filled. A black wedge, a shield, ten or twelve men and women abreast, with heads and shoulders that kept filling that space where others had been — a black curtain of mourners just suddenly there. Mammoth black body now unfolding up the other side of the Plaza Principal.

'I was shooing away flies,' said Eleanor, 'and you know how that is. You see them but you don't.' She was speaking in a hush, although she showed a certain excitement now. The mourners had begun their song; their dirge was halting and uneven, without harmony or even melody, this interrupted now and again with piercing cries of lamentation. 'I was shooing away flies,' said Eleanor, 'without seeing them, and suddenly there they were all coming at me, all the mourners, and for a moment I saw them all as flies, upright but still flies, all silently winging toward me, the men with their patched black suits and the women with their black rebozos and black lace and black veils.'

'And then they turned', sighed Frank, 'and headed for the church.'

'So here it is,' said Eleanor, 'the bleak wedding of all our murdered souls.'

Gómez left his table and came up to take a quiet chair at theirs.

They had been viewing this same spectacle every morning for six days now.

'Look at him,' said Frank. 'The only man in town who before the flood already had a proper suit.' He was speaking of the priest, Father García, who stood alone on the cathedral steps waiting for the dead to come to him. He was wrong, of course. Here even the poorest family had its mourning clothes; they were passed down from generation to generation for there would not be a generation that did not have a need for them.

They could see — behind the glass walls, behind the black wrought-iron frames above the carriage wheels — the new wooden boxes holding the dead.

'Now I understand it,' murmured Eleanor. 'El Flores is where you come when you die. It's where they're sending the people this year.'

Gómez chuckled and kissed her hand. The white tie on his white shirt was the same white and Eleanor noticed now that he even wore a white polish on his nails. 'The Mademoiselle is perhaps upset? The Mademoiselle would perhaps like a pill?'

She retrieved her hand and raised it to shield her eyes.

'Don't let me see it,' she said, 'whatever it is.'

'See what?' Frank asked.

'Whatever it is.'

She could see across the plaza one of Father García's attendants dusting and arranging the Father's full black gown.

Gómez rose and returned to his former chair. Madeline appeared now out of the small office and stood by the door, though she wasn't looking at any of them, nor at the procession either. She stood with her legs apart, pressing a hand against her stomach, sweat beading her brow, a look of panic in her eyes.

Eleanor saw her but did not think to interfere. 'They let them into El Flores,' she was telling Frank, 'but they allow no one to leave for fear they'll spread what is so catching here. The señor and you and me and Maya with his art of the see-through dead and probably your cool Indian as well. What is it, Frank, that the spit-and-polish paratroopers say? The buck stops here.'

Past the coffin mounts, over the kneeling figures at the head of the procession now halted in front of the cathedral, she had a clear view of Father García high on the steps, his jewelled staff raised in benediction, his other grasping the shining silver cross and sweeping to embrace all who might be so contained — intoning over these dead and the vast previous dead whose spirits had now passed into heaven — and all the time heedless, it would seem, of the sobbing men and women at his feet with tumefied and unctuous kisses for his perfectly arranged gown.

She saw above and to her left, walking the high flat roof of the Banco Nacional, a thin Mexican in a tight business suit, field glasses over his nose and trained on the field of mourners below. His sight was settling on this one, on that one, and passing on to another, and not until she saw the glitter of the lens in the sun did she again address Frank.

'I'm Pisces,' she said. 'A Pisces, as you may know, is insecure and unreliable. A Pisces is as apt to go to pieces in public as she is to fall asleep while a lover is kissing her hand.' Her voice was high and perilous but secured by nothing she could account for. 'That's what they tell me about what a Pisces is when they share my birth date and hour. The chart doesn't lie but the birthday can. Do you believe that, Frank? Am I unreliable and insecure? Actually, I'm quite the opposite. I'm so secure in my breakdown that it frightens me. I'm like the ice skater must feel when he's at the bottom of the pond.'

She looked over at the roof of the Banco Nacional and observed that the field glasses were still fixed on her table.

'Do you know that statue of Morelos in Janitzio in the middle of the lake? It's so high a person can't climb it. Do you remember Nüno de Guzman, the avaricious conquistador? They say he liked to roast people alive, especially local Tarascan chiefs who refused his commands. There are murals painted inside the statue of Morelos and in panel after panel the artist is roasting Nüno de Guzman, avaricious conquistador. Does it do any good? Is his roasting too late? Anyway, I once climbed up Morelos, for that was always a thing I vowed one day I'd do. Not climb Morelos — whose statue I didn't know about — but stand up straight inside the skull of a man who had been emptied of everything he might ever have had — for that's what statues are. Standing up in Morelos was the next best thing to standing up inside you. But do you know? I got dizzy, I couldn't even take my hands from my eyes to look at the view. Don't let me see it, I said, whatever it is! The Morelos ticket taker was waiting at the foot of the stairs when I came down. I asked him if anyone ever fell. 'Fall?' he said. 'That isn't necessary, as no one climbs.' Do you suppose I dreamed it, Frank? Have I still never found myself in a position to look out through the eyes of a man? Not through Morelos' and never through yours because I've never been cool Indian enough. Actually I'm not Pisces, but if I am, I'm a Pisces who isn't sure.

Not Pisces and I'm not twenty-eight or thirty years old, I'm more in the vicinity of 405. Look at me, Frank. Have I aged? I'm 800 now and, like Methuselah, I've outlived all my wives. Now I'm 5,010. In another second I'll be 28,000 and if I don't slow down soon I'll be older than all the dead out there. That's what it means being a Pisces. You can never catch up with yourself because you're always in a race with something else that doesn't slow down. Maybe I'm trying to catch up with the cool Indian I once thought I was and which I continued to believe I was until the morning last winter when I woke up and discovered that the body I had been sleeping beside didn't exist, that the person I was bedding with all those years was totally imagined. Where were you? — all those years?'

Frank did not trust himself to reply. He felt uneasy and sullen and even sinned against. It was unkind and unfair and against the rules for Eleanor to unburden herself of all this. He had agreed to come here and sit with her and review this ridiculous passing of the dead but he had not come here to listen to Eleanor's fanciful insults and obscure accusations. Yes, yes, it was perhaps true and she had cause. No doubt she did feel her youth was behind her, that it had somehow been violated, but how could she blame him for that? Doubtless her dissatisfactions were real, they might even be urgent, he didn't question that she sometimes suffered, but she had no right to blame him for her own failures.

Yet he could remember now certain strange mornings when he awoke in bed beside her, the two of them silent and staring at the ceiling, at the walls, the sun streaming through their window and each of them listening for the low groan of life that was elsewhere — that was always elsewhere, *anywhere*, never there in that room in that bed they shared. They had never liked each other or respected or trusted each other — perhaps that much was true — but they were married and he knew — he would insist on this — that he had given his best.

The man on the roof of the Banco Nacional was no longer in sight. The first glass coffin was moving on ahead, another was moving into place. The dirge the mourners sang rose in volume; after the priest's flash of jewels it would die down again. Their march was less orderly now, an inelegant straggling face — without the cohesion of purpose now that the first dead had been blessed, now that the ritual had prepared his body for its escape from earth — now that only the cemetery lay ahead.

The priest raised his arms over the second entrapped soul and several women rushed up to kiss his gown.

The procession passed slowly in front of the Bodega. Eleanor could see the women eyeing their table through their veils. The march would circle the plaza and wind up Calle de San Francisco and eventually empty into the *cementerio* high above the village where the lake could not get to it. Then some of them would reassemble at the *funeraría* on Calle de la Noche de la mil Lunas and others would join them and the death procession would begin all over again.

Frank stamped out his cigarette on the red tile floor.

Gómez quit his table and went into the Bodega kitchen, reappearing a few minutes later with a cup of hot coffee which he took in to Madeline.

Eleanor could hear Madeline's harsh voice lifting in resentful commentary even as she watched the mourners filing by. The dead, in their coffins behind the polished windows, had surely never known such comfort when alive. They rode over life now, a due and proper reward. A dog ran in a bewildered way along the outer column of marchers and someone kicked him spinning over the stones. The dog crawled on his stomach, debated a moment, and trotted awkwardly back to sniff once more the mourners' heels. Those at the procession's rear were being urged along by one of the health inspectors but it was the priest, of course, who determined the pace and he seemed to be in no hurry. The business of God could not be rushed by the inspector from Morelia with his talk of plague and pestilence, for the inspector from Morelia was a stranger here and unused to the pace of life in El Flores. Let him post his notices and place his guards around the baneful waters of the lake and around those pernicious fountains in the village but there the responsibility of the inspector ended.

How many now? It was bad luck to count the dead and Eleanor

believed in bad luck, but in six days now she had counted enough to keep her bad luck running for some time to come; no, it would not do to change her luck now.

The roof of the Banco Nacional was still empty. Only the mossy configuration of madonnas carved in relief against the stone was looking at her.

Madeline was crying aloud inside Gómez's office. She was pleading with the Mexican but what she wanted exactly Eleanor couldn't say.

The worst was over. Everyone was saying the worst was over; indeed, they had been saying it from the start. Soon the heavy tourist buses of Tres Estrellas de Oro would roar around the plaza corner, the *mercado* peddlers would appear, the Posado de Don Vasco would fill, La Chica would open its doors and the Alameda whose *pescado blanco* was quite acceptable. The coffin mounts would be returned to Morelia and eventually, all in good time — *mañana, por cierto mañana!* — the workmen or the rain would clear the rubble and scent of death in El Flores.

'For heaven's sake,' complained Frank, 'why does she continue to put up with that man?'

Eleanor felt no compassion for Madeline with her desperate tears. They were urgent, but ask her and she would not know herself why she was crying and Eleanor could not tell her. Gómez could not tell her either and Frank could only ask her to shut up.

'Oh, look!' exclaimed Frank, 'here comes Nora Meyer Jones!' He rose quickly, waving to the girl striding gracefully toward them down the Street of Moons.

'Sit down, Frank,' Eleanor instructed him. He stared at her out of curiosity, but then did sit down. Eleanor meant nothing by this. She simply preferred that Nora Meyer Jones be left free to find her own way to them — to them or to someone else or some other place. It was this, the accidental design, that gave pattern to a life.

The mourners hid her away. Eleanor grasped Frank's arm, as much as to say, *Frank, I want your attention now*. She had a glimpse of binoculars above the *banco* wall: Maya, painter of the dead, getting down to serious work.

'Frank,' she said, 'the time from exposure to illness to death is all within a period of thirty-six hours. The illness results from one or a combination of any of the three known means of exposure. First, you may be exposed through the food you eat. Second, through the water you drink and, third, through contact with anyone who has been exposed to the previous two.'

'Oh, Christ,' moaned Frank, 'Eleanor, can't you sit still?'

'This is the way it works. You feel a little worse each day, you run a fever, the fever rises, you suffer alternating or at times concurrent chills. You sweat horribly. You get headaches, you get diarrhea. Finally, all the vast and perpetual body pains accumulate and force you into a kind of drowsy stupor and your senses gradually wear thin. You waste away, you're able to watch your own death taking place and finally when it happens you're ready to welcome it, you go peacefully as the clouds on a sweet summer day because there's nothing to stop you any more. It's the way I felt last winter when I woke beside you and you said you were leaving me. Frank, how do you feel?'

'I feel fine,' replied Frank, 'though I thank you for all the information.'

'Thank heavens you did. Since then, day by day, I've felt the scales lifting from my eyes.'

The bells in the three steeples at the head of the plaza struck and Frank listened to the tolls, wondering whether the bell ringer would this time confuse his count. He looked over the heads of the mourners for sight of Nora Meyer Jones but she was evidently hidden away somewhere within their maze.

'The Saint is loco, the Saint is terrible. Death here is all leisure, Frank. You can walk up San Antonio at your leisure or make love to Nora Meyer Jones if that's your pleasure. But no matter how extended it is it finally has to empty into something else, if only into more leisure. This breakfast has been at our leisure, a slow leisure on its way to becoming our own version of the El Flores death.'

Frank lit another cigarette and stood, smiling down on her. 'Speak for yourself, Eleanor.' The bells on San Antonio pealed, replying quickly this time to those in the plaza. The last coffin was being blessed. Very soon now the plaza would be empty and they would see the mourners gathered at the *cementerio*. Already the diggers were up there waiting, trapped in their own penthouse ritual above the *posada's* roof.

Meanwhile, on the roof of the Banco Nacional, the painter Maya was now in clear view. He had erected his easel, he had his sketch pad and pencils, his oils, his binoculars too.

Nora Meyer Jones stood by the fountain at the plaza's centre, pointing to him. 'Look! The ghoul! The ghoul!'

Abruptly she wheeled and charged across the street toward them, weaving through the mourners — entering the Bodega in a splash of enthusiasm. 'God!' she cried — 'God, I hate walking alone, it's like waking up on an island by yourself!' She advanced on Eleanor, holding out her hand. 'Are you *it*? Are you the wife? I thought he was lying! Hello, my name is Nora Meyer Jones. You can call me one but don't call me all!' She took Eleanor's hand and shook it hard. She had bright, beautiful eyes and could not get all her smile into them. She straddled the chair, quickly rose again. 'Who's crying? Is someone crying? What's going on here?' She strode across the floor, yanked open the office door. 'Hi!' she said, 'what's the trouble here?' Madeline raised a startled head; Gómez turned slowly in his chair. 'Are you the waiter?' she said to him. 'Can I get some food around here? I'm starved! Plumb famished through to bone.'

She didn't wait for an answer. She came quickly back to their table and draped her arms around Frank. 'You don't mind?' she asked Eleanor. 'Good! I've always been nuts for older men!'

Frank blinked good will at Eleanor. Eleanor blinked it back at him. The dirge ended in the plaza. The mourners advanced on up the hill. Up on the bank's roof, with extended arm, thumb uplifted, Maya was sighting down on their table. Eleanor sat erect, her expression beatific, hands laced across her bosom as if she held there the scarlet rose which only Maya, she herself, and Death's Angel could see and enjoy.

3. *For Love of Gómez*

THE BELLS in the three steeples in the plaza cathedral were first to announce midday and a minute or so later the rather timid bells from the poor church of San Antonio on the hillside pealed their thin acknowledgement; very soon afterward, as had become their custom, Señor Gómez and his American companion Madeline appeared noisily out of the side wooden door so long weighted by its many black iron bolts and wide encrusted bars — to which Gómez had recently added the black metal crucifix which Madeline, among others, found so obscene — and made their way in unforgiving silence over the beautiful grass to the three lawn chairs which Don José and Manuel had today at the señor's instructions situated in a shadeless area some little distance up from the pool.

Madeline was brooding, which was not unusual, moving along sluggishly and with an intentionally unpleasant whine, her head down, now and again summoning sufficient energy to enable her to cast a malevolent glance over the spacious grounds, past the two Mexicans working in shoddy disgrace at the pool, and over the elegant Gómez who now was hastening on in front of her, either to evade for a moment the girl's harsh noises or to arrange the glass lawn table between their chairs with the precise symmetry he required for these occasions.

Approaching distantly behind them was the señor's loyal doña, Señora Pesuna — carrying their noon provisions close to her stomach and with the fixed attention of both hands, in the first place because she much admired the artistry of the silver tray on which their refreshment rode, and in the second place because she could well remember spilling, some three weeks ago, a full pitcher of sangria over the demented girl's dress. True, it had not been her fault, as the señor had elaborately insisted, but it had since been the doña's intention to avoid the skinny and implacable *gringita* whenever possible.

The doña arrived at the chairs in time to hear the American

girl's shrill voice complaining about something, about the sun perhaps, for she was flinging emaciated arms up to the sky, much as if God Himself had somehow offended her in the creation of this beautiful day. The doña emptied her tray promptly, responding with a grunt to the señor's kind expressions of gratitude — wanting to hurry back to the safety of the señor's grand casa, for she had a fear of what she might see today in the crooked eyes of the señor's moody guest. She was herself without luck, burdened by the unfortunate hoof of the bull — each of her three husbands had died — but the impossible señorita was truly damned, *maldita*, for she had at once the eyes of the cow still nursing and those of the angry bull in a rage to kill.

As it happened, however, Madeline immediately calmed down, turning to them a pointedly bemused expression that seemed to be saying, 'You see, I do have control, nothing you may do to me today shall affect me!' — thus accepting with uncharacteristic grace the gay multicoloured chair which the señor, by the sweeping of his hand, indicated might serve her needs this afternoon. She unfolded the chair to its full length and reclined in it without additional ceremony, accepting too the tall beautiful drink in the embossed silver glass which Gómez now had poured for her. 'Thank you,' she said civilly, in a voice even approaching happiness, and the señor responded with '*De nada*,' it is nothing, his voice low, only the faintest amusement showing in his eyes.

The girl stretched out languidly under the sun, and the señor also leaned back, clearly relaxing, pulling his wide-brimmed hat down low over his brow until the sun was obscured. She was in her bathing suit as was customary at this hour, and Gómez wore his usual white ensemble: the perfectly tailored white suit, his high brushed-suede boots and the magnificent sombrero. She tasted and had no immediate complaint against the sangria which the señor today had especially prepared for her; for himself his doña had brought a bottle of Santo Thomas wine, the San Emilion label — and he too tasted his drink and declared it palatable, though somewhat to his surprise, for this native wine had never been a favourite.

'The Mademoiselle,' he inquired, 'is she comfortable?'

'I'm just peachy,' the girl replied; and while this expression was familiar and offensive to the trained ear of Señor Gómez, it was delivered without the girl's usual insistence of acrimonious wit, and so the señor was content for the moment to smile agreeably and pat her warm knee.

The sun droned overhead and for half an hour neither had much more to say. Manuel and the elderly Don José looked up from time to time from their work at the pool to reassure themselves of this fact and to renew their individual wagers as to how long this unexpected situation might continue — while Señora Pesuna paused occasionally at the window in the kitchen where their *comida* was being prepared, there to issue another of her muttered and tainted prayers to the Virgin. The doña's prayer, however, concerned neither the wickedness of Señor Gómez nor that of his mistress, but was meant solely for the relief of her third husband whose life the recent pestilence of the lake had claimed.

The sun thickened; it expanded and seemed to hang ever nearer; it poured down in waves, hugged the señor's beautiful garden, came weighted and as if spooned into the air in ripples; more and more Madeline began to shift and groan in her chair. Her sight turned longingly toward the pool, and she raked spiteful glances at the señor sitting so composedly, so blissfully, close by.

'The Mademoiselle,' the señor said, smiling lazily, '— she finds the sun too hot? It is — how to say it? — *la sartén*, the frying pan?'

Despite her intentions, Madeline could not resist this clear invitation to tell Gómez what he could do with himself. 'You', she muttered bitterly, pausing to wipe damp hair from her face, 'can go to hell!' The señor smiled and nodded his head idiotically, as if he were one in a pair singing harmony. 'Damn you and your stupid swimming pool,' declared Madeline. 'You do it this way only to spite me. You can't stand the idea that I might ever enjoy myself.'

The señor laughed, which further irritated her, though she fully understood this to be his intention. 'But I don't care,' she concluded, her voice lifting to the high nasal pitch that the señor and all who were acquainted with her so much deplored — 'Nothing you do can bother me!' Sighing now, satisfied that her integrity remained intact, Madeline rolled her back to the sun, drawing up a slow arm across her enervated and sweating face so that her eyes might be shielded.

The señor casually lit up his filtered Delicado, and let his gaze float blithely about.

'Once more,' he said softly, 'I will explain to the Mademoiselle, for I know she has not been herself lately and finds our customs unfamiliar. Today we must drain the pool —'

'With buckets!' interrupted Madeline, who could not help herself.

'Then the pool must dry. Afterward, we must whitewash the pool and then again it must dry. With these necessities successfully concluded, Don José will attach the garden hose and the swimming pool will begin to fill.'

'It's outrageous!' shrieked the girl.

The señor said no more until her contortions had subsided. Then he lifted his left hand and slowly counted off the days on his fingers: 'Once more I will explain. Three days to empty this pool. One to dry. Another to whitewash the floor and walls. Perhaps two for this whitewash to dry. Three additional days for the hose to fill.'

'Yeah!' said the girl. 'With your little half-inch hose. I could spit and fill it up quicker.'

'At that point,' continued the señor, 'the Mademoiselle may have her swim.'

'Screw it,' whispered Madeline.

'So,' said the señor. 'Ten days, less or more. Who is to say? But ten, I should think. Though we cannot be certain. My men have many other jobs to perform. They may tire of this business with the swimming pool. They do not understand the Mademoiselle's urgency, you see.' He shrugged, extending his arms to full length. '*Por que no?*' Why not?

He blew cigarette smoke toward the girl, and laughed contentedly. He liked to think that he differed from his countrymen in that he measured time by the future rather than the past; it was this trait, he believed, that had enabled him to tolerate this vain and belligerent and altogether ludicrous girl for so long.

Madeline had turned away. She was not, in fact, listening. She had already thought this matter through, and was in no mood for his mocking explanations: she wanted to swim; she could not; someone, therefore, was to blame. She stared across the lawn at the tasteless crucifix mounted on his door, and kicked irritably at the flies, at the very air. Soon. A few more hours. Then she would be going home. Purging all reminders of her humiliation here: this miserable Mexico with its ignorant cacophony of misery and guile and neglect — of this drab wrecked village with its endless and blissful acceptance of everything from natural physical disasters — wind, fire, flood and plague — to the meanest and most crucial of personal deprivations. A stagnant, blistering place that lacked even the saving grace of what one might term a higher tragedy because it was throughout base and impotent — and surviving only because tourists such as herself came and spent their money here.

'*Qué pasa?*' the señor asked. What is the matter? He rubbed his hands together, winking. '*Fuma usted?*' Perhaps the enchanted Mademoiselle would like the cigarette?

Madeline, regarding him coldly, did not reply. She thought: Smoke, by all means. Never mind my feelings, what could my feelings or wishes possibly matter? His long fingers, extended, secured the cigarette elegantly, his teeth closed on the oval shape, and her own cheeks sucked in as he pulled in the smoke. Loathsome! she thought. God, I hate this man!

She hurled herself flat against the chair's webbing, again yanked the clinging hair from her face ... and found herself staring in sudden fury at the thick shaded grass beneath the vacant third chair. Nowhere else in El Flores was there a lawn so luxuriously verdant and thriving. Throughout the village the earth was parched and decaying, all dry stubble, putrid debris all over. She was convinced that Gómez went to such extremes in the care of his garden not out of any pride or love of grass but simply to deny her the one pleasure available to her here. The pool! she thought. His goddamn pool! He is happy only when I suffer!

A whine escaped her briefly and she thrashed against her chair's scratchy webbing. Sticky! Everything so God-awful primitive and depressing! She rolled on her back, lifted herself, and stared with consuming hatred at the two men working at the pool. Look at them! she thought. Those disgusting idiots! Those fools. Bailing out that huge pool with their two yellow leaky buckets! God, they're insane! It will take weeks!

One of them, young Manuel, down on his knees at the pool's edge, saw her looking and grinned his toothless grin, jabbing a dark finger at his dripping bucket.

She took up her glass from the table and drank to its bottom. Gómez was watching her, but she didn't care. She would endure him these last hours. She would not let him upset her. Today, she thought, I'm in the driver's seat. She would tell him, before it was over, what a monkey she thought him to be. She lay back down, groaning. She would have to pack soon. Too bad she had put it off. But she couldn't have anyway, or Gómez would have noticed. Let him remain ignorant, she thought. When I go it will blow him out of the park. She wondered about the doña. Had that lazy bitch washed her clothes? Were they ironed? Gómez, she thought, lets that woman get away with too much. She steals. I'll tell on her before I go. Last week she returned my new shirt with all the buttons gone. Every one.

But they all steal, she thought. She would tell them all off before she left: Gómez and his doña and that trash down at the pool. She hated them all. Ignorant, filthy, shiftless — she rolled over and reached for her glass — *foreigners*, she had almost said. But she was the foreigner. She was in their grimy country and at their mercy. Dependent on their sickening, toadish hospitality. Had to put up with their imbecilic grins and that stupid green shit in her eggs. Had been forced to put up with *him!*

She stared at the señor, squinting; her mouth screwed into a grimace, and she found herself speaking:

'Tell that fat cow of yours to bring me more sangria!'

The señor said nothing. He did not even look her way.

In a little while she lay back down, stunned and depleted by the heat, in agony from the unrelenting monotony of this dull hour. 'Now,' she said, her voice slurring. 'This very minute! I'm thirsty! It must be 100 degrees out here.'

'*Desde luego*,' she heard him reply cheerfully — of course — and knew that he would be beckoning to the two idiots labouring so ridiculously at the pool, one of whom would presently appear and be sent to the casa where he would tell the slovenly doña that the señor desired another pitcher for his señorita.

Again her sight took in the vacant chair and it occurred to her to wonder if Gómez was expecting anyone. Well, no matter. She would have a use for it if he didn't.

She closed her eyes, and waited. The sun was insufferable, they were all pigs, this country was an unholy terror, but she could abide it — or so her thoughts went — this last day.

SO HERE THEY ARE. Since noon they have been reclining in gay lawn chairs out under the sun in the señor's large beautiful garden, Madeline in her bathing suit, the señor in his impeccable white suit, boots and sombrero. The doña arrives to replenish the sangria and the señor informs her pleasantly that they will be having their *comida* here at these chairs under the sun. Señora Pesuna recognizes this as madness but reflects on it not at all; it is not her duty to suggest alternatives to the señor. Old Don José and Manuel quit their labour at the pool and disappear briefly into deep shade to drink Coca-Cola and chew on crusty *bollillos* in advance of lunch, for though they are hungry it would be impolite of them to dine fully before the señor has been served his. The señor, as if transfixed, stares at the pool and over these lovely grounds which the recent flood has fortunately spared. His view embraces his fine stand of trees — pecan and orange and avocado — which his grandfather had planted and through which is visible now the shore end of Calle de la Noche de la mil Lunas and the placid blue of the lake. Occasionally he will remove his sombrero and fan his dark handsome face which has dampened not at all in this high sun. He smiles, and also waits. Madeline dozes. The señor will periodically turn and regard her perspiring face almost with tenderness. He bends forward sometimes and brushes flies from her legs that glisten under heavy applications of coconut oil. The air here is thick with its smell. Don José and Manuel resume their duties at the pool. The señor sips at the Santo Thomas wine. In one hour its volume has dropped scarcely a thimbleful.

They have been together eight weeks now.

The señor smokes and the smoke wraps overhead in the windless air; all of El Flores, all of Mexico, seems to have connived with them in the making of this sultry hour. From where he sits the pool shows a surface of green scum. The speed with which the algae overtake this body of water never fails to amuse and intrigue Señor Gómez. For weeks — for two or three — it will stand — clear, lovely, unspoiled — but within a few hours after the first patch forms, the pool's entire surface will surrender to this slime. No, this speed the señor does not understand. But although he cannot accustom himself to it, he is on the whole not displeased. Such is the way of nature and he will deal with it in his customary way: he will empty the pool, feed the scum back into the earth, and his garden will prosper. His companion may shake her pathetic fists and screech, she may further degrade herself with these innumerable insults and accusations — but such behaviour too presents no special problem. This also is the way of nature. These stubborn Mesdemoiselles must be dealt with as his pool is. They must first be emptied — humiliated — and then they may be filled.

MADELINE WAS STIRRING. Again he filled her glass, placing it at the table's edge where she might reach it without struggling. He consulted his watch, nodded, and contemplated the empty chair. His pleasure in arranging this chair for the use of the Mademoiselle's father was considerable. It would remain vacant — at any rate it would never be occupied by the señor from across the border — and Gómez regretted this somewhat for he admitted to a mild curiosity about the sort of parent who could sire someone of Madeline's selfish, venal, and deluded nature. He had not enjoyed these eight weeks, but his time with the truculent Mademoiselle had fortified him in his views. His actions with regard to her and her predecessors were perhaps questionable on some abstract level, but he was now more than ever confident that his methods were both necessary and deserved.

Madeline waked, grumbling, and reached for her drink.

In Mexico, it seemed to the señor, the *norteamericanos* were constantly so reaching.

She brought the glass down, took several deep breaths, then swallowed the remainder in her glass.

The señor promptly refilled the tall container, and watched the girl rub her eyes in petulant drowsiness. With her knuckles, like a child. He smiled compassionately. She was of course unappreciative of his foresight in lacing this mixture with a quantity of Oso Negro Ginebra sufficient to propel her ahead of time into her afternoon siesta. No. The unruly Mademoiselle would not know that she had been drunk since ten minutes after spreading herself so possessively into his chair.

'Where's your lackey?' she now demanded.

He raised a curious brow, finding the word unfamiliar.

'Your donkey,' she said. 'Your slovenly doña. Where's our lunch, or whatever you call it?' The señor blinked consolingly, and she blinked back. 'What time is it?' she asked, screwing up her eyes at the sun. 'God, I'm about dead. I don't see how you can *breathe* in all those clothes.'

Gómez turned to her the patronizing smile she found so exasperating. He did not trouble himself to inform her that in his view there was very little the infirmed and irrational and atrociously impaired Mademoiselle from the USA did understand. Once more he noted that whenever the girl became sullen her eyes crossed ever so slightly. He found himself pondering whether this was a trait shared by most *norteamericana* women.

'This is not as sweet as the first pitcher,' the girl complained, indicating the sangria. 'I don't like it.'

The señor refrained from observing aloud that she had been consuming the liquid with what appeared considerable thirst.

She fell exhausted back into the chair.

Her bikini top — a Casa Rosa creation from the señor's own

shop — had stretched, leaving one breast now fully exposed. Gómez shifted in his chair to avoid this unnecessary distraction. She scratched irritably at one uplifted knee, and wiped the oil from her fingers by stabbing her hand repeatedly into the grass. She winked at his sour face. Buster, she thought, you think I have a contemptuous nature, but you haven't seen the half of it yet. Just wait till my Dad gets here.

The thought delighted her and for a moment she was mindless even of the heat. Her father was coming; he was coming this afternoon. He would fly down, was in the air this very minute; he would take her out of this pigsty called Mexico. Perhaps then this nasty man in his vile white suit would not be so cruel and smug and indifferent to her needs.

A finger poked into her rump. She turned her head to find him grinning at her. 'Ah! The Mademoiselle has secrets, no? The Mademoiselle has the little bird?'

She frowned, moving away from his touch. What was he getting at? Did he suspect? I'm telling you nothing, she decided. Nothing! — and gained a moment's pleasure from this practice — as she thought of it — of uncharacteristic guile.

'You can't keep me here, you know,' she said, taunting. 'I can leave anytime I like. I'm not your cringing little nubile white slave.'

The señor pulled the white sombrero down over his brow. He slid deeper into the chair and placed one boot heel-to-toe over the other. They were beautifully made boots and he treasured them greatly.

'You'll see,' said Madeline, enjoying herself. 'I'll walk out on you and you won't be so preachy and superior then!'

Gómez had no interest in this. He found the girl's declarations trite and pathetic. He rose, and flicked a spot of ash from his suitcoat — stared off into the trees for a moment, and then sat back down, sighing, lifting his face to meet the sun. He was enamoured of this house, of these grounds, and was capable — such times as this — of believing the sun existed solely for him.

'I might!' Madeline said. 'I might not even be here tomorrow!'

With this remark her voice lost much of its control. It carried, high and brittle, to the two Mexicans working at the pool. They held their buckets by their sides and their attention lingered on her as if they believed that by sight alone they could explain the baffling presence of this naked *gringita* with the skinny legs and *la grande boca*, the big mouth, and the crazy love for the unpleasant swimming pool.

The señor spoke with his eyes closed, his hands laced over his chest. 'The Mademoiselle has acquired confidence. I congratulate the Mademoiselle. Perhaps the Mademoiselle has received news?'

Madeline had been swatting flies. She turned quickly and gave his face a confused search. 'What do you mean, news? What are you talking about?'

He waved a slender hand, disarmingly. His expression was untroubled and adoringly innocent. He tipped himself forward, helpfully, and whispered: 'The Mademoiselle has perhaps engaged the services of the *teléfono*? The financial affairs of the Mademoiselle are perhaps soon to be in order?' He relaxed back into his chair, radiant. '*Qué bonito!*' How nice.

Madeline felt herself swept along by a tide of familiar resentment. She retreated into thoughtful silence. She had no way of knowing that the señor had arrangements with the señorita at the telephone office whose services Madeline had yesterday engaged; that he was in daily communication with agreeable unshaven Filipe at the telegraph office where she had for so long been expecting money; nor that the untidy employees at La Casa de Correos routinely reported — and often sent on ahead for his perusal — to him on the contents of *apartamiento* 29, her private and secret letter box.

The sky remained absolutely clear, and the sun seemed larger and nearer, like a giant living thing lured by the need for human company. On the street outside the señor's walls an *helados* vendor could be heard rattling his cart over the stones, crying with a cadence.

Madeline dipped her fingers into the pitcher, searching for ice, but the ice had melted, so she smeared cold liquid over her brow and throat. 'Americans,' she exclaimed suddenly, 'should not be allowed into this stupid country!' She felt a renewed surge of contempt — of utter hatred for everything that moved before her eyes — and settled back again against the chair's webbing, calmed and enriched by the insights this attitude afforded her.

The assertion brought no change to the señor's features. Just now his interest was in the two workers down by the pool. Such foolish men — worthless! — yet they gave him much pleasure. He admitted to a certain pride in them. They were slow, they were witless — they in fact had not a single brain in their heads — but it pleased the señor to consider that he would not exchange one of them for ten ... for a hundred ... vapid *inmigrantes* such as Madeline. They, after all, could work. But the Mademoiselle! What a waste! One longed to turn the skin on all of them, to shout *Márchese! Salga! Vaya!* — Leave! Go home! — and drive them across the border as the *leñadores* drive their burros past the watering-hole. *Por qué no?* Because they always came, alone and in pairs, by full car, boat, plane and train, with their full pocketbooks and forever crying Thief! Thief! I have been robbed! or crying out wherever one saw them, *Ne entiendo! No entiendo!* Speak the *inglés*! ... or, like Madeline, abandoned though yet unweaned, stunted and purposeless and most often in tears, they came to his door begging, crying I am hungry, I am cold, I have no place to stay, no money, oh, señor what will I do? and always with the same explanation. It is not my fault señor *no es culpa mía*, the fault is with your bank which will not honour my cheque, it is the fault of your post office which has lost my mail, with your water which is not pure and your food which has made me sick oh, señor *Socorro Socorro!* help me señor and I will do anything ... but rarely remembering to say *gracias* and injured if they should be compelled to say *please* — for all that belonged to anyone else in this country was theirs anyway and in any case their money would soon arrive and they would be independent, they would be themselves once more, they would need no one's help.

The situation was desperate, Señor Gómez reflected — whenever was it not?

He sipped at his wine, smiling at Madeline in sombre fascination, and in fact feeling something akin to a fondness for the deep worry lines in her brow and the narrow slitted eyes that could not see exactly straight ... glancing away from her now and then to nod his head in acceptance of the attention of Don José and Manuel who stood with imbecilic grins in the scum-coated water at the shallow end of the pool, lifting their twin buckets and jabbing deliriously at the dripping sides so that he might better understand and appreciate the zealous intent with which they were applying themselves to reducing the level of water in the pool, so that all might be happy once more.

'Dopes!' fumed Madeline. 'Idiots! At home we'd shoot people like that.'

'Ah,' said Gómez, 'but if I shoot them we should have to do the work ourselves.' His melodic voice chided her.

'God!' she cried, her teeth clenched. She sighted Manuel's glum pudgy wife, nineteen and looking forty, seated under one of the pecan trees, nursing her youngest child while her two small sons sat obediently beside her, staring across at them. 'She's filthy,' Madeline said, pointing to her. 'Make her go away.'

'On the contrary,' said the señor, 'I myself know she bathes once a week. Quite on the other hand the dirt is good for them. How otherwise will they build up an immunity against the germs?'

Madeline groaned in disgust. She was sick of talking to him. She was tired of this kind of nonsense and even feeling a nostalgic longing for her parents' house in Los Angeles and for the one or two intelligent friends she had run about with there. She sat up with a new fervour, turning and planting her feet in the grass, directly facing him.

'I want a cigarette,' she said.

His chin showed a blue crescent of beard cut smoothly down to skin. His long black lashes curled. They were, in her view, disgusting on a man. For a time she had even believed them artificial. She clenched her fist, waiting, determined this time to have a cigarette, and at the same time thinking *soon, soon, in a few hours my father will be here*. But she didn't want to think now of her father who didn't trust her enough to merely send the money. No, he had to come down here himself and preach to her, tell her what an aggravation she was to him — and finally drag her home the way one would a child. As if she would stay in this stupid country one minute longer than necessary.

'But I sent you money before,' he had told her yesterday on the phone. 'What did you do with it?'

'That was Raymond,' she had said. 'Raymond spent it.'

'Someone always does. You always have one excuse or another.'

'He was no good, a pig, how was I supposed to know?'

'You never know,' her father had said. 'It's always punks that attract you.'

She stared at the closed eyes of Señor Gómez — at his nose, at his thin lips now purple in the sun — and recoiled at the faint stirrings of desire. It's disgusting, she thought — furious not at herself but at this reminder of all the men whose mouths had ever touched her. Of Raymond, for instance, with his petty moods and cheap tricks and lousy Spanish and the sneering belief that he was invincible. *You never know*, her father had said. Well, that was a lie. She knew all too soon: scum, pigs, each of them, not one worth wiping her shoes on.

She looked across the lawn at the two men bailing water from the pool. Impossibly ignorant, but at least they didn't have to suffer as she was suffering now. At least they could stand in that putrid water and stay cool. She felt unbearably hot and sweaty, and reached for the sangria. The ice had thinned the bitterness, it tasted delicious now. Sangria was a wonderful drink. You could sip it all afternoon and through the evening and when you finally went to bed, sleep — or whatever — was what you were ready for. And if you wakened the next day drowsy and stunned, what did it matter — because this was Mexico and Mexico was ...

She felt dizzy, and put the pitcher down, wondering whether she was getting drunk. Surely a little wine couldn't ... but no, it is the heat, she assured herself. Only the heat. In a civilized place there would be air conditioners but in El Flores even the street lights flickered and dimmed at night or the power went off altogether.

She swayed forward, touching her fingers to Gómez's cheek.

Her fingers slid over his eyelids, his nose, touched lightly on his mouth. His expression did not change. You pig, she thought — but for the moment there was no vehemence in her mood. He was worse than Raymond, worse than her father — he was despicable and evil to the core — but his eccentricities were at least amusing. And he had money. His wardrobe was filled with white linen suits. The white boots he drooled over. His famous tinsel-sheeted front door. His stupid Café Bodega where no one could eat without dying halfway through the meal. His beautiful garden with the crazy swimming pool that wasn't for swimming ... Malignant bastard.

She lifted his hand and touched his fingers to her lips. 'Gómez,' she begged softly. 'May I have a cigarette?'

His eyes opened and he shook his head.

'Please ...' She reached for the package; he smacked her hand away. Her flesh stung, and tears came to her eyes. 'But you promised me!' she said, her voice rising. 'Yesterday you promised me I could smoke today!'

'What the señor gives he may take away,' he said smoothly.

'I want a cigarette!' she cried, and wrenched at the pack — but again Gómez stung her hand. 'The Mademoiselle is overanxious,' he murmured. 'The Mademoiselle forgets herself.'

She began shouting. 'Let me have them! They are mine! You promised!' She caught his wrist and tried to tear them from his palm. Her body twisted and she tried to reach him with her teeth. 'Give them to me! They're mine!'

'*Lo siento*, Mademoiselle,' he whispered. Without warning his flat hand struck her across her face. '*Lo siento.*' He smacked her again. '*Lo siento.*' Again. I am sorry. I am sorry. *Perdone*, Mademoiselle. He kept on slapping her. She continued to kick and wriggle about, her neck snapping each time he struck. Finally she stopped struggling. She did not attempt to dodge his blows. Her head was erect, she was smiling, inviting him to go on hitting her for as long as he wished.

Down at the pool the two workmen — and Manuel's wife and children under the tree — watched with tolerant unconcern, their faces masks of indifference, as though they were awaiting the coming of rain or flashes of lightning in a closing sky. *Por qué no?* Why not? Or so they thought. If these had come once they would come again later. If not soon, then soon after. If not then, then never. If never, then *tanto mejor*. So much the better.

'Ah,' sighed Don José. '*El fumadores*.' Is it the cigarettes?

'*Sí-sí*,' replied Manuel, '*El vino*.'

'*Le grande amorio*,' murmured Don José, nodding.

To want the smoke, to have the wine, to be in love. *Bueno, bueno.* Nothing here ever changes. The coyote still runs through the señor's garden.

They laughed softly together and spoke with a sorrowful and polite indecision of *el blanco* señor and his *malnutrida gringita* — and after a few artless attempts to empty additional water from the pool they agreed it would be wise now while the señor was engaged to abandon their hard work for a good lunch and perhaps *más tarde*, later, a private moment or two in the shade, for this was good and exactly what two such hard-working men owed to themselves.

The señor was bad, *malísimo*, but only a little bad, for it was a man's duty to occasionally smack the face of his *puta*, for it was well understood that only a man's fist could keep the good whores gentle.

The señor was once more arranging the lawn chairs to their desired formation. Madeline was down on one knee in the grass, hacking for breath, and loudly sobbing. '*Cómo está usted?*' whispered the señor. '*Sí, sí*, have the cigarette, what am I thinking of? *Cómo quiero usted?* Of course you may have the cigarette. Have all the cigarettes.' He crushed the mangled package into her hand. 'Light up, have the smoke. By all means. The Mademoiselle will be herself again.' He talked on in this way, grinning, quite calm himself, adamantly solicitous. She dropped the package and he replaced them in her unresisting hand. Her shoulders were now shaking a little less noticeably. She was on her knees crawling away from him. 'Salud! To your health. The Mademoiselle is beautiful when she smokes. When she does not, the Mademoiselle she is *el toro de lidia*, the fighting bull.' He lit one of his cigarettes, and placed it between her lips. 'Ah. Now the Mademoiselle is happy!'

Madeline was now whimpering. He gave her a shove away from the chairs. 'Bravo. Let us take the little bull into the casa.'

She stumbled ahead.

'I will advise the señora that our *comida* is to be delayed. Do you agree? Does the Mademoiselle find favour in this idea?'

Madeline whirled. 'Don't touch me!' she screamed. 'Don't you dare touch me!' Her fists were raised, and her red face contorted. 'I'll kill you if you come near me!'

But she stood, waiting — with growing interest — and when the señor came abreast of her and wrapped his arm over her shoulder she walked along with him, meek, but not unwillingly, into the señor's casa and to his bed.

A SHORT TIME LATER — after twenty minutes or so — the side wooden door again opened and the two made their way without incident to the waiting chairs. Madeline had retained her swim suit — indeed she had showered and seemed more than a little refreshed — while Señor Gómez had exchanged his rumpled white suit for another identical to the first. With a courtly manner he now seated her. He held a flame to her cigarette, adjusted her head-rest, and encouraged her to lie down and relax in the sun in these few moments before the *comida* came.

She murmured her thanks in a faraway voice and the señor replied '*De nada*' and for some minutes kneeled beside her to spread the coconut oil over her skin.

He strolled down to the pool and there, stooping low, measured with a finger the water's descent from its original surface line. His workers had not yet returned and he saw no visible signs evidencing their existence in the adobe hut beyond the avocado trees. He looked up at the sky which was a cloudless lovely blue, consulted his watch, and reasoned with some certainty that he and Madeline would yet have time to eat before the coming of the afternoon rain. He loved this rain which arrived now each day and at about the same hour without fail, and found it unfathomable that the unpredictable Mademoiselle as a rule did not.

From her chair Madeline watched him stealthily. What had just happened in the señor's bedroom she had decided to ignore. She did not begrudge him these love-making acts — in this respect at least he was no more perverse than other men. And better, she conceded, than most. She poured coconut oil in the palm of her hand and rubbed the heavy liquid — Gómez would not allow her the purchase of a decent suntan oil — over her exposed stomach and shoulders and limbs. She smiled vacantly, her eyes wide, admiring the hard flatness of her stomach, the curve of her legs, the tight muscles of her thighs. Her full breasts, the smooth beauty of her skin.

Overhead, sputtering in slow flight, a single-engine plane appeared, flapping a message for the town. Madeline could not read the trailing banner, but she had seen the El Flores posters and correctly reasoned it to be advertising the bullfight in Morelia scheduled for the coming weekend. Dull grey in colour, cruising low, an antique. That, or junk, like all things here. The plane passed in front of the sun and momentarily disappeared; Madeline gasped and threw up her hands over her eyes, wounded by the sun's incredible glare. The plane knocked along miserably, and once more she looked up, hearing the flutter of the sign directly above her; the cloth was whipping about violently because the stupid pilot had not known enough to cut air holes into the thing.

The pilot was quite visible too and she could see him waving.

'Crash ... I hope you do,' she murmured aloud, and wrenched her arms behind her back to tighten the bikini strings. The friendliness of these people, as she had told Gómez more than once, she found personally nauseating. God knows what deceit it was intended to hide.

Gómez was not in sight. She had a moment of panic, thinking herself alone, but then she located his white figure near the wall at the street door which was now open. With him stood the El Flores padre, Father García, his black gown hanging wide at the ankles, his monk's cowl pushed back over his shoulder, his bald head shining in the sun. Both of them, like fools, looking up at the sky. Madeline turned away with a curse. Next to Gómez, the padre was the man she most despised in all of El Flores. Serving God, what a laugh that was! Since the day of the storm, after Raymond had taken her money and abandoned her here, her hatred for the priest and his church was without compromise. On that day, pelted by the rain and half out of her mind from the grief of Raymond's betrayal, she had battered on the cathedral door and implored the father to let her in — to help her — but he had refused. So if she was slut to Gómez now, the blame lay entirely with the church and that hypocrite.

I've been through hell, she thought, but everyone will have to admit that I never looked better.

It had crossed her mind that she ought to send colour postcards of herself to all the men she had ever known saying *Grieve, bastard, for all the good times you're missing now!*

She looked back again at the door and saw Father García with his arm around Gómez's shoulder. Gómez was giving him money. Madeline flung herself back against the chair, her eyes closed, her fists shaking.

A few minutes later the plane again circled overhead, as if it had forgotten something on its first run; it hammered on away, taking its ragged message to another of the tiny villages hugging the lake.

The señor once more claimed his chair.

'I saw you,' Madeline said, 'giving a big wad of pesos to that monkey!'

The señor was obviously surprised at this outburst, but waited for her to continue.

'It may interest you to learn,' said Madeline, 'that yesterday I was seated on one of those benches in the plaza when your resident saint came up and sat beside me with that "my child my child" routine of his.'

The señor lifted a brow.

'He put his hand on me,' she said. 'He put his hand right here between my thighs.'

This statement clearly disconcerted the señor. His hands fluttered hopelessly up and down, his view swept over the garden, went from tree to tree, before it came to rest again on Madeline's bent and glistening knees. Once or twice he started to speak but each time his hands fluttered up and whirled about and fell again with nothing spoken. It was not the Mademoiselle's story that aroused this discomfort. That the Mademoiselle was lying was assured. Did she go anywhere without first securing his permission? Did she speak to anyone without this being immediately reported to him? And did the Father not spend all of yesterday in Erongarequaro across the lake where some hint of the recent pestilence still remained? Had the Father not revealed as much a moment ago while requesting money to aid those in Erongarequaro still infirmed? No, that the Mademoiselle had fabricated this ugly assertion the señor instantly perceived. But his hands lifted and fell, he searched the high branches of these trees, because he could not comprehend or even imagine why the Mademoiselle should feel so compelled.

It did not occur to the señor — nor did Madeline admit to it — that she made this assertion merely because Gómez had given away money she had come to consider as partially her own.

Señora Pesuna approached across the grass, bearing their *comida* on the beautiful silver tray earlier employed and which boasted now a large earthenware *olla* filled with a mixture that yet bubbled in its brown juices.

'What's this puke?' Madeline asked. But a second later she sniffed at the bowl and laughed as if to convey the notion that she had been joking — prompted to this move by the severity of the señor's expression and the realization that such a rudeness was no longer necessary. This would very likely be her last meal at the señor's table, and she had no doubt that once she departed Gómez and his servants would richly regret her absence and be forced to admit that she was something other than the shallow, naïve American girl they had supposed her to be. They could go on thinking whatever they wished, however. She knew herself to be an altogether candid person, open and friendly and generous — and if she was ever considered anything less this was only because so few people really understood her or ever made an effort to get to know her.

'I give up,' she said. 'What is it?'

'*La sopa*,' the doña replied. Soup. Only soup, señora. Soup, as anyone with eyes can see.

The bowl contained chicken giblets cooked with numerous unidentifiable vegetables over which floated, for good luck, scores of hot jalapeño chiles. Madeline tasted hers, frowning, and quickly reached for one of the two Tecate XXX beers the doña had provided. It was delicious, she told the woman, which was the case, and Señora Pesuna, no longer offended, hurried away to secure their second course, a fine pescado blanco taken from their own lake now that the health officials had declared the local fish free of contamination.

The señor dined lightly, in silence, with no apparent hunger. An inaccessible grief appeared to have overtaken him. He poured his beer into the lovely glass, and sat in jaded contemplation of the foam. He toyed with glass and bowl, clearly interested in neither. His fingers laced above his chest and now and then again his eyes rolled heavenward. It was Madeline, of course, who brought this on. The spirit of this woman would yield but it could not be broken. And yet what a curiously ignoble — what a marvellously vain and worthless — spirit it was. It withstood everything and in fact the more one attempted its mutilation the more it thrived. He could not accept Father García's timid boast that God was in every person, that the soul even of his volatile mistress resisted all such transgressions for the simple reason that the soul belongs alone to God. Even if one could overlook the banality of such a claim, the señor asked himself, why should God continue to have an interest? No, not even the *norteamericano* God could be so long-suffering. The explanation, the señor concluded, lay entirely with her native origins. Only her native country could produce citizens of such interminable wretchedness and conceit, and in such numbers. Here in his country they might degrade themselves, they might behave with utter abandonment — secure in the knowledge that here it did not greatly matter. Their vanity still prevailed. They could be beasts but — *Están con los angeles* — their souls resided with the angels because they came from where they did. But inculcated how? By what? One could account for its prevalence neither by economics, their religion, nor by the racism always lurking in their blood. One could account for it not at all. '*No sé*,' muttered the señor. I don't know. Perhaps the issue was less complicated, after all. Perhaps it was to be explained by their diet, by the curious customs by which their appetite was appeased: because they had so few reminders of the low order of life from whence they came.

'*Perdone?*' I'm sorry, what was it you said? He lifted his head; the Mademoiselle was speaking to him.

'I said,' repeated Madeline, her voice thinning in a haughty cascade '— it wasn't the first time either!'

The señor, released from his reverie, laughed heartily, enjoying the vision of Father García, whose sexual penchant was so well-known, with his hand on any woman's leg.

Madeline picked moodily at her fish. The fish had been steamed, and looked undercooked, which was why she didn't like steamed fish in the first place. 'My father will pay you,' she said.

The señor raised an interested, puzzled eye —

'... for what you spent on me,' Madeline said.

This too the señor thought very funny. He lifted his glass and toasted the thought.

'What's the matter with you?' asked Madeline. 'You're nuts, you know. But you'll miss me when I'm gone.'

The señor seemed to reflect on this. He poured another inch of cerveza from the Tecate can, ran his fingers under the lapels of his white suit — all the while appraising her across the table. 'The señor,' he said finally, 'has been posing the question. The señor has been deciding what he must do with the poor Mademoiselle.'

Madeline did not immediately take this in. Now that it had occurred to her, it seemed quite natural that Gómez should miss her. Raymond too had surprised her in this regard. Some weeks back she had received a brief letter from him, postmarked San Miguel de Allende and written in a grade-school scrawl, in which he had whined generally about the state of his poverty and specifically about all the crude Americans there and ended with these hilarious words: *you were a* BITCH *Mady and I guess I* LOVED *you and* MISS *you and was a* DOPE *to cut out on you just because of worrying about where the old $ was coming from.*

The señor was again ignoring her. He soberly regarded the sky while one finger tapped repeatedly on his watch crystal, much as if he supposed he could predict the very minute the afternoon rain would commence.

Madeline twisted in her chair and clutched at his arm. 'Listen,' she said. 'My father is coming. I am leaving with him this afternoon.'

The señor replied with enraptured good will. 'Ah,' he said, 'but the Mademoiselle's father is not arriving. The excursion of the father of the Mademoiselle has been cancelled.'

Madeline sneered. But she searched his face and in a moment the sneer gave way to uncertain panic:

'You have talked to my father?'

The señor responded with his most engaging smile:

'*Sí*, Mademoiselle. Many times.'

Madeline was stunned. For a time she sat trembling, poised on the edge of her chair as if awaiting explanation. Then her fists knotted at her sides, a quiver went through her body, and suddenly she pitched forward into the grass, moaning and twisting, beating her knuckles against her head. 'You did this!' she cried. 'Why? How much did you pay him for me?'

And she continued so, crying and pleading, as if already proof existed in support of this extravagant claim.

The señor vacated his lawn chair and strolled down to the pool where Don José had been idly standing for the past few minutes.

The doña, oblivious to Madeline's frenetic behaviour, returned a final time to collect and remove their dishes. Señor Gómez sent Don José out to scratch beneath the rose bushes planted in triple rows at the lower end of the garden. He then withdrew into the casa to procure his white umbrella. The children of Manuel, who were allowed by their parents to enter the pool when it was empty, ran up to timidly estimate the progress made that morning against the water — and ran away with contrived urgency a moment later when their mother called. Manuel could be seen pacing out a small plot of earth in the unbroken ground up from the path to the garbage dump — for here today with the señor's permission he and his wife were to plant the spinach and the tomatoes and the corn ... and over there perhaps, why not, a new place where the pig might root to his satisfaction ... for his was a decent family which held the señor's love and was not therefore required like the unfortunate poor to eat the leaf of the cactus all year long.

Madeline grappled back into the chair, there to mutter curses while scratching and slapping at her skin, separating blades of warm grass from her oiled body.

A few white clouds drifted in, momentarily screening out the sun.

Señor Gómez reappeared. For a time he passed aimlessly up and down his wide slate walk, the rolled umbrella swinging in energetic rhythm from his left hand. Several times he seemed determined to approach Madeline who was now softly weeping in her chair, though on each occasion some new thought seemed to impede him. Finally he contented himself by taking up a position under the shade of one of his most formidable trees, from which point he stared glumly across the lawn at his erubescent companion. His view was drawn particularly to Madeline's long red fingernails which he had ordered her to so paint soon after their first meeting. The colour in his opinion was altogether appropriate. Tiny pools of blood that had cooled and deepened — and which served at once to signal her value. The nails of all her predecessors had in fact been coloured the same. The blood of such women was infamous, symbolic of a thing so callous that he could see it always in his mind's eye, especially those late nights after Madeline had drunk herself past rancour and fatigue, past all attempts to fasten blame — those hours when she lay in his arms and all her whining delusions of supremacy were surrendered.

The señor did not pause to consider that at such times he lay in her arms with a similar calm, sharing in the advantages of that temporary truce. It would have displeased him vastly to consider that in their mutual pleasure they in any way significantly accommodated each other. Nor for that matter did the señor find it convenient to reflect on his own eccentric fascination with these *inglesas*, a fascination that was eccentric not because they were women or *inglesa* but because he harboured no equivalent scorn for their gringo compatriots. Were one to pursue with him the inevitable sequence of such reasoning he might have readily conceded that such sexual distinctions as frequently he was disposed to utter originated out of a most extreme bias. He might have agreed that the Mexican male's opinion of their women was not of the highest, and that on this account his guest had every reason to express fury. He would have pointed out, however, that Madeline had not the slightest concern for Mexico's women, and had failed even to notice their inequality.

He was content now to remain under his tree and dwell to his satisfaction on one aspect of the labyrinthine nature of these *inglesas*. It was perversely true, and a mystery past his ability to comprehend, that Mexico's sun was terribly unkind to these visitors. They had a tendency to disappear when confronting the sun day after day in his garden. With great confidence they shed their clothing and surrendered themselves, thinking perhaps that one sun was so much like another. Their hair dulled, their eyes glazed, flesh slackened on their bones. They became speckled and dirty, as if the sun sucked the filth out of them and left it to rot on their surface.

They reminded him, in fact, a bit of the El Flores dogs.

The señor's speculations along these lines were interrupted by the arrival at his door of an unfamiliar *vendedor* who happily announced the availability now of *la bonita fresas* and who held up two pails which had arrived he said that very day by autobús and which were for sale now *muy borato*, very cheap. The señor examined the strawberries with much delight, agreeing with the *vendedor* that they were indeed beautiful and at last instructing him to journey inside the casa where he might conclude arrangements with the doña. After numerous expressions of gratitude and remarks on the perfect weather, the man departed to fulfil this mission.

Waiting outside the señor's walls on the cobblestones of Calle de la Noche de la mil Lunas was yet another person desiring the señor's attention. Sighing, he noted there the familiar and insistent señora who lived in the hut behind the *mercado* now with her seven children and her dead husband whose mouth also would not be filled. Her wrinkled and dark Tarascan face with its fateful eyes was shrouded behind a mantilla, and wrapped within the rebozo slung over her shoulder rested the inert form of her youngest child who might only be sleeping but who also might be dead. The señor advanced, realizing full well that the woman had nothing more to show him than her usual inconsequential and artless embroideries depicting, as she would herself tell him, the *bonito mucho bonito* rooster in the red thread or the blue and each such a good gift for the señor's white *novia* or such a practical aid to the señor's doña Anna when she wipes the dishes in the kitchen.

The señor refused her goods but gave her a twenty-peso note and suggested she visit him again in a few days when she might have for sale a serviette in the yellow.

He walked past Madeline — drawn up now with her head between her knees — and returned to stand by the pool.

He heard her once shouting to him:

'You could have put chlorine in the goddamn water!' to which he silently replied that the Mademoiselle's chemicals would retard his garden and, moreover, had a disagreeable odour.

The rain came with its usual suddenness.

Madeline dashed across the garden, shrieking, and disappeared through the side wooden door.

The señor walked under his umbrella to where the lawn chairs were positioned, and with Don José's assistance, removed them to the shed where they were customarily stored and where they would now remain until tomorrow.

He walked with Don José out to the pool and together they stood on the white wall watching the rain spatter down and drum on the green surface. The rain was wondrously cool and thick — it seemed to whir through the air and ten feet in the distance one could see nothing — and the two exchanged pleasant remarks on this daily phenomenon, reminding each other repeatedly that tomorrow the garden would be even more beautiful.

Shortly afterward, his linen suit adhering to his thin frame, the señor turned leisurely through the side door and entered the casa to explain to the Mademoiselle the exact nature of his single dialogue with her father.

For half an hour it rained.

Then the sun again came out, as dazzling and as blistering as it had been before. Señora Pesuna emerged from the casa and went home to attend to her own many children. Don José, in the room where he had sought shelter, hunched on the floor and for some time investigated the condition of his shoes. Manuel and his family assembled by the path to the dump, from there proceeding to perform mysterious duties over the earth where their vegetables would be planted. Señor Gómez, if one knew where to look, would be found at his desk giving attention to one or the other of his numerous business affairs.

A light steam hovered loyally over the surface of the pool and for some hours the señor's beautiful garden remained empty. Eventually Madeline made her appearance and trudged still in her bathing suit down to the pool. She secured a long pole and with it attempted to separate the slime which the sun was already drying. A clearing barely large enough to accommodate her body was soon effected: she sat poised on the wall, closed her eyes, and slid gently into the water. She stretched face-down and for a moment floated there; then she kicked out from the wall and, so propelled, disappeared underwater.

From his window in the casa the señor watched her. Periodically her head broke through the green cover, her mouth gasped open; then again her head submerged, the legs shot through the water, the scum rearranged itself above her, and for another minute or so he would see nothing of her.

He was pleased with her, for the first time in his memory.

Wintering in Victoria

YESTERDAY MY WIFE LEFT ME, no word of warning, no scenes, I walked in the bedroom and found her packing.

'That's right, jerk,' she said, 'I'm getting out of your life, you prick, I can't get out of this house fast enough.'

Fine, I said, are you taking the kid?

'The kid, the kid, the kid!' she said, 'do you even know her name? You bet I'm taking her, she isn't safe here with you!'

What have we done to our women?

Years have gone by since I met one who believed a child was safe with its father.

Not that it bothered me.

I waved them down the hall and out the door, told them if they changed their minds it would be all right with me.

If you want to come back, fine, if you want to make this permanent, fine — no hard feelings on my part.

My wife came running back inside a few minutes later to tell me she'd like to kick me silly, nothing would give her more pleasure.

'Someone', she said, 'ought to knock some sense into you before it's too late. If I was only big enough or strong enough or stupid enough, I'd do it myself. Man, would I give it you!'

I put down the latest issue of *Swampstump*, got up out of the easy chair and bent over.

Go ahead, I said, this ought to make it easier.

The kid was crying, however.

The kid stood in the open doorway, her coat bunched in her arms, saying 'Daddy, Daddy, Daddy, bye, Daddy!'

Something is wrong with me, I was touched but barely enough to tell it.

My wife ran up to her, shook her, picked her up in her arms and said 'Don't talk to that S.O.B.'

Then they went.

Walking, who knows where or for how long, probably without a dime between them.

Too bad, I thought, it wasn't raining.

Since it wasn't I decided to go out for a while myself. Take a walk, Jake, I told myself, be good for you.

My pal Jack was in his driveway the next block down, polishing his Austin Mini. Across the street Mr and Mrs Arthur C. Pole were raking up wet leaves, trying to set fire to them.

Look at those idiots, I said to Jack — wasting perfectly good mulch.

Not that I cared.

Jack threw down his chamois cloth.

'You're my friend,' he said, 'right?'

Right, I said.

'I can talk to you,' he said, 'right?'

Right, I said.

'And you'll not take offence, right, you'll not want to punch my head in if I level with you?'

I told him not to worry, we were pals, we had been good friends for a long time, if he had something to say to me to come right out and lay it on me, no hard feelings on my part.

'O.K.' he said, 'I been wanting to say this to you for some months now.'

Go ahead, I said.

'All right,' he said, 'I will. You've become a big pain, Jake, you've gone wing-wingy on us, nobody can stand your company anymore. It isn't that you don't have feelings, no, I'm not claiming that, but nobody can reach you anymore, Jake, it's a pain being with you, you've become a first-class down-at-the-heels shit-in-the-mouth and I can't stand the sight of you, I wish to hell I could never see you again.' He stopped then and hitched up his pants and glared at me.

I told him I understood, that I wasn't upset, to get it all off his chest right now if it would make him feel better.

'All right, Jake,' he said. 'The fact is you've become a bloody cipher, a big zero, a big hulking zombie-fish that I get queasy just talking to! For your own sake you ought to seek professional help, talk to your minister, do something about your lousy condition.'

Good, I said, I'm glad you told me, Jack, is there any more?

'That about sums it up,' he said. 'I've talked it over with my wife, I've talked it over with all the guys, and we are all in mutual agreement that we don't want to have anything more to do with you, we wash our hands of you.'

Fine by me, I said, and turned and strolled away, not bothered in the least.

In fact, I felt relief — if anything.

I walked down to the billiards hall and broke a rack and dropped in seven balls the rotation way and quit then, hung up my stick, leaving the rest on the table, it's always that cruddy eighth ball that breaks my streak.

I went over to another table and broke another rack and ran seven more.

I felt all right, pretty good, but I can't claim much elation.

I picked up a pot roast from the butcher shop and walked home and put it in a pot with a potato and an onion and put this in the oven on a slow bake.

I thought it might feel pretty good to sit at home and enjoy a good dinner alone with maybe a glass of wine, take off my shoes, maybe afterwards have a quiet snooze.

In the meantime I checked through the mail, got out my cheque-book, paid off some old bills.

I figured it cost me twelve thousand and eighty-four dollars a month just to be comfortable.

To have heat, lights, phone, seven rooms, a car and clothes.

The only thing I have even a faint objection to is the bird, a canary, that business of eating like a bird is utter nonsense, I can recall times in the past when I've thought the bird was eating me out of house and home.

But he does the best he can, I don't blame him, he's got to get along, I bear no grudges, I enjoyed writing those cheques, I thought that maybe tomorrow I'd go down and watch some of the people when they opened their mail, Stocker's Moving Company and B.C.

Hydro and B.C. Telephone and the oil people, thinking surely they'd crack a smile to see that old Jake B. Carlisle had paid his debts in full, no need now to barrage him with further calls, threaten law-suits, power cut-offs, all that crap.

So there was some mild elation, not much, nothing to shout about, and afterwards I enjoyed a hot bath.

I'm a little tired, I guess, of bathing with other people, of sharing the tub with wife or daughter, I stretched out, closed my eyes, sort of dreamed for a while.

The phone was ringing, it was some guy named Mr Zoober, something like that.

These people who announce themselves as Mr Such and Such, I can remember the times I'd strangle the phone and sometimes tell them to go to hell because people who say Hello, this is Mr Such and Such from Such and Such give me a pain, they're rotten people obviously, they either want to sell you something or tell you they're cutting off your water, in the past such people have really got to me, but this time I was civil, I said, why yes, good of you to call, how can I help you, Mr Zoober?

He told me he'd like to sell me some insurance, was I interested, and I thought about it for a second or two and then told him well I might be, tell me what he had in mind.

Which he did, and made an appointment to come over that very evening.

I put a few carrots in the pot roast, buttered a bit of bread, poured a glass of wine, and shortly thereafter sat down and had a very nice dinner.

It was during this that the doorbell sounded and I opened it and Jack stood there with his wife beside him.

Hello, Jack, I said, how are you, how are you, Alice, what can I do for you?

'We were thinking,' said Jack, 'that perhaps I was somewhat hard on you.'

'Yes,' said Alice, 'you poor man, you see we didn't know that June had left you.'

I tried to explain to them that I valued Jack's comments, I

appreciated his honesty, that as far as I could tell June's leaving me had nothing to do with it.

'No,' insisted Jack, 'under the circumstances it was a mistake for me to come down so hard on you.'

'You see,' said Alice, 'we didn't know you and June were having marital difficulties, that changes everything, now we know why you've been such a drip, Jack wants to apologize.'

It isn't necessary, I told them, the truth is we hadn't been having any special difficulty, no more so than other couples, that it would be a mistake for them to assume that such small differences of opinion as we had in any way accounted for my recent failures as a person.

No, I said, you're very fortunate to be rid of me.

They stared at me for five minutes or so and then went back to their car and drove away.

I thought it was nice of them to come by like that, a decent gesture, but it didn't matter to me.

I went back in and finished my meal which was cold by that time though I didn't care, if you ask me hot meals are very over-rated.

I noticed about that time that I had cut my finger and figured it must have happened while I was slicing the carrots.

I watched the CBC news on television and nothing much was happening in the world, which was fine with me. I watched a special next, Highlights in the life of Doris Day, and finished off the bottle of wine without much thinking about it.

At eight Mr Zoober called, right on time, and told me about the various plans and policies a man of my age and income and family status ought to have. He seemed a little worried that I was alone, he asked a few veiled questions about my wife, had a few suspicions about the empty wine bottle, but was obviously most disturbed by the dirty dishes still on the dining table.

On the whole he wasn't a bad fellow, I can't say I much objected to him, and we finally agreed that a policy for fifty thousand or so would do me fine.

I think he was quite surprised when I got out my cheque-book and wrote out a big one for him, he seemed to think I had been stringing him along.

He made some joke or other about never losing a customer, and left right away, apologizing, saying he had a few more customers to see tonight, he was aiming for the Million Dollar Mark this year because his company was giving all the Million Dollar salesmen and their families a free trip to Honolulu.

I thought about inviting him back in to write out a bigger policy, what the hell, it didn't much matter to me.

Not much else happened that night, June's mother called and asked what the trouble was, couldn't things be sorted out, she'd always liked me or anyway had liked me pretty much until recently, what had happened to me, was it another girl?

I said, no, it's been years since I felt much attraction for anyone other than June, that her daughter was a fine woman and I hoped she wouldn't worry too much about this, to try to go to sleep and forget it.

'But little Cherise!' she said, 'What will happen to little Cherise, don't you love little Cherise!' and crying on and on like that about the kid until I got bored with it all and hung up and got myself a cup of coffee.

I've never much understood how people can go through their lives drinking that lousy stuff they call coffee in the supermarkets, Eight O'Clock, and Yuban and Chase and Sanborn and Maxwell House and Nabob, it's enough to make a person sick, whereas I drink only the dark French roast because there is no better coffee in the world and standards ought to begin with these most common of practices otherwise there is little likelihood they will exist in more important affairs. People all over the world are drinking those lousy brands and thinking this stuff stinks and likely as not going out to murder and rob and cheat, all because of the lousy coffee they drink, though I've long since given up getting worked up over such trivia, it doesn't matter to me, I had my French roast the filter way and stretched out on the sofa and dozed a while before getting up to draft a few letters to people I had been thinking about that day, my mother whom I have always respected and admired and my boss the business man and the girl I had known back in college named Cissy Reeves though I wouldn't know where to send her letter to.

Dear Mom,

I said, and told her of the insurance policy of which she was co-beneficiary and enclosed Zoober's card in the event anything unfortunate happened to me and no one got in touch with her because it has been my belief that those guys will not pay off unless a gun is held at their throats.

I doodled a bit on her letter, not knowing what to say, wondering idly about her life and about mine and about her nine other sons and daughters all of whom had turned out to be fairly average people through no fault of hers.

I sealed it up after a while and drew a few kisses on the envelope, it wasn't much of a letter but what the hell.

Next I wrote my boss, telling him not to expect me to show up for work the following few weeks, I was going to take time off, if he didn't like it he could find another guy.

Then I wrote Cissy and that took some time because I found I didn't much remember anything of value about Cissy, she was a fairly regular girl, fairly routine, not especially attractive I guess if one wanted to be objective about it, hard to tell now why I had found her exciting enough to chase all over campus and storm and rage whenever I saw her with another guy, Cissy with her ordinary body and ordinary clothes and a mind certainly that no one would notice in a crowd, married, the last I heard, to some guy who was expecting big things from Simpson-Sears or The Bay, hell, who could remember? Dear Cissy, I wrote, I just thought I would get in touch after all these years and tell you that I have been thinking of you today for the first time since our graduation dance when you cried on my shoulder and told me you had decided to marry this business administration guy because you really loved him and you knew I'd be hurt but it was probably best for all concerned and how you walked with me out to the car and got in the back seat with me and how even as we were undressing it came over me that I had not the slightest interest in having you naked under me so I said crap on this and said goodbye Cissy Reeves and drove away and have not thought again of you until this very day when mostly all I want to say is how are you Cissy, how has your life been though I can't really say I care one way or another and I know I'll never give you another thought once I seal this letter.

I sealed it and it was the goddamn truth, poor Cissy, probably a good thing I didn't know where to send it.

But it was pretty boring about that time, I wasn't sleepy, so I made another copy and sent one to the head office of Sears in Toronto and another to the Vancouver Bay because I wasn't up to searching out their master quarters, it didn't matter that much to me one way or the other.

I finished off the cheque-writing chores, writing a letter for each cheque, telling B.C. Telephone and Hydro and the like how much I valued their services and hoped we could continue now with a good relationship, that I wasn't one of those who believed for a minute that their profits were excessive, that they were money-grabbers and impolite and sticking it to their customers wherever they could.

I fell asleep pretty soon after that, must have, because about twelve I was awakened by the telephone, I was asleep on the sofa in my clothes when this great jangle came, and it was June of course calling me an S.O.B. prick and a lot of other things and she hoped I was enjoying myself, who did I have with me, she wasn't surprised, naturally I had never thought one minute of her, I was a self-indulgent prig without any feelings for anyone else and she had always known it would come to this — and I let her talk on, it didn't seem worth it to interrupt, I was even enjoying it in a mild way and appreciating June because normally she is such a steady person, level-headed, routine, somewhat ordinary, I guess, never saying much, taking life easy, you wouldn't think she was the type to have a thought in her head nor much emotion either.

'I'll kill you, kill you, kill you, you bastard!' she screamed that several times and I shrugged more or less, I asked if there was anything specific I had done to enrage her, to compel her to leave, that I'd be happy to apologize if that would make her feel better, that I'd promise to change, do better, try harder, if that would help her cope any easier with the situation. But she of course just continued to scream, not even using words any longer, the rare one like "Pig" or "S.O.B." but mostly just scream scream scream as though someone was slicing down her back with a butcher knife and finally her mother took the phone away from her and said Jake you've got to come over here, I can't do any more with her, and I sighed around a bit, I complained and tried to find excuses, said I had a lot to do, a lot of chores, but June's mother is an insistent woman and eventually I agreed I'd come over and do what I could.

That's how it happened that I came across Jack and his old glum-chum wife Alice another time. They were sitting outside my house in their car, just sitting there watching my door as if they thought it might suddenly burst into flames.

I opened the door on Alice's side and asked what they had on their minds. I don't know, it seemed to me that once I saw them there, it was as if I had expected it or should have, I wasn't very surprised.

So hello, Jack, hello, Alice, have you been here long, what's on your minds?

Alice, in the past I've felt some sorrow for Alice, she has always seemed so miserable, so glum, but always without reason, no explanation for what's troubling her, that's just the way she is, glum and miserable, as if poor Jack has never kissed her and she had never wanted him to, as if nothing has ever happened to her and why should it, the truth is that Alice hasn't any imagination or interest, I suppose if she goes through her day and finds time to wash her hair or sweep the floor then that has been a pretty good day for her, nothing to complain about, about what she expected from the day, in fact it occurred to me as I opened her door that here was the first time I had found Alice out of her houserobe and slippers and now it had happened twice today so something very strange must be going on here.

They didn't say anything right away so I told them that I hoped they hadn't been brooding about Jack's comments to me, that truthfully I didn't mind a bit and Jack was absolutely right in telling me I was developing into a first-rate cipher, that I didn't mind in the least and was only just mildly surprised that anyone had noticed any difference in me, I certainly didn't intend to go around as if I had some sign hung on me saying NOTHING BOTHERS ME.

'Jake, Jake, Jake,' Jack moaned at last, 'Get in, let's drive around a while.'

I thought he had in mind going down to the S&W drive-in for maybe a hamburger and Coke, because we do that together sometimes with Alice and June and the kid along, so I had to tell them I didn't think I could make it, I'd received an urgent telephone call a moment ago and had to get across town fast.

'From June?' asked Alice, and I admitted that was the case.

She hugged me then, quite suddenly, I didn't so much as see her arms reaching out for me, she simply pulled me to her with the strength of a wild beast and pressed my head against her neck, thumping me on the back and repeating 'Poor Jake, poor Jake, oh you poor man, oh let us help you, I'm sure you will feel better if you'll only talk about it.'

It was Jack who had to make her let me go, who pried her arms from around me. 'For God's sake, Alice,' he said, 'how can he talk with you strangling him?' and she sat back quietly after that, sulking, biting her lips like a retarded child because she doesn't like him speaking to her in those tones, I guess.

'Now the reason we are parked in front of your house like this', he explained, 'is because June called us, she was worried.'

Worried? I said, and he said 'Yes, she was afraid you might do something to yourself.'

Like what? I asked.

'Something criminal,' said Jack, 'and June said she would never forgive herself for it.'

'She figured she'd be to blame,' said Alice, 'that she wouldn't be able to look at herself in the mirror ever again if you went and did something stupid to yourself like slicing your wrist, oh Jake you know she worships the ground you walk on, if only you weren't so peculiar!'

They continued to talk in that vein for some time, I couldn't say anything to calm them down. Finally I said, 'Look, I thought you understood me; suicide is the last thought from my mind, who can bother, no, you don't need to worry about me.'

Alice gave me a consoling look, she kept reaching for my hand or my face or my leg and I kept trying to move out of her reach, lately I have just not liked at all people wanting to touch me. 'So look,' I said and it seemed to me my calm ought to have been blissfully penetrating — 'Look, why don't the two of you toot along and look after your own lives, I'm fine, and I'm confident June and I can handle this without your help.'

But they wouldn't accept it, they were offended, they insisted I get in the car and they'd drive me over to June's mother's house, June needed their help now even if I refused it and they wouldn't dream of walking out on a friend.

I got in the car, what the hell.

During the ride I tried to relax, not lose sight of this new life I'd found for myself. The truth is I couldn't help feeling some resentment, a guy comes along who isn't bothered by anything and right away everyone starts losing their wigs.

'Who was that man who came by your house earlier?' asked Alice, and I told her it was Mr Zoober from the insurance company, and I saw them exchange glances and a moment later Alice broke into tears, she was quite nasty, how stupid, she said, and how mindless and vindictive and self-centred suicides were, they never thought of other people, of wives and children left behind, what would happen for instance to poor little Cherise who had never done anything to anybody? She'd hate me forever, she said, if I killed myself, that would really show me up for the kind of jerk I was, and I could tell Jack pretty much shared her feelings, he looked like he wanted to punch me, kept staring at me in the rear-view mirror as if I might do it right there in the back seat of his station-wagon with its smell of dog.

All the lights were on at the house, I saw that as we turned the corner. All the doors were wide open and even as Jack made his slow approach I could see someone running out into the yard and back in again every third second, run out and pull her hair and yell and then run in again. Naturally it was June, in her housecoat, in her stocking feet, her hair stringy, a thousand lines in her face that I had never seen before. She looked a mess but the truth is I hardly noticed. Before the car came to a stop she was already coming at me with her fingernails, spitting and clawing and screaming, punching me around until everyone except her was satisfied. Her mother is a genteel lady, she hates scenes, she appeared at last and pulled June off me and led her back inside.

'Don't think you don't deserve it,' Alice told me, and Jack added that I'd better not try anything, he was watching me. They all went into the living room to look after June and June's mother came out to pat my arm and lead me upstairs to where the kid was.

'She couldn't sleep, poor child,' she said, 'she was calling you and finally June got angry and locked her in the closet but I managed to find a spare key and get her out, be kind to her, Jake, she doesn't understand.'

I smiled and told her I would do the best I could and she patted me again and returned downstairs.

I entered the room, usually a guest room but hardly ever used now because June's mother says she's tired of people, and the kid was seated in a child's rocker that was much too little for her — rocking in the dark, not saying anything. She was cute, I was touched in a distant way, I really didn't feel much of anything, no more than the simple aesthetic response to a child's silhouette in a tiny tot's chair.

'Is that you, Daddy?' she asked, and I replied it was, and she said, 'Don't turn on the light, please.'

I asked why, had her mother been pinching her again.

'Not much,' she said, 'on my legs and on my stomach some but it doesn't hurt very much.'

I turned on the lights. She had a few welts on her skin, a zig-zag of purple wounds down her legs, nothing to get upset about.

'Everything was fine,' she said, 'once I was locked in the closet, I hope you haven't been worried.'

I told her I wasn't, I knew she could take care of herself. I noticed her hair was wet and asked her how that had happened. She told me her mother had made her take a bath but she hadn't wanted to and so June had held her under the water.

I'm glad you didn't drown, I told her, and she said she was glad too but that someone still had to clean up the bathroom because June had gone through the room pulling everything out of the cupboards and the medicine cabinet and throwing it all in the bathwater, she really had made a wreck of the place.

I told her not to mind, someone would see to it, that June probably had got confused and thought she was at home because normally she was spic and span and especially in her mother's house.

The kid said she didn't mind, she'd tried to clean it up herself but June had kept on pinching her. 'But are we really leaving you, Daddy?' she asked, 'June says we are and that you don't mind, that you are itching to be alone.'

I asked her how she felt about it.

'I don't ever want to be alone,' she said, 'but I can manage if I have to.'

She had a blanket around her shoulders and was shivering, it seemed somewhere between the bath and the closet she'd lost her clothes.

I stepped out of the room to look for them and found June snarling at the foot of the stairs, restrained by Jack and Alice and her mother, furious to get upstairs and sink her teeth into me.

Let her go, I told them, and after a moment or two they released her. She charged forward, taking about five or six steps before her breath gave out and she gasped down on the carpet, sobbing. Now take her back to the sitting room, I told them, and Jack came up and got her and led her back down.

There comes a time in your life, you start giving orders and no one in the world will stop to question them.

I found the kid's clothes in the bath water and wrung them out. I drained the tub and put to one side those things that hadn't been ruined.

I could hear Jack and Alice talking downstairs, though June and her mother were silent and there seemed to be some sort of fight developing between Jack and Alice. No one had thought to close the doors and the house was under a distinct chill.

No go, I told the kid, you're going to have to make do with the blanket.

She turned her face away, hoping I wouldn't notice that her cheeks were swollen.

I crossed the room and slid up the window. It looked clean outside, brisk, an open sky, a hatful of stars — a fairly regular scene for this time of year.

'I'm going to cut out now, kid,' I told her.

She sniffed a bit and hugged the blanket tight around her.

I climbed over the sill and felt for the fire escape rung and started down.

The kid came down behind me. I looked up and she was all naked above me, distorted like a dummy.

'My shoes,' she said, when we were on the ground.

The ground was cold, even icy. I stooped and she climbed on my back. We ran across the yard, jogged under the trees. Her knees wrapped tight around my waist, one hand gripped my shoulder — she rode light and handsome as an apple.

How far can you go with a kid on your back? I don't know. After a while she began giggling, I giggled too. After a time, you don't feel anything, a slow giggle is good for you, the giggles give you wings.

'How far do we go, Daddy?'

Not far. We spent the night here: a fairly routine, a fairly ordinary place. Not much happens here. We can get along. Tomorrow — maybe the next day — we'll go out, ring up her mother, run a quick check on our affairs. But there's no hurry. There never is. Our lives are routine, normal: you won't find much that bothers us.

The Broad Back of the Angel

WHAT MORE CAN WE DO to ourselves? Is this the question that keeps lights burning in this house through till morning? One might think so. We make a clean target. But is this appreciated?

Having tired of the blue umbrella, Gore now elects to have a silver ring inserted in his lower lip. Matila complains.

'Gore, Gore, I don't want metals on your face!'

Gore is himself uneasy: he goes out, he returns. He's up, he's down: a man in my condition notes the uneasy play of limbs. Here he comes again, his eyes bloodshot, his lips hanging low. The finish is silver, but anyone can see there's lead inside. For the expression, he says. Just the right lip for my day and age. I like it fine, he says.

Ta-dum, ta-dum. Who reaps the harvest of this merry-go-round? Is anything so cheap — and yet so expensive — as this way we live?

'Ah, friend,' he says, '— you're not fooling me!'

What can the poor bastard mean?

Weeks go by. Months. No one in this house is sure. But this we know: the ring interferes, it affects whatever we do. Gore pines for soft foods, to mention one: for those that do not require the grip and churn of his lower lip. To appease our hunger we are obliged to take furtive walks in the cold night. In this neighbourhood? We remark to each other: how many others have you seen? Are those human — or inhuman — shapes? And these uphill routes are hard on a man in a wheel chair. I prefer to remain inside, gnawing on the forbidden thumb.

And Gore? What a tease! Last night he stabbed the fork into his nose. For the expression, he said. Is not my countenance much improved? He can't eat — but puts on weight, even so. Look now how he drags the floor, how the boards creak and bend! You would think his feet were carved from this very wood. 'I like it fine,' he says. His motion arrested, how he drools! Saliva thickens on his chest, but is that a grin? My wife thinks it is.

'Get rid of it,' Matila pleads. 'Do!'

She commands, she entreats. Her desires have no effect and soon she is adding to the moment with her tears.

'Mrruff-mrruff,' Gore remarks, his lower lip having stretched. 'Mrruff-mrruff!' What is the man saying? Better he should say nothing, or go out and barter with neighbouring dogs. His voice is a throaty mutter that Matila hears in her sleep. My wife confesses: 'Oh, Sam, I hear it too!'

Yet he continues to sing when he bathes, and I notice a glint of logic not evident in his eyes before.

We meet at the dining table and Matila holds aloft her fork — 'What need have we for these?'

You would think our lives had no form but for this scheduled food.

But why am I telling you? My past life was more elegant, but was it more refined? I ask you now: how is yours?

Matila whines. Each new emergency ushers in the familiar notes *'Do-re-me . . . !'* My wife marvels: 'Are your ears so condemned? She's in agony! Can't you at least project a friendly smile?'

The fact is I proffer what I can. I listen, but who am I to intrude? Indeed, Matila is whining — but is hers not the voice which brought me to this chair? The voice that keeps me here?

Whose screaming bullets are these that ignite my groin? Is it me — or Matila — on the receiving end?

But oh, how she howls. 'I won't put up with this! Metals on his face! I'll sue for a divorce! Why should I suffer these mad extremes?'

And from some place in all this a practical — a reasonable? — voice is heard. 'On what grounds?' It is my wife speaking, and her words reach me as if through a tube. Is it Matila, or myself, whom she addresses now?

Later, bedroomed, I can put this question to her face. 'Oh,' she says, 'I am soft and patient with Matila's moods. I am with her, in her skin. I love her for her temper. For her moods. I find nothing objectionable in her incessant whines.'

And I am asked whether I share these views. 'It is Gore', she says, 'whom I find too miserable to tolerate!'

Me? I take no sides. Though a love for Gore engulfs me even as she speaks. I too would have metals on my face. I too would have my expression improved. I poke out my lip and am disconcerted at finding nothing there. 'Oh, *Gore!*' — that's the one sentiment my mind reveres. 'Gore! Never mind that he's the fool! Never mind that he's the product of what he wears! That what he wears is what most wears at him!' This chair, I think, would fit him almost as well as me.

Delirium has its pause. I have not served in seven wars without learning something from them. A tolerance for the other side.

My wife is unmoved. 'You cripples!' she says.

And thus I am wheeled again into the dark. 'Think this issue through,' she says to me. 'I'm sure you will come to your senses soon.'

And here in the darkness, what are the thoughts that occur to me? That women are unpredictable. That women pursue where nothing leads. That wives willingly betray whoever first betrayed them. That for a friend they would forsake either the gallant or hideous dead. That breasts and legs and man's imagined lust combine to create some holy orifice. That nothing eludes them like sweet sympathy. That no womb, empty or full, is worth the smallest sacrifice. That men are perhaps different after all. That the same darkness which greets me here drove her to drive me to its dingy embrace. Or that it is sleep which finally captures all.

Thus I nod.

How curious it is that in my black dream sweethearts continue to promenade in pairs. A hand inserts itself in mine — warm, fragile, a mysterious hand. We walk and walk and no one speaks. We never tire. Our pace never alters. But after a while our footsteps are heard passing on in front of us.

When I was a boy ... but how distant I seem to myself. Was there ever a moment when I was not this clunking bull? When these two wheels did not frame my eyes? And my raw hands did not shove these knobs? Yet a boy's vision endures. There was magic in those innocent coils between heart and brain. Its presence makes me shudder in embarrassment, looking back.

This obnoxious spasm in my legs! I slap cruelly at my thighs, at my dancing knees. My wife sighs irritably in her sleep. My feet clatter loudly against the steel shoes which support my legs. I continue to box at these limbs, squirming high in my sweaty seat. This monstrous chair knows the disgust I feel.

My friend Arturo, dead now, had a story he liked to tell. 'There was this poor man,' he would say, 'who owned nothing except one sorry mule. And the beast cost more to feed than he brought in. "If I could teach this brute not to eat," the poor man decided, "my situation might gradually improve".' Here Arturo always paused. 'You must understand,' he would say, 'the significance this story has for me.' And his lidded eyes would make their appeal. I would strut here and there, no doubt uncorking and pouring wine or slapping down yet another ale. I had no patience for Arturo's stories. He took life much too seriously, in my view. 'So,' I would finally insist, '— so, did this poor man teach his animal to go without food?'

Arturo's melancholy face would draw nearer. His hands would clutch my arm. 'Yes, yes!' he'd say, greatly excited. 'The mule learned to go without food! Took to it without complaint! But then the sonofbitch up and died!'

Morning. I have passed another night in this chair. It occurs to me, wheeling myself past an open window, that this was a story I told Arturo. Nothing cheered Arturo so much as a story with a rousing punch-line. His fingers would lift and there would be his bloodprints on my arm: 'Impossible! How people can be such fools!'

Poor Arturo.

My wife sleeps soundly now. She is bedded under a spangle of white daisies and yellow butterflies. My trembling limbs can make her toss, but Matila's rage bothers her not at all. Matila is fiery at daybreak, a person back from desperate frontiers.

'I want a divorce!' she screams. 'I can't live with that idiot another day!'

Gore stumbles by, in one hand his razor, in the other scissors for close work about his hidden chin. His lip ring flashes brilliantly, but it is his silent tread that ignites my wife: 'What is it?' she exclaims, on her elbows — 'What's happening here?' She settles back, contented, secure, as Matila's screams erupt once more.

'I hate it! Hate it! Hate metals on your face!'

We are guests here, I remind my wife. Offer comfort, yes — but on no account should we interfere. I go on speaking while clothing from her closet is flung out. My wife at night is tented under seven layers of wool; in the day flimsy playthings decorate her flesh. 'You kept me awake', she says, 'with your groans. Arturo's dead mule story, I suppose.' But then she's gone.

My wife is a committed woman. She is committed to these people. Her life, she would say, is wrapped up with theirs. Some measure of concern is due them, to be sure. They have provided us with a home. Elevator and washtubs have been installed. They do not deny us their food, such as it is. They would even give up their best bed did we not constantly refuse. Yet I am puzzled each time I labour to change my clothes: was I crippled when I arrived here?

Once again I wheel myself into their midst. Gore sees me and his eyelids fall. 'On what grounds?' my wife is asking them. 'You people have always been peculiar and extreme. You have always been somewhat ridiculous, as you know.' Matila nods. Gore's head weaves from side to side. 'Mrruff-mrruff', he appears to say, '— I like my expression fine.' Matila groans. 'There!' she says. 'You can see how impossible he is!'

I have no opinion on this. One outrage is so much like another, and in any event no one thinks to inquire about my view.

My chair's shadow paints every wall.

'There are', my wife is saying, 'your children to be considered.'

And that completes it for this hour. Traffic is heavy for an instant and then I am alone.

Weeks pass. Months. How much time who can tell? Can more be done to ourselves? Through many of these days my chair is positioned dead into the corner walls. I marvel at this joining of walls. Cruel seam which divides my two eyes while wanting to overlap them in the making of the single eye I would have, the one eye that would have me. My neck aches. Muscles throb. So much wanton checking of activity at my rear — so much weary searching for intersecting lines that have no origin anywhere in this room. All lines begin — or end? — at the front door. I nod ... and dream of passing through it into a sea of mud. Dreaming is the word we give to the life that frog eyes perceive. Body and head become one from there.

'Oh, Sam, Sam!' my wife laments. 'Oh, Sam!' Her backside oils silently through the open door. These people are magicians: they appear and disappear and the air which made space for them is never satisfied. Shock waves flow tirelessly within a radius approximately four feet of this chair. I observe it, drab lump between two gleaming wheels. I try to move from this sterile centre and the void goes with me. Matila, drenched by her own tears, enters and places a peeled orange in my lap. Fat wedges so beautifully orbed. They repose on blue china like old lace, like a roadmap of the planet Earth. I lift the orange in my palm and hold it inches from my face. It stares back at me. It catches the light and for a moment I am able to probe its lovely depth.

Matila vanishes with a stricken cry: 'He won't eat it! He's unmanageable! He's worse than a child, I can't do anything with him!'

The house shudders under the siege of feet running to her rescue.

Liquid dribbles through my fingers and down my arm.

I hear my wife's raucous protest in a distant room: 'God! Haven't we seen enough of his obstinacy! Must he drive us all crazy before he'll be content?'

The drapes are drawn. I sit in a dark pool, and what the eye perceives is a bed of decaying leaves in a stagnant pond. My flesh stinks, yet I would hold out for something finer: the drive of birds in silent flight.

What can I say for myself? I speak of Gore, of Matila, of my wife, I make passing reference to this chair — although nothing is further from my mind than these. I stare at my hands but it isn't these deformed knots I see. The eye is wretchedly endowed: images form prematurely along the optic nerve, introducing mystery patterns on the eye's darker side. It is this which accounts for the sensation often felt: that we are retreating even as our bodies move ahead. It explains too why a dog will chase his own tail.

We meet at the dining table and I find myself asking: Who are these people? What curious forces unite us here? My wife shoves me to the toaster. I am invalid but someone must perform these chores. With his new lip Gore cannot eat toast. He shoves soft bread into his mouth and groans.

'My new lip', he announces, 'is catching on.' Mrruff-mrruff.

He speaks the truth. Earlier today the postman rang the bell, wanting to display the polished ring he wears. Next week we may expect his wife to appear with her breasts exposed, drinking champagne through silver straws, wearing a hat cut for donkey ears. What lengths we won't go, to transmogrify these tiny lives.

When Arturo was a boy he had wanted a dog. The dog died, run over by a car while Arturo stood in the pastry shop buying a loaf of bread to support his mother's stingy meal. *'My dog my dog!'* he cried, and stood out on the pavement, ruined, holding the mangled dog in his arms: stopping traffic, stopping pedestrians who were properly horrified. *'Little boy, don't you know? . . . Little boy, you! . . . Little boy, don't you know you'll get blood all over your clothes? . . . Little boy!. . .*

In the meantime . . . well, it's always in the meantime, every moment that we breathe . . . in the meantime the dog's guts have spilled all over the boy Arturo's arms, the blood flows in a puddle around him, and Arturo — stricken! — what could he do except cry out in the most profound and absurd grief: *'No no no no you can't take him this dog is mine!'* And, weeping, squeeze the sopping beast more tightly to his chest.

Finally someone shows some sense — we are not total morons after all — someone says to someone else, 'This boy is in a state, can't you see he is? This boy needs looking after!' And someone else has roughly the same idea and eventually the boy is approached: 'Little boy, what's your name, where do you live, little boy? Your parents!. . .' And so on, though of course the boy is perplexed with grief, oh, you should have seen the tears wash over him. Even so, he intends to fulfil his purpose here, he's got the loaf of bread still in his arms, mixing with dog to the extent that no one can tell which is which. It requires three people to pry the dog from the boy's arms and three more to restrain him as he attempts to get the dead burden back. 'Little boy, can't you see! ... Little boy! ...' And all the time the boy is screaming, yanking dog fur and guts back to his embrace: *'my dog my dog my dog my dog my dog my dog my dog my dog!...'*

My wife wheels me out into the yard. 'Stop muttering,' she says. 'What is it now? Your dead dog story, I suppose.' She abandons me to the open sky. Had one the vision, I think, one could see through it and beyond. The weather contents me, although it was in this very spot that yesterday a rock struck my chair. Thrown by the small child who lives next door. The fence here is high, I could hear his laboured breathing as he climbed. And his father's quiet encouraging voice: 'Did you *get* him? Did you hit him *hard*?'

We are intelligent, we have emotions, we have will. We have strength. Power innate and much of it at our fingertips. We have all this but we are helpless in every way.

Gore, for instance, makes a rare appearance beside my chair. 'Our wives,' he whispers, 'are looking distinctly odd. I prophesy there soon will be trouble in this neighbourhood.' Mrruff-mrruff. My wife arrives, elbowing him aside. 'I am sorry,' she tells me, 'I have let you remain in the sun too long. Your poor face is on fire, do you hurt?'

She administers a white salve and I find myself struck anew by our pathetic efforts to cajole love out of where it hides. The salve worms under my skin, she delivers bromides, anodynes — tears wet my cheeks in gratitude and pardon me I nap.

When I was a boy....

When Arturo....

When....

The boy's mother was telephoned. She came running over, found no one there, the street empty of traffic — no evidence of madness except for this puddle of blood in front of the pastry shop. She goes running back to her own house, and as she bursts through the front door she sees a half a dozen people she's never seen before, and hears one of them saying, 'He's dead.' He's dead, he's dead.

He's dead.

She rushes forward screaming, lamenting, wailing, pulling her hair, shoving everyone. Grief vanishes the moment she sees her boy standing in the room with the dead dog dripping from his arms. She hurls herself against the boy, shakes him, slaps him, twists and pulls him, all the time shouting I TOLD YOU TOLD YOU I TOLD YOU DIDN'T I TELL YOU I WELL MARK MY WORDS YOU WILL NEVER NEVER NEVER HAVE ANOTHER NEVER ANOTHER DOG! DIDN'T I DIDN'T I WARN YOU TELL YOU SO! She tears at the boy's ears, chops his head, pushes him, shakes the dog out of his arms onto the floor and stays there herself kicking at the dead thing, screaming at it, and now shoving the boy into the bathroom, ripping off his clothes, while the boy shouts back at her *my dog my dog my dog my dog my dog my dog my dog my dog!...*

On and on.

I awake in my chair in the familiar corner, shivering, a grey blanket over my legs. I stare at my hands and for a long time cannot make my fingers move. Behind me Matila is weeping. She and my wife, like twins born only for such emergencies, are pacing the floor. Matila strides a short distance, my wife chases after her. Matila whirls, comes back again. My wife remains at her heels. Each time the distance shortens. Finally they are face to face. They exchange expressions of surprise, they cry out, and fall wounded into each other's arms.

'What can I do now?' moans Matila. 'What now? It's no good telling me this is my own fault!'

'It's our fault,' my wife replies, 'for being here. You could have been sleeping in our bed.'

'I couldn't stand it if you were not here,' sobs Matila. 'What was I thinking of? I must have lost my mind!' Her voice rises, levels off, follows an uncharted route filled with groans, demented appeal for compassion which she cannot grant herself. 'At night it's so different! That ring! His lip! In the dark!' Tears burst forth anew with this declaration, her neck thickens. 'I'm ashamed! I can't bear this humiliation I feel!' Her body folds, and my wife leads her to a chair. She sits and for an instant the grief recedes, Matila's body goes erect, she glares menacingly and shakes a fist at the vast wrongs done to her: 'Another *baby*! The last thing this marriage needs! Now it will be months before I can divorce the prick!'

My wife pulls up another chair, sits so that their knees are touching now: 'I don't know,' she asserts. 'Perhaps the responsibility will bring your husband to his senses. I've never felt that Gore was a hopeless case.' She smiles, sends it crashing to where I sit. I respond with the simple movement of a single finger, which exercise suddenly arouses my stick legs. Lifeless, they thrash about in their hideous dance.

Days go by. Weeks. Lamps know all the wrong hours in this house. Matila's stomach swells, her belly is as immense as her new pride. Oh, Matila, the stiff-legged kangaroo. She smiles and the gleam is on us all.

'I have been neglecting you,' my wife remarks. She brings hot water in an enamel bowl, plops herself on a cushion in front of me. Sponges my legs.

Gore moves from room to room, distracted, muttering to himself. 'A child's perceptions are limited,' he explains. 'All the same a man would be a fool to take unnecessary chances.' He has had the ring removed, wears a black cloth over his chin, is never seen now without the walking stick slung over his left arm. 'The snow,' he says. 'Yesterday I fell, badly bruised this knee,' Snow? Was it not yesterday I sat out under a high sun, sipping juice through a tube, recalling Arturo's dog? Arturo ... afterwards, the next day perhaps, that very night ... out in the backyard burying his dog, going at the earth with a splash of grunts, throwing soil the length of the yard, going down deep, throwing it up hard: *My dog! My dog! My dog!...*'

Snow is indeed packing us in. To my mind we are stuffed here like souring Judases' in a crate. Gore limps from window to window, tap-tap advances his cane. He halts beside Matilda, takes her fingers to his lips: 'And how's my little girl?' Matila blushes, bows her head: she is capable only of whispered speech. Gore moves on to my wife whose hand likewise gracefully awaits. Her face, tinted, with its softened eyes, with its shadowy cheeks — do I recognize it from someplace? Yes, like features imperfectly chiselled at the centre of some clouded moon, viewed through my own foggy telescope. These quarters, from where I sit, are cast in aphotic gloom, much as if Mary Magdalene had come in out of two thousand lonely years of mud and snow to express herself through their wistful eyes. As if she had come in to say: 'The life He gave me was not all He promised it would be.' To be forgiven signifies a dubious advance; to forgive is to ripen into fulsome pain. Gore, too, by his affectations, by his doleful show of warmth, so perceives. Yet I envy him. Once I too must have limped, employed sticks, worn a pinned ascot; with some alacrity and conviction could lift and tease a woman's hand. Now these doorknobs I call hands crawl upward from my lap and scratch to recognize whatever growth exists above or beneath the skin: this circle of raised or indented dots, these fuming pools I call eyes nose and mouth.

Arturo before he died spoke of giving birth to a dozen perfect beasts . . . but before that buried his dog and pitched a tent for half a year in his back yard. His mother nightly stationed herself at the nearest door, shouting her restless warnings into the cruellest darkness she had ever seen: I TOLD YOU TOLD YOU DIDN'T I TELL YOU WHAT WOULD HAPPEN IF YOU GOT A DOG?

Come out here, Arturo replied, and I'll bury us all.

Seasons flush us from these careful holes in which we hibernate. Witness Matila flushed from hers. Arturo's photo removed from the mantelpiece. His mother forming wings or horns for whatever is to be her brief afterlife. Arturo and Matila, Matila and Gore: marriage is whatever our best locket holds. Our lives before we attain them come wrapped in dust. Arturo, brother and friend: in his family and in mine we arrived condemned. My bones are last to survive these wicked, privileged hours. Dust is all-knowing, all-powerful. It appropriates, even engenders where nothing else will. It has the weight of a thousand copper pennies over my eyes.

'But you must eat something!' insists my wife. 'You're snake-thin, you're not getting enough nourishment to keep a frog alive!' She snaps her head away, startled by the note of triumph her voice can't conceal. The words, too, discomfort her: this frog shape is mine. This sack of snakes, dormant always, which forms my body from neck to thighs. My head twists up, I allow an arm its furtive crawl — my wife recoils, finds escape in the busy arrangement of silverware, while I acknowledge with found indifference that vanity thrives under the most obscene of conditions. Gore laughs. I look to find his face at the usual chair and for a moment can discern nothing in that space. Only a swirl of dust on the other side of some milky field. Gore goes on laughing. 'I've got his number,' he says. 'Old Sam is not fooling me!' My hand twitches back to hide again under the grey blanket which supposedly dignifies me. 'Look,' someone exclaims, '— he's crying!' 'Oh, look!' another says, 'what a rush of tears!'

My eyes are indeed aswim. But whose voices are these? How is it that strangers come to be seated here? Has someone invited them? Do I know those voices from somewhere? My wife is making the easy excuse for me: 'Don't let him disturb you. He's probably thinking of Arturo's buried dog.'

'Arturo?' One of these newcomers speaks Arturo's name.

'A previous occupant of this house.' It is Matila bringing dishes, addressing the table with a festive air.

'Ah, Arturo,' responds Gore, '— whatever happened to him?' He lifts his cane, pokes its tip to that space where I breathe.

'Everyone dig in,' Matila says. Her apron falls casually over my knee.

'Eat, eat!' encourages my wife. 'God knows how he lives.' A murmur goes around.

I get enough. I get, in fact, more than my share. I get hers, I get Matila's, and Gore's. I get Arturo's too. I get whatever potion our dead mule most enjoyed.

These newcomers are ravenous. They can't remember when they've dined better or imagine how soon they're likely to have it so well again. Yet while juices drip from their lips they are already recalling the simplicity and beauty of life where they come from. What a glorious future, they assert, one may have there! My wife scoffs, but is too polite to ask why, if so, they have come here. Matila and Gore hold hands, speaking delicately of their tender hopes. 'One child, a single child,' Matila maintains, 'may change the world!'

When I. . . .

I once. . . .

'Arturo's dog —' I begin to say . . . but my wife's laughter drowns me out. 'Mrruff-mrruff!' she barks. 'Mrruff-mrruff,' Gore rejoins. Their laughter spreads around the table and orbits there. My knees quiver, my legs thrash under cover. This weeping does nothing to extricate me. Snakes snooze contentedly in the warmth of my groin. This frog tongue thickens when it greets air. This blanket is dead earth borrowed from a grave. I speak to you of my wife, of Arturo, of Matila and Gore, I make passing reference to mules, dogs, and this chair — yet nothing is further from my mind.

I remember a large house, panoramic grounds. The solemn expressions of ancestors in oval frames. The abiding sovereignty of one massive glass chandelier. My mother in her ghostly. . . .

But someone's hand is resting lightly on my shoulder now. It occurs to me that it has been there for a long time. I look up into the face of one of our dinner guests. She has red hair, I notice, and a small pretty space between two front teeth. 'I'm so tired,' she says to me. Her voice is gay, her eyes amused, as if she means to tell me that she would not exchange this fatigue for anything in the world. 'I'm plumb tuckered out!' Her words waltz merrily, she has the mood of a schoolgirl who has never known this condition before. Behind her other guests are expressing this mutual exhaustion — they stretch and yawn, yet it seems to me this dinner table has rarely seen such ebullience. Chairs are pushed back, the guests rise, and the air makes room for them. It shifts in a frenzy, eventually to settle where they stand. The woman's hand tightens on my shoulder. Her dress, cut low, is of darkest green, and I stare at her close, freckled cleavage. I would be content, I think, to let my head hang there. 'We are new to the neighbourhood,' I hear her say. 'Will you consent to walking us home?'

The moment is awkward. My wife is stacking dishes, Matila and Gore sit as though dazed, staring at their wine glasses. So it is that I volunteer. I rise without difficulty from my chair. The woman smiles as if enchanted and wraps a hand over my arm. I glance back to see my wife's head cocked, her eyes large, her mouth rounded in mute surprise.

I lead our guests out the door, I advance with them along the sidewalk that led them here. I walk with the woman's arm light upon mine. The night has no scent, it has neither colour nor substance of any kind, yet there is nothing I do not recognize. We reach a certain corner and their footsteps pass on ahead.

I see them in the far distance and marvel at the broad backs they have.

Once Arturo, in passing, spoke of his mother: 'She advances, with pail and mop and broom, to clean up battlefields. She —'

I return to find my wife crying, tears plopping into the white beauty of her half-consumed dessert. 'How humiliating this is for me!' she is saying. 'I'm worn out from all that man has put me through!' Gore lifts one drunken eye: 'I told you,' he says. 'Old Sam wasn't fooling me!'

Matila rocks, arms joined over her breasts as if to force down the climbing child. 'It was Arturo,' she moans. 'He would never forgive me for leaving him.'

They return to their despondent watch of my empty chair.

The elevator chugs, it rattles, but it delivers me to this room. Matila's bed is perfectly satisfying. Far more comforting is it than the other in that adjacent room.

I like it better, to tell the truth.

I can stretch out in my full ease here.

It has the scent of talcum and fresh earth. It has Arturo's handprints on every wall. He and I: we were born and raised in rooms such as this. What has become of those oval portraits which were here? Whatever became of our glass chandelier? It cried — we all said it did — whenever anyone moved in rooms above or below. And someone, where I lived, was moving all the time.

'It is weeping', my mother would say, 'for all the nice children you shall have.'

Its beads caught the sun and flashed radiance everywhere.

This flesh is chilled. Eyes seek the darker side.

What is the hurry? The question is immaterial now, yet it is one which engages me.

In our family we were discreet: we mapped out our paths of solitude, and then we fled.

We followed wind gusts — always with an eye alert for the old family trails. 'You go far,' my mother would say, 'but you do come home.'

Matila is first to enter. Her shrouded face, in this light, seems rouged. She too has been crying and now her face further distorts. She whimpers, drawing up a chair. In a moment she will tell me that Arturo was no better than other men. That she could not live — could not survive — with him. That no woman could. She bends nearer, fixing her sight on mine. He wet eyes glisten. She has not two eyes but pieces in a chain of jewels which could secure the world. The depths which open to me are incalculable; were I of a mind to I could follow this chain to places both beautiful and horrible.

The chain weakens; slowly it vanishes there. We see only what fronts us here. Matila bows her head and gnaws at the fist in her mouth. Her shoulders heave. Tears burst from her.

'It's your fault!' she cries. 'You would not share yourself! Don't expect me to grieve! Everything was always such a secret with you! I feel nothing! Nothing! And Arturo would say the same!'

This vindictiveness is so shallow it barely touches me. I speak calmly of the futility of such assertions and denials. She pretends to hear nothing. She grinds both fists against her teeth, now sobbing all the more. To my mind it is fear and guilt convulsing her. It is Arturo trying to leap inside. 'You deserve this!' she cries. 'You deserved it all!'

My dog! *My* dog! *My* dog!

I am the mirror of her enraged eyes. We would both sweep me

up like some long dead fly, poke me with sticks until I am driven to the most remote garbage pile. A person's eye is monstrous, it sees around and beyond the woman in this room. It sees the space that is missing here. It sees space tumbling in upon space, the rubble of waves where nothing upright moves. The ear expands. It asks the value of this daily sacrifice. Defending one's self is the last indignity. The ear is magic: it listens to nothing. Yet these bones continue to anoint themselves. The longest war is one of nerves. Love bends to its pleasure as it flees towards another transient ache.

The eye widens.

Flesh is all mouth and devours itself.

'Oh, Sam, Sam, you've done it at last!'

My wife's form shivers between these high bedposts at the foot of the bed. Her finger spins a meaningless insignia, while her nostrils flare with a poison old in her.

Incantations are aswirl throughout this house.

Her hands smack together, they clutch and wring. She would murder the last duty that has forced her here.

What have we done to our lives? What brings us to this mad rapture we call remorse? Snakes crawl out from my guts and I feel little more than a tingle in that cavity where they were. My own remorse is waiting to crawl inside. I lament these times. The dreadful vigour of seasons, the shove of year into year.

I can recall a large house, panoramic grounds. During his last years my father slowly cruising the fenced-off yard in his motorized chair. Myself at a high window watching him.

My wife claws at bedposts. 'Why? Why? Why did it have to be like this?' Who am I to say which of us is haunted most?

The moon's pull is stronger than my own. These people by size are life-like. They walk, they speak, they will go on doing so. Others will take the place of those who stand here. I will reappear among the dust motes and give the kiss to every hand.

But now....

When I....

Mrruff-mrruff....

My face takes the oval frame. Nothing is obscured. I see back all the way.

I rise, and return to my chair.

'This is madness!' the two women shout. 'Why does he do this to us!'

What have we done to our women to so incline them now to these accusations? To this loyalty? To this melodrama? What have we done to ourselves that induces us to notice?

The single eye of the swivelfish, confronting phenomena, enlarges. The eye becomes all.

All that is outside will now come in.

Say no more, I tell myself.

Reveal nothing.

By morning no trace shall remain.

My dog! My dog! My dog!

Biographical Notes

BRIEF BIOGRAPHICAL NOTES on some of the people called to give evidence for or against me:

MARCELINE ABLE (1964-) Material to come.

WANDA LEE CASSLAKE My Dead Friend.

Wanda Casslake came into my life nine years ago when I was thirty-five and branching out and never left it although she quit her own for reasons that remain to be extricated by someone better equipped to deal with biographical history than I am. Natural actor and wonderful human being. A pleasure-loving woman with a generous heart who always made the most of her appearance, on-screen or off, and only wanted everyone to think the worst of her. Bust like a boy's. Married to:

ROBIN HARVEY (1935-) Actor.

On camera, he rarely knew what to do with his hands: one had to take enormous care with angles because his head tended to photograph excessively large. The Floating Wedge, as this is called in the trade. The best a critic could ever think to say of him (*Great Speckled Bird*) was that he knew 'how to undress casually while indifferently smoking a joint.' He could at times surprise us, but he was, for the most part, an awful bore. Robin found little in life about which to be enthusiastic. He was fond of reminiscing over the recent past. If I went out with Robin and Wanda for a night of drinking and relaxation after a gruelling day on the set, Robin's sole delight was in reminiscing over what the three of us had done the previous evening. Actually, he was never sure what we'd done and would remain unsure even after we had told him. Powerfully built, but with a slow, uncomplicated mind.

Canadian. Most of the people in these Notes are. I cite this with some hesitancy, since in my view the information yields little that is vital. Circumstance is relevant, origin is not, and accident is the father of mankind. National origin has significance relative only to transitory phenomena. It was for this reason that the stork, flying through skies belonging to no one, was selected to carry our early burden (trademark, by the way, of our first eight films). Such oddities of persuasion received frequent airings by Wanda and me. Robin Harvey found these musings of no consequence and normally went off to talk and drink with other individuals, some of whom no doubt were only too happy to tell him what he had done the previous evening. Wanda — who made a point of never telling me where she was from or what her family situation had been, just as she would never reveal her age or why she had married Robin or admit that she had ever read a book — Wanda, being the argumentative type, naturally disputed all notions relative to the common brotherhood of living beings exclusive of any vital differences incurred through country of origin, religion etc., foo-fawing for that matter *any* lofty ideas I might propose.

'Why then', I might ask her, 'do you continue to work? Work without a higher purpose is a pokey thing indeed.'

I do it for the money, came her inevitable reply. *I do it because I enjoy titillating the hicks, and because being denigrated by a society made up of people who are not as honest about themselves as I am affords me considerable masochistic kicks.*

'If I thought that', I would tell her, 'I would fire your can tomorrow. You are a great artist and through your art we are reshaping the planet.'

Oh, Martin, she would say in her fiery yet sad little way, *you are only trying to find an excuse for this terrible thing we do.*

Wanda Casslake took the opposite view on every question I ever raised, from the simplest to the most abstruse, even arguing that her breasts were 'of quite the normal size' — this despite ample proof to the contrary which for years flowed through 16mm projectors every Saturday night at a hundred private cinema clubs and societies around the world. All now confiscated, I should explain. Scheduled for destruction the minute my last appeal is refused. Nothing of her remains in my possession except ten stills shot one sour, forlorn evening a week before her death. But not shot by me. These photographs, incidentally, I have wanted unpublished for the good reason that Wanda's flat chest does not lift them above the obscene. They have no redeeming social value. They are as dirty as they come. Which is why I held on to them. The point I would make about their existence is that filth remains filth until someone with a humanist perspective comes along and transforms it, often through art, into a thing that takes the measure of the beauty and depth of human life.

Police continue to snoop about, paid informers lurking on every corner.

'I want those pictures, Martin,' Robin tells me.

'Oh, shove it,' I tell him. 'Wanda was adamant in maintaining that she owed nothing to you, that her marriage to you was largely accidental, regrettable, barely worth the paper that made it official.'

I'll sue you, he says.

Opportunist, 5′8″, balding, something of a card shark, proponent of the *laid-back life* and for that reason a happy choice for roles opposite Wanda as his every indifferently delivered line and gesture served to symbolize a) the dehumanization of oppressed working classes everywhere; b) twentieth-century man gone soft through luxury; and c) that intelligent women will always give themselves to brutes too dense to value what they are receiving.

Drinks too much. Recently converted to Catholicism.

Her co-star through the twenty-three films comprising the *Night* series.

Less said of him the better.

RITA ISLINGTON (age approximately 42) Education, occupation, marital status, etc. unknown.

A short time ago, fresh on the heels of my incarceration and release on bond, a woman showed up at my door, announced that her name was as listed above, and that she had an interest in buying her sister's photographs, no questions asked — though she hoped my price would not be unreasonable.

'Who was your sister?'

Wanda Lee Casslake.

'I never would have known.' A shrug of her shoulders. 'Who told you I have them?'

I can't say.

'Did Robin send you?'

I suppose you mean her husband. I have never met him.

'How did you find me?'

Through your lawyer.

'Are you acting on behalf of yourself or for others?'

I want only to salvage what remains of my sister's reputation.

'She was a great actress.'

I do not agree.

'Where was Wanda born? What were her parents like? For a long time I've been very interested.'

Such questions are not pertinent to this negotiation.

'Are we negotiating?'

I hope so. I do not like to have my time wasted.

'Have you ever worked in cinema?'

You are prying. Let us talk price.

'What in your view constitutes a reasonable sum?'

I think you will find my offer liberal.

She opened her purse. As it turned out, the sum offered was liberal indeed. My black onyx bowl was soon stacked high with her currency. 'No,' I said.

No?

For the first time she seemed to be about to lose her temper. I sensed, if I may say so, a whiff of danger.

You will not sell them to me?

I sensed, emanating from her, an uncompromising hatred. Her skin had gone white. A moment later she smiled and my suspicions seemed ludicrous. On an impulse I decided to let her have the negatives. *Without charge.* The last is important to the view I have of myself, which is why I have it italicized. I have never made money unfairly off any person and would certainly not do so off Wanda. I did what I could for Wanda. I tried to make her happy, without becoming too involved.

Don't get too close to me, Martin, she would say. *Don't get involved.*

I gave her a job, propped her up when her faith in herself was low. I lent her money and saw to it that her child was taken care of when Robin wouldn't and Wanda herself was in no shape to do so. The material we had to work with professionally was often of dubious quality though I did my best to imbue it with substance. (This is equivocation: the fact is I yearn to burn my bridges and start over.) But I did these things with no intention of acquiring credit for myself. I did them out of the simple belief that we owe loyalty to those we would call our friends, and with full knowledge that had our situations been reversed she would have done as much for me. Wanda was argumentative, she liked to make people believe that she had not a brain in her head; in fact she was an extraordinary woman who repudiated her own vast gifts out of a deep-seated psychosis I could never probe but which the camera often understood.

'Would you care to see the child?' I asked Rita Islington.

I believe not. I do not care for children.

Strange Rita Islington.

I surrendered the negatives to her for no other reason than that she intrigued me. In the years I had known Wanda she had never mentioned having a sister. Yet how frequently do I mention my six brothers?

I trusted her.

She reeked of scent — an exotic perfume almost as permeating as incense. She wore spiked heels made of a lovely soft leather the colour of the sky. Her co-ordinated purse boasted a musical signature. Her hair was fully a yard long, with a high sheen even in my dimly lit reception-room. She refused to take off her glasses, the lenses of which were so curved and dark I never saw her eyes, despite my frequently assumed stance to this or that side of her.

Pardon me. Am I making you nervous? You appear unable to stand still.

Her voice was throaty, mellifluous — as if it liked to recline on a velvet cushion when not in use. Her language was precise, which characteristic heightened an already regal bearing, reminiscent of that developed by Marlene Dietrich while under the baton of Josef von Sternberg. Moreover, having once offered payment of money (there was never any hint that she was prepared to go further), she seemed not at all surprised that I refused it:

Gallantry still lives, n'est ce pas? — and allowed her ungloved hand to rest in mine longer than form would concede necessary. Nor did she make any objection to my stated intention to retain as my personal property the single set of prints made from those very negatives and which occupied in plain view the walls enclosing us. *Mmmmm,* I recall she said, *I find this affection you have for the small bosom incomprehensible.*

'I was fond of Wanda.'

I noted that she appeared herself to be normally endowed, though her dress was not of a style to call attention to this.

She had visibly lovely legs, and the most beautiful lips I have ever seen.

Since she gave no indication of hurry, I offered her coffee. She declined. She did not drink of the bean, she said. I then offered alcohol, and this also she refused. Though she did say a moment later that she would drink with me if I insisted. By this hour she had arranged herself comfortably on my sofa, and had already, without looking at them, dispatched the negatives to her purse.

'Why should I insist?' I asked rudely. 'I would hardly be likely to compel a total stranger to drink with me.' As a matter of fact, my composure was broken. Prior to her arrival I had been drinking steadily.

Is it true, she wanted to know, *that you were my sister's lover?*

'Never,' I said. 'I am married — or was — and treasure fidelity.'

How odd, she laughed, *for a porn king.*

Such statements intimidated me.

She wore a fur hat, in addition to other finery. I vividly recall this because my estranged wife had only recently lost a similar hat. My impression, before making a proper study, had been that this woman was wearing my wife's property.

'How did you come by your nice hat?'

It was the gift of my first husband.

'You have been married then ... more than once?'

You are notoriously inquisitive. This, I would guess, is of value to one of your calling.

'It wasn't a calling. It was simply something to do. Easy money. Corn for the butterballs.'

That does not correspond with my sister's image of you.

'A rabid fanatic?'

She rose to go, once more offering her hand. I kissed it. I don't believe I have ever done that before. Even in jest. I opened the door. A drab light spilled in from the hall. I suddenly did not want her to go. I felt like a man about to go over a cliff on a bicycle (*Night Plus Morning*, 1973). I could hear loneliness rushing at me in full stampede.

'Don't go yet. Please.'

Goodbye. You have been most kind.

That remark turned the trick. My spirits lifted. I no longer had any interest in keeping her.

Her ankles disappeared inside the Rolls Corniche Mark II parked at the curb.

ELAINE HIGHTOWER WOLFE (1942-) Female Caucasian, born in Manhattan, matriculated at Wyoming State Christian College for Women (BA) and Colorado University at Boulder (MA in Human Resources). A former waitress, car-hop, interior decorator, receptionist, currently part-time media/projects critic for erratically published journals. Emigrated to Canada in 1967, married five years later, no children.

My estranged wife.

Writes from time to time an uninspired, thematic, therapeutic verse which is then set to music and given the occasional performance at well-attended feminist meetings. Does a nice softshoe when drunk (rarely).

The most marvellous of women.

Identifying scars: on her lower abdomen, which I shall not tell you about.

For the period of time with which these Notes are concerned, she was living apart from me, though in the same neighbourhood, until such time as, in our counsellor's phrase, 'we got our priorities sorted out.' The above disclosure has hidden reference to a) the vanity of Elaine Wolfe which drives her to want and need an independent life, and b) the relative insecurity of Elaine Wolfe which drives her to want and need a husband, together with c) outside pressures which insist that she not throw away her life. We are both entrapped and our emotions made banal by the afterburn of love achieved through six years of matrimony.

Eyes: blue.

Chin: erect.

That she is a pretty woman, an intelligent and humorous woman, and a powerfully intense personality is affirmed often enough by

EDWARD HIGHTOWER (1919-) Father of the above

OLIVE HIGHTOWER (-) Mother of the above

GERTRUDE HIGHTOWER MEWS (1896-) grandmother of the above

and sundry relatives and friends (see Notes below). A wealth of additional values has been likewise aggressively advanced, to wit:

Elaine is a fine woman, a tower of strength.

Elaine has only your happiness in mind.

Elaine is selfless to the extreme. There is nothing she wouldn't do for you.

You had better get a hold of yourself or you are going to lose this veritable jewel who is unabashedly still in love with you but is no one's fool, who adores the ground you walk on and has never looked at another man but who cannot forever be treated as a doormat. Moreover, she has charm, a sweet disposition, money of her own, and a character that is positively radiant. You are going to wake up one morning an old man alone if you don't soon come to realize and appreciate that an angel is what you have.

Agreed, and then some.

No sooner had my mystery caller, Rita Islington, departed than did Elaine Wolfe arrive to remind me of these many paragon qualities (not that *she* would; her presence, I am saying, did so), while at the same time hoping to wring out of me the identity of the woman in question, together with that mission which had summoned her to my door.

Who was she? What did she want? Oh, Martin, you're not going to make those films again!

Because we can't stand to make another unhappy we often opt for the quickest cruelty. I immediately took to the telephone, not at that time disconnected, dialling one

PETER MAHONEY (1918-) Noted attorney, city council member, twice unsuccessful candidate for mayor on the NDP ticket, author of the monographs *Divorce in Las Vegas, The Scottish Decree, Totem and Taboo,* etc.

'She is harassing me,' I told this man, and he immediately divined that my reference was to Elaine Wolfe. He asked that I summon her to the phone. I complied and judge that he reminded her of the delicacy of the situation, that he and her parents' lawyers were working diligently to iron out an agreement which he could promise her would in due time be resolved to everyone's satisfaction, including the court's.

But I don't want a divorce, she told him. *I don't even want this separation.*

I was then recalled. *Guard against depression*, he warned. *Don't do anything silly.*

'I'll get twenty years.'

He laughed. *We shall see.*

'If we thought we had some chance of getting Angelia,' I said, 'we could hold on.'

My wife wept. We both wept.

Does it have to be like this? she cried.

'I don't know.'

I forgive you. If that's all that's standing between us. If there is anything to forgive.

We hugged, fondled and continued to weep. 'It helps,' I admitted, 'but you know very well there is no way out. You have your future, not to mention your reputation, to think about.'

I don't care about that! It's my place to stand beside you!

I reminded her that her parents' hearts would be broken, their health thrown in jeopardy, if she took up with me again.

'Already your father has had one mild attack. That comes directly to my door.'

Yes, but Angelia! Unless we're together Angelia will surely be taken away. It's that bitch Marceline's fault! I could wring her neck!

'She's a friend of the court. We can't touch Marcy.'

Oh, Martin, why did you ever have anything to do with her!

We wrung our hands, moaned until our throats hurt, ranted over the injustices done to us by society and friends, searched about helplessly for a ray of sunshine, and finally threw ourselves together on the floor and found brief happiness in that physical union which assuages the bleakest hour.

Oh, love, oh, beauty!

Christ, I love a passionate woman.

Weeping without hope, she then fled.

I was utterly distraught, a crawling wound, too worn out even to endure the long struggle toward bliss via alcohol. In my self-pity I reached for the one kind review my work has ever received, seeking pathetic recompense from

MICHEAL OBLE (-) Semi-reputable freelance art and film critic, Assistant Librarian at the Spadina Street branch of the Toronto Public Library, author of the celebrated article (*en Route*, the in-flight magazine of Air Canada, June 1978, pp.29, 40, 51), *Pornography with a Message: The Underground Films of Martin D. Wolfe.*

The most recent of the *23 films of M.D. Wolfe opens with a massively detailed, nearly interminable sequence made up of the same repeated, gradually expanding scene. Fade in on a barren plain where a clump of ant-like creatures congregates. Viewed by a single hand-held camera at considerable distance, a lone figure appears. Puffs of smoke drift up lazily into an overcast sky. The figure falls. As the smoke wafts away we have superimposed, the camera infinitesimally nearer, an all but exact re-enactment. This time one can faintly hear the pop of gunfire a few seconds after the figure has again collapsed. Superimpose and begin once more, the same scene imperceptibly nearer, the action extending a few frames longer.*

Our audience begins to fidget and some to demand a return of their money.

It turns out before long that our victim is a woman; with each rebirth of the scene more and more flesh is exposed. Is Wolfe giving us, then, an elaborate striptease? Those hesitating in the aisles decide to reclaim their seats. This may after all be the show the posters promised.

More smoke and gunfire. We are well into Biographical Nights *before it comes to us that what we are perceiving is not what have perceived; and by the time this 90-minute feature drives to its close the original seven-second opening takes all of one hour to recount and has become another narrative indeed. Along the way, the distant, rather pretty gunfire has given way to machine-gun bursts, rocket fire, and in the end to full-scale battlefield explosions which are integrated with the sustained shrieks and howls of ferocious dogs. Overheard fragments of speech become diatribes, though here too there are surprises, for the language is no longer English. The once barren plain has become a mirage in which any environment is possible. Wolfe can even manage to find in it room to continue his obsessions with factory interiors. Figures seen initially in military uniforms, later in priestly robes or in the elegant attire of heads of state, are next seen as beggars, convicts, amputee veterans, and eventually as the working-class representatives without which no Wolfe film is complete. Nothing is secure, Wolfe appears to be telling us. Nothing is to be counted on. Place is totally unreliable. Who we are is the most specious of inventions. Wolfe's few converts will know, however, that whatever else this director may be, he is not a mere illusionist. His scene employs mirage as metaphor but inside that mirage much is hardcore naturalism. Thus when the camera swings away from a tight shot of the face of our old friend Wanda, looking more enigmatic than ever, we are not altogether astonished that the wide lens reveals the familiar over-large, bobbing head of Robin Harvey as he does his sexual labour over her. Blue-collar Harvey this is — hungover, laid-back, no doubt thinking of his wages as he looks indifferently out at us. Clearly his mind is not on Wanda. He sees us, it would seem, and nods a non-committal greeting. The camera withdraws farther. We are inside Wolfe's infamous textile factory. As far as the eye can see, a thousand looms are projected, repeating this act of bestial rape, of intermittent harmony. The factory hums with vicious lust, though the greater horror resides in the machines which roar on in the production of more and more undistributed profit.*

Wolfe has moved out from the most distantly objective portrayal of one victim's story into the dark and tangled heart of material in which perpetrator, victim and spectator blindly collaborate. He confronts his audience with the bitter notion that misconceptions which apply to his subject matter apply to our own lives as well. Guilt weighs heavily on us all, he would have us acknowledge, but the eye which finally perceives truth is the one that must make the largest sacrifice. His is the one to educate priests, reform heads of state, dismantle the military, deliver us into good and secure biographical night. A sense of shifting guilt permeates this film, as indeed it does much of the Night *series in its entirety. All parties absorb a share — the working classes, for instance, with which Wolfe is most allied, in their* need *for heroes, even in their* need *for God. Yet he repudiates the belief that they have a need for someone, human potentates, to tell them how to run their lives. Better God, he argues, than us. Their virtues are seen as constant and surpass the ill or goodwill of those who would so instruct. Identities shift in his films in order to dramatize a theory of universal brotherhood but once that is seen he wants us to recognize that the main weight of guilt never shifts. It is an incorrigible property of that elusive party so rarely physically present where atrocity prevails. The people who exploit and kill Wanda in this film are indicted but the burden of guilt flows elsewhere. This ultimate source is nameless but one can never doubt that it exists, or that it is plotting new crimes even as this one transpires, or that at all cost it must be tracked down. Wanda, unfortunately, does not suspect. She believes in her heart that this is happening to her because of something she has done. She does not aggressively resist her destruction partly because she views this end as rightful payment for her vanity, for her few moments of pleasure, for wanting something better. It is this twisted nobility of spirit, this forlorn innocence that moves us so and for which she earns our begrudging respect. We leave the theatre with sex-drive diminished, with the lust to revenge her permanently intact.*

But are Wolfe's films high-class porn, or are they art? One is beginning to hear murmurs of support. More than a few have passed up Swedish Hotbox *and* The Devil in Miss Jones *for* Biographical Nights. *Martin Wolfe, we can suppose, does not live in hell; his films, however, remind us that he would be vastly happier if the public his films are aimed at were less content to do so. Despite their intensely sexual nature, his films make deeply religious statements so arduous in their pursuit of change that, left to their own devices, they might in time confound the Pope, foment revolution and topple governments. That they are made in the first place is an expression of the director's optimism and faith.*

Biographical Nights *exposes with startling clarity the design which has persisted through the whole of this man's cinematic career. He radically marries pornography with earnest morality. Base lust is his symbol for greed in all its forms. Pornography is the vessel which transports his devious socio-political message, geared to lure an unsuspecting public into the theatre — and out of it a different person. It is for this unique premise that he might be justifiably attacked. Undoubtedly, his defence would be that while the New Wave gave us masterpieces, it politically affected little. One can almost hear Wolfe laying down the ground rules to his incredible and infinitely patient Wanda: 'The most permanent revolution begins by gathering its harvest from the bottom. If we can reform drunks and degenerates, if we can turn a nation of confirmed voyeurs into activists, we can reform anyone. Your hot breath, your boy's chest, and Robin's glazed eyes, will render them susceptible.' His aim, I believe, is to crack heads wide open. To this end he disposes of Freud, incorporates Masters and Johnson, and goes Marx one better.*

OBLE, OBLE, my eternal thanks to Oble. A review I was all but tempted to send to my mother. A few thoughts are wrong but I cannot quibble. When this item first came to our notice, my wife and I, with Robin and Wanda, booked a table at Antoine's and held an extended post-mortem. Elaine read it, read it again, cried, and went back to it once more. 'It's so right', she gushed. 'Beautiful, it's beautiful.' Her eyes shone. She wriggled close, unable to touch me often enough. I couldn't eat my escargots or dip my bread in their juices without poking her in the ribs. 'You're wonderful, oh, Wanda isn't Martin wonderful?' The pleasure this man Oble gave her, how I wish he had been at the table. She had never been more radiant, so much the Pike's Peak of Love. It grieved me that I had no more reviews to show her, no trophies to pull from my pockets. I felt wretched, thinking of all the years I had made this fine woman endure public disgrace. And how I, too, needed that praise ... doubt piled upon doubt, scorn heaped upon scorn, all receding now.

Robin's mouth silently shaped this or that imponderable word. 'I don't get it,' he muttered at last. 'What does this turkey mean? Was I hung over? Why can't he just call it a good skin flick and let it go at that?'

When Wanda read it she howled. She laughed so hard and so long we were obliged to apologize to Antoine and his other guests. 'Oh-oh-oh!' she gasped, 'this is killing me! What a hoax! Oh, Martin, did you have to pay him a lot of money?'

Elaine, wounded for my sake, turned on her in a fury: 'That isn't true, you're a beast to say that.'

'It is true, our pictures are garbage, that's all they are, Martin's not a saint and I'm not Garbo, if the public had any sense we'd all be in jail.'

Elaine burst into tears. She wrenched at the table-cloth, spilt her water, shook violently all over, quite fed up with our companions.

Robin appealed to us all. 'Look, we're here to have a good time, forget our troubles. Let's behave ourselves. I'm confused about that mention of rockets. I never saw any rockets.'

'If they want to call *smut* political and a means for social change,' stormed Wanda, 'that's their business. All the *Nights* pictures are trash! *Dirt! Filth! Slop!* Nothing more!' She was in a rage, bristling, her beautiful eyes steaming with venom.

'You're frightened,' I told her. 'Why? Why does it scare you that the films might be good? That they might be worthwhile?'

'I know who *I* am! I know *what* I am too. I don't need any jerk cinephile to justify my existence!'

Elaine too was primed for war, in no mood to let this coarse assessment slide. She banged the salt shaker on Wanda's salad plate, picked up a fork and raked it over the table like a dagger. 'You were wonderful in that picture!' she shouted. 'You are a fine human being! A wonderful mother! Martin's too modest, I don't suppose he's told you that he gets letters from strangers saying how you have changed their lives!'

'One,' I corrected. 'One letter.'

'Yes! From a man reborn! From a man martyred in Ethiopia because of what the *Night* pictures did to him.'

Wanda reddened. But she did not speak, her thoughts deflected by Ethiopia's unknown dead. I was devising a theory about Wanda. It would destroy her, I sensed, if she ever came to realize that she'd somehow come out of whatever foul, stench-infested, brutalizing place she'd started from and developed into the extraordinary person she now was. If it ever dawned on her that she *was* out of it now. No one is ever *safely* out of it. There is no green benign place, no happily anointed field, no sanctuary where one may cast off the memory of what one was. No amount of sophisticated cinema talk, none of the high-fashion clothes or expensive restaurants or the nice car and lavish apartment she could now afford could convince her that she had not been murdered once upon a time. These outer trappings were fine, they gave pleasure, but the heart and soul that is murdered once is one that stays murdered forever. It marches on . . .

Look, Martin, I heard one of them say, *he's plotting out our next picture.*

... it marches on in our false bones, enjoying good food, good music, physical love, the company of friends, it takes luxuries and comforts as they come, but it will not be deceived. It knows this delicious camouflage can't resurrect what has been permanently destroyed. Wanda would allow no one to tamper with this horrible, abiding vision. That vision must not be altered because to alter it she would have to forgive. And nothing — whether person, place or God — deserved forgiveness of those crimes committed against her, the mundane stench of which she breathed daily. They deserved reminders. The steady vigil of accusation. This was the film I had always wanted to make of Wanda and never had. Eternal victim. Everpresent accuser. Perpetual riddle of human life. A straight narrative, no tricks, no gimmicks, an old-fashioned tale, one that parents could take their children to see.

The ardour of expression at our table had thinned. Elaine was squeezing Wanda's hands across the table, her shoulders routed between two candlesticks. 'One letter,' she was saying. 'But such a letter! Lives made over — that's what art can accomplish!'

Wanda squeezed out a thin laugh.

'What I object to in all this review business,' said Robin, 'is how critics can only talk about directors these days. One mention he gives me, one stinking line! If I hear another word about Russ Meyer or Bertolucci or that crowd I'll throw up.'

'Not here, I hope,' teased Wanda. 'Not tonight.' She smiled at my wife. Eyes gone lazy. Her enigmatic face. 'I apologize. Pay no attention to me. You know I never know what I'm saying.' She lifted the champagne bottle out of its ice-bed and poured our glasses full. 'I didn't know I was part of a revolution. Guerrilla action, is that what it is, Martin? Me, a poor girl off the farm in ...' She paused, batted her eyelids at me, inserted a thumb briefly in her mouth: 'Look at Martin, he's suddenly all ears. I almost gave away where I was from. You're such a pest, Martin, so boring — as if it matters where I was born or how poor or rich my parents were. For all the years I've known him he's been itching to hear me confess that I was born an orphan, raised in a church home where I was beaten and went unfed, or that if I had a father I was kept out of school and raped and made to sleep under the front porch with dogs.'

'That's Martin to a T,' piped in Elaine as if this remark struck her as a sudden revelation. 'He's got theories about us all. Because I was overly protected in my youth he's convinced that even today I need a nanny in my room and the light on when I sleep. It's only through subterfuge that I ever got to see his films. I had to lie and claim I was shopping or seeing friends.'

I raised my glass in a toast to these two teasers.

'What do *you* think?' Robin asked me, jabbing a finger at Oble's review. 'Do you take this brainy stuff seriously?'

'Yes,' the women chorused. 'Tell us what you think!'

My wife's hand cruised along my thigh as she snuggled her head against me.

The truth is that, between one thing and another, I was close to tears. 'I do think,' I said, 'that except for Elaine, this is the first truly nice thing anyone has said about me since I was twelve years old.'

'Boo!' croaked Robin. 'He's drunk.'

The women regarded me with wonder, smiling tenderly, warmed to see so much sentimentality exposed. 'Oh, God,' mourned Wanda, 'he's going to cry now. He always does on the set.'

'When *I* was twelve,' joked Robin, 'I was looking to reform school as a step up in the world.'

'You still are,' observed Elaine, shushing him. She turned to me. 'What was said to you at twelve? Can you remember?'

'Vividly. My mother came in from work one day and found me sweeping. Into the corner where I had the dust-pan waiting ...'

The women's eyes never left me. They were enjoying this moment, yet at the same time feared the cavalry would charge over the next hill and whisk me to safety before I could reveal my secret.

'He was desperately poor,' said Elaine by way of illumination. 'His mother, alone, had to raise seven children. Martin had no shoes and when his teeth rotted they were extracted by slamming doors. He won't forgive anyone for this. He holds us all responsible.'

'What did your mother say?' asked Wanda.

'She said I was beautiful. That I had a beautiful soul. She told me I had the spirit of an angel.'

Wanda sighed, not masking her disappointment, murmuring, 'Now that's true deprivation' — no doubt recalling her own forced labour as a child and finding my gallantry feeble by comparison. 'To hell with this,' remarked Robin. 'I'm tired of hearing about disadvantaged people.' He excused himself and left the table. My wife contentedly massaged my thigh. I survived the brutal confession. We stuffed ourselves with food and kept the champagne flowing.

It was a fine evening. Our last together with Wanda.

MARY NAPELS (b.d. & description withheld by request)

Helpful neighbour, homemaker and good sport, nicknamed 'Mosie' by her friends: 'Hello, Mosie.'

Hi, Martin, how is my favourite convict this evening?

Contributor of $500 toward my bail. Overweight, but doesn't like to be reminded. Confronts every issue with brutal fact.

You deserved it, Martin. I hate your films. I don't care that they are part of our sexual liberation. I'd rather be uptight with Queen Victoria. I don't care about your good intentions. Your condemnations smack of the celebratory. I recall with a shudder that scene from Peppermint Nights *when you have Göring meditating on his victims like Narcissus bent over his image at the pool. I bathe a long time after viewing your films.*

'Why did you put up money for my bail?'

One feels protective of fools. And you've toned down the vulgarity, you've become more tasteful of late.

Dropped by only yesterday evening, by appointment, and helped me cook a succulent dinner.

Don't worry. I won't jeopardize your chances for getting Wanda's kid returned. I'm perfectly willing to tell the judge you'd make a lovely parent.

For this repast we were joined by

SANDRA OLSON (1939-)

A semi-official visit. Former enemy, now new-found supporter and co-conspirator, a Family Affairs investigator.

How's tricks, gang?

she asked, plopping down beside the crab dish a bottle of Spanish burgundy with a home-made label.

I come with greetings from Angelia Latishia Casslake who pines for her return to the pornographer's bosom. Now, don't weep, Martin, but this altercation with your wife worsened your case.

'There is no altercation. She left because her parents promised her they'd die of a broken heart if she stayed with me.'

We can hardly tell that to the court. Nor can we tell it that her father has threatened your life. We are up the familiar creek, honey bunch.

We weep, all three. One good cry leads to another and soon Sandra is regaling us with vivid reports of her own fanatical and brutal father whose stated mission in life had been the terrorization of all females and the blowing up of all foreign embassies and banks on home soil. To succeed in the latter he was often obliged to be out of town, for which his family gave incessant thanks to their dimly perceived saviour. I held her hand while she told me of the nightly humiliations, and how reprieve came at last when one of his Montreal bombs prematurely exploded. Later on, with Mosie off to her bed, I told Sandra Olson something of my own story.

Martin Martin Martin I feel so sorry for you!

'Oh, I don't know. Other people have survived worse nightmares.'

I should have curled up and died! It's awful, awful!

That my tale was more terrible than her own she conceded, and this, I judge, made her feel better — as it did me — about facing the dawn which by this hour was nearly upon us.

I'm going home now. Try not to worry.

'Oh, you're a joker, Olson, you are.'

I could not sleep. Donning a disguise that would fool no one, least of all myself — slouch hat, upturned trenchcoat, a walking stick to complement an imagined limp — I aimlessly followed footpaths, lanes and alleys in the neighbourhood, gaining forlorn solace in thinking about

MIRANDA PROBST (now in her eighties) My high school French teacher. Children's counsellor and church organist, retired. She befriended me when I was a youth and isolated from my peers. *You were such a nice, awkward, almost backward child. Much too sensitive for your own good. So shy, so honest. I told you I would pass you but you said you deserved to fail. You must come and see me again before I die. What have you done with your life, dear boy? You must tell me sometime, I know it would make me proud. My friends here will be green with envy over this new shawl.*

'POOPS' THOMAS (about my age) Obese boyhood chum, the only person I was ever able to torment without fear of reprisal. Nothing known of his adult life. Where are you, Poops? Have you found happiness?

LEO YSELOVICH (-) My high school history teacher who pushed the cycle theory with such malice and vengeance that I have not abandoned it to this day. Born a Dukhobor, old religious sect exiled (7,000 of them) to Canada from Tsarist Russia in 1898 after years of famine and persecution (*Night of the Tsars,* 1974). He wore the same sweater year after year and seemed always to walk over the same path dogs had taken a moment before. Tall, bespectacled, a chain-smoker. Elderly now and possibly deceased. I like to think he influenced lives more complimentary to him than mine. Hounded out of the public school system at age fifty-six for alleged homosexuality, not heard of since.

RUDOLPH PUCARD (1926-) A servant of the people. RCMP vice detective. Pucard had but one goal, to 'send smut merchants back where they came from.' Grim, bedevilled little bachelor a shade up from Maigret. Attended perhaps fifty screenings of the *Night* films in search of a psychological edge to be used against their perpetrators. Became, as a result, confused. Grieved deeply over Wanda's suicide.

Wanda: *I like him fine. Have you ever noticed that his right eyelid droops? I like that.*

My arresting officer, January 1978. *We've got the Able girl's statement, sonny-boy. It's a crock of scum but the department wants you and they don't care how.* Refused to testify under oath at the pre-trial hearing that the accused had unlawful carnal knowledge of one Marceline Able, minor, and that he did thereafter with reprehensible greed force her to work for him on the street as a common prostitute.

My lawyer: *Your Honour, I object to the nasty manner in which the prosecuting attorney has dropped this ugly charge.*

Me: *It's all a filthy lie, Your Honour.*

The Judge: *I would advise the honourable defence attorney to restrain his client or I shall have him gagged.*

My lawyer: (whisper): *Shut up, you fool.*

The Judge: *Detective Pucard, to your knowledge was the accused this child's pimp?*

Pucard: *Your Honour, I uncovered no such evidence.*

The Judge: *Hang the evidence. In your line of inquiry did you assume he was so engaged?*

Pucard: *No, Your Honour.*

The Judge: *Well, we've got to stop this vile business somewhere. Objection denied.*

ALBERT ROSEN (1931-1978) Fascist, rabid anti-Semite and lifelong cinema freak.

The only documented case of a man whose character was reformed through film. After seeing the *Night* series, this stranger wrote me, he was committing his life to a war against evil. Shot down outside a mosque in Addis Ababa, Ethiopia, Sunday, 21 March, 1978, by guards of the red terror, while attempting to distribute food and medicine to the poor. A nail driven into his chest, attached to it a note which named him the people's enemy. One of 148 verified dead, mostly children, shot or hacked to death that day. Another day after so many and so many. His body and theirs littering the streets, removal forbidden. Notes pinned to bodies read: *This mother's son put the people's well-being above ideology.* (Amnesty International Bulletin.)

—— WOLFE (1936-1936). Born dead. My sister.

SISTER MARY OF ST. DAVID (-1978)
Raped and murdered on this street corner one month ago, criminal party not yet discovered. One Christmas eve three years ago she passed Elaine and me right about here, transporting on her shoulder an undecorated tree.

It is an evil thing that you do, Martin. My prayers go with you.

'Mine with you, Sister.'

SO MANY OTHERS
Nameless and unknown, disfigured in the memory, strangers, friends and shadowy walk-ons. The truck driver for Maple Leaf Foods who on a road past Long Beach, BC, pulled Wanda Lee Casslake too late from her carbon monoxide end to everything.

The motor wasn't running any more. I reached in, turned off the ignition. She toppled over. I don't know how long she'd been dead.

On the front seat a note: *Let Elaine and Martin have Angelia, she'll be happy with them.*

So many more. Over the faces of all these, superimposed, enduring year after year, the innocent, amazed eyes of a boy from nowhere, looking forward through time at me. My own eyes. My own, the same eyes, looking back at him.

'How goes it, old friend?'

My eyes never close. There is nothing you do that I can't see.

'Will you never be satisfied?'

You may have fooled Oble but you shall never fool me. A thousand people have passed before me, Martin, but you are the biggest disappointment of all.

'I'm tired now, old friend. I'm going home.'

You've disgraced me, Martin. People like you have no home.

Dawn. True dawn. A red wash above the city, the air fresh for a change. I tell you much is to be said for living one's life by the sea. The milkman making his rounds. A street cleaner high in the orange cab of his giant machine. Rows of parked cars, the occasional cat or dog. Another night survived.

When I get back to my building I find my wife curled up on the hallway floor. Asleep. The hall isn't heated, a thin coat stretches from her head to her feet. Mouth a little open, her eyes puffy, her hair a mess. Her hands are ice-cold.

'Elaine,' I say. 'Elaine, you have got to stop doing this.'

She awakens in a fright, then sees it is only me. She stretches her arms, yawns noisily, and scrambles to her feet.

You keep moving the key.

'Yes, to keep you out. But you've got to stop camping in the hall.'

I know. This time I think I caught a cold.

She walks in behind me, turns on the lights, and begins immediately to clean up the place.

Sloppy housekeeper. Whoever is looking after you now.

She tires, however. She fluffs up a pillow, sits on the sofa, plops the pillow on her lap.

I've decided. Martin. Hell or high water, I'm not leaving again.

'We've been through all this before.'

I sit down beside her. Her head lolls, or mine does, and her arm falls softly around.

We're so tired, she says.

She sneezes, grabs a tissue and blows her nose. The tissue floats down. We stare in front of us. There is nothing to see but bare wall.

It's our chance of getting Angelia back. If my parents die of shame they'll just have to. I'm staying, Martin.

'I guess so. If you're sure.'

I'm going to bed now.

'I'll join you if I may.'

We do not bother to undress. We drag ourselves to the bed and tumble in. Our backs curve, our knees bend. We are twins, lengths of soft curving flesh harpooned to the mattress by a single throw. To diffuse the light Elaine sweeps hair across her face.

Be quiet, she moans. *Don't say a word.*

I have grit in my eyes; it's this that causes tears.

Five minutes later we irritably sigh, kick like gypsies in a dance. Sob and sink down again. A pillow smothers her.

You're thinking, she accuses. *You've got to stop it, Martin, I can't sleep.*

MARCELINE ABLE

Viper. Liar. Killer of this sleep. Amorphous runner, derelict from the lost lagoon, guide for the lunatic's museum. Freelance jibber-jabber who single-handedly brought my mogul's empire tumbling down. *He put his hands all over me sir and when I said I wouldn't I wasn't that kind of girl he hit me and threw me down and then he did it to me so help me God I wouldn't lie about a thing like that and it went on for days and days until I was so sore I couldn't move all my pleading with him done no good and finally he was tired of me I guess and he said if I worked for him on the street he'd look after me he said a girl like me pretty and young and kind of classy you know I could make a lot of money on the street and he'd see to it I got a good share I told him I didn't want to but he made me sir he said it was all I was good for...*

Discovered by Wanda, loitering on a street corner one day (*Hey, Miss, could you spare a quarter*?) and hired by her for part-time child-minding work.

You can see that she needs help, Martin. She's loony, she's a bit confused, but she isn't dangerous, I'm only doing what you would have done for her in my place, and you know all the trouble I've had getting someone to look after Angelia.

'She's bad news, Wanda.'

No, she isn't. You should have seen me when I was her age. The responsibility will be good for her. You're always preaching compassion, I should think you'd show a little now.

A runaway, as it turned out. Hitch-hiker, acid-dropper, vagrant, groupie, Moon disciple, racist, back-stabber, shop-lifter and compulsive whiner:

Everybody dumps on me!

Hating above all things the square and the phony.

I hate a phony, don't you just hate a square, Martin?

I went without appointment one day to Wanda's place and knew something was wrong the minute I knocked on the door. It was Marcie who finally came. 'Where's Wanda?' I asked and she said *Wanda's shopping, how would I know where Wanda is?* Strange, something about her that wouldn't let me go away. 'What's going on?' I asked, 'where's the kid?' *Oh, the kid*, she said, *the kid, I guess she's around somewhere.* And then giggles leading into hysterical laughter as she backed against the wall and slumped down. Angelia in the kitchen, weeping hopelessly, barricaded inside the cramped cabinet where the garbage was stowed. *Well, she was freaking me, Mister, suppose you just motor on out of here.*

'Wanda, Wanda, you've got to get rid of that nut you hired.'

What harm can she do, be patient, she's only trying to find herself.

Charlie Manson's great granddaughter.

He was always coming on to me grabbing at me wanting me to ball with him I wouldn't of minded so much except he was always coming on so righteous like you know and know-it-all just like my parents he was always dropping by the place when Wanda was out and I could tell what he was after but I gave him the cold shoulder I wouldn't have nothing to do with him I guess he's got a thing about young girls or something he's kinda uptight about sex you know weird. But me I was just looking after the kid the way I was s'posed to and I did good too which wasn't easy the kid was always wanting something a real attention-grabber if you know the kind I mean well the kid was like that something awful but I was looking after her see and ignoring Martin. It wasn't till later I found out he was in the porno business that nearly blew my mind when I heard that because he'd always seemed so straight to me him and Wanda was real close and at first I thought they had a thing going but I don't know you never can tell with people and I was looking out for myself I mean I had my own life to lead right? But then him and Elaine they started ganging up on me they told all sorts of stories on me to Wanda and I could tell the way she was looking at me she had her doubts and then there was that time when she lost her money I know she thought I stole it though she never said nothing about it she was real tight you know wouldn't spend a dime on herself anyway they told Wanda I was really fucking up the kid which really freaked me they said I was mean to the kid I even beat her but that was an outright lie. What's true though is that I was after Wanda to get me a role in one of their pictures I could be a pretty good actress I think if anybody ever gave me the chance I'm very photogenic to tell the truth. I know what they'll tell you they'll say I told them I'd do anything to be in the movie business I'd even do it with a black or a Chink any kinky thing they wanted but that's just a rotten lie like I told you I didn't even know that was the kind of picture Martin makes. So when I told them they could chuck it I wasn't having anything to do with dirt like that well that's when Martin raped me nearly as I recall I'm a little confused now what with it being such a terrible ordeal I went through and when the policeman arrested me for soliciting that's when I told him how come I was in this bad spot which I'm telling you about on my own free will...

Deranged, demented, vicious. An idiotic little jerk. Empty-headed for the most part. Even ordinary at times. Even at times, God help me, amusing:

I was with a Moog Synthesizer man before I come here.

'With who?'

We were really grooving on each other for a week or two, crashing out at this deserted house he knew about, about ten of us. Funny thing was, every morning we'd wake up and nobody could find their shoes. We'd all be walking around dopey-like on the freezing floor asking each other where's my shoes, what happened to my fucking shoes?

'What had happened to them?'

Well then one night I saw him. He had this toesack and he was scooting from bed to bed cramming all the shoes he could find in this bag. And then he went outside in the snow and threw them every which way far as he could, every one of them. Then he came back inside and went to sleep.

'Would he throw away his own?'

No, that's why he was doing it, that was his whole idea. So we'd have to wear his, taking turns, I mean wearing his while trying to find our own. Hiking boots, about size twelve.

'Didn't anyone suspect him?'

Well we were pretty stoned, most of us either coming off a trip or taking off on one. No, he'd sort of stay in his sleeping-bag all day grinning, he really got off on it, seeing us walk around in his shoes. He was trying to make friends is what he said, loaning out his shoes. He said it made him feel real good, like Jesus when he threw bread upon the water and the crumbs turned into swans, that's the funny way he talked.

'Why did you leave him?'

Oh, they practically killed him when they found out he was throwing their shoes out in the snow. And he was kind of a drip you know.

She could be nice, she could lay a faint finger on the heart-strings when she was in a sentimental or depressed mood:

You people, you and Elaine and Wanda and even Angelia sometimes, I know you want to love me, I know you try to. It makes me feel kind of creepy, you want to know the truth, I never felt that way before. I keep asking myself when's the hatchet going to fall.

Mindless. Totally without conscience. Yet we rarely felt her evil was intentional, that it was motivated, that she had any reasons for the way she behaved. One day Elaine and I, talking about her, worked ourselves into a nervous state, and went running over. *Hurry, Martin, she's doing something terrible, I can feel it, can't you?* Horrible scene. Marcie in the bathroom trying to stuff Angelia's head down the commode.

Why did you do it, goddamn you, Marcie, what's wrong with you?

A shrug. *I don't know.*

I don't know either. It's God, I think.

GOD

God is the proven traitor. I sometimes think his body is the rot in this air. That the battle for our souls was lost, our fate sealed incalculable ages ago. At the very minute we looked and began to fabricate something better than ourselves. That's when we killed God, at the very instant we in our image created Him. Not, as is usually supposed, to explain our origins or sweeten our destiny — but simply to shift the blame elsewhere. We strung the bastard up. That's when we did it and that's why.

It is Elaine, rising petulantly out of sleep, who first hears the banging on our door. *Quick*, she says, *get it before I wake up.* She flops back down, groaning, hand over her ear. I get to the door somehow. My neighbour Mary Napels is there. She glares at me, striding inside.

Have you seen it? Have you seen this vile rag? It's hideous, you'll never be able to adopt Angelia now!

She thrusts a rolled newspaper in my hands. I look stupidly at her and ask her what time it is.

Open it! she shouts. *Let's see you explain your way out of this.* She grabs the tabloid back, yanks the sheets flat, and drums a finger violently on the page. *There! It's disgusting, how could you let them do this?*

DEATH STALKS THE BEACH

the headline reads

AS SMUT QUEEN HAS LAST PARTY

Wanda with her flat chest, in her birthday celebration with Robin, black boxes to obscure genitalia and to hide Robin's eyes, smart lawyer's device for staving off libel suits. My photographs, last gift from Wanda. At last victorious, giving the one performance she always claimed for herself and giving it in *The People's Inquirer.*

Elaine sways barefooted in the doorway: *What is it? What has gone wrong now?*

Mary rushes to her. *It's Martin, he's sold those photos to a scandal sheet.*

Nonsense.

A bottom-of-the-page insert claims my attention: a grim, cloudy photograph captioned HER DEATH CAR. Not Wanda's car, not even a real beach, but a studio blow-up of what a real one is. Through the early morning mist I can just make out the grey curved stem of a woman's neck, the dead face lodged between window and seat, so elegiacally turned. 'Professionally posed,' the parenthesis informs. 'Meanwhile, her long-time director and bosom-chum Martin Wolfe, awaiting trial for the alleged rape of a juvenile, continues his efforts to adopt the queen's small child. Get 'em while young, eh Martin?'

MARTIN DEWITT WOLFE (1934-) Film-maker (now retired). *Night with Wanda*, etc.

'I give up, Elaine. I quit.' I pass this new bouquet to my wife, to let her have a whiff. I give her such imaginative gifts, she might say. Human smut skilfully disguised as a gift to all mankind. Thank God for the press, which keeps us abreast of ourselves. Thank God. The last picture show. It's over.

How could you do *it, Martin?* Mary Napels is weeping at the tombside. Somebody has swiped the last crumb off God's plate.

'I didn't. Somebody else did.'

That woman, Elaine cries. *Rita Islington! Wouldn't that be it, Martin? You gave her the negatives. But why? Why would she do such a thing to her own sister?*

'Why not?' I say. But then I look at the two women, both of them horrified. Weeping and yet ready and able to give solace. I know well that look in my wife's eyes; it is frequently there, frequently inquiring: *Have you lost faith, Martin? Oh, no, Martin, you couldn't!*

I'm sorry, Martin, my neighbour says. *It just seemed too much, the final straw. You know? I had no right to suggest ...*

She comes over to give me a hug. Elaine comes too and the three of us stand holding on to each other. One more word and we would weep like a fountain.

My wife breaks suddenly away from our triumvirate, shaking her fist at the sky: *Angelia!* she shouts. *How are we going to save her?*

ANGELIA LATISHIA CASSLAKE (1974-) An innocent child. The star of my next film:

The most recent film of M.D. Wolfe opens with a massively detailed, nearly interminable sequence made up of the same repeated, gradually expanding scene. Fade in on a barren plain where a clump of ant-like creatures congregates. As the scene comes closer we notice that these figures are strangely reminiscent of demons on a canvas by Brueghel, gnomes leering from behind haystacks etc. Each time the scene is replayed our vision is improved. For instance, we observe that the item being wagged by each of a crowd of chanting, hydrocephalic idiots is in fact the grotesque and elongated human penis. Another group whom we had originally supposed to be gossipy old women becomes eventually a chorus line of judges, each one of them bewigged. We are ten minutes into the film before it is possible to see that the idiots surround a fire. Bound to a stake in the centre of this blazing pyre is a little girl, not more than four years old. Off to the left is another victim, who looks remarkably like Wanda Casslake. She is being stabbed repeatedly with pitchforks, wielded by two other women, one elegant and austere, the other a mad-eyed juvenile. The Wanda-woman rises again and again, bleeding and struggling over to the fire as if she would give succour to the child at the stake. At last Wanda expires, her death rattle being amplified stereophonically throughout the theatre. One of the idiots, however, is seen on closer inspection to be a film director — he wears dark glasses and an Italian open-necked shirt; he has a folding director's chair strapped to his shoulders. With him are two women, very impressive types. We soon discover that these three are in fact attempting to rescue the little girl. Pretending to add faggots, they in fact remove the most treacherous. The director loosens the cords which tie her while the two women create a diversion — they writhe provocatively around the bodies of the idiots, licking their own lips and cupping their naked breasts as if to offer a drink of milk — he takes the child from the fire and places her piggyback where the director's chair was previously strapped. He adjusts his dark glasses and gives a blast of the whistle round his neck to alert his friends that the mission has been accomplished. Unfortunately, this also alerts the enemy — so that the two women and the director have to run like hell, the idiots barking after them while the judges blow tin bugles and stomp their heels. But they make it. All the way across the expanding screen they run, miniature angels seemingly getting nowhere, so tiny the camera's eye barely perceives them. The idiots and the judges abandon the chase and attack each other. In this way is the foe at last vanquished, harmless dots bleeding into the barren plain.

FADE OUT.

FADE IN: EXTERIOR. FLYING STORK, SWADDLED BABY. PAN.

CUT TO: DISTANT 'X' ON BARREN PLAIN.

CUT TO: SWOOPING BIRD.

The Heart Must from Its Breaking

THE POSTMAN: This is how it happened that morning at the church. Timmons was speaking on a topic that had us all giggling, 'What You Do When and If You Get To Heaven and Find It Empty,' and we were all there and saw it. How suddenly before Timmons got wound up good the wood doors burst open and there in the sunlight was someone or something, like a fast-spinning wheel made up of gold, though it couldn't have been gold and was probably some funny trick of the light. Anyway, there it was, and beckoning. Must have been beckoning, or calling somehow, because two children got up from their seats at the front and quiet as you please marched right out to him — to him or it — and went through the door, and that was the last any of us ever saw them. Then a second later that other kid — Tiny Peterson was his name — went out too, but his mama was in time to save him. Now I'd lie about it if I could or if I knew how, but it was all so quiet and quick and then over that I wouldn't know how to improve on the actual happening. Out that door and then swallowed up, those two kids, and that's all there was to it.

A SISTER: He can say that's all if he wants to. Roger Deering sees an affair like this the same way he sees his job, which I would remind you is delivering mail. He drops it through the box, if he can be troubled to come up the path, and then he's gone. What he's left you with don't matter spit to him. But I live in that house now, my sister's house, and I can tell you the story don't end there.

They were my sister's children, Agnes and Cluey. Sister was home in bed sick so I'd taken little Agnes and Cluey to church to hear Timmons give what we hoped would be a good one, and right after the second song, with Timmons hardly begun, Cluey who was on my left stood up and whispered 'Excuse me', and brushed by my knees, then Agnes on my right stood up, mumbled 'Me too' and they went on down the row, scraping by people, getting funny looks, and then going on down the aisle pretty as you please. I thought Cluey had to go to the bathroom. He was always doing that, never going when you told him to and it embarrassed me. But you do get tired of telling a boy to wait wait wait when he's squirming and crossing his legs, trying to hold it in. I don't mean he was doing it that day, I'm only saying that's what I thought he got up for. He'd been nice as pie the whole time, both of them, both while walking along with me to church and while sitting there waiting for Timmons to get primed. So I was in a good mood and bearing them no malice, though they were a long shot from being my favourite nieces and nephews. Sister had been ailing for some while and they were feeling dopey about that, we all were. That was the day Sister died, in fact the very minute, some said. Some said they'd looked at their watches when that door burst open and Cluey and Agnes went out never to be seen again and that very second three blocks over was the very second Sister passed on. It was close, that's all I'm saying, and my skin shivers saying that much, especially when I remember about the blood. But I'm not saying anything about the blood on Sister's window, being content to leave that to the likes of Clayton Eaves who is still dunning me for that ten dollars. I don't like to think any of it is the truth, for I'm living in Sister's house now and I know sometimes I hear her and that she hears me. Sister dies and her two children disappear the same minute and it does make you think. Though I didn't see any whirling light or gold spinning at the door. I felt a draft, that's all. Like most people with any sense I thought the wind had blown it open, and when people say to me there wasn't any wind that day I just look through them, since any fool knows a gust can come up. Still, it's strange. I can't think what happened to the children. No one wanted them. I couldn't, and Sister wasn't able. Their daddy couldn't have come and got them because none of us hardly remembered who their daddy was, or wanted to, because even in his best of days he hadn't been what you'd call a solid citizen. He wasn't right in the head, and not much in the body either, and even Sister knew that. So she had her hard times, raising that pair without a hand from him who hadn't been seen I think in nine years when all this happened. No aunts or uncles would have come for them. We don't have kidnappers around here. No, it defies explanation and I've given up trying. When Sister wakes me calling in the night I sit up in bed and answer back and we go on talking that way until her spirit quietens.

I hope Cluey and Agnes are all right, wherever they are, that's all I hope. I don't agree with those who say they're long-since dead, nor those who say they're in heaven either. Timmons might.

THE PREACHER: Sure they're dead. I don't know how, or how come, or why, not having the divine intervention on it, but you can't tell me two children dressed for church and without penny or snotrag between them are going to get of out this town without anyone knowing it. There are just two ways for entering or leaving and that's by the one street that leads off to Scotland Neck at one end and Enfield at the other, and they didn't go either of those ways. Couldn't have, because a hundred people rocking on their porches that fine Sunday when they should have been at Spring Level hearing my sermon on 'The Empty Hell' would have noted their progress and likely turned them around.

So they're dead. Yep, and their bones plucked by now. Dust to dust and the Lord's will abideth.

Somebody picked them up right off the churchgrounds, I'd say, right there at the door, and spooked them away. Why I don't know. They were ordinary children, no better or worse than most. Funny things go on in this town the same as they do anyplace else and I figure those two are buried this minute down in somebody's cellar or in a backyard where a thousand things hidden go on day in and day out. I've preached till I'm blue in the face, the same as one or two other ministers have, and it's done no good. Not a lick. You can't stamp out the devil's work for he's like a mad dog once he gets going. That's what it was, of course. The old devil keeping his hand in. If it hadn't been those two children it would have been something worse.

We searched the woods, every rock, weed, and clover.

Nothing. Not a hint.

About that door. I saw *something* but *what* is something else. It wasn't gold, though. It was more like a giant black shadow had spun up over the stairs and filled the doorway. I remember remarking to myself at the time: it's got so dark in here so suddenly I'm going to have difficulty reading my text. I was going to ask Minny at the organ to turn more light on, when Cluey and Agnes got up and distracted me. A second later it was light again. If I'd known what was to happen I would have called out. But who knew? That's how you know it's the devil's work, I say, because you don't. You just don't. You never will.

THE ORGANIST: Timmons is right. I was at the organ. I didn't want to be, having a bad cold, but I was. They couldn't get anybody else. My nose was runny, I told them, and I had aches — but so what? 'Minnie, now Minnie, you come on down.' So I did. Yet it's the same story every time and nobody even bothering to keep up. I've heard cows mooing in a meadow had more rhythm and feeling than the people in that church. But I saw nothing. Saw and heard nothing. No light or gold. No shadow. No children either. It takes a lot in that church to make me turn around. Back trouble, leg trouble, I wore a neck brace for ten years. I keep my back to that lot and that's how I like it. One time a curtain caught fire back there when Orson Johnson — the crosseyed one — was playing with matches. I looked around then. That's about the only time.

ORSON: I'm the one she's talking about. What I wished I'd done that day was burn the whole building down. But I didn't and I growed up and I was there the day those two walked out. There whittling on a stick with this Fobisher knife I have. With the wife and hoping it would wind up early, though I knew it wouldn't, so I could go home and have dinner, maybe grab some shut-eye. But, yes, I saw them, and I felt my neck crawl too, before they ever stood up, because something was behind me. Maybe not at the door, but behind me certainly. My skin froze and I remember gripping my wife's wrist I got that scared. I thought it was Death back there, Death calling, and He was going to lay his cold hand over my shoulder and speed me on off. 'What date is it?' I asked my wife. 'How long we been married?' Now I don't know why I said this, but I know it scared her too, though she just kept shooshing me. I didn't want to die. Hell, it seemed to me I'd only started living. But 'shoosh' she says, so I shoosh. I shoosh right up; I couldn't have said another word anyway. I sat there with my knees knocking, waiting for Death's hand to grab me. Then I see the kids coming down the aisle. They got their faces scrubbed and that ramrod aunt of theirs, Gladys, she had slapped some worn duds on them and got their hair combed. Death's hold on me seemed to loosen a bit and I thought how I might slip out and ask them how their mother was doing — whether she was still in her sick bed or out of danger yet, that sort of thing — maybe slip them a quarter because I'd always felt pity for those kids — and I tried to move, to wiggle out the side and sort of slink to the back door, but what it was I found was I couldn't move. I couldn't stir a muscle. And a second later my hair stood up on my head because a voice was hissing in my ear. 'Don't go,' it said. 'Don't go, Orson, it will get you too.'

Though I didn't think then that 'too' business was including the kids. I might have got up if I'd known that. I might have headed them off, tried to save them. If anyone could have. I don't know. Oh, they're dead, no question of that. I think they were likely dead before nightfall. Maybe within the minute. It's too bad too, especially with their mother going that same day.

ORSON'S WIFE: I felt Orson stiffen beside me. He looked like death warmed over and he started jabbering beside me, shivering so hard he was rattling the whole row. I put my hand down between his legs and pinched his thigh hard as I could but he didn't even blink. He was trying to get out. So I put my hand up where his man parts were and I squeezed real hard and told him to hush up. 'Hush up, Orson, stop playing the fool' — something like that. He was freezing cold. He had sweat beads on his brow an inch thick. I brought my heel down on his foot, trying to get him quiet, then I heard him say 'Death, Death, Death.' And 'Don't go, don't go.'

He didn't know he was talking. I saw Aaron Spelling, in front of us, lean over and say to Therma that Orson Johnson had a briar in his behind. Therma turned and looked at us. Her mouth popped open. Because Orson was such a sight. I got my hand away real quick from where it was; I just clamped my fingernails into his thigh and kept them there the rest of the service.

Later on we had to get the doctor in, I'd hurt him so and the infection must have lasted a month.

I didn't notice the kids; I had my hands full with Orson.

It was three whole days in fact before I so much as heard of the children gone missing or dead and of their mother's death.

THE NURSE: I was nursing Tory when she took her final breath. By her bedside I was with a tea cup in my lap and watching the window because I thought I'd heard something running around out there. Like a galloping horse it was. But my legs were bothering me, and my sides, so I didn't take the trouble to go to the window and see. I sat sipping my tea, listening to the galloping horse.

It was a day like many another one up to that time except that the house was empty, it being a Sunday, and other than that horse. A few minutes before, when I got up to get my tea, I'd put my head down on Tory's chest. I was always doing that, couldn't help it, because although I've sat with hundreds of sick people I'd never heard a heart like hers. It was like water sloshing around in a bowl; she hardly had no regular heartbeat is what I'm saying. So I'd put my head down over her chest and listen to it slosh like that.

I couldn't see how a human being could live with a heartbeat like that.

The horse it keeps right on galloping. Now and then I'd catch a whir at the window, white-ish, so I knew it wasn't no dark horse. Then all at once my blood just stops, because something has caught hold of me. I look down at my wrist and there's the queerest hand I ever saw. Thin and shrunk and mostly bones. The hand is all it was in that second, and I shrieked. The china cup fell to the floor and broke. Saucer too. Tea I splashed all over me, so I afterwards had to go in and soak my dress in cold water. There were the long red nails though. A vile colour but Gladys said Tory liked it. That she wouldn't feel comfortable in bed, sick like that, without her nails painted, because how would you feel to be in bed like she was and looking like death, in case anybody came in. So let's keep her looking civilized, Gladys said, and one or the other of us kept her nails freshly painted. So after my minute of fright I knew it was Tory's hand, her who hadn't moved a twitch in three months, suddenly sitting up with a grip like steel on my arm. It was practically the first sign of life I'd seen in her in the whole time I'd been minding her. She was sitting bolt-up, with her gown straps down at her elbows so her poor little bosom, the most puckered, shrivelled little breasts I ever hope to see, was exposed to the full eyes of the world.

She had her eyes locked on the window.

And there went the horse again, gallop, gallop.

I got hold of myself, got her hand off me, and stooped down over her. I was about to say, 'Now little lady let's get that gown up over your bosom before you catch your death' — but then that word got caught in my throat so I said nothing. And I'm glad I didn't or I might of missed what she said. Her eyes were on fire and she was grabbing at something. At the very air, it seemed to me. 'You'll not get my children!' she said. 'No, you'll not get them!' Well, my skin crawled. I don't know why, don't know to this day. Just the way she was crying it. 'You'll not get them, not my Cluey and Agnes!' She was screeching that out now, as frightened — but as brave too — as any soul I hope to see. *'You can't have my children!'* On and on like that. And she was twisting around in bed, flailing her arms, striking at something with her poor little fists. *'No, you can't!'* she said. Then this even worse look come over her face and for the longest time she wasn't making human sounds at all. Half-animal, I thought. Like something caught in a trap. I thought she'd finally bit the noose — that her mind had gone. I kept trying to get that gown up over her breast works — you never knew who would come barging into that house without knocking or breathing a word, even her sister has crept in sometimes and scared me out of my wits. And she's fighting me, not letting me get her back down in the bed. She's scratching and yelling and kicking — her whose legs the doctor claimed was paralysed — and she's moaning and biting. Then she shrieks, *'Run! Run! Oh, children, run!'* And this perfect horror comes over her face, pure agony it is, and torture worse than I've ever known a body to feel. *'No!'* she screams, *'No! Please! Please don't!'* and the next second her breath flies out, her eyes roll up, and she sags down like a broken baby in my arms. I put her head back on the pillow and fluff it some. I pull her straps back up and smooth out her gown over her chest's flatness. I pat the comforter up around her neck. I get her hair looking straight. I close her eyes, first the left then the right just as they say you ought to do, and I root in my purse and dig out two pennies. I go in and wash them off and dry them on my dress, and I put them nicely over her eyes. Then I sit watching her, trembling more than I ever have. Wondering what has gone on and thinking how I'm going to have to tell her sister and those poor children when they come in from the church. Not once giving mind to that broken china on the floor. I reckon I never did. I reckon someone else must have come in and cleared that mess up. Maybe Gladys did. Or maybe not. I plumb can't guess, because one second I'm there sitting looking at my hands in my lap and the next second I'm thinking, What about that galloping horse? Because I don't hear it any more. No, it's so quiet you can hear a pin drop. And I hear it too. Pins dropping, that's what I think. This shiver comes over me. I have the funny feeling I'm not alone in the room: that there's me, a dead person, and something else. I look over at the bed and what do I see? Well, it's empty. Tory ain't there. I hear more of these pins dropping and they seem to be coming from the window so I look there. And what I see is this: it is Tory, come back to some strange form of life, and sliding up over, over the sill and out of that window. That's right, just gone. And I guess I fainted then, that being the first of my faints. The next time I open my eyes my sight is on that window again and this time Tory is coming back through it, sliding along, and her little breasts are naked again, she's all cut up, and blood has soaked through her and she's leaving a trail of it every inch she comes. 'Help me, Rosie,' she says. Well, that's what I'm there for. So I get her up easy as kittens — she hardly weighs an ounce — and I get her back to bed. 'They're safe,' she says. I say, 'Good.' I say a lot of comforting words like that. 'Don't let anyone see me like this,' she says. 'I'm black and blue from head to toe.' It's the truth too, she sure is. 'Have Gladys quietly bury me,' she says. 'Closed coffin. Can you promise that?' I said sure. She patted my hand then, poor thing, as though I was the one to be comforted. Then she slips away. She slips away smiling. So I get the pennies back on. I straighten the covers. Then I sit back in the chair and faint away a second time. I'm just waking up when Gladys comes in from church to tell me that Agnes and Cluey have gone and there's been a mighty mess at the church and some are saying the children are dead or gone up to heaven. I pass out the third time. I can't help it. I fold down to the floor like a limp rag and I don't know what else is going on till there is a policeman or a doctor at my elbow, I don't know which.

OFFICER CLIVE: It was me, Sam Clive. Clive, C-L-I-V-E. Officer Sam Clive. I wasn't there in any official capacity. I lived then just two doors down from Tory and that day I felt in my bones how something was wrong. I was out in my yard mowing and this funny feeling come over me. I looked up and it seemed to be coming from her house. It was shut up tight, the house was, but there was this whirring disc in the sky. A flying whatayacallit I at first thought. Anyway, it seemed to sink down in the woods just behind her place. So I strolled over. I saw curtains fluttering at her sick room window and I was brought up real short by that — because that window had always been closed. Every day, winter and summer, on account of Tory was holding on by such a thin thread. Heart trouble, kidneys, pneumonia — the whole shebang. I stepped closer, not wanting to be nosy and more because of this eerie feeling I had. Well, I saw those curtains were dripping blood. It was pouring right off that cloth and down the boards, that blood. And I thought I saw something sliding up over the sill the minute I come up. Flutter, flutter. It was the curtains I guess. Though I don't recollect it being a windy day. But that blood, heck, you can still see where it dribbled down the side of the house, because they never painted it over. They painted the rest of the house, the sister did after she got it, but for reasons known only to them they painted up to the blood and stopped right there. Anyhow, I hurried on over. I looked through the window and there was this fat nurse down in a heap on the floor beside this broken china and Tory in the bed with bright pennies over her eyes.

THE PAINTER: I done the paint job. I give the old gal a good price and me and one other, my half-brother who was helping me then, we went at it. White, of course, that was the only colour she'd have. And she wanted two coats, one put on vertical and one crossways. I said why. She said her daddy told her when she was a kid that's how you put paint on if you wanted a thing to stand up to the elements more'n a year or two. I said I'd never heard that. I said Tom Earl, Have you ever heard that and he said, No, no he hadn't. She said, Well, that's how she wanted it and if I wouldn't or couldn't do it or didn't think I was able then she reckoned I wasn't the only painter in town and a lot of them cheaper'n me. Ha! I said. I said it's going to cost you extra. She said, I don't see why. I said, Because, Miss Gladys, it will take me a good sight longer painting this house the fool way you want it. You can't hardly git no speed painting vertical because the natural way is to go crosswise following the lay of the boards. She said it might be natural to a durn fool like me but that weren't how her daddy done it and I could do it and at the price quoted or I could shove off and go out and stick somebody else. So I got the message. Two coats? I said. Two coats, she said, Hank Sparrow can't you do that neither? I shook my head a time or two. There weren't any way I was going to make one red cent out of it. I'd be doing well just covering wages and gitting the paint paid for. But her sister had passed on and hide nor hair of her kin had been seen, those two children, so I said well it won't hurt me none to do this woman a favour.

I got Tom Earl and him and me took at it. It went right smooth and we did the same top job we always did. Till we got to that window. I brushed the paint over them dark red streaks and said to Tom Earl, Well, it'll take a second coat, but that ought to do her. But when it dried, even after the third and fourth coat, them bloodstreaks were still there same as they were when we started. Tom Earl said, Well, she ain't going to pay, you know that, until we get these streaks covered over. I looked at him and I said, You're right there, you done spoke a big mouthful. And I went out to the truck and got me my tools. Got me my hammer and chisels, my blowtorch too: one way or the other I was going to git that blood removed.

Well, she comes running. She have got her head up in a towel, one shoe off and the other one on, and she's dripping water, but still she comes running. What are you doing, what are you doing, she keeps asking, are you going to take hammer to my house or burn it down? Is this what you call painting, she says. So I looked at Tom Earl and he's no help, he just shrugs his shoulders. I look to her and say I've painted and I've painted and it's still there. What is? she says. Hank Sparrow are you trying to two-bit me? No'm, I say, but there's something peculiar going on here. There sure is, she says, and it's you two with no more sense that a cat has pigeons. Now, hold on a minute, I say. So I take her round the house and I show her how we've put on a good seven coats minimum. But still that blood where your sister crawled up over the ledge. You leave my sister out of this, she says. She says, Hank Sparrow I have known you Sparrows all my life and there has never been one of you didn't try to weasel out of work and didn't lie with every breath scored. Now give me that brush, she says.

Tom Earl and me we give it to her. We coat it up good and we wrap a little tissue over the handle so she won't get none on her hand, and we tell her to go to it. We stand back picking our teeth and poking each other, laughing, because one, the way she held that brush in both hands with her tongue between her teeth and bent over like she was meaning to pick up dimes, and two, because we knew it was a lost cause and no way in hell that paint was going to do it.

See there? She said. See there? Now is that covered or isn't it?

Give it a minute, we said. You give them streaks about two minutes and your eyes will pop out.

Well, she stood right there with us, insulting us up one side and down the other every inch of the way. But we took it. We said nothing hard back to her. We knowed she was going to get the surprise of her life and be walking over hot coals to beg pardon. And in two minutes, sure as rainwater, those streaks were back. They looked fresh brand-new, even brighter.

She went back and stood under the tree studying it, thinking her and distance would make a difference.

It's this paint, she said. This is shoddy paint you're using.

Well, we saw there was no end to it. So we got her in the truck between us, her with her hair still up in this green towel, and we drove down to the hardware. She got Henry Gordon pinned in the corner not knowing which way to turn but no matter how hard she pinned him he kept telling her that the paint we had was the best paint made and there weren't none no better including what went on the mayor's own house. I'll see about this, she said. And danged if she didn't call the distributor, long-distance, charging it to Henry. What is the best paint made? she said. And he said the very one we'd put on her house. She slammed down that phone. All right, she said, but Henry Gordon you have sold these two so-called working men a bad mix. I want another. Help yourself, Henry told her. She marches in his stockroom, says eennymeeny-minnymoe over the cans, and comes out with one. All four of us now go back to her house. She has me git the lid off and she dabs over that blood again, so thick it just trickles down to the ground. We wait. She is now fit to be tied. I have lost a dear sister, she says, and lost my precious niece and nephew, and now you are telling me I've got to live with the curse of this blood?

We said it looked like it. Every one of us did, jumping right in with it. Because that blood was coming right back up. It was coming up bright as ever.

Well, I never, she says.

So we go inside and stand in her kitchen and she gives each of us a co-cola. It surpasses meaning, she said. I don't understand it. I don't guess I'm meant to.

We said, Yesmam.

All right then, she said, I will just have to leave it there. It's meant to be left there. It's meant to be some kind of sign or signal. A symbol.

We didn't argue with her. I didn't even raise a hand when she said she was holding back ten dollars' paint money because I never finished the house. There was something spooky about that place. All I wanted was to git shut of it. Me and Tom Earl took her cash and I give him some and me and him went out drinking.

THE PAINTER'S APPRENTICE: He drank. I didn't because I was only thirteen and the law wouldn't have it. But I knew Cluey, had seen him around, and that Agnes too because she was always at his heels, and I'd heard the stories of how the woman had died and Cluey and Agnes had gone up in thin air. I had beat up some on Cluey, being something of a bully in them days. I had bloodied his nose once and left him sobbing. I remember it and know it was him because he threw a rock at me and got me on the kneecap. And because of what he said: 'My daddy will git you,' he said. I was nice enough not to say 'What daddy?' And I was glad I didn't. Because that night something tripped me up as I was walking home along the dye ditch, and I fell off into that ditch and broke my left leg. It was somebody there all right, that's all I'm saying, and it wont Cluey or any other thing with two legs. It tripped me up, then it put a hand in my back, and I went tumbling over. I was with Tiny Peterson. He can tell you.

TINY PETERSON: It's every word true. But what I want to get to is that church. Timmons was being his usual assy self, playing up like he was doing a cameo role for Rin Tin Tin, yammering on about emptiness this and emptiness that, when the wood doors burst open. I was already turned around, trying to smack at a little girl back there, when Cluey come by me. I had my legs up high and he couldn't get past. So I dropped my legs. I'd just got them back up when his little sister tapped my knee. 'Excuse me,' she said. 'Me and him are going out to see my daddy. That's him at the door.'

I raised up high in my seat and looked again at that door. People behind me started hissing but I didn't care. There was something in that door all right, but it wasn't hardly human. It didn't have two arms and two legs and it didn't have a face either. But it was beckoning. I saw Cluey and Agnes walk into the thing, whatever it was, and then they simple were not there any more. There was nothing. I thought it was a vision. Timmons just then got his smart voice back and was saying something about 'Heaven is empty.' The empty heaven, something like that. I admit it. Goose bumps rose high on my arm as a kitchen window. I was really scared. Now, why I did it I don't know to this day, but I went running out after them. I figured that if maybe their daddy was out there then maybe mine was too and he might save me from my empty heaven. I went flying out. I sped out over everybody's knees and trampled on feet and the next second I was outside in the yard. Cluey and Agnes couldn't have been five seconds in front of me. And what I saw there gave me a chill I can feel to this minute. There was this woman there in a white gown which was down to her waist so I could see her nipples and these real wizened breasts. I reckon to this day it's why I like big-bosomed women. But what she was doing was struggling with this creature. Creature is what he was, make no mistake about that. She had her arms and legs wrapped around him, pulling and tugging and chewing — pure out-and-out screeching — while the creature thing was trying to throw her off and still hold on to poor Cluey and Agnes who by this time were just bawling. They were just bawling. The creature was dragging them along and that woman was up on the creature's back, riding him, biting into the thing's neck, punching and clawing. Well, it let go of the children. It gave a great howl and tore the woman off itself and practically bent her double. I mean it had her with her back across his knees and it was slamming her down all the while she screamed 'Run! Run! Oh, children, run!' And they streaked off. I've never seen nothing tear away so fast.

'Run! Run!' she cried. And they did and it was about this time that I heard this galloping, and a great white horse came out of the woods. The prettiest horse I ever will see. It galloped up to the children and slowed down and Cluey swung on its back, then got Agnes up there with him, and that horse took off full-speed, faster than I'd think a horse could. Then gone, just flying. The creature still had the woman. He slammed her down one last time and from where I was, hiding behind the tree, I could hear it: her back snap.

Snap, like that, and the creature flung her down. It let out a great roar — of hatred, of pure madness at being thwarted, I don't know which — and then it took off too. But in the wrong way, not after the children. It seemed to me, the longer I looked at it run, that the closer it came to having human form. It had arms and legs and a face, though that face looked a million years old and like it hated everything alive.

That's all I saw. My own momma came out then and fixed her finger over my ear and nearly wrung it off. 'Git yourself back in yonder,' she said, 'and don't you move one muscle lessern I tell you you can. When I git home I mean to put stick to your britches and you are going to wish you'd never been born.'

I whimpered some, though not because of her ear twists or any threats she made. I never told anyone till now. Hell with them.

THE FARMER'S HUSBAND: The horse came by my place. I was out on the porch rocking away when it come by. Mary was in her chair with peas in her lap, shelling them. It was white, that horse was, it had two riders. They were up in the hills though. They were out a good far piece. There was something unnatural about it, I thought that. About how fast that horse was running, how it didn't get slowed down none by tree or brush. I said to Mary how I'd never seen no horse like that, not around here. Not anywhere else either, I reckon. My dog was down between my legs and he got up and took off after them. About a quarter hour later he come back whimpering, his tail drawed up under his legs. He went under the house and moaned. It took me two days to git that dog out.

THE FARMER: See that horse? He told me. And he pointed. I went on with my shelling.

Wonder why they don't take the road, I said. Wonder whose it is?

I never saw no children. Didn't see what the dog did either. I didn't look that long. I can't set out on the porch all day like him, watching what goes on. I got my own concerns to look after. Still, it was unusual. In the kitchen washing my hands I found myself staring out at a blujay in a tree. Was that a horse, I ast myself, or was that a ghost?

TINY PETERSON'S MOTHER: I thought when I went out and tweaked his ear that the sobbing Tiny was doing wasn't on account of that ear. He was snow-white and trembling and it was all I could do to hold him up. If I hadn't been so mad and set in my ways I would have known he'd seen something. It wont no way for me to behave, whether it's to your own flesh or another's — but my husband had run out on me again and I imagine that had something to do with it.

But I'm sorry for it. I think it was the last time I wrung that boy's ear.

THE DOCTOR: You are all looking at me. Keep looking, then. You've always come to me with your aches and pains, now you're coming to me with this — is that it? I've told you my end before. I've never held anything back, and I won't now. Yes, I signed the certificate. She'd been slipping a long time and we'd all expected her death. I spent more time than most worrying about her. I said to her one day, 'Tory,' I said, 'my medicines are doing you no good. I know you are in terrible pain all day and we both know you haven't got long. If you've a mind to, and want me to, and realize I am only raising this issue because I am aware of your misery, then I could give you something to help you go out easy and gentle and without the smallest pain.'

She always told me she'd think on it. She'd let me know, she said. Then one day, after I'd given her every painkiller I could and none of it was helping her the slightest bit, I raised the question again.

'I'd like to go off, doctor,' she said, 'in a nice and swoony dream just as you describe. But I can't go yet. I've got to hold on for my children's sake because I know one day he is coming back. I've got to stay and save them from him, if I can.'

I knew, of course, who she was talking about. You can't live here as long as I have without knowing that. But I said: 'Tory, if he *does* come back, we will take care of his hide. You don't have to worry about his harming your kids.'

'You don't understand,' she said. 'There will not be a single thing a living soul can do. No,' she said, 'I will have to take care of this myself, if I'm able. But I thank you.'

I didn't mean to divulge this. Though I don't see how it alters anything. It tells us something of the spirit she had, I suppose, and confirms the love and concern she had for that boy and girl. The rest of it I'd discount. I never saw evidence of anything to the contrary while I was in medical school. Nor since, either. Yes, I signed the death certificate. You know as I do that it was a natural death. The heart couldn't any longer do its job. Yes, she was black and blue all over. Yes, there was blood on the curtains, and not merely her own blood either. I ran a test. The report came back to me and an idiot at the laboratory had scribbled on it, 'Please provide more information.'

Well, I didn't. I wasn't about to let myself be made a fool of up there.

I'm done. Let Tory and her children rest in peace, I say. Let these stories stop right here.